Chap
4.02

A TANTALIZING TRUCE

Her lips softened in a smile. Reaching out, she trailed a knuckle along his cheek, faintly stubbled with the shadow of a beard.

"In the meantime, shall we call a truce, Boss-man?" she challenged quietly.

He seemed unable to resist touching her in return and took her hand. He drew his palm over her wrist to her elbow.

Sonnie held her breath, transfixed by the sheer tenderness of his caress. He did not stop but continued toward her shoulder and onto her back, his work-roughened skin a pleasurable contrast to hers.

His hand splayed, slid along her shoulder blade, one side and then the other, before ending his journey at the barrier of her corset. He seemed hungry to explore, to learn of the feel of her.

Her gaze melded with his. She couldn't pull herself away, though the intimacy of the moment suggested she should.

He fingered the pink satin ribbons, as if he contemplated undoing them as slowly as he'd undone the back of her dress. His whiskey-shaded eyes, smoldering with the desire he held in check, settled on her lips, and his breathing took on a definite ragged edge.

"Truce, Sonnie," he whispered.

WYOMING WILDFLOWER

PAM CROOKS

LEISURE BOOKS NEW YORK CITY

Dedicated to:
Doug, Ann Marie, Katie, Kristi and Amy—the loves of my
life. May you always have romance in your heart.

A LEISURE BOOK®

March 2001

Published by

Dorchester Publishing Co., Inc.
276 Fifth Avenue
New York, NY 10001

ISBN 0-8439-4843-4

The name "Leisure Books" and the stylized "L" with design are
trademarks of Dorchester Publishing Co., Inc.

Printed in the United States of America.

Visit us on the web at www.dorchesterpub.com.

WYOMING WILDFLOWER

Prologue

Summer, 1872

The stench of raw sewage rolling in the gutters permeated the steamy night. Drunken derelicts shuffled past the aging tenement buildings squeezed onto the city block; thugs and thieves, like hordes of cockroaches, lurked in the darkened alleys to wait for more innocent victims.

But Lance Harmon felt safe enough in his tiny room, as safe as any ten-year-old living in New York's Lower East Side could be. He didn't like life in the slums much, but at least he had Mother, which made him more fortunate than most. She always protected him.

Well, she used to, anyway.

Mother hadn't been herself since Father had left. Lately the role of caregiver had fallen onto his young shoulders, and he'd accepted the responsibility with a man's aplomb. He and Mother had only each other.

She needed him—needed him more than ever.

He stared upward at the sagging ceiling and listened to the sounds seeping from the thin walls of her bedroom. He couldn't sleep when she was so restless, and knowing that she'd started drinking earlier than usual worried him all the more.

The baby was coming. Though Mother hadn't said as much, he knew. Her time was past—almost two weeks now—and just thinking about it spawned a troublesome fear deep inside him. He didn't understand most female things, but anyone could see how small and frail Mother was and how big her belly was.

"Lance! *Lance!*"

He bolted from the flea-bitten mattress and flew to her room. He froze at the sight of her upon the rumpled bed. Perspiration caked her auburn hair to her forehead and neck, and her skin had an awful pallor.

"Mother?" he said hoarsely. "Are you all right?"

"No, I ain't all right!" she snapped with uncharacteristic sharpness. Her speech, normally refined and cultured, turned coarse and primitive when laced with liquor. "I'm hurtin'. Hurtin' bad."

Grimacing, she raised herself up and reached toward the nearly empty bottle on the nightstand, but collapsed backward with a loud moan. Her arms gripped her abdomen, and her legs clawed the covers.

Panic rooted Lance to the floor. He tried to think of something to help her, to make her feel better, and failed.

After what seemed an eternity, her pain appeared to pass. Her bosom heaved as she gulped in air. Her head turned upon the pillow, and she fixed her exhausted gaze upon him.

"Lance," she said in a whimper. "Lance, honey."

He moved closer. "Mother, tell me what to do."

"I need a drink." She ran her tongue around her lips. "Give me the bottle . . . so's I can have a drink."

He hesitated. The cheap wine wasn't good for her. So many times he'd told her that. Now—especially now—she needed her wits about her.

"Lance!" The sting had returned to her tone. "Get me the bottle!"

He obeyed hastily, knowing he shouldn't but needing to comfort her any way he could. Her arm lifted slowly, as if she hadn't the strength for even that, and she grasped the neck of the container. Trickles of wine ran down her cheek and chin as she swallowed.

She made an odd choking noise. Her eyes rolled to the back of her head. The bottle fell from her grip, its meager contents spilling onto the pillow, and she curled away from him to her side. Again she clutched her belly; again she moaned and writhed in agony.

It seemed to Lance, this time, that the pain was never-ending. How much longer could she go on? Tears smarted his eyes; his pulse pounded in terror. What could he do?

Finally, breathing heavily, she eased back onto the mattress. Her lids drifted closed, fluttered open, then closed once more.

Something wasn't right, Lance realized. Mother was so tired, so weak. When would the baby come? In minutes? Hours?

When?

He fell to his knees beside her and took her limp hand. His fingers stroked hers feverishly. "Mother? Can you hear me?" Only silence mingled with her raspy breathing. "Mother? I'm going to find someone to help you. I won't be gone long."

Her eyes flew open wide. "No!" she shrieked. Her hand grasped his wrist in a burst of strength. "You mustn't go out there! Sadists . . . everywhere!"

"But Mother—"

"Stay here!"

"Mother, Mr. Hawthorne can help!" Lance had always thought their landlord had taken a fancy to her after Father went away. Often he'd seen him smile his crooked little smile at her.

Mother's face, normally so beautiful, but now so weary, contorted in contempt. Her hand fell away to clasp the bedcovers. "Hawthorne! Oh, God!" Her back arched at the onset of another pain. "His fault! He did this to me!"

Confusion and distress warred within Lance. He rubbed her arm, her shoulder, and blinked furiously at rising tears.

"For the rent, he said," Mother gasped. A trickle of perspiration snaked down her temple; a strange, demonic gleam flared in her eyes. She seemed to see right through Lance, as if he weren't there, as if she channeled her hate toward someone he couldn't see. "You men. You're all alike, y'know that? Talk fancy about love to a woman, fill her with your disgustin' seed, then leave her to die with your brat tearing her apart."

Full-blown terror exploded within Lance. What was she saying? What did she mean?

Her scream rent the room, and he broke into a sob. She struggled for air, for control; her pain-racked body twisted on the mattress.

"Stay away from 'em, Lance," she ranted. "Y'hear me? Be strong. I don't want . . . no son o' mine hurtin' a woman like your father or that . . . beast Hawthorne hurt me."

"Yes, Mother," he cried, not quite sure what she bade him or what he promised.

"Men are disgustin'." She blinked at him, as if trying to focus on his image; he watched the rage drain from her. "Where is your father? I need him," she whispered. "Stay with me, my darling son."

"Mother." He tried hard to swallow his panic and remain calm. "You need a doctor. I'll find you one."

"Stay with me!" she screeched. "Don't leave me!"

"All right, Mother. I'll stay, I'll stay."

Her mouth opened. Her body jerked. Her shrieking wail sent wave after wave of shudders down Lance's spine.

And then, he looked down in horror. A puddle of deep crimson oozed from her body and soaked into the sheets.

Dawn broke over the old tenement building. A hazy sun peeked through the faded curtains and warmed the little room grown cold from death.

Lance huddled in the corner, oblivious to the blood on his hands and the stain of tears on his face. His numb, haunted gaze riveted on the two forms, one infantile, the other finally at peace, lying silently on the bed.

He was alone. Completely, totally, irrevocably alone.

Chapter One

Autumn, 1890

> *Dearest little sister,*
>   *With deep regret I write this to you, for I ab-hor casting a shadow over the wonderful time you are surely having at university in Europe. However, I fear you would never forgive me should I not let you know the news immediately.*
>   *Papa suffered a heart attack this morning. He is still in crisis; we are most worried about him. The doctor won't leave his side; nor will the rest of us, for he has not yet gained consciousness.*
>   *You must come, Sonnie. Come back home to us. Papa needs you now.*
> *Barbara*

Sonnie Mancuso didn't have to read the telegram again to know its contents. She could recite every paragraph, every word, from memory.

She'd been strolling St. Peter's Square in Rome when the message had finally caught up with her. Accompanied by her aunt and two of her cousins, she'd raced through the great piazza back to their hotel; within hours they'd boarded a train to Paris, then another to London, and finally a steamship back to America. Aunt Josephine's wealth and influence had been invaluable in arranging their harried return.

With gloved fingers, Sonnie refolded her older sister's message along lines so creased the edges had begun to tear. Her gaze fell, as it had many times before, to the date typed three months earlier.

Three months. Had Papa recovered since she'd received word of his attack? Or had he . . . ?

Sonnie refused to think of the possibility of his death. He was too strong, too smart, too . . . stubborn to die.

And she had missed him terribly since he had sent her away.

Vince Mancuso had not been blessed with sons. Sonnie was his sixth daughter, an "afterthought" born nearly ten years after Barbara. Cholera had claimed her mother when Sonnie was yet a baby, and after her passing, Vince had channeled his energies and time into building the Rocking M ranch, while leaving the care and responsibility of raising Sonnie to his older daughters.

Sonnie's mouth dipped ruefully at the rush of memories. She'd been a hellcat in those early years, much to the exasperation of her sisters. Willful and too much of a hoyden, she'd resisted their attempts to domesticate her, to teach her of cooking and sewing and cleaning the big house, when all she'd ever wanted was to brand cows and ride horses and feel the clean Wyoming air blow across her face and through her hair.

She'd longed to be one of her father's men.

It had been impossible, of course. Vince had been determined she'd be a replica of her sisters, a proper young lady with all the feminine attributes inherited from her mother. He'd been appalled at her tomboy ways, and had thwarted her keen interest in the workings of the ranch, right up to the day the last of the Mancuso sisters had married and moved away.

Papa needs you now.

Sonnie didn't think Vince Mancuso had ever needed anyone, least of all her. What use did he have for a tagalong daughter? He'd already raised five. If he'd ever needed her, or even wanted her, he never would've sent her to Boston to live with Aunt Josephine, to receive her schooling there, to learn of social etiquette and fashions and the arts, all the things her sisters survived just fine without.

She'd been devastated when he had presented her with his decision. He'd refused to listen to her protests, her rants and ravings. She'd thrown a full-blown tantrum, but in the end he'd won, as he always did, and Sonnie left the Rocking M ranch.

She'd been back only once. Once for the holidays in all those years. And even then Papa had plopped her right back on the train headed east.

Papa needs you now.

Sonnie realized she still held Barbara's telegram between her fingers and slipped it inside the satin-lined leather of her bag. A determined vein of hope brought an uncertain smile to her lips.

Maybe Papa *did* need her. It'd been so long since she'd seen him. Surely he missed her. And perhaps it'd taken a heart attack to make him realize he wasn't invincible, that he wouldn't live forever, that the world didn't revolve around Vince Mancuso and the Rocking M.

Ah, dear, stubborn, headstrong Papa. She couldn't wait to see him.

She only hoped she wasn't too late.

*   *   *

The Union Pacific Railroad passenger car swayed along the rails with a rhythmic hum that would've been almost lulling had Sonnie been of a mind to relax. All day she'd stared through the window at the golden wheat fields and endless sand hills of Nebraska. Since they left the North Platte and Ogallala Depots, the topography of the land had changed from the gentle swell of the bluffs to the jutting snow-capped Rocky Mountains.

Cheyenne would be their next stop. In growing anticipation, she fidgeted with the seams on her gloves, clasped and unclasped her hands. She tried to maintain an aura of composure, but as the mighty steam engine chugged to a stop, she wanted to throw all dignity to the wind and bolt to the doors like an exuberant filly.

Instead she smoothed the striped silk of her dress over her knees. She sat up straighter and tugged at the black bands of velvet trimming her waist. Her fingers gripped her bag primly on her lap, and she waited for the conductor's signal allowing them to leave.

From Boston she'd sent a wire notifying her father—or someone—of the exact date and time of her arrival. What if the wire had never reached the Rocking M? The ranch had always been self-sufficient. Days and even weeks passed before one of the men made a trip into town to receive mail and telegrams.

What if they didn't know she was coming?

Chewing on the inside of her lip—a most unladylike habit, Aunt Josephine always declared—Sonnie stared into the throng of people crowding the platform. The blur of faces revealed no one familiar, and she battled a rising wave of disappointment.

At the conductor's direction, she maneuvered into the aisle with the other departing passengers. She stepped from the train into the crisp autumn air and rose up on tiptoe to search again for someone she recognized.

"Miss Sonnie? Miss Sonnie! Over here!"

So many years had passed since she had heard the wizened old cowboy's voice, but the sound washed over her as though it had been only yesterday. Feeling a delighted smile fill her features, she turned, instantly spotting his arm waving over the heads of the crowd. She returned the wave, then nudged her way through the throng toward him.

"Took yer own sweet time in comin' back, didn't you, young lady?" Cookie scolded with a frown on his face and a twinkle in his eye. "What's the matter? Ain't cow country good enough fer you anymore?"

Knowing there was no malice in his reprimand, Sonnie laughed. Dubbed Cookie for the ready supply of treats he'd kept in his saddlebag to surprise her with as a child, he had worked for her father for as long as she could remember and was as loyal and dedicated as any man could be.

"That's not true, you grouchy dear, and you know it." She dropped a quick kiss upon his stubbly cheek. "How good to see you again!"

"What do y'mean 'grouchy'? Me? Heck, anyone'd turn grouchy standin' 'round waitin' for you and that iron horse to roll in."

"Don't you pay him no mind, Miss Sonnie. We hardly waited at all, and Cookie was plain fascinated by that there train."

Sonnie's glance lifted upward to the tall cowboy beside him. She smiled. "How are you, Stick?" Painfully shy and obviously infatuated, he'd earned his nickname from his lanky height and bony features, but not a finer wrangler did Vince Mancuso employ. "My, I do believe you've gotten more handsome since I saw you last."

16

"Aw, Miss Sonnie." An embarrassed·blush crept from the collar of his new shirt upward to his slicked-down hair. "You always say that, leastways you used to, and both of us know it ain't true."

"Oh, but it is." She laughed again and gave him an impulsive peck on the cheek. "Thank you for coming to meet me."

"My pleasure, ma'am." His blush deepened from her show of affection. "I'm real glad to see you again, and I'm sure your pa will be, too."

She searched both weathered expressions.

"How is Papa?" she ventured, her smile fading. "He's all right, isn't he?"

"Reckon he is." Cookie patted Sonnie's shoulder in somber reassurance, and she murmured a fervent prayer of relief. "The heart attack took a bite out of his strength, but he's gettin' better. The doc says he'll need a few more weeks of recoverin'."

"Your sisters were all here one time or another," Stick added. "Took their turn takin' care of him. They've gone home to their families, though, now that the worst is over."

"Yep." Cookie eyed her shrewdly. "All that's been missin' is the baby of the bunch. The littlest Mancuso."

The littlest Mancuso. Daughter number six. The last in line, the one who always seemed to be nudged aside, sent away, unneeded.

Not anymore.

Sonnie met the old cowboy's bold perusal.

"I'm a grown woman now, Cookie. With a mind of my own." She squared her shoulders with renewed resolve and turned. "Stick, please retrieve my trunk when it's unloaded. Ask them to hurry. Oh, and leave word that the rest of my things will be arriving shortly. Cookie, bring the rig around. I can hardly wait to see Papa!"

17

As both men obediently wove their way through the dissipating crowd, the older of the two mumbled and shook his head in a well-practiced scowl.

"Dadburned bossy woman," he said. "The way she's taken to givin' orders, you'd a-think she was plannin' on stayin' fer a spell."

At the thought, a sudden wide grin spread and softened his grizzled features, and his steps quickened to do her bidding.

Sonnie eyed the interior of the small stagecoach with admiration, noting the tufted leather seats and gleaming wood. The exterior sported a coat of black and gold paint; even the wheels were trimmed in matching hues. In her time away from the Rocking M, she'd been exposed to various displays of wealth and luxury, and this coach, obviously new, ranked among the finest she'd seen.

She wondered at her father's reasoning in the purchase. Had his preferences switched from traveling by horseback to a mode more sedate? Had his health demanded it? Or had he taken a liking to a more flamboyant lifestyle?

For not the first time, Sonnie realized how little she knew him anymore. They had lived worlds apart for too long. The ties they shared as father and daughter had grown fragile, so fragile that in her loneliest moments, she was sure they were nonexistent.

But she was going home now. She would learn to know him again, just as she would know the ranch and all the cowboys who worked it. Vince would love her as he should, as she loved him.

Because he needed her.

The shiny stagecoach door swung open on well-oiled hinges. Cookie stuck his head inside and squinted at her.

"Stick and I are gonna ride on the box. You gonna

18

be okay inside here by yerself, young lady?"

Sonnie smiled at his concern. "Of course. Why wouldn't I be?"

He shrugged. "There's been trouble 'round these parts lately. You know how to use a gun?"

His question startled her. "Why, yes, but—"

He leaned forward and grasped a small wooden case from the seat opposite her, then tossed it into her lap. "There's one if you need it. Already loaded and everythin'. Brought a basket of vittles, too. The boss thought you might be hungry after yer trip. Anythin' else I can get you?"

"No, thank you. I'll be fine."

"Don't worry 'bout nothin'. Stick and I'll take good care of you." He grinned. "Boss-man would skin us alive if we didn't."

As he stepped away, Sonnie noticed the ominous rifle in his hand. The door latched firmly, and she frowned. What kind of trouble brewed that demanded they be heavily armed?

She glanced at the case in her lap and lifted the lid. On a bed of velvet lay a shining, silver-barreled derringer and a ready supply of miniature copper-colored bullets. Somber, she closed the lid again. Years in the city under Aunt Josephine's protection had sheltered her from the violence that was part of everyday life here in the West. The land was prone to outbursts of lawlessness—she'd do well to remember that—and while there was a time in her life when the sight of a gun and bullets wouldn't have troubled her overmuch, today it only served to remind her yet again how her father had distanced her from their home at the Rocking M. She thrust the case in a far corner of the seat.

More than ever, she was determined to prove to him how valuable she was, that she belonged on the Rocking M. From the satchel at her feet, she retrieved the latest edition of *Special Report on Diseases of Cattle* and opened its pages thoughtfully.

How hard she had studied these years! Papa didn't know of the classes in animal husbandry she'd taken—and excelled in. He would never meet her professors in veterinary science or horticulture. He wouldn't understand how she, as a woman, struggled to learn in a man's world, to be accepted for her intelligence and not her beauty or gender.

How could he, when he couldn't accept her himself?

A flicker of hurt and resentment flared before she quickly banked it. No, she had never told him of the studies she'd chosen; indeed, she had sworn Aunt Josephine to secrecy. She would surprise him. She would prove to him she was as good as he was.

The rig lurched forward. Her pensive gaze drifted to the window. Cheyenne had grown, she realized. Businesses flourished; traffic rumbled heavily in the streets. Wyoming had been admitted to statehood only a few months earlier and had prospered from the great westward expansion. The Eastern newspapers often reported the problems that same growth had caused, vexing wealthy cattlemen like her father and threatening the massive lands they owned.

Compared to Boston's civility, Cheyenne seemed harsh, even crude. The women dressed plainly, quite unlike herself. Sonnie conceded that her tendency to favor the current fashions raging in London and Paris would cast her as an oddity here. Hadn't she turned more than a few feminine—and masculine—heads at the train station?

The team lumbered past the outskirts of Cheyenne. Lush grasses blanketed the rangeland; grazing cattle roamed the hills and valleys for as far as Sonnie could see. She drank in the sight, which was vastly different from the congestion of the city, and she wondered if the herds of Hereford cattle carried the Rocking M brand.

Eventually, however, her belly reminded her how long it had been since her last meal. She laid aside her book and found the basket Cookie had left for her.

A checkered towel covered the top, and beneath, Sonnie discovered fruit, cornmeal muffins, raisins and nuts, even an india rubber water bottle with a drinking cup.

Papa's thoughtfulness warmed her. His consideration of her comfort increased her longing to see him all the more.

And when had his men begun to call him "Boss-man"?

The basket's fare soon eased her hunger. Munching on the last of the filberts and walnuts, she settled into a corner of the coach and eased back into the tufted leather. She propped the book in front of her and began reading of the most recent findings of the United States Department of Agriculture.

The rig jerked in a sudden spurt of speed, and Sonnie frowned.

A shot exploded in the distance. From the box, Cookie shouted a harsh command. A whip snapped; Stick bellowed, and the team heaved forward even faster. The rutted road bounced the stagecoach without mercy and toppled her book to the floor. Sonnie was forced to grip the edges of her seat lest she fall with it.

Alarm wadded in the back of her throat. Someone had given them chase, but why? A second gunshot erupted closer still. Dear God, what had they done?

Rawhide cracked again and again. Desperation threaded Cookie's yells as he urged the team to their limits. The coach pitched and tossed, and Sonnie was sure the frame would be ripped in two.

A flash of color merged with the blur of the countryside. A rider, his revolver raised to take aim, galloped terrifyingly close. Another, this one on the rig's opposite side, did the same. Gunfire burst in her ears. The coach careened wildly, thrusting Sonnie helplessly to one side. She cried out and tumbled with a thump to the floor. The awful sensation of spinning, of growing dizzy and disoriented, assailed her. She slid and banged against the seat, the basket, the door.

And then . . . nothing—absolute stillness for second after heart-pounding second.

A savage epithet shattered the silence. She blinked at the door above her.

The door. A rational part of her understood that the coach had fallen to its side, and that she lay with legs spread, hat askew, and skirts askance, in a most unladylike position.

"By Gawd, now look at what you went and did." Outside, Cookie's voice grated with horror and dismay. He pounded on the rig's undercarriage. "Sonnie? Miss Sonnie? Oh, Gawd, you all right?"

She couldn't speak. Shock numbed her.

"We gotta git her out!" Stick rasped.

"Git over here, you sons of bitches, and help us. We got a woman inside, and she could be dead!" Cookie yelled.

Sonnie's mouth moved. She wanted to reassure him nothing was broken, that she was only bruised, that if they could just give her a few moments to catch her breath and tattered composure—

The stagecoach began to rock and sway anew. A wave of nausea nearly upended her stomach. Horses whinnied, men grunted and swore, and she slid and bumped all over again. The rig settled upright with a bone-jarring thud.

The door flung open; her edition of *Special Report on Diseases of Cattle* slid out. Breathing heavily,

Cookie appeared in the opening with Stick craning over his gray head.

"Miss Sonnie?"

"She's alive! Thank the good heavens!"

"Come on, honey. Me and Stick'll help you out. You okay?"

She managed a wobbly nod. Assured no blood had spilled and all her bones were intact, she righted her petticoats and sat up. Her Italian heritage had gifted her with a fine temper, and she resecured her hat with its diamond-studded pin with increasing annoyance, and though Aunt Josephine had taught her to curtail most outbursts, this time even she wouldn't deny that a full-fledged scolding was warranted and acceptable.

"What's takin' her so long in there?" someone demanded with a snarl. "Git her out here where's I can see her!"

"We gotta git you out, like he says," Cookie said in a terse voice. He patted her shoulder in grim reassurance. "We're in a bit of trouble right now, but you jest let me an' Stick handle it, and you'll be jest fine."

Sonnie scooted to the doorway on her backside and slid her feet to the ground. She drew in an irate breath. "Well, I *never* in all my born days—"

A big, filthy hand grasped her wrist and yanked her from the coach. She scurried to keep her balance and spun in fury toward the brute.

Her angry outburst swirled back into her throat. He possessed a body as powerful as the strength in his hand. Coarse black hair hung down to his shoulders; eyes dark as coal scrutinized her with contempt. He was bare-chested and wore only trousers and boots, and his skin was a shade of copper she'd never seen except upon the pages of her cousin Jeffrey's dime novels.

An Indian.

23

Her indignation left her in a whoosh. Savages. All of them. So many times Jeffrey had described their war parties and methods of torture, their expertise with tomahawks and penchant for scalp raising.

Dear God.

"Anyone else in there, Snake?"

The Indian grunted a negative reply to his partner's barked question. He crossed his arms over his mammoth chest and stood in menacing silence.

"Where's Mancuso?" the other man demanded. He reminded Sonnie of a weasel with his elongated features and crafty eyes. He sweated profusely, though the air carried a chill. His body stank with old perspiration.

"He ain't here," Cookie hedged, one eye narrowed.

"This his rig?"

"Maybe."

"It is." The man smiled without humor, revealing two missing front teeth. "Nobody else 'round here's got a getup as fine as that 'un."

"So? What're you gonna do about it?"

"I want Mancuso!" he snapped.

"Well, runnin' innocent folk off the road ain't gonna git him fer you!" Cookie snapped back.

The animosity shimmering between the two men was a tangible thing. Why the weasel and the Indian wanted her father Sonnie couldn't imagine, but instinct told her no good would come of their meeting.

"Innocent?" The weasel smirked and waved his revolver in their direction. "I know you two're part of his outfit, and that makes you no more innocent'n he is." He shifted his attention toward Sonnie. She drew a wary breath inward. "What I don't know is . . . how this here little beauty fits in."

Cookie lifted his clenched fists into fighting position; his wiry body shielded hers.

24

"Git any closer and I'll tromp yer hide. Don't think I won't!" he warned.

"You just leave her alone, mister," Stick declared tightly. "She ain't got no part in any of her pa's doin's."

"Shut up, Stick," Cookie said in a growl.

"Her pa? Well, now. How 'bout that?" To Sonnie's surprise, the weasel cackled in sudden glee. "Didn't know Mancuso had another piece of fluff tucked away somewheres. An' now she's here. Well, well, well."

Offended, Sonnie lifted her chin. She didn't like the way he looked at her, or spoke of her father, or found such amusement in her return. She had no idea what it all meant, and her confusion stifled the scathing retort she dearly wanted to make, but didn't dare.

The weasel returned his revolver to his holster and gestured to the Indian.

"Let's go, Snake. We'll catch up with the old man later," he said, still smiling. "I'd say our time here was well spent, even if we didn't get to the old man, wouldn't you?"

The Indian returned to his palomino in silence. He halted, one foot in the stirrup. His cold glance touched her like a slimy hand. His hard mouth curled in contempt. Sonnie swallowed and endured a new fear.

Everything Jeffrey told her could be—would be—true with this man.

He mounted and let loose with a shrill, yipping yell that sent shivers down her spine. He kicked his mount's ribs and tore off into the hills. The weasel followed.

"Oh, Miss Sonnie." Stick groaned. "I feel right terrible that your homecomin' was spoilt like this."

Cookie swore and yanked off his hat.

"You dadburned idiot," he said in a hiss. He drew back and swatted him against the shoulder once, twice. Stick yelped in surprise. "What'd you go and do a stupid thing like tellin' 'em she was Mr. Mancuso's young'un fer? Don't you know when to keep yer fool mouth shut?"

The young cowboy blanched in genuine distress. "Aw, Cookie, I didn't know . . . didn't think—"

"Damn right you didn't think!"

He looked as if he intended to land Stick a few more blows with his hat, and Sonnie hastened to intervene.

"It's all right, Cookie. News of my return will spread quickly anyway. No harm done. Truly."

"Yeah, you'll think 'no harm done' when them two are back stirrin' up trouble for yer pa," he muttered, plopping his battered hat back onto his gray head.

Misery cast a pall over Stick's face. "I'm sorry. Real sorry. We'll get her on home just as fast as we can, and she'll be safe there."

But Cookie's thumb jabbed the air in the direction of the stagecoach. "We ain't goin' nowhere fer a spell. The rig has a dadburned broken axle which ain't goin' to get fixed whilst we're standin' here exercisin' our jaws! Now you git Miss Sonnie's trunk so's she has somethin' to set on, then haul yer butt back to help me, y'hear?"

"Yes, sir!"

Stick hurried to retrieve her trunk, thrown from the coach a short distance away. Cookie bustled off to gather tools from beneath the driver's seat. Sonnie stood frozen, awash in guilt and dismay.

If she'd been born the son Vince Mancuso had always wanted, then none of this would be happening. She'd never have gone out east, wouldn't be returning home now. She wouldn't have fallen at the mercy of those two shifty men. Cookie wouldn't be upset and concerned; Stick wouldn't be mortified from a mere slip of information. And perhaps, if she'd been a son, Vince Mancuso would have confided his dealings, the

reasons their assailants hated him so. She'd be knowl-
edgeable, strong enough to fight back, trusted.

Instead she was just one more of her father's
daughters. Another Mancuso "piece of fluff."

She drew in a slow, purposeful breath.

No, not "fluff." She was educated now. Useful.
More capable than any of her sisters.

Maybe even more capable than any of his men.

Thus bolstered, she gave Stick a reassuring smile
as he presented her with the trunk. Opening her hand-
bag, she removed the telegram tucked inside. Barbara's words, her plea to come quickly, reinforced her
resolve.

Papa *did* need her.

With growing determination, she rescued her
abused edition of *Special Report on Diseases of Cattle* and reverently brushed the dirt from its cover.
Since she didn't know the first thing about repairing
a stagecoach's axle, she would learn of poisons and
parasites, medicines and cures, and return to the
Rocking M as the most intelligent daughter Vince
Mancuso had.

Chapter Two

Winter, 1877

*The wind howled and whistled outside Omaha's Old
Opera House, but the men and women crowded inside
had long ago forgotten the snow-driven cold. Children occupied their full attention, orphan children
newly arrived on the train from New York.*

*Already, under the scrutinizing eyes of the adults,
they'd paraded through the aisles before standing in
a semicircle on the stage, and already most of them
had been picked.*

Only Lance remained. Unchosen. Alone.

*Humiliation seared him. He stared straight ahead.
So what if no one wanted him? So what if no one
cared enough to take him in for a little while? He
was fifteen, the oldest of the orphans here. Only two
more years and he'd be on his own.*

So what?

He'd survived nearly five years at the Children's

Aid Society. Nearly five years without Mother. Nearly five years of selling matches and newspapers and helping the Reverend Brace take care of the younger boys.

He could survive a couple more.

The western agent in charge would simply take him to the next scheduled stop. And there, as now, he'd stand perfectly still while everyone gawked at him in his stupid orphan uniform and tried to decide whether or not to take him.

Alone. He would survive.

Lance dragged his gaze to a burly-chested man waiting expectantly before him. Snow dusted the shoulders of his thick sheepskin coat and collected on the brim of his big hat. He moved closer, emanating an obscure vapor of cool, fresh air.

After a long moment, the man reached out and poked Lance's biceps, then tilted his chin upward as if to inspect his coloring.

"A little scrawny," he murmured. Offended, Lance stiffened and pulled away. The man smiled. "But nothing honest work and square meals won't cure. You got a good appetite?"

Lance didn't tell him he couldn't get his fill at the orphanage, that there always seemed to be someone younger and hungrier than himself at the table. He tried to ignore the glimmer of hope flickering within him.

The man stroked his pencil-thin mustache. Lance, growing uneasy from the silence, shifted from one foot to the other.

"So you're looking for a home, eh?" the man asked finally.

Lance swallowed his pride. "Yes, sir."

"And I'm looking for a son." His features softened, and he nodded in approval. He extended his hand. "Name's Mancuso. Vince Mancuso."

*   *   *

They were late. Damn late.

Lance leaned a hip against the porch railing and inhaled deeply of his cigarette. Smoke billowed from his lungs in an impatient swirl. One more time, he scanned the road leading up to the big house. One more time, he found it empty.

Cookie and Stick had better have a good reason, a heck of a good reason, for being this late.

He'd give them ten more minutes, then mount up and ride into Cheyenne himself. His mind agonized over every mishap, every reason he could think of that might have caused their delay. He vowed to find them and bring them all back home again.

Sonnie. Oh, to see her again.

The blood heated in his veins. It always did when he thought of her. It mattered little that she didn't know who the heck he was. From the moment he'd first laid eyes on her years ago, he'd stayed in the background, out of her life.

And loved her.

A smudge on the horizon gradually formed into a definite shape. Lance recognized the stagecoach. He pulled his glance from the road and tried to quell the leap of anticipation in the pit of his belly. Flicking his cigarette into nearby shrubbery, he straightened from the railing and turned toward the man seated halfway across the porch.

"They're coming, Vince."

Sonnie's father peered at him over the rim of his reading glasses, nodded, and folded his newspaper neatly in his lap. He rose, wobbly at first, and steadied himself with his cane. He slid his glasses into a shirt pocket and waited at the top of the stairs.

Lance considered him. Mancuso presented a fine figure of a man. Sturdy in stature, he was handsome and formidable. The heart attack had cost him some weight, some strength, and his age had slowed his recovery, but his eyes were shrewd, his mind sharp and quick. The running of the ranch had never faltered after his illness.

Even so, Lance noticed the subtle dependence he had shown toward him. He'd taken Lance into his confidence, showed him the inner workings of the Rocking M, displayed the financial ledgers few before him had seen. He'd asked for, and Lance had given, advice. They'd talked for hours of subjects they hadn't the time for in the past, and the bonds, already begun that cold day at Omaha's Old Opera House, had grown even stronger.

Lance knew Mancuso had misgivings about Sonnie's return. Why, he didn't yet understand, but Vince didn't show the elation a father should have upon his daughter's return home. Sonnie was the one topic Vince rarely discussed, and the one Lance wanted to the most.

The stagecoach lumbered into the yard. Cookie barked the team to a halt and pulled the brake. Stick leaped down, and without a glance toward the porch, hurried toward the rig's door.

Lance remained at the railing. Expectation rooted him to the floor, rendered him motionless. The door opened wide, and he caught a glimpse of a small, kid-leathered foot stepping to the ground. Teasing snippets of petticoats tumbled about shapely ankles before they were lost in the volume of rose-and-green-striped silk.

A rushing sensation, not unlike a thousand waterfalls, erupted within him. His heart pounded—no, thundered—in his head and chest. Blood flowed hot in his veins.

She always did this to him. The pitifully few times he'd been near her, it happened without fail. He gripped the railing behind him, gripped until he feared the wood would snap, until he achieved a measure of control.

Control.

He wouldn't let her see the effect she had on him. What would she think? That he was a coward?

Seconds passed. She never gave him a passing glance. She hadn't noticed he was there.

The rush faded, grew more manageable. He released the railing, flexed his fingers behind his back.

She was beautiful. As beautiful as the most exotic wildflowers growing free on the Wyoming range. More beautiful than any woman he'd ever known.

With a gloved hand, she touched a finger to her hair, which was black as sable, lustrous. Her hat was perched forward on her head in the latest fashion and sported ostrich feathers that floated and swayed with every movement. Luscious red lips quivered with emotion.

"Papa?" she whispered.

The little sound tore at Lance. She abandoned her dignity and flew up the porch stairs. Vince caught her in his arms and murmured her name.

Moved by their reunion, Lance looked away. The carriage door clicked shut; Stick's boot sole crunched the dirt.

The sounds tugged Lance's attention. The two cowboys were disheveled and somber. His gaze darted over the stagecoach, the scratches creasing the once-gleaming paint, the broken spokes on two wheels, the bent steel of the frame.

Lance shot a sharp glance back toward Sonnie. She appeared unhurt after whatever battle the vehicle had endured.

He vaulted the railing. Two long strides carried him to Cookie and Stick.

"What happened?" he asked in a low growl.

"Had a scare," Stick declared.

"Heck of a scare," Cookie said. "Two men jumped us. We tried to git away, but they was faster'n us. Wrecked the rig in the process."

"What did they want?" he demanded.

"Mr. Mancuso."

His mouth tightened. Reprisals were not unexpected on the range, but never before had vengeance struck so close to home. Worse, Sonnie had been caught in the crossfire.

"Who were they?"

"Clay Ditson was one, but I didn't let on I knowed him."

Ditson. Lance narrowed an eye. "And the other?"

"His Injun. Snake. Looked mean as ever, too."

"Heck." Foreboding thick as mud filled him.

"If any harm comes to Miss Sonnie, I reckon I'm to blame." Stick's announcement carried a definite vein of guilt, and Lance raised a questioning brow. "I shouldn't a-told 'em who she was, but it just slipped out. I feel right terrible about it, too."

"We ain't seen the last of 'em, neither!"

The young cowboy's obvious shame deepened from the reproving frown Cookie tossed at him.

Lance made no attempt to salve Stick's remorse. Cookie had reason to be concerned with the revelation of Sonnie's identity, and though Lance understood Stick's regret, loyalty to the Rocking M, and Vince Mancuso and all his kin, was paramount and expected. Anything less would not be tolerated.

"Lance," Vince said, his tone sharp and insistent.

As Lance turned to reply, his gaze clashed with Sonnie's. She stared at him with a mixture of curiosity and disapproval.

"Who did this?" Vince barked, indicating the coach with a terse gesture.

Why did she look at him that way, as if he'd done something wrong? It unsettled him, and he angled his body away from her, as though to shield himself from all she did to him. He concentrated on channeling his attention toward her father.

"Clay Ditson and Snake. They wanted you."

"Hunting me down on the road like a common criminal?" Vince roared.

"Appears so." Lance had learned long ago that calmness weathered him through Vince Mancuso's storms.

"And with my daughter in the coach." The cane thumped the porch floor in Vince's agitation.

"Papa? Do you know them?"

Sonnie clung to her father's arm, as if now that she'd finally arrived, she couldn't let him go.

Seemingly with effort, Vince focused on her. "They're for me to deal with, *mia bambina*. Don't give them another thought."

"How can I not? They gave us quite a chase! What need did they have of you?"

"Business."

"What kind of business?"

"Later, Sonnie."

The command in the words brooked no argument, and she obediently gave him none, but her uncertain glance skittered toward Lance.

Again he looked away. His cowardice regarding Sonnie had been a part of him for as long as he could remember. Vince could handle her far better than he, and Lance steeled himself not to meet her gaze.

"Stick," he said instead. "Take the rig to the machinery barn. We'll fix it up there."

"Okay," he mumbled.

"Got the mail fer you," Cookie said. "Had a wire come in, too."

Lance caught the small bundle sailing toward him from the driver's seat. "Good. Thanks."

The two cowboys tipped their hats to Vince and

Sonnie in polite farewell. Lance moved to join them, but Vince called him back.

"Aren't you coming inside, Lance?" he asked, frowning.

"Thought I'd check on the new foal," he said, grasping the first excuse that popped into his head. He needed time away from Sonnie, needed to be able to breathe the very air she stole from him.

"Pah!" Vince scoffed, waving a dismissing hand. "You just checked him this morning. He's doing fine. Have a drink with us to celebrate my daughter's homecoming."

Lance's pulse beat a little faster inside him, grew bolder with every second he hesitated. To be in the same room with her . . . He tried to think of another excuse, a logical reason to stay away, and failed.

Sonnie released her father's arm. She spoke softly and held the door open for him. Vince, never doubting that Lance would follow, went inside.

The door closed. Lance stood frozen at the bottom of the porch stairs. He'd do whatever Vince Mancuso wanted. He always had. If Vince wanted him to go inside and be polite to Sonnie and engage in normal conversation like any other man and woman, then he would.

But first . . . first he would wait until his heart ceased its pounding roar, until the rush of a thousand waterfalls quieted to a low hum, until the blood cooled in his veins.

Only then could he panic.

Papa's office hadn't changed in the years Sonnie had been away. Oh, a little more cluttered, maybe. A little less organized, certainly. But for the most part, the room had remained just as she remembered it.

She glanced lovingly about her, reacquainting herself with the massive map of the Rocking M that took prominence on the wall behind his desk. On another hung a tanned hide emblazoned with the Rocking M brand. Assorted photographs of her mother, sisters, and herself mingled with those of prized bulls and stallions. Rifles and revolvers filled a nearby gun rack. The room reflected Vince Mancuso's life, his passion for the Rocking M, and the years of hard work he'd put in to make the ranch a prosperous operation, and Sonnie thrilled to see it again.

"What would you like to drink, Sonnie? A glass of wine? I have raspberry brandy, too. Your favorite, eh?" her father asked, propping his cane against the cabinet.

"Yes, Papa. Still my favorite. A glass sounds heavenly. Thank you."

Sonnie slipped the diamond pin from the crown of her hat and set the headpiece on a table. She watched him add a portion of water to the glass, a little idiosyncrasy she'd forgotten. Papa always believed a lady didn't take her spirits full strength. To this day, Sonnie couldn't tolerate them when they were.

"You look wonderful, *mia bambina*," he said, handing her the glass. "As lovely as ever."

"Do I?" She sipped, thoughtful of his use of the endearment. "After traveling so far so quickly, I feel in need of a relaxing bath."

Her father settled himself in the burgundy leather chair at his desk. He considered her a moment.

"You needn't have come, you know. It's dangerous for a young woman to travel alone."

You needn't have come.

A tremor of hurt flickered through her. Her lashes lowered. "Everyone expected the worst after your attack. I couldn't possibly have stayed away knowing you were deathly ill."

"Your sister shouldn't have worried you. Matters were always well in hand."

Sonnie sank slowly onto a brocade settee. Her grip tightened on the glass. Papa hadn't really needed her after all, she realized, despite Barbara's message.

"Who ran the ranch when you couldn't?" she asked in a strained voice.

Papa appeared taken aback at her question. "Lance, of course. Who else?"

"Lance." A niggle of resentment escaped in the single word as she matched the name with the man on the porch.

"Does . . . Lance have a last name?"

"Sonnie," he began with faint exasperation. "Harmon. Harmon's his last name. Don't you remember?"

"Oh, Papa, how could I possibly?" she challenged in defense. "I . . . there have been so many men who've worked for you over the years, and I've been gone—"

The front door opened, and she halted. Bootsteps approached, and Papa's gaze slid toward the hall. Without rising, he motioned *him* inside.

Lance Harmon had presence, Sonnie conceded with a barely disguised sniff. That much she'd give him. Tall and lean, he strode into the room with a grace that belied the power he exuded. Thigh muscles rippled beneath the denim of his Levi's. Spurs jangled from the heels of his boots. In perfect symmetry, narrow hips broadened upward to wide shoulders, and beneath the pale blue shirt he wore, his biceps stretched the fabric almost to its limits.

He tossed the mail, several newspapers, and the telegram onto Papa's desk before helping himself to a bottle of whiskey. He moved about the room with confidence and ease, as if he'd staked ownership. Given Papa's high opinion of him, perhaps he'd done just that, and at the thought, her resentment flared anew.

"Evidently introductions are in order, Lance," Papa

said. A smile formed beneath his mustache. "Sonnie doesn't remember you."

Harmon looked directly at her. Eyes as heated as the whiskey in his hand touched her briefly before flitting away again.

"I'm not surprised. I wasn't around much when she was growing up."

Sonnie bristled. He made her sound as if she were a mere babe from the cradle. The man couldn't be thirty yet, twenty-eight at the most. Being almost twenty herself, she was a full-grown woman and hardly a child.

"This is my daughter, Sonnie Mancuso." Amusement danced in Papa's tone. "And Sonnie, meet Lance Harmon."

She didn't think the matter funny. Her chin lifted, and she waited for Harmon to acknowledge the formality. His eyes lighted on her for another burning scan of seconds, but he remained where he was.

Obviously it would be up to her to follow proper etiquette.

"I'm pleased to meet you," she said coolly and almost held out her hand. In Boston, the men *always* took her hand, often with an added kiss, but this one certainly showed no inclination to do anything similar.

Remaining near the liquor cabinet, his stance relaxed, his demeanor controlled, he simply inclined his head. She was glad she hadn't offered him her hand, after all. His attention left her to focus on her father instead, and the mail he'd begun to open.

Sonnie watched Harmon and nursed her burgeoning animosity much as she nursed the raspberry brandy.

Yes, he was handsome, she mused. Handsome in a rugged way that made the Eastern men she'd met seem like pale-skinned dandies. He had clearly weathered an abundance of sun and physical labor. His tawny-shaded hair shone with highlights of gold; his features were bronzed and defined. He exuded masculinity—sheer, raw masculinity.

Sonnie lifted her glass and took a long swallow.

"Senator Hickman will be attending the Association's meeting," Papa said, scanning the telegram through his reading glasses. "He wants to set up an appointment with us." He held up an envelope and sifted through several others. "But nothing from Mr. Horn."

"Don't expect him to write, Vince," Harmon said, and set his drink aside. "He's not the type to bother."

"A man of Tom Horn's caliber should at least give us the courtesy of an answer," Papa retorted, tossing the mail onto the desktop in frustration. "We've been waiting for weeks."

"Give him a little more time."

"Time! Every day rustlers steal a few more head of cattle or them darn squatters take a little more of our land. The stockmen are being squeezed out of business, and we don't have time to waste."

"I know, Vince."

Papa fell silent for a moment. "We'll wait until the first of the month; then we'll clean up the range *my* way."

His avowal dragged Sonnie's thoughts from Harmon to the matter at hand. She sat back in the settee in puzzlement. Was this the trouble Cookie and Stick had hinted at? Rustlers and squatters were thorns in every cattleman's side, but to what extremes had they gone to force her father into retaliation?

She knew the name Tom Horn. He was an Indian scout and an interpreter, a Pinkerton agent and a deputy sheriff. Yet the Eastern papers had touted a different side of him, one the West had applauded: his notoriety as a gunfighter.

Sonnie nearly shuddered.

Papa had obvious need of his services, which meant the man couldn't be as despicable as one might think. Papa always gave careful thought to everything and everyone, and if he needed Tom Horn's gun, he'd certainly have good reason. Who was she to question his choice?

She didn't appreciate being ignored, however. Papa and Harmon conversed as if she'd vanished into another room, as if, as a woman, she'd be incapable of intelligent conversation, or worse, totally incognizant of the seriousness of the situation.

But she understood. Being chased down in the stagecoach this afternoon and having her life threatened clearly defined the ruthlessness of the Weasel and the Indian and the measures they'd take to get to her father.

Papa scowled and snatched another letter to open. The front door slammed. A definite thunk on the foyer floor suggested her trunk had been set aside.

Stick peered into the office. His searching glance settled on Harmon. "I brought in Miss Sonnie's stuff, boss. And here's the little peashooter you sent along for her. Anythin' else I can do?"

At first Sonnie thought he'd made a mistake in addressing Harmon. She glimpsed her father, but he showed no reaction to the young cowboy's presence; indeed, his mail engrossed him completely.

Boss? Lance Harmon?

The one who'd given her a derringer to defend herself with, who'd sent her a lunch, who'd promised havoc if Stick and Cookie didn't bring her back safely wasn't *Papa?*

Numbness encircled her. Hadn't Papa cared enough to attend to those things himself? Hadn't he worried for her as she'd worried for him? Surely his health would have allowed him to!

Lance Harmon. Not Papa.

Tears burned the back of her eyes. The disappointment pierced her breast like a smoldering coal. Had he taken over her father's life, his men, and the Rocking M as well? Why would Papa let him?

Through the roiling haze of hurt, Sonnie saw Stick put the case containing the gun onto a shelf, heard Harmon speak quietly in turn. Stick seemed eager to please, to make amends for the slip of her identity, and she took immediate pity on him.

After the cowboy's departure, Papa ran a hand over his face. Fatigue etched deep lines in his forehead, and he slumped tiredly in his chair. The stagecoach's broken axle had delayed Sonnie's return by hours, and the wait had obviously taxed his stamina. She clucked her tongue in sympathy.

"Papa, why don't you lie down to rest?" she asked, moving to his side and laying a hand on his shoulder. "When you awaken, you'll feel much better, and we can visit then. I have so much to tell you."

"As much as I hate to admit it, a nap is what I need." He sighed and reached for his cane. "Your papa isn't as strong as he used to be."

"You will be again. In time." Sonnie gently pulled his glasses from the bridge of his nose and put them in a drawer. "Come. I'll help you to bed. Are you still in the little room down the hall?"

He nodded, and she took his arm. She kept her stride even with his as they walked slowly across the room. Papa halted at the door and gave Harmon a wan grin.

"Every father should have a daughter like Sonnie to fuss over him, eh, Lance?"

A corner of Harmon's mouth lifted, but he said nothing. His gaze merely touched her in that heated, intense way of his.

Sonnie's heart swelled from Papa's compliment.

The pleasure his words gave her smothered the hurt she'd endured earlier. How could she have doubted him? He really did need her. He just hadn't said so exactly.

Within moments, Papa had settled himself comfortably in his bed. Sonnie pulled the covers to his chin and bent to kiss his cheek.

"If you have any questions, Lance can help you," he said, his voice already slurring with sleep. "Just ask him."

Sonnie had no intention of asking Lance Harmon for anything. Papa obviously valued the man, but soon he would see he didn't need Harmon as much as he thought. Not while she was here.

She returned to the office to retrieve her hat. Harmon stood at the window, his back to her. He appeared deep in contemplation as he stared out over Mancuso land; indeed, he hardly seemed aware she'd entered the room. Not that he'd react any differently if he *were* aware, she thought with another sniff. He'd yet to speak to her directly since she had arrived.

With hat in hand, she slipped from the office and headed upstairs to her bedroom. Spread along the entire front width of the house, it had once been her parents'. After her mother died, though, her father had moved downstairs, leaving the room unoccupied for years. As her sisters married and moved away, the rest of the upstairs bedrooms had all emptied out as well—except for Sonnie's childhood hideaway at the end of the hall.

When she was fourteen, though, Sonnie had decided to abandon her old, youthfully decorated room, with its clutter of toys and dolls, and unobtrusively moved in to the old master suite. She loved its spacious and cheerful feel, lent by the abundance of sunshine spilling in from windows lining an entire wall. A sitting room on the right had once doubled as a nursery but now bore a chaise, vanity, and book-shelves, and presented a wonderfully private retreat. The crocheted coverlet, thick floral carpet, and heavy furniture offered a quiet elegance her maturing tastes favored.

She tugged the draperies farther apart and opened a window. The cooling breeze freshened her skin, and, exhaling a pleased sigh, she turned and spotted a pair of boots, their leather tooled and shined, propped at the foot of the bed. With a frown tugging at her lips, Sonnie let her gaze sweep the room. A stack of folded shirts lay on the dresser, and a jacket was carelessly draped over the back of a chair. A small bowl held a pile of cigarette stubs and cold ashes.

She pivoted at the sound of movement in the hall. Harmon balanced her trunk on one shoulder and headed toward her former room at the back of the house.

"Lance?"

His step halted at the sound of her voice. Slowly, as if not expecting to be called from behind, he turned, narrowly missing the walls with the corners of the trunk.

"May I call you Lance? Or would you prefer Mr. Harmon?"

Sonnie couldn't help the haughty tone of the questions, but her resentment of him smothered her good manners.

A wary guardedness leaped in the chiseled planes of his expression. "Lance is fine."

The sensual timbre of his speech drifted over her. She steeled herself against any slip of a reaction and glided away from the windows to indicate the baggage he carried.

"I believe that's mine. Set it by the bed, please. I'll unpack later."

For a moment he didn't move. His glance swung from her to her old room, then back again.

"I thought—" He stopped. "I was under the impression you—"

"I haven't slept in there since I was fourteen. It seems, however"—she lifted her nose loftily—"that someone has laid claim to this room in my absence."

His silence obliterated any doubts she might have had. Above the open collar of his shirt, his throat worked in a spasmodic movement, as if he tried to swallow and couldn't.

His corded muscles bulged from the strain of carrying the trunk. He entered the room and slid it from his shoulder to the floor before straightening.

"Your father couldn't be left alone after his attack. I moved in to stay closer to him."

"My sisters were here, were they not?" she challenged.

"Yes," he said. "But after he regained consciousness, he asked that I, in particular, stay."

"I see." Her lips clamped in barely restrained irritation. "Well, he's feeling much better now, isn't he?" She scooped up the pair of boots in one arm and the mound of shirts in the other. "If you don't mind, Lance Harmon, I prefer to have my room back." She thrust them all at him and snatched the jacket to add to the pile. "Find some other place to sleep, won't you?"

A vague spark of rebellion, so minuscule she might have been mistaken, flared in the honey-gold depths of his eyes, yet receded as quickly as it appeared. Her glare seemed to unnerve him, and, wordlessly, he strode to the doorway.

"Wait," Sonnie demanded.

His arms full of clothing, his back ramrod straight, he halted without turning.

"Stick and Cookie did their best to protect me this

afternoon. They'd have given their lives had it been necessary," she declared with firm emphasis. "Any mistakes they may or may not have made should not—and will not—be held against them." She paused. "Do I make myself clear?"

He waited so long to reply she thought he'd deny her altogether.

"Yes," he finally said, the terse word hanging heavy in the air. "Crystal clear."

Sonnie remained unmoving long after he left. She'd expected to feel a stirring of satisfaction from wielding her authority over him. After all, she was a Mancuso, and he was only one of Papa's men.

But satisfaction evaded her, leaving in its stead a nagging certainty that Lance Harmon was more, much more, than simply one of her father's ranch hands.

Chapter Three

Land, miles and miles of land, stretched toward the horizon and beyond. Covered with a thick shawl of brilliant snow, caressed by a deep azure sky, this place called Wyoming Territory presented a raw challenge as breathtaking as the swirling January wind.

Mancuso land. All Lance could see and more.

How could one man own so much? He thought of the congestion, the slums, the filth of New York. How could a part of one country be so ugly and another so beautiful, so limitless with opportunity?

"Impressive, eh?" Vince Mancuso watched him closely, a confident smile curving below the line of his mustache.

Lance could only nod. Words escaped him. The awe of it all held him transfixed and wide-eyed.

"I'm offering you a new life here, son," Vince said. "One that won't be easy, one that'll make you dog-tired at the end of each day." Pridefully, his glance *swept the wintry horizon before he resumed. "But I'm telling you, too, that you'll be rarin' to go every morning, and you won't do without." He hitched the collar of his coat higher about his ears. "Mind if I call you son?"*

The shift in conversation left Lance pensive. He'd be nobody's son except Mother's—he hadn't been Father's since the day he left—but if it made Vince Mancuso happy to call him that, then he could see no harm in it.

The horse beneath him pawed the snow. Lance ignored the discomfort the action caused, discomfort born of thigh muscles unaccustomed to a saddle. Once more, his enthralled gaze roamed the expansive meadows and hills sprawling in every direction.

"You're fifteen," Vince went on without waiting for a reply. "I'll pay you a fair wage, even though I've got the papers saying I don't have to. We'll get a formal adoption later if you want. Either way, I'll be taking care of you from now on."

Lance wiggled his toes inside the stiff leather of his just-bought boots. Eagerness spiraled through him. Long nurtured within the walls of the orphanage, the yearning for a home of his own triggered a deep thirst to learn of this unfamiliar land, to work it with his sweat, to belong.

Finally, to belong.

She hated him.

Lance dropped the heap of shirts and boots into the nearest chair and strode out the door with long, frustrated strides. He leaped down the porch stairs two at a time, his foul mood tattooing a scowl on his face.

He'd taken her room, her haven in the big house, the one place on the entire spread she could claim as hers, the only part of the Rocking M Vince hadn't taken away from her.

But *he* had.

The knowledge mortified him.

He cursed himself for not thinking of her side of it, for not having her homecoming in perfect readiness. He despaired of not asking Vince or Barbara or any one of her sisters which bedroom was hers before he'd moved in.

He strode toward the barns and outbuildings scattered beyond the well-tended lawn of the house. Several cowboys slid him curious glances, but he ignored them. A worktable was set up outside the main barn, and Charlie Flynn, on the Mancuso payroll for almost a decade, intently repaired a maze of harnesses.

"Charlie!" Lance barked without a break in his gait. "Mount up. We're riding into town."

Charlie glanced at the sky and the sun that would set in a couple of hours' time. He set the harnesses aside and followed Lance into the barn.

Both men saddled their horses in silence. Lance avoided Charlie's questioning gaze.

"Gonna be dark soon," Charlie finally said.

"I know."

"You got a hankerin' for some of Gracie's cold beer or something?"

"Or something."

Charlie grinned and pushed his hat higher over his short, sandy-shaded hair. "You got a hankerin' for Gracie?"

Lance tightened the cinch around the sorrel stallion. It'd been a while since he'd been needled about the woman who took his virginity, but he was in no mood to tolerate a round of teasing. He stabbed a boot into the stirrup and swung into the saddle. "No. I need her help."

Charlie followed suit. Dipping their heads beneath the wide door as they exited, they guided their horses from the barn.

"I reckon this has something to do with Miss Sonnie's accident," Charlie said, an eye squinting once more to the sky.

"Yeah, it does."

"Then I'm happy to be along. She didn't deserve to get her pretty little neck nearly broke just 'cause she wanted to come home and take care of her pa."

News had spread of the afternoon's ambush. Charlie's loyalty would mirror that of every other hand who worked the ranch, Lance knew, and the cowboy's comment toughened his intent. A trip to see Gracie might net a chance to learn the whereabouts of the men who'd caused it all.

He spied Stick brushing down the last of the horses unhitched from the stagecoach. His strokes were grim and brisk, a purging of his soul. Lance sensed the regret still haunting him.

He pulled up close to the corral. Stick spotted him; the currycomb went still in his hand, and he straightened.

"Sonnie spoke well of the care you and Cookie gave her today," Lance said. "You did the best anyone could under the circumstances."

"Anyone else mighta kept their mouth shut about who she was," Stick retorted sullenly.

"It's done. Ditson would've found out sooner or later." Lance held Stick's gaze. "I wouldn't hesitate to put her in your protection again."

"You wouldn't?"

"No."

Stick drew up taller. His remorse fell away like an unneeded blanket. "I'd die for her if I had to, Boss. Any of us would."

Including himself. Lance gave him a tight smile. "Let's hope it doesn't come to that." He reined the sorrel into a turn. "We'll be back late. Leave a light on in the barn for us."

"Sure thing."

"See to Sonnie's needs, too. She's been gone a long time. She—"

"Say no more. She's had me sufferin' from Cupid's cramps for as long as I can remember. She won't lack for nothin' if I can help it."

Lance guessed Cupid's arrow had pierced the heart of most any man who knew her. But no heart had been pierced as deeply as his own.

He gave Stick a curt nod of farewell and poked his spurs into the horse's ribs. With Charlie beside him, he rode hard toward Cheyenne.

Gracie's Spirits and Eatery occupied a corner of Sixteenth and Thomas Streets, directly across from Wightman Livery and right in the midst of the town's bustling business district. Gracie Purcell had opened her little café to cater to customers who were few but regular, consisting mostly of saddle tramps and cowboys too dusty and dirty to frequent a restaurant demanding more respectable clientele.

Maybe because Gracie herself had never gotten respectable.

Former dancer. Former singer. Former madam. Some said she'd even been a prostitute in her younger days. She had a smile as big as the wide Wyoming sky and a heart to go along with it, however, and Lance'd liked her from the moment he'd met her.

The hitching post in front of the eatery was full of tethered horses, their riders most likely lingering over coffee after eating supper or indulging in the first of a long night's string of beers. Lance and Charlie added their reins to the row, and, slapping the dust from the brims of their hats, they ambled toward the door.

Out of habit, Lance scanned the horses' rumps in the gathering dusk. Gracie's had long been a favorite watering hole for cowpunchers from the Mancuso outfit. He recognized many of the local brands, but none wore the *M* and half-circle of the Rocking M. Only two horses, a mealymouthed bay and a rangy palomino, didn't carry a brand, an oddity in a land where stockmen diligently marked all that was theirs.

Inside, blue gingham tablecloths and frilly matching curtains offered the only feminine touches to a room usually dominated by men. Women and children rarely entered, a fact most likely attributable to the colorful painting hanging over the well-polished bar. Sheathed only in a gossamer veil and reclining seductively upon a bed of roses, a naked lady watched over every patron. Gracie had staunchly defended the piece, proclaiming it noble art, and kept the work in its place of prominence, even at the cost of losing coveted, respectable customers.

The tables were partially filled, and Lance and Charlie paused a moment, their glances flicking over the men scattered about the restaurant. No one paid them any mind, and they headed toward an empty table near the bar. Their movement caught Gracie's eye, and she managed a wave despite the stack of dishes in her grasp.

Beauty did not come naturally to her, but Gracie transformed herself into a fetching woman with the aid of lotions and cosmetics. Too-dark brown hair and a thickening waistline gave credence to her years, yet her zest for life made her seem much younger.

"It's about time you two stopped by," she called out in a cheerful voice. Her voluptuous bosom bounced beneath the fabric of her blouse as she approached. "How long's it been? Three, four months?"

Lance smiled and did a quick calculation of the weeks that had passed since spring roundup. "Nearly five, Gracie."

"That's five months too long." She ran an appreciative gaze over him. "You're lookin' good, Lance."

"So are you."

"After runnin' myself ragged in here today? I must look like a limp mop." Despite her words, she beamed from his compliment.

"You gonna quit jawin' and get us a beer, Gracie?" Charlie demanded with a teasing lilt. "Or do we have to get one ourselves?"

"Oh, hush, you old coot!"

"Old coot?" Charlie made a show of being offended. "I ain't a day older'n you, darlin'."

"That's a lie, Charlie Flynn." Any cowboy knew that the way to raise Gracie's hackles was to mention her age, and any cowboy worth his salt mentioned it any chance he got. She shot him a murderous glance and swatted at him with a towel. Chuckling heartily, Charlie ducked, and she missed. Sputtering under her breath, Gracie pivoted in a huff and left them with a blatant wiggle of her hips.

Amused, Lance slid into a comfortable slouch in his chair. He propped one foot on the opposite seat and tilted his hat back. While he waited for Gracie to return with their beers, his assessing gaze swept the room again.

In a far corner of the room, Snake wrangled his dinner as if there were no tomorrow. He sat alone, his attention focused on the meal he shoveled into his mouth. A long-bladed knife lay within reach near his plate.

Gracie set two tall bottles on the table with a thunk. Moisture beaded on the brown glass. Lance took a long swallow of the cold brew and kept the Indian in his range of vision.

"I hear Sonnie Mancuso is back in town," Gracie said as she groped for a paper and pencil in her apron pocket.

Lance made no comment. Merely hearing Sonnie's

name spoken stirred a flurry of emotion within him. Charlie lifted his drink and guzzled, then let out a loud, satisfied sigh.

"Yep," he said. "Purty as ever, too. Maybe more so. Came back to see her pa."

"How's the old man doing?" Gracie watched Lance. He knew she had long suspected his feelings for Sonnie—perhaps had even envied them.

"Gettin' better every day," Charlie answered for him. "Lance takes good care of him, don't you, Lance?"

A woman screamed. A sound, like a piece of furniture falling over, followed, and several heads turned toward the second-story loft.

"Where's Clay Ditson?" Lance demanded. Snake continued to work over his dinner as if nothing unusual had happened.

"Up there," Gracie replied, a frown marring her red lips. She motioned to a closed door at the top of the stairs. "With Daisy."

Lance finished off his beer. The mousy-haired young woman had worked for Gracie in all capacities at the eatery; evidently her duties included seeing to the customers' intimate needs as well.

"She was willing," Gracie said defensively as Lance stood, scraping the floor with his chair. "And Ditson was flashing some big cash. She needed the money. We've all got bills to pay, you know."

Lance ignored her. He strode toward the stairway and up the steps with cold determination. At the door, he halted and turned the knob. The lock had been turned into place.

He lifted a knee and kicked.

The door swung open with a crash. Daisy screamed.

Sheets were tangled between the two on the sagging bed; a nightstand had fallen on its side. Ditson

53

lay prone with Daisy struggling beneath him. His perspiration soured the air. Grimy tendrils of his dark hair escaped from the brim of the hat he hadn't bothered to remove.

Revulsion churned in the depths of Lance's belly. It was times like this when he was ashamed to be a man—when men like Ditson took advantage of a woman even if she was willing—or worse, when she was innocent and vulnerable.

The way Mother had been with the landlord Hawthorne all those years ago.

Or the way Sonnie had been this afternoon.

He thought of Sonnie lying on the sagging mattress instead of Daisy, imagined her being there against her will, her skin soiled from Ditson's touch, his breath, his lust, as he spilled his disgusting seed into her.

The image sickened him.

He snatched a threadbare robe from the floor and tossed it toward the bed. Daisy wriggled free of Ditson and lunged for the garment, covering her thin form with its folds.

"Get out of here, Daisy," he said softly.

She mumbled something resembling acquiescence and darted to the dresser. She plucked a bill from the top and skittered from the room.

"Come back here, you no-account female! I ain't got my money's worth from you yet!" Ditson roared, trying to disentangle himself from the covers. "Harmon, curse you! What the heck're you tryin' to do?"

Lance shut the door behind him. Gracie's patrons had no need to hear his business with Ditson, or to know he intended to take his revenge for the scare Ditson had given Sonnie. He wanted the pleasure all to himself.

"Stay away from Vince Mancuso's daughter," he said.

The deep-throated command appeared to take Ditson by surprise. He eased from the mattress; his features slowly twisted with mirth.

"So that's what this is about." He seemed oblivious of his nakedness as he stepped warily away from the bed. "Wantin' her for yourself, are you? Tell me, Harmon—been under her skirts yet? Given her a right welcome home?"

A mighty snarl erupted from deep within Lance's chest. He grabbed Ditson by the arm and slung his fist into the man's stubbly jaw. Ditson flew into the wall and slumped to the floor.

Lance relished the sting on his knuckles and knew sweet gratification from Ditson's pain.

"Mancuso took what was mine," Ditson rasped. Hate emanated from him. He licked at the blood dripping from the corner of his mouth. "I'll take what's his any chance I get, and if that means gettin' to him through his daughter, then I sure as heck am gonna." He roused himself, but apparently thought better of it, remaining, instead, exactly where he was. "I want my land back, Harmon. All of it. And I'm gonna get it."

"You touch her and I'll kill you."

"You don't scare me. You're as underhanded and connivin' as the old man."

"Silver Meadow was never yours," Lance said in a growl. "Silver Meadow is Mancuso land. You squatted on prime grazing range and stole Mancuso stock to start your own herd. We ran you off once. Next time we won't be so patient."

Ditson's fleshy, sunken chest, sprigged with curling hairs, shook with joyless laughter. "Quite the twosome, ain't you? Mancuso's got so much land, he don't need my little patch. The man's got to learn to share."

Lance straightened grimly. Talking to Ditson had

proved fruitless in the past; now was no different. He moved toward the door.

"I got a right to be a cattleman, just like Mancuso, you son of a bitch!" Ditson yelled. "He ain't got no right to run the rest of us off!"

"Consider yourself warned," Lance said in a low voice. "Stay away from the lady and from the Mancuso range."

His hand gripped the knob and pulled.

"Harmon."

Lance stopped and waited.

"Consider yourself warned that I'm not gonna."

Damn the man to hell. Tight-lipped, Lance yanked the door open and slammed it shut behind him. He met Charlie at the bottom of the stairs.

"Everything okay, boss?" the cowboy asked, concern drawn into his tanned face.

"Fine. Just fine." Lance made no attempt to curb his biting tone. The jangle of his spurs muted the clomp of his boot soles across the wooden floor. He halted at the table where a wide-eyed Gracie still waited, pencil in hand.

He dipped his fingers into the hip pocket of his Levi's and pulled out change. The coins clattered to the table in payment for the beers.

A chair scraped the floor. A harsh sound, sharp and guttural, raised the hair on the back of Lance's neck. Slowly he turned toward the Indian waiting in the shadow-wrapped corner of the restaurant.

A gleaming blade hissed past him, fast as lightning. Snake's knife slammed into a heavy beam scant feet away, its handle still vibrating from the force of the throw.

"Son of a bitch!" Charlie choked, his jaw agape.

Lance didn't flinch. His muscles were frozen, his heart robbed of its normal beat. Snake stood in a wide-legged stance, the crude, angular planes of his copper face arrogant, silent with scorn.

And Lance understood: Clay Ditson possessed the brains, Snake, the muscle. A dangerous pair. A deadly combination. Throwing the knife implied a message, a foreshadowing of . . . later.

Of business not yet finished.

His jaw tightened. Without a challenge to Snake, without thanks to Gracie, without a motion to Charlie, he pivoted toward the restaurant's doors.

Sonnie couldn't have come home at a worse time.

A vague glow from somewhere in the back of the Big House peeped through the dark sitting room window and offered Lance a timid welcome home. His thoughts grave, he perched against the porch railing and slowly finished his cigarette.

He was in no hurry to go inside. Sonnie and Vince had apparently retired early; there would be no one up to talk with, even if he wanted to. Besides, he'd already made a decision. All that was left was to figure a way to see it through.

Somehow he'd have to get Sonnie on a train back to Boston. She'd hate him for it, but it was for her own protection. He winced as he remembered the looks of adoration she gave her father, and anyone could see her happiness to be back on Mancuso land.

But he knew Clay Ditson. Lazy and shiftless, he'd put down stakes in grass-rich Silver Meadow, and then brazenly rustled Rocking M steer over the past winter. After the spring roundup, Lance figured nearly a couple hundred head couldn't be accounted for, and he was convinced that, with Snake's help, Ditson had pilfered the majority.

Vince had been furious. He'd ordered Lance and a dozen of his trusted men to burn Ditson's ramshackle cabin to the ground. Only fast talking on Lance's part had prevented Vince from hunting the two down and hanging them on the spot.

Shortly thereafter, the heart attack felled Vince, and things had quieted down. With no retaliation from Ditson, Lance had put him out of his mind and concentrated instead on nursing Vince back to health.

Then Sonnie came home, and all hell had broken loose.

Not that it was her fault. No, the opposite. She'd been an innocent victim, but at least she'd been a *living* victim. Lance vowed to do everything in his power to keep her safe from harm.

The only way to do that was to send her back East, keep her as far away from the Rocking M and Clay Ditson as possible. Unfortunately, that meant keeping her away from himself, too.

He tossed aside the tiny stub of his cigarette. What chance did he have with her, anyway? He couldn't think straight when she was near. He couldn't breathe, couldn't act like any other man in the presence of a woman. For his own peace of mind and for her safety, he had to send her away.

He breathed a soft curse at the unfairness of it.

The ranch had quieted for the night. The bunkhouse sheltered cots filled with snoring cowboys, dead to the world until just before dawn, when the cook's rousing holler would beckon them to breakfast. Even the livestock were silent.

His growling belly demanded the meal he'd denied it since the ride into Cheyenne. He entered the house, latching the door behind him, and headed for the kitchen, the lamp left burning there drawing him like a beacon. His tread echoed within the walls of the hushed house; his spurs jangled inordinately loudly.

He dropped his hat upon the table before rummaging through the contents of the cabinets. Finding nothing quick and appealing, he turned to the stovetop and the pot perched on one of the burners.

Lifting the lid, he grimaced and sighed. Bean soup again, with congealed bacon grease, chunks of pork, and an overload of spices. Celia Montoya, who volunteered to cook for Vince while her husband, Ramon, prepared meals for the rest of the men, favored fare with a kick to it. Vince never seemed to mind, but Lance himself preferred plainer food, with nothing stronger than respectable dashes of salt and pepper.

Too tired to bother fixing himself something different, he set the pot to warming before searching out a loaf of rye bread. Regardless of her perchant for spices, Celia managed to bake to perfection, and Lance sliced himself a thick portion. Another trip to the cabinets produced a jar of apricot preserves and a dish of soft butter.

A slight sound, like bare feet shuffling across the rugless floor, stilled his actions. Unbidden, the roar of a thousand—a million—waterfalls blasted through him. He clutched the preserves so tightly the glass should have broken. His thumb slid unnoticed into the butter.

Without looking, he knew it was Sonnie. He could smell the fresh, carnation scent of her even before he turned. His senses exploded with awareness of her presence.

"Oh. It's you." Surprise tinged her tone.

He forced himself to face her, to assume a facade of control. Luxurious sable tresses flowed about her shoulders and back with careless abandon. He never realized how long her hair had grown over the years until now, and the nearly overpowering urge to bury his face into her neck and stroke his cheek against the silken tendrils shook his battered composure as Snake's flying knife had failed to do.

"I thought you were Papa," she said, a hand grasping her satin robe tighter to her bosom. "I thought maybe he felt ill or . . . or something."

She appeared uncomfortable to be with him. Maybe it was the lateness of the hour or the intimacy of being together in the dimly illuminated kitchen. Lance nearly groaned from the irony of it.

She showed none of her earlier pique with him. From that, he took relief. The roaring eased to a low hum inside his head; he even managed to set the preserves upon the counter with a semblance of coordination.

"Where did you go tonight?" she asked after a long moment.

Belatedly, Lance realized he'd made no comment to her explanation. He glanced down and noticed his thumb stuck in the butter. With a flare of impatience, he yanked it out again and reached for a damp cloth.

"Into town," he said.

Her dark brows arched. "Cheyenne? Whatever for?"

"Business." He saw no reason to concern her about Ditson. Her return home had been marred enough because of the man.

"Business." A flicker of hurt flittered over her expression, and she gave a defeated shake of her head. "You're as closemouthed as my father. I'm not a little girl anymore, Lance."

He remembered how Vince had answered her in the same vague manner earlier this afternoon, and regretted his own reply. He scoured his mind for a more suitable one, yet his keen desire to protect her from further worry or dismay prevented it.

Sonnie slipped her hands into the robe's pockets and glanced at the pot on the stove. The pungent aroma of chilies and garlic hovered in the air while the soup warmed. She returned her gaze to him.

"After my father woke from his nap, we spent the

evening talking and getting reacquainted." She paused; her chin lifted a little higher. "He speaks highly of you. In fact, he speaks of little else. The Rocking M and you are synonymous, it seems."

Lance grew wary of the resentment in her words. "We've been close for a long time," he conceded.

"As close as a father is to his son." Her voice carried no questioning inflection. It appeared she was convinced of the observation.

He frowned. "I could never replace you. You're his daughter, his flesh and blood. He loves you very much."

"He loves you as well. And I don't even know you."

Her bitterness galled him. Needing the distraction, Lance turned away and stirred down the little bubbles in the simmering broth.

His relationship with all five of Sonnie's sisters had always been friendly, though, he had to admit, short-term. Only recently had he spent any duration of time with them, and only then because of Vince's heart attack.

He understood Sonnie's hurt. She feared losing her father's love to him, that somehow Vince's heart wouldn't hold enough affection for both of them, that after being gone for so many years, she'd been replaced by someone she viewed as a perfect stranger.

She couldn't have been more wrong.

Sonnie reached over the pot of soup and the spoon he used. Her fingers curled about his wrist, tilting the back of his hand toward herself. "You've been in a fight."

Never had she touched him before. He stared at the smoothness of her flesh, creamy with a hint of the olive tones of her heritage, and how it contrasted with the callused bronze of his. He tried to comprehend what she'd said.

"Your knuckles have little cuts in the skin. You hit someone tonight." Her gaze roamed over his face, as if searching for some sign that a similar blow had been returned. "And he didn't hit back. Is this what your business in town was about? A fight?"

Her disapproval left him powerless to defend himself, to deflect her criticism with a sound explanation, to point out that the whole purpose of his ride into Cheyenne was to hunt Ditson down and warn him within an inch of his worthless life to stay away from her.

She released his wrist without waiting for a reply. The coolness of her touch scalded him much as the scathing look she speared him with for a long, agonizing moment.

"I would like a tour of the ranch," she said finally. "First thing in the morning. And since my father is incapable of accompanying me, I suppose"—she hesitated—"I suppose I shall have to settle for you."

His belly did a flip-flop. A tour of the ranch. With Sonnie.

Alarm soared through him.

How would he breathe? How would he endure the sting of her resentment of him, of knowing she despised him so?

But before his mind could form the words to reassure her, to convince her he could never replace her as Vince's own, that the Rocking M was as much her heritage as his, she'd already begun moving away from him.

"Good night, Mr. Harmon."

The satin shimmered over her hips as she left the kitchen. A frosty chill hung in the room afterward, a chill not likely to be warmed by Celia's spicy, steaming soup.

She despised him. In spite of everything.

Lance eyed the fare with growing distaste. His appetite gone, he dropped the lid onto the pot with a clatter. The clanging sound drowned out the curse spilling from his lips.

Chapter Four

Vince Mancuso's home stood as majestic as a palace in an island of snow. The Big House, he called it, a structure aptly suited to the name, and a finer house Lance had never seen.

It was almost too fine. Imposing, actually. He swallowed. Even scary. He'd lose himself in all those rooms. After a lifetime of tiny, squalid apartments and the stark simplicity of the orphanage's dormitory, the grandness of Vince's residence was daunting.

"You don't like it, do you?" Vince asked with keen perception.

Lance didn't know what to say. He didn't want to seem ungrateful, not after all Vince offered, but a lie of disagreement just wouldn't come forth.

"I didn't either at first," Vince admitted ruefully. "The place grows on you, though." His face, reddened from the cold, blowing wind, took on a faraway look. "I built it for my wife. She wanted to fill it with a dozen babies, and she would've, too, if I hadn't lost *her.*" A surge of emotion quieted him for a moment. "*She gave me six. All daughters.*" He stirred himself from his reverie. "*You'll be more comfortable in the bunkhouse with the other men.*" His gloved finger pointed toward a low-slung, rectangular building a short distance away. "*The bunks are nothing fancy. Main thing is they're warm, and you'll have plenty of companionship.*" His glance settled approvingly on Lance. "*You'll make friends here. You'll fit in in no time.*"

Again, eager anticipation for the future coiled throughout every nerve ending in Lance's body. How would he ever repay Vince Mancuso for the chance he'd given him to begin his life anew?

The front door to the big house opened, and a squealing young girl dashed out.

"*Papa!*" A pair of pink ribbons tied back her wild sable curls. Oblivious to the need for a warm coat or to Lance's presence, she ran down the porch stairs. "*Papa! Papa!*"

Chuckling heartily, Vince dismounted and swept her up in his arms for an exuberant hug. Five more girls, obviously sisters of varying ages, appeared on the porch, and within moments he embraced each of them.

The men came next—hordes, it seemed to Lance: Cowboys with their wide-brimmed hats, scuffed boots, and bandannas around their throats. They came from the bunkhouse and the barns and every structure in between, all to greet Vince Mancuso.

Lance was excluded from their welcome, but he hardly noticed. The pair of pink ribbons, and the little girl who wore them, held his attention.

They'd forgotten her. Though she tried to break into the wall of male bodies and older sisters to get to her father, no one seemed to care she was there. Not even Vince.

Especially Vince.

She appeared devastated, stricken by his rejection. Lance's heart constricted. He, too, knew what it was like to be forgotten. Unneeded.

He ached for her. Then her sisters remembered she didn't wear a coat, and when they led her, shivering, into the Big House, Lance learned her name. It was a peculiar name for a daughter so beautiful and feminine.

Sonnie.

The supple suede of Sonnie's split skirt whispered in the air with a lightness that matched her step. Her fingers trailed along the polished balustrade of the stairwell as she left the hall and approached the kitchen, which was alive with the lingering smells of brewed coffee and seasoned sausage.

The low timbre of male voices slowed her step. Her mind flashed a memory of dim lighting and Lance standing over the stove, a wooden spoon in his hand. Her heart beat inexplicably fast.

He'd be in there, of course, planning the day's chores with her father. It was a habit with them, most likely. Did her father ever make a decision without him anymore?

Resolutely, she entered the kitchen and found them seated at the table. Both were immersed in the numbers scrawled on the pages of a huge, leather-bound ledger.

Papa's eyes smiled at her over the edges of his reading glasses. "My little girl finally decided to get up, eh?"

She sensed a vague hint of disapproval in his greeting, so faint she might have imagined it. She pressed a kiss to his cheek. "It's early, Papa. Just after dawn. And I'm not little anymore."

"You'll always be my little girl, Sonnie," Vince said, and absently patted her hand.

She banked a twinge of annoyance. She didn't want to be reminded of her placement in the long line of Mancuso daughters.

Not with Lance Harmon sitting there, witness to every word.

She hadn't fallen asleep last night with ease. She'd been tortured by her immediate resentment of him—and his hot glances that flowed over her face and skin, much like Papa's expensive brandy heated her throat with every swallow.

She forced herself to look at him, to be polite and civil and pleasant.

"Good morning, Lance," she said smoothly.

He smelled of shaving soap and the fresh Wyoming wind in his clean shirt. He looked vibrant and masculine, strong and powerful, and he rattled her composure to no end.

He returned the greeting in his low voice, warmed her with his whiskey gaze, and she had to turn away.

"Are you hungry?" Papa asked. "Celia made us a pan of scrambled eggs with sausage this morning. Help yourself."

She was grateful for the distraction and served herself a plateful. She reached for the pot of coffee.

"Lance tells me you asked for a tour of the ranch," her father said, watching her. "This morning."

"Yes." She carried her plate in one hand, the pot in the other, and strode to the table. "I've missed the Rocking M, Papa. I want to see the land again."

"He's been waiting. The sun has been up for an hour already."

The coffeepot hovered over her cup. Again she heard a note of censure in his tone, noticed her father's and Lance's finished breakfast plates, knew Celia had been up and working long before she had.

She poured the black brew with controlled dignity, first her cup, then her father's, then Lance's, despite the dismay building inside her.

"I won't be so lazy tomorrow, Papa," she said. "I'll get up earlier. I promise."

"Your journey home wore you out yesterday. You are used to sleeping so long, eh?"

"No," she murmured, frowning. "Rarely."

Lance leveled her with an assessing gaze. "He wanted to wake you. I told him to let you sleep."

"I expect no special treatment from either of you," she said.

"It's still early. The sun hasn't been up long. Don't fret over it." Lance's glance swung to her father. "Either of you."

Reproval hung in the command, which had been given in a quiet voice, but with respect. Papa nodded and flashed her a quick, conciliatory grin. "You deserve to be pampered. It's not every day you come back to visit. Relax all you want while you're here."

Visit? The word echoed in Sonnie's brain. He thought she intended to return to Boston, that her stay here would be temporary.

Before she could untangle the misconception, Celia Montoya, one arm around a bag of flour, the other toting a small child, emerged from the pantry.

"Miss Sonnie! How good to see you again!" The dark-eyed woman beamed.

Delight coursed through Sonnie at the sight of the young woman, and she rose to her feet. "Oh, Celia, the last time I saw you, you were a blushing bride on Ramon's arm." Her arms circled Celia's slender shoulders in a quick hug before she relieved her of the flour. "And who's this? What a beautiful little boy!"

Gently, she brushed the child's hair from his forehead. At her touch, he whimpered and pulled away to bury his face in Celia's neck.

"Our son, Juan. You must forgive him, Miss Sonnie. He's not normally so unsociable." She shifted him to a more comfortable position on her hip. "He's not feeling well this morning. I think he's coming down with something."

Sonnie reached out with her free hand and felt his forehead. The fever met her palm, and she crooned in agreement. "He should be in bed resting."

Celia tossed a helpless look toward the table. "I didn't know if I should come today, but someone must cook for your father."

"I can cook for him."

"You?"

"Women in Boston cook every day," Sonnie said. She tried not to sound defensive at the uncertainty in Celia's voice. "My sisters taught me my way around this kitchen long before I ever left."

"And you hated every minute." Her father chuckled at the memory.

Sonnie took the ribbing, knowing it was true. "I've taken several excellent cooking classes, Papa. And Aunt Josephine's chef was superb. He's taught me many things."

Juan whined and fidgeted in his mother's arms. Compassion for the toddler tweaked Sonnie's own maternal instincts. "Celia, he needs to be in his bed. Take him home. I'll take care of my father."

The young woman appeared torn between her son and her duties. She glanced worriedly at Lance.

He stood, taking his coffee cup with him.

"Sonnie's right," he said. He moved toward the door, power and masculinity sheathed in the lean contours of his body. "Your place is with Juan. Vince won't starve with his own daughter cooking for him."

"I'll be fine." Vince looked askance at them from

his ledger and waved her away. "Take the time you need to care for the boy."

"I'll have Stick bring around the surrey for your drive home," Lance said, and left.

Celia tucked an errant strand of dark hair behind her ear and smiled. "I will go then."

Sonnie lent her assistance in bundling Juan into his small coat. Within moments Celia and her child had settled in the carriage waiting in front of the house. Sonnie draped a blanket about the toddler's chubby body as he rested his sleepy head on his mother's lap.

"Remember to fix plenty of food, Miss Sonnie," Celia said. "There's always extra mouths at the table. Your father is tending to like his coffee a little weaker than he used to. And try to get him to eat something in the middle of the afternoon."

"Don't worry. You just take care of Juan, and I'll take care of my father."

"Thank you, Miss Sonnie."

With a slap of the reins, the surrey took off. Sonnie acknowledged a bittersweet victory in her quest to take care of her father. The decision had been hers to send Celia home, though it had been Lance who finally convinced her to go.

Still, it was a start. She experienced a thrill of pleasure at the thought of being the mistress of the Big House, a voice of authority on the Rocking M.

"You can't do it all, you know."

Sonnie whirled. Lance tossed the dregs of his coffee into the bushes lining the front porch and approached her.

"Whatever do you mean, Mr. Harmon?" she demanded.

"Cook for your father. Take care of his house. Take care of *him*. All that, and take over the Rocking M, too."

She stiffened. "The ranch is my home. I have no intention of 'taking it over,' as you claim."

"Don't you?"

Beneath the brim of his hat, his shrewd gaze studied her, as if he could probe into her innermost secrets, each of her hopes and dreams.

And lay them all out on the table, like playing cards to deal at his whim.

"I've been here less than a full day, Lance. I'm a stranger to you. Just as you are to me. You're wrong to judge me as if you've always known me."

He went still at that. She sensed his restraint, as if he held inside more than he allowed her to see.

She sensed, too, a weakening in him, as if some of his impatience had vanished.

"Then why the tour of the ranch, Sonnie?" he asked quietly.

"Why do you deny me the pleasure?" She met his challenge, held his unwavering gaze, gave no more than he gave her.

"I've denied you nothing," he said, the words suddenly rough, emphatic.

"But you'd like to."

He swore and stepped away, the impatience back in him. "I'll give you your damn tour of the place. Meet me at the corral in twenty minutes."

A smile touched her mouth, sweet in its victory.

"I'll be there in ten."

The shortgrass prairie grew wild and free and sprawled along the Wyoming horizon in glorious, untamed beauty. Miles and miles of blue grama and buffalo grass blanketed the Rocking M rangeland and fed Vince Mancuso's cattle their fill. Sonnie marveled at the hundreds of black, brown, red, and white hides clustered in the distant hills.

Her father's livestock. *Impressive,* she mused. *Very*

impressive. He'd built up the herds from those she remembered, and what she could see was only a small portion of the whole. The numbers were staggering— too many to count, too many to fathom. She doubted even Vince himself knew how many cattle he owned.

Beside her, Lance sat in the saddle and inspected them, too, an eye squinted against the midmorning sun. He studied them in earnest, and Sonnie wondered what he was thinking.

She refused to ask. He'd been aloof during their ride from the Big House onto Mancuso rangeland. Polite. A perfect gentleman. And so silent she thought she'd go mad from the frustration of it.

A sigh escaped her, and she shifted in her seat. The saddle leather creaked and drew Lance's glance.

He regarded her for a moment. "You ready to go back?"

"Not for a while yet."

"It'll be time for dinner soon."

She shook her head, protesting his argument. "Another hour or so."

As if against his better judgment, he shot another glance toward the sun, then nodded in concession. "What else do you want to see?"

"Everything." Sonnie nudged her horse forward and dragged her gaze along a bunch of little bluestem growing amid the buffalo grass, the flowered tips brushing the bottoms of her stirrups.

"Reckon we can't see everything in one morning." His horse kept pace with hers. "Most likely we couldn't see it all in a month, either."

"Too bad. I'd like to see all there is to see on the Rocking M. Did it rain much this summer?"

"Not enough to make the cattlemen happy. Or the farmers, either." He shrugged, appeared willing enough to keep the conversation going. "But we've had worse droughts. Heck of a lot worse."

They rode into bottomland, devoid of trees and the prairie's shortgrass. A breeze whipped up, and Sonnie's hand flew up to keep her wide-brimmed hat on her head. Dirt kicked into pesky swirls. Prickly pear cactus and yucca thrived in the barren soil.

"The cattle have overgrazed here," she said, her mouth pursed in consternation. "The land will erode away if something isn't done."

A corner of his mouth lifted. "Such as?"

Was he mocking her? She sat a little straighter in the saddle. "A fire. A controlled one. The ash will replenish the soil and clear away old grass shoots so that new growth may thrive. By next spring, the cattle will be able to graze again."

"You're a smart lady, Miss Mancuso."

"You're making fun of me, Mr. Harmon."

"I'm not."

"Has my father ever considered drilling a well?" she asked.

"Here?" He appeared taken aback.

"Yes." Her nod was emphatic. "It would be expensive, true, but the water would enable the forbs to survive."

"Forbs."

"Herbs that aren't grass. Wildflowers, if you will."

"Sonnie—"

She tossed her head and lifted her nose into the air. "There are more than two hundred species of flora in this part of the country, and more are being identified every day. One of my professors predicted that upward of seven hundred species will be recorded in the sand hills alone. Fascinating, don't you think?"

He stared at her, his shadowed gaze incredulous and a bit amused. "How did a girl growing up in the East get to know so much about ranching in the West?"

"I studied long and hard, that's how."

73

His brow raised.

Her chin lifted.

"I took horticulture and veterinary classes, if you must know. When my father ordered me to study music and foreign languages, I learned about animal husbandry instead."

For a moment Lance fell silent.

"It was important to me," Sonnie added, not quite sure why she was telling him so.

"You didn't want to be like your sisters," he said. "You wanted to be the son Vince never had."

Sonnie met the heat in his whiskey gaze. "You make it sound ridiculously simple. It's not."

"I understand more than you give me credit for."

"How can you possibly?" she demanded, puzzled. She'd only met him yesterday.

But he ignored her question, his attention snared, instead, on a half dozen head of cattle huddled together. Sonnie studied them, too.

Something wasn't right. The certainty filled her with foreboding; she knew it as surely as Lance did. The animals appeared listless. Unsettled.

Sick.

They dismounted and approached the cows; their big, doleful eyes watched them without interest.

"They've got no appetite." Lance scrutinized the grass in the rangeland not so far distant. "They've wandered here because they don't care if they eat or not."

Sonnie pressed a hand to the hide nearest her, felt the rapid beat of the cow's pulse, heard the labored breathing.

Lance stepped around a large stain in the dirt.

"Diarrhea. What the hell happened?" Grimly he held a brown-and-white face in both of his hands, opened the cow's mouth wide, and looked inside.

Sonnie bent closer and looked, too. "Her tongue

and throat are irritated and sore. She's eaten something she shouldn't have."

"She's been poisoned." He growled the words, fury blatant in his tone.

"Oh, my God," Sonnie said under her breath, horrified at the realization.

Again his sharp glance darted over the larger herd grazing on the shortgrass in the hills. Worry that they might have been affected as well darkened his features.

A chill took Sonnie. Her brain searched and sifted through the memories of scores of ailing cattle she'd seen and examined over the past few years.

Lance grasped her by the elbow and hauled her toward her horse.

"Did the professors in your fancy school teach you about hate on the range, Sonnie?" he demanded. "Or how men will sabotage and kill to get their revenge?"

Sonnie yanked her arm free and spun to face him.

"They taught me about yellow phosphorus," she said, thinking not of what Lance warned her about but only of the diagnosis so clear in her mind. "The cows have all the symptoms."

He halted. "Phosphorus. Christ."

"Look at them, Lance. They stand there in a stupor. Convulsions will set in soon. Every one of those cows there could die today. Or tomorrow."

"Do you think I don't know that?" His hands clamped around her waist, and he lifted her bodily into the saddle. "Rat poison. My God."

"We must oxidize the phosphorus to overcome the systemic effects of the poison." She scrambled to get her seat in the saddle, to slide her feet into the stirrups and grasp the reins. "I suggest old oil of turpentine. Potassium permanganate may be given as well."

"You sound like you jumped right out of a textbook." He swung into the saddle with controlled speed, with agile grace.

With anger.

"I intend to tell my father my opinions," she said, defiant that Lance paid no heed to all she tried to tell him. "I'll convince him my diagnosis is right."

"You do that, Miss Mancuso. And while you're at it, you can tell him Clay Ditson and Snake are responsible for poisoning prime beef. And that his youngest daughter has no business getting herself involved in a range war and needs to be sent away somewhere safe, somewhere far away where she won't get herself hurt."

"I'll do no such thing!" she gasped, but her glance swept the horizon for signs of the harsh-looking Indian and his sour-smelling accomplice.

She shuddered in spite of herself.

Lance leaned over, tugged her horse's bridle, and forced the mare into a turn toward the ranch. A mask had fallen into place over his features, that iron-clad control she both hated and admired.

"I'm staying right here," she grated, and spurred her horse out of Lance's reach. "I can help my father. Together we can solve the problems on the Rocking M."

The vow didn't include Lance. The slight narrowing of his eyes revealed that he understood the omission.

"You don't have a notion in hell about the problems on the Rocking M, Sonnie."

"I'm learning." Her nostrils flared. "He'll teach me what I need to know."

Lance swore, reached into a shirt pocket, and withdrew a rolled cigarette. He tucked it into the corner of his mouth.

He didn't bother to light the tobacco. The hard line

of his jaw gradually eased, but his expression remained distant, unfathomable.

"Well, Sonnie," he drawled. "I reckon you got one more problem waiting for you when you get back to the Big House. I reckon, too, Vince won't be happy about it."

Wary, she eyed him. "What's that?"

"Dinner." He indicated the sun, sitting high in the sky. "You're late."

Sonnie slid from the saddle, hurried up the stairs, and dashed into the kitchen. The door slammed behind her.

Lance was right. Dinner should have been ready and waiting.

The realization of it galled her. Cookie stood in the middle of the room, his hands propped on his hips, a perplexed frown on his grizzled features. Stick stared uncertainly at the cold, empty kitchen.

Both men turned at her harried entrance.

"I'm sorry." Breathless, Sonnie began to hunt for an apron to protect her suede skirt. She had no idea what the pantry shelves held, but she tried to form a menu of what to fix on such short notice.

"Reckon we might be at the wrong place at the wrong time, Miss Sonnie," Cookie said, still frowning. "Ain't we supposed to eat about now?"

"We most always have dinner at the Big House when we get the hankerin'. Celia never seems to mind. Is that gonna change now that you're back, Miss Sonnie?" Stick asked.

"No, no. Of course not," Sonnie said, aghast that he would think so.

The back door opened, and Lance stepped in. Frazzled by her tardiness, by him, Sonnie avoided his gaze and rifled through a drawer filled with towels.

Papa's cane thumped along the hallway. He appeared in the doorway. His sharp-eyed perusal scoured the room.

"Sonnie, haven't you a meal ready?" he asked.

She gave up on the apron and turned to face him. She blanched at his frown. "I'll have something ready shortly, Papa. If everyone would like to make themselves comfortable, I'll—"

"These men have been up and working hard long before you even awoke," he interrupted. "They're hungry. They need to be fed."

Sonnie froze. His scolding tone mortified her.

"I should have watched the time, Papa." She wanted to die from embarrassment, from shame. "I shouldn't have been so careless."

"This isn't Boston," he reminded her with an impatient thrust of his cane. "And you're not on holiday in Rome. This is the Rocking M."

"Yes, Papa."

She sensed the discomfort of the other men. Cookie shuffled from one foot to the other. Stick cleared his throat and stared down at the toe of his boot.

"Ramon will have plenty of food, Vince." Cool and calm, Lance reached for a bar of soap at the sink. The low timbre of his voice sounded controlled, without censure. "We'll eat in the bunkhouse with everyone else."

"Sure," Cookie said. "We'll eat in the bunkhouse. You bet we will."

He gave Stick a pronounced jab in the ribs.

"Bunkhouse grub is good," Stick added quickly, his head bobbing. "Mighty good, Miss Sonnie. We don't mind 't all."

Sonnie endured their sympathetic looks as each lifted a finger to his hat and left as if hellfire licked his heels. The room fell silent, so silent she could hear the dull pounding in her temples.

"You won't forget again, will you?" Papa asked,

more softly this time, sparing her the indignity of another reprimand in front of Lance.

She shook her head. She felt like a child caught in a forbidden prank. She wanted to beg him for forgiveness.

"It's my fault, Vince," Lance said. Water dripped from his arms. "I should have brought her back sooner."

Her father's gaze rested on him briefly.

"We rode out too far, lost track of time. We both knew better."

"Seeing the ranch was important to her," Papa mused, as if Sonnie were no longer there.

Lance nodded and found a towel. "Nice morning for a ride."

Papa's irritation clearly dissipated. He turned back to Sonnie.

"I'll come back in half an hour," he said. "Would that give you time to fix *me* something to eat?"

"Yes. Of course," she murmured.

He gave her an approving half smile, then left. She stood stiffly, listening to the sounds of his cane as he retreated to his office. She didn't need to turn around to know Lance remained, that his burning gaze rested on her, that he felt her regret almost as much as she did.

"Thank you," she said, and drew in a breath.

She heard him move closer.

"For what?" he asked.

"For defending me to him. For taking the blame." She blinked, trying hard not to succumb to a girlish bout of tears. "For not laying into me when you had the right."

"Lay into you?" he repeated slowly. "Because dinner wasn't ready?"

"You're the 'Boss-man.' A good scolding would've been well within your realm of duties."

"Sonnie." Her name fell from his lips in a protesting growl. She held up a hand before he could say more.

"But then, my father did well enough, didn't he? He's a hard man. He didn't build the Rocking M into the spread it is without stepping on a few toes when someone didn't pull his share of the load." She endured a new stab of hurt. "Not even his daughters."

She whirled away from him, found a skillet, and set it on the stove's burner with a noisy bang that suited her wounded mood. She rummaged through another drawer in a determined hunt for an apron but found two bowls instead. She set them upon the table with a thunk rivaling the skillet's.

Lance halted behind her, so close she could smell the leather from his saddle, the soap just rinsed from his skin.

"You needn't have taken the blame for me," she went on. Her voice broke with a betraying quaver. "Please don't next time. I-I mean, there won't be a next time."

She broke off. She refused to show her despair. Not to him. Not when he inspired her father's respect more readily than she did.

She wanted him to touch her. The need came out of nowhere. The idiocy of it, the futility, spurred her to reject the fantasy of his arms closing around her in comfort and enabled her to bolt well out of his reach.

"You said nothing of the poisoned cattle to my father," she said abruptly, and snatched a plate of sliced roast beef from the icebox.

"No. I didn't want to upset him any more than he already was."

Sonnie bit the inside of her lip.

"I'll tell him later. When the time is right," he added.

Knowing Lance's reasoning was sound, that he

kept her father's health uppermost in his mind, she nodded jerkily.

A long moment passed. Then his boot soles trod upon the floor, halted at the door. She waited for him to speak.

"If you're in need of an apron," he said quietly, "try the third drawer down on the left."

A moment later she stood alone in the room. Without looking, she knew he'd be right, that an apron would be just where he'd said, in the one place she had yet to check.

She closed her eyes. The man knew Vince Mancuso's kitchen better than she; she was more the stranger to her father's house. A nearly overwhelming feeling of inadequacy stung her soul.

A feeling of total, unequivocal failure.

Sonnie rolled the last walnut-stuffed date in sugar and set it neatly in place upon the silver tray. She stepped back from the table, sighed, and considered her handiwork.

It was a peace offering, of sorts. She hoped the sweet treat would make up for her negligence about dinner and would soothe whatever annoyance Cookie or Stick might still be feeling toward her.

Not that she'd seen anything of the sort in their expressions. And Lance . . . well, Lance had been absolutely gallant about the whole thing.

Sonnie sighed again.

Even her father had been his usual loving self at dinner. Most likely he and the others would go about their business and pretend the whole thing had never happened.

But it had. She wanted the sugared dates to win them over again, to remind them she was still a Mancuso and very much a part of the Rocking M—not a city girl gone too long to easily fit into their lives.

She glanced around the tidy kitchen and figured she had enough time before starting supper to bring the treats to the men herself. Her spirits lightened at the thought.

A quick trip upstairs to her bedroom produced the jacket that matched her skirt. Brisk brushstrokes livened the shine in her hair, and she decided to leave the long black tresses down, unbound but for a pair of pearl combs placed high on the sides of her head.

She studied her reflection in the mirror, pondering the suede skirt that flowed from her thighs to her calves and hugged the slimness of her hips and waist. The tops of her boots hid beneath the skirt's hem, but what leather showed gleamed, a fine testament to the boots' quality and price. She looked like a rancher's daughter, she decided, not displeased. A daughter worthy of the name Mancuso.

Making a good impression was imperative. For many of her father's men, this would be their first meeting. For the others, those who had been on the Rocking M payroll for years, it would be a reacquaintance with those she remembered, renewed introductions for those she didn't.

Her nerves fluttered with anticipation, with pleasure, at the prospect.

After returning to the kitchen, she balanced the silver tray in one hand and, careful not to disturb her father's nap, quietly shut the door with the other and stepped outside.

The crisp Wyoming air nipped at her cheeks, but the sun warmed its bite. Sonnie halted at the bottom of the porch stairs, and her gaze caressed the lay of the land surrounding the Big House for several long, appreciative minutes.

Fruit trees lined the lane leading to the main road heading into Cheyenne. Split-rail fencing encased the sprawling lawn and formed a handsome yard ablaze with crimson and gold leaves on the maple and cottonwood trees, brilliant mums and prolific hollyhocks.

More fencing divided corrals. Livestock barns housing horses, hogs, and mules loomed in the near distance. Red-coated Hereford cattle dotted the range beyond, the air punctuated by the cries of bawling calves. Chickens flitted about; roosters screeched; imposing blackbirds cawed and complained.

Oh, how she'd missed this, Sonnie thought with a swell of emotion: the sounds, the expanse, the beauty of the Rocking M. She inhaled a lazy breath.

And she'd missed the smells, too.

It had been inevitable that she'd come back. A twist of fate. A stroke of luck. Papa's health had failed him, but gifted her with a reason to come home. And though her return had not been without its rough moments, the future promised a smoother road paved with determination and gentle persuasion.

The tray of sugared dates testified to that. She strolled toward the barns, feeling more content than she had in a very long time.

Chapter Five

The flames of the campfire jumped and danced, the only flare of light within sight on the boundless Wyoming rangeland. The cold night closed around Lance like a black cloak, oppressive and unnerving. Huddled next to the fire in their bedrolls, three men snored in sleep, oblivious to their lack of quarters.

He shivered. He'd never spent a night outside before, had never set up a camp, had never worked a roundup. There were many things to learn in this new country. Only by listening to the others spin tales, by trying to understand their strange way of talking, could he quell his unease.

"Yep," Shorty said. "Ain't no skunks anywhere like we got right here in the Territory. You ever seen a skunk before, Lance?"

Lance grew fidgety under their attention. He didn't yet feel a part of them. He was too new. Different.

"Sure," he said, not flinching from the little lie. Certain a page from the orphanage's encyclopedia

didn't count, he met the cowboy's gaze directly. "Lots of times."

Shorty nodded. "Reckon they all smell the same, but out here, they're bigger, meaner. Plumb crazy."

Unable to stop it, he let his glance dart to the shadows, then back to Shorty. "Crazy?"

"Yep. Crazy. Come right up to you with no fear. And they'll bite any chance they git. Ain't that right, Mr. Mancuso?"

Lance swallowed. An unseen coyote howled a warbling cry and prickled the hair on the back of his neck.

Vince took a leisurely drag on his cheroot, his silence indicating agreement.

"Saw a man get bit once," he said. "Went mad before my eyes."

"Mad?" Lance choked.

"Started slobberin' at the mouth," Shorty added.

"Screeched and hollered like a banshee," Vince put in.

If Vince said it was so, Lance believed him. His heart started a slow pounding. A noise in the foliage beyond quickened the beat.

"By Gawd!" Shorty shrieked. "There's one now! Do you see it, Lance?"

Something moved closer. The firelight caught a hazy stripe in the dark. No one moved. How could they all be so brave?

"Don't let him git you, Lance."

Too intent on the slinking creature, Lance hardly heard the warning voice. The stripe grew more distinct, drew closer.

"Watch him! He's gonna jump!"

At that precise moment, the skunk lurched and lunged. Out of nowhere, it hurtled from the air and landed in his lap. Lance yelled out in horrified fright. His hands frantically clawed the awful thing away.

85

His chest sucked in air. By the time his head cleared and his heart slowed, he realized he'd bolted to his feet, ready to run.

He realized, too, that Shorty was laughing, writhing in the dirt. The others, those he'd thought were sleeping, rolled with laughter beneath their blankets. Even Vince's shoulders shook in lively mirth.

Their hilarity surrounded him, and Lance knew their joke. A skunk skin, stuffed with rags and crudely tied together, lay on its side where he'd thrown it. Another cowboy held a long line of balled twine, one end attached to the skin.

A self-derisive grin stretched across Lance's lips. He felt foolish, stupid. In spite of himself, the grin turned into a reluctant chuckle.

Everyone watched him, gauging his reaction. His laughter slowly deepened to match theirs, and one by one they began to nod in approval.

He'd passed their test—a difficult one, one at his own expense. But he didn't care. He'd reached an important plateau.

Acceptance.

"What've you got there, young'un?" Cookie called out. He gave the patent leather on the stagecoach a final rub of oil, then tossed the piece of muslin aside. Straightening his wiry frame, he beckoned Sonnie closer.

"Has Ramon given you dessert?" she asked. Her admiring glance skimmed across the repaired rig, which was gleaming and looking like new again.

"Ramon? Dessert?" A huff of tobacco-tainted breath slipped through the old cowboy's mouth. "Nah. He don't bother. Celia's the one who does the bakin' 'round here."

"Perhaps these will do, then." She held the tray out to him.

"What are they?" He eyed the treats suspiciously.

"Dates," she replied, a little surprised he didn't recognize the fruit.

He appeared doubtful. "I ain't never seen a date all gussied up like these are."

"They're rolled in sugar to make them look pretty," she said. Tendrils of amusement lightened her tone.

"You didn't stick nothin' funny in 'em, did you?"

She laughed, tickled by his boyish wariness. "No, you dear. They're filled with walnuts. Try one. And if you don't like it, I'll find plenty of men around here who will."

At her dare, Cookie plucked one off the tray. He took a tentative bite, chewed, then popped the entire piece into his mouth.

"Well?" Sonnie's mouth twitched.

"They'll do." His grimy fingers snatched several more. "Hey, Red. Frank. Want one?"

Two cowboys scrambled from underneath the coach. Wiping their hands on their pant legs, they approached her, their shy gazes not quite meeting hers. She greeted them warmly and offered them the tray.

"What's the matter with you boys?" Cookie snorted in disgust and gave the closest a slap to the shoulder. "Ain't you got no manners? The least you can do is wait to be introduced proper before feedin' yer faces. This here's Mr. Mancuso's youngest. Her name's Miss Sonnie."

"Miss Sonnie." Awe filled the words, spoken by the bravest of the pair. "Red Holmes, ma'am. Right proud to meet you."

Sonnie noted the color of his hair, and she knew it must be the reason for his nickname.

"I'm proud to meet you, too, Red." She smiled.

Beaming, Red landed a not-so-subtle nudge to the young cowhand beside him.

"And I'm Frank Burton," he said hastily, and blushed furiously.

Sonnie immediately sought to put them at ease. "Are you hungry? Help yourself. There's plenty."

Their enthusiastic compliments warmed her. A few moments later a new group joined them, their eagerness to meet Vince Mancuso's daughter obvious. A second round of introductions were made, and Sonnie committed each name to memory. In seemingly no time at all, their easy conversation transformed them from hired hands into friends.

She hadn't realized how much being accepted into the Mancuso outfit had meant to her until now. Their appreciation, masculine and respectful, touched a part of her heart she hadn't known needed touching. Their welcome was spontaneous and enthusiastic. Their acceptance nearly completed her return home to the Rocking M.

If only the Boss-man would do the same.

Through the open barn doors, Lance watched the huddle of men surrounding Sonnie grow larger by the minute. Her laughter drew them like thirsty cattle to water. They came from everywhere, heedless of the work they left behind, eager for a morsel of her attention.

He scowled darkly. They seemed drunk on her, every one of them.

He'd just returned from Mancuso rangeland with Charlie Flynn. They'd been forced to put down the half dozen poisoned cows too sick to save. His mood worsened just thinking about it.

Now, seeing Sonnie with damned near the entire Mancuso outfit panting at her feet . . .

Any other man would walk out and join them. No other man would keep himself from the pleasure.

No one except him.

Charlie entered from the corral and dropped a handful of hen quills on the workbench. Lance turned away from the entranceway and busied himself doing nothing.

"Looks like Miss Sonnie's out there gettin' to know the hands," Charlie said, peering out. "I wonder if she remembers me."

His hopeful tone grated on Lance's patience. He dragged his glance back through the open doors and watched Sonnie bend over to pat one of the ranch dogs on the head. The mutt—dubbed Moose— wagged his tail furiously, as smitten as the rest of them.

"Mind if I go out and jaw with her a spell?" Charlie asked.

But before Lance could reply, Charlie was on his way out, leaving Lance alone in the barn to fight a wave of disgust for his own cowardice.

He refused to think of her, and fished a knife from the hip pocket of his Levi's. With the tip of the blade, he cut oblong holes a quarter inch from the small end of the quills, then slathered them with petroleum jelly.

He heard her enter.

The soft tread of her footsteps warned of her approach. The now-familiar rush, the sensation of her presence, roared through him. His fist closed, opened, then closed again.

"I thought . . . maybe you'd like a sugared date, Lance. I saved some for you."

She was uncomfortable with him. Uncertain, as if she couldn't gauge his response to her. He snatched a milk bucket in one hand, the quills in the other, and spied the silver tray with the remaining confections.

How could he eat when she tied his stomach into knots?

"You're busy," she said when his hesitation stretched into long moments. She set the tray on the

89

bench. "You can have one later if you'd like."

"I will." The roar lessened. "Thanks."

Moose had followed her in. He rubbed against her, his wagging tail thumping her skirt. She scratched his head absently.

She seemed nervous, yet she made no attempt to leave. Maybe she wanted to stay. Maybe she wanted to be with him.

He squelched the hope. He was crazy to think it. To want it.

He entered the nearest stall and dropped the quills and bucket inside before sitting on a low stool.

"What are you doing?" She followed him in, curious.

His hand lifted and stroked the rust-shaded coat of the cow before him.

"She has sore teats. Her calf's a rough nurser." He found it easy to talk with her about something as ordinary as cows. "Been chewing on her pretty hard. I'm keeping them separated so she can heal."

"Oh." She moved closer, then fell to her knees in the hay beside him. "She's full. She needs to be milked."

"That's what the quills are for."

"To empty the udders?"

His mouth softened at her choice of words. "Yeah. To empty the udders."

Her expression turned wistful. "I haven't milked a cow in years." She turned hopeful eyes toward him. "May I?"

In all his life, he'd never be able to deny her anything. He was sure of it.

He managed a brisk nod. "Trade places with me, then."

She shifted to oblige him, placing a hand on his thigh to steady herself as they switched positions. The casual movement, that thoughtless act of touching him, branded him clear to his bones.

The roar inside his head threatened. Iron-clad control held it back.

Sonnie tucked the suede skirt primly about her and settled herself on the stool. Lance squatted on his haunches, angling his body toward the cow's rear legs in case she had a notion to kick. He took a quill and gently inserted it into a teat.

Sonnie made a sound of sympathy.

"Are you hurting her?" she asked in a voice hardly above a whisper.

"No." The cow hadn't flinched, showed no sign of pain. "This'll help the milk's flow."

"Oh," she said again, intent on his actions, fascinated with them.

After he'd done the same to the other teats, he straightened. "Are you ready?"

She nodded. Grasping the forward teat with her left hand and the opposite with her right, she pulled and squeezed. The cow shuffled and swung her head toward Sonnie, her big brown eyes doleful and wary, her jaws working her cud.

"Easy, Rosie," Lance crooned. He rubbed her broad side in long strokes. "Try again, Sonnie."

She did as he told her, to no avail.

"Nothing's coming out." She heaved a frustrated sigh.

"Do it this way." Without thinking, Lance leaned toward her and covered her hands with his, guiding her in the proper motions. Milk trickled, then increased to a steady stream.

"Oh, it's coming out fast now!" she said softly, the airy sound amazed, triumphant.

Her skin felt smooth and cool—delicately veined, fragile-boned, unaccustomed to hard work. Lance barely heard the victory in her voice. She filled his senses with awareness.

He'd never been this close to her before.

He pulled away. He had to, for his own sanity. For control. She continued milking and didn't seem to notice his reaction.

A coiling tendril of hair tumbled over her shoulder and rested across her breast. Lance stared openly, shamelessly, at the rounded curves. A growing heat spread within his loins. He jerked his glance away, his imagination of the womanly flesh hidden beneath the suede vivid and rampant.

"Ta-da!" Her dark eyes bright with delight, Sonnie turned to him and presented him the bucket brimming with foamy milk. "Now what?"

Lance inhaled slowly to clear his head of the lusty visions.

"We clean her with tincture of myrrh." He set the milk carefully aside and left the stall in search of the bottle.

"May I help? How often do you apply it?"

"Twice a day," he said, and stopped dead in his tracks.

Moose, half dog, half billy goat, ate anything he found worth eating, and most times his stomach tolerated none of it. One paw held Sonnie's silver tray firmly in place on the ground while his long tongue vigorously licked at the last traces of sugar.

She gasped in dismay.

Lance turned. Her expression was one of horror, of absolute incredulity. Full-blown amusement erupted within him.

He held it in. He wanted to spare her feelings. He knew how she'd hoped to please everyone with her treat.

"Oh, bad dog! Bad, bad dog!" She tried to shoo

him away. Moose didn't budge, too engrossed in stealing one more lick from the tray.

She found a broom and took a wild swing. Moose yelped in alarm. His tail fell between his legs, and he slunk into a corner. She snatched the tray from the ground.

"And what is so funny, Lance Harmon?" she demanded, her eyes sparking ebony fire.

"Nothing," he said hastily. He choked down his laughter and kept a close watch on her broom. "Nothing. I swear."

"Do you think I can't cook just because I lived in the city?" she asked. "Is that why you refused to eat the dates?"

The chuckles died inside him. Her unexpected accusations blindsided him.

He sputtered a denial.

"Maybe you're glad the dog ate them all." Her nose lifted with an audible sniff. "Well, Boss-man, I'll prove to you I can cook. Tonight. Six o'clock. Come hungry."

With that, she left.

Lance stared after her. It had all happened so quickly. He had no idea why he was blamed for Moose's crime or why Sonnie's mood had turned so blatantly testy. He swore in frustration and sent the dog a glowering scowl.

Moose, properly chastised, whined in apology and promptly threw up.

The table was ready.

Sparkling silverware and fragile, hand-painted china adorned the starched white tablecloth. Crystal glasses etched with the Rocking M brand stood in their places above each plate. Pressed linen napkins were folded perfectly at every place setting.

Not even Aunt Josephine could prepare a finer table

than this, Sonnie mused with satisfaction.

She'd decided against using the dining room for supper. It was too large and formal. Though they'd rarely eaten in the same room where food was prepared at her aunt's house, memories of eating at the heavy wooden table here in the kitchen lingered from her youth. She was certain Papa and the others would prefer it.

They'd be here in only a few minutes. Her nerves fluttered, and Sonnie pressed a hand to her belly to quash the feeling. Everything was ready. The meal promised to be superb, and, she assured herself, there was nothing to be apprehensive about.

Bootsteps and the low drone of male voices from the back porch announced their arrival. The door swung open. Cool air scurried inward, and with it, Cookie, Stick, and Charlie Flynn.

But not Lance.

Sonnie ushered the men in with a gracious welcome and tried to hide her disappointment. So what if he decided to eat with Ramon and the other hands in the bunkhouse? They'd enjoy her meal without him.

She concentrated her attention on arranging a large platter with quail and rice.

She'd made him angry. That was it. Her little temper outburst after Moose devoured the last of the sugared dates had soured Lance to her supper invitation, and he'd refused to come.

Maybe she shouldn't blame him.

Male conversation billowed around her. He was getting to her. That low voice of his. The strength he exuded. Blatant, raw masculinity. And his dedication and expertise in ranch matters was something she envied—and admired.

No wonder Papa favored him.

Sonnie's teeth found the inside of her lip. Lance

was the reason for her apprehension, she knew. She wanted to prove to him she could be all that he was, in the kitchen and out.

But now that he wasn't coming, she felt oddly deflated. Robbed of the opportunity.

Robbed of him.

She spooned sauce over the golden, plump birds and tried not to think. As she drizzled butter over tender asparagus spears, a crisp swirl of air blended into the kitchen's warmth.

Her gaze flew to the door.

Lance stepped in. He removed his hat and raked a hand through his tawny-shaded hair. He looked rushed, out of breath.

Wherever he'd come from, he'd been in a hurry to get here.

She swallowed down her pleasure and met the wary guardedness in his gaze.

"The others have only just arrived." She lifted the heaping platter and extended it toward him. "Put this on the table, won't you?"

Tossing his hat aside, he reached to take the dish from her, and their glances locked. From within the depths of his eyes, the guardedness disappeared. In its place was a hot whiskeyed flame—assessing, powerful.

His gaze broke from hers, lifted to the hair she'd piled in a coif on her head, slid down over the pale blue wool of her dinner gown, and up again.

The whiskey flame flickered, burned.

She almost shook from the heat of it. The platter swayed in her grip.

He took its weight, smooth and easy. "Whatever you want, Sonnie."

The provocative tone of his words, barely above a whisper, nearly shattered her composure. Shaken, she turned back toward the stove.

Whatever you want, Sonnie.

She would have to be stronger against him, against the effect he had on her. Tougher. She didn't want to think about the things Lance Harmon was beginning to make her want.

She had to concentrate on the meal she'd prepared. She had to be accepted by her father's men, to prove that she belonged on the ranch and not conveniently tucked away in a city clear across the country.

She had to prove it to Lance.

The men clustered around the table. Sonnie set the bowl of buttered asparagus in the center and sensed their hesitation to sit.

"Ain't never seen a table set as fine as this 'un." Cookie grunted, both hands stuffed in his pockets.

"Almost too fine to spoil by eating at," Stick added, his tone awed and admiring.

"Oh, that's silly," Sonnie said. "Find a chair, all of you. The food is growing cold."

"Want me to light this here candle, Miss Sonnie?" Charlie queried.

"Please do, and thank you."

"Well, look at this." Her father's voice boomed into the room. "Josephine has taught you well, *mia bambina*." He moved forward with his cane clicking along the floor and took his place at the head of the table. "Looks real nice. Smells good, too."

His compliments made all her labors worthwhile. "I hope you're hungry, Papa. I've made your favorites, with peaches for dessert."

She set a bowl of pasta, topped with a sauce of tomatoes, anchovies, and olives, in front of him.

"Ah, pasta." He smiled. "It's been a long time since I've had any."

"I thought so." She retrieved a bottle chilling in ice and began pouring into each of the glasses.

"Wine?" Cookie asked skeptically.

96

Sonnie nodded. "Full-bodied, to complement the meal."

The old cowboy shook his head and covered the top of his glass with his hand. "I'd rather have a beer."

The kitchen fell quiet.

"I think, Cookie," Lance said, his tone soft as he settled his long, lean frame into a chair next to her father's, "that if Sonnie wanted beer served, she would have provided it." His steady glance hooked with the other man's. "Try the wine."

Slowly the gnarled hand pulled back. "Now that you mention it," he said with a loud clearing of his throat, "wine *does* sound good. Fill 'er up, Miss Sonnie."

Sonnie's confidence wavered momentarily. She wasn't sure if she should be grateful or appalled at Lance's intervention with the old cowboy, but as the dishes began their rounds about the table, and the men's praising comments filled the conversation, her aplomb returned.

Miniature loaves of crusty bread completed the meal, and she removed her apron before she sat down. With a start, she realized all the chairs were occupied except for one.

Next to Lance.

She hadn't counted on that error in her careful table arrangement. She'd assumed her place would be at her father's right.

Clearly Lance was accustomed to taking that particular seat. No one seemed to question it.

She stoically took her place beside him and laid her napkin over her lap.

"Mangia! Mangia!" her father declared with a rare enthusiasm. He picked up his fork to dig into the food on his plate. At his example, the men followed suit.

"Papa!" Sonnie's eyes widened; her glance swept over the others. "We must say grace."

In unison, the forks were laid back down again.

"It seems we have forgotten that," her father said, his expression deadpan. "Shall we say one aloud or silently?"

Masculine expressions waited for her reply. Their lack of practice in something as basic as saying grace at mealtime exasperated Sonnie.

"A silent one will do."

All heads bowed in individual reflection. When her own prayer was complete, Sonnie straightened, and, as if waiting for her signal, the others did the same.

She tasted the quail. Each had been simmered to perfection, and Sonnie was pleased with the tenderness of the meat. She had painstakingly figured the amount she'd need, since the birds were small and at least two would be needed to satisfy a manly appetite. But several remained on the platter. A little frown teased her brow.

"Papa?" She sought his assurance. "How is your quail?"

"Very good," he said, his head bobbing between bites. "The best I've had in a long while."

Her glance slid toward Lance.

"The quail is fresh," he commented in his low voice.

"Stick bagged them for me." She sent the young cowboy an appreciative smile. "He worked hard to get as many as I asked for."

"So that's where you were all afternoon," Charlie said. "Thought maybe you were snoozing in a pile of hay somewheres."

"Naw. But I heard tell I missed some mighty fine-tastin' dates whilst I was out huntin'," Stick said with obvious disappointment.

"You did." Charlie grinned. "Reckon Moose got

your share." He relayed the dog's offense for Papa's benefit, which left them all roaring. Sonnie's cheeks warmed at the memory, but she accepted their teasing with a few giggles of her own.

Only Cookie remained silent. He toyed with his food, and at her query he flicked a piece of anchovy across the plate with his fork.

"Can't tell what this is," he muttered.

"It's an anchovy, Cookie," she said.

"An-cho-vee? For dinner?"

"Why, yes. They're very popular in Italian dishes." Dismay began to build within her.

"Can't see why you like 'em so much," he groused. "They taste funny."

"Cookie," Lance said, a wealth of warning in the single word.

"Well, I can't stomach 'em, boss," he blurted. "I ain't used to city slicker's grub."

"You don't have to eat anything you don't like," Sonnie said. She wanted to apologize for everything that made him unhappy. "Would you like me to fix you something else?"

"He eats what the rest of us eat," Lance said in a growl. "Or does without."

At the terse command, the table fell silent.

Sonnie slid her hand over his forearm, felt the muscles tense beneath the fabric of his shirt.

"Maybe Ramon would have something he'd like better, Lance," she said. Her dismay grew in leaps and bounds. "Or I have potatoes in the drawer. It won't take long to fry him some—"

"No."

The single word silenced her, as it must have done to countless recalcitrant ranch hands before her.

She bit her lip.

The sauce was perfectly spiced. Indeed, it rivaled that of the most exclusive restaurants in Rome and

Paris and was a wise foil for the quail. But Cookie's failure to appreciate it dulled her success and drained her own appetite.

"My daughter has become accustomed to the finer things in life, Cookie," Papa explained, breaking off a chunk of bread. "She's developed a taste for a wide variety of cuisines." His dark-eyed glance held the old cowboy's. "You'll like the anchovies when you eat them."

No one could mistake the hidden order in his words, a command to support Lance's. Sonnie's throat constricted. She wanted to throw the entire meal out the window.

Cookie lifted his glass and took a good-sized swallow of wine. He grimaced and blew out his breath. "Reckon a man's gotta git away from steak and potatoes once in a while. Lookin' forward to them thar anchovies, Miss Sonnie. I'll get used to 'em. Yessirree."

And he took another drink of wine.

Sonnie's hand balled into a fist on her lap. She hated being patronized by her father and Lance and all the men. She picked up her fork and resumed eating without tasting a bite.

The meal progressed, and the tension around the table dissipated as the men fell into their usual camaraderie. Sonnie's attention wandered to the graceful way Lance held his knife as he buttered his bread, to the fine sun-burnished hairs on the backs of his hands. She noticed how callused they were, how clean. He had manners, a style of eating and drinking that made the men around him seem rough and clumsy.

They weren't, of course. No more than she. But he was different. A notch above. Somehow better.

Her glance drifted downward to the soft blue wool of her dinner dress. With its bordered skirt finished with navy bands and wide point de Genes lace, she was different, as well. She seemed far too overdressed when set against the men with their rolled-up shirt-sleeves and denim jeans. She'd given little thought to her attire until now—Aunt Josephine always insisted upon formal wear at mealtime—and, for the first time, she understood the men's initial discomfiture after their arrival.

Yes, she was different, too. Something out of place at the Rocking M. Mink among ordinary cowhide. And because of that, the men treated her warily, like a fragile object, and with high esteem and respect, as if they feared she'd break.

She didn't want their wariness or discomfiture. She didn't want to be out of place. She wanted to be a part of them. Their equal. Their partner.

More red wine slipped down her throat.

". . . back to Silver Meadow. A few more head came up missing."

Lance had her father's full regard. "How many is a few?"

Sonnie's attention sharpened.

"Twenty-five. Maybe thirty."

"Bastard doesn't learn, does he?" Papa snarled.

Grimly Lance shook his head. "Ditson and Snake have been camping out in the cabin's burned-out shell. Some of the debris has already been cleared away." He touched his napkin to his mouth, then dropped it on his empty plate. "Looks like they're planning to stay for a while."

Sonnie held her breath at her father's angry frown. There was more Lance had to tell him.

"You think they might be out there now?" Papa demanded.

"Could be. Saw him and the Indian at Gracie's last night, but I don't think they're staying in one of her rooms."

"We'll find them. They need to be taught a lesson."

He reached for his cane and thumped it hard on the floor for emphasis.

"Vince."

Her father stilled. His razor-sharp gaze bored into Lance.

"This morning Sonnie and I came across a half dozen cows. They'd wandered from the main herd." For the first time, Lance hesitated. "They'd been poisoned."

"What?" Her father's voice thundered to the ceiling. He swung toward Sonnie, his features harsh.

"It's true, Papa." Never had she seen him like this. "They were very sick."

"Let's ride out," he said abruptly, pushing back his chair. "We'll surprise Ditson, the son of a bitch."

"It's cold and dark," Lance said, his brows furrowed. "You haven't ridden since your attack."

"And by God, it's time." A ruthless expression darkened her father's face—one that held no mercy. "Stick, saddle our horses."

The men rose.

"I'm coming with you," Sonnie said.

"No." Lance and Papa spoke the denial in vehement unison.

"But, Papa." Her gaze jumped from him to Lance, then back again.

"It's not safe," Lance said, answering for him.

Unease rippled through her for her father's health, for all he intended.

"Let Lance go, then," she said to him. "And the others."

"Keep out of this, Sonnie!"

She recoiled from his abrasive tone. Unbridled hurt soared through her. Still, she tried again, half rising from her chair in her appeal. "Stay here for dessert, Papa. Please. I've fixed peaches, your favorite. Remember?"

Cookie was the only one who seemed to hear. "Peaches, did you say?"

She nodded, her gaze glued to her father's retreating back. "Steeped in wine and sprinkled with crumbled—"

At the cowboy's blanched expression, she stopped.

"Your pa's in a real hurry. Maybe later, Miss Sonnie."

In the blink of an eye, the kitchen emptied.

Except for Lance.

He stood at the door, its knob gripped in his fist.

"Supper was good, Sonnie," he said, his voice low, rough. "I want you to know that."

She sank back into her seat.

"My father is waiting, Boss-man," she said bitterly. "Go before he does something he shouldn't."

A muscle in his jaw leaped, but Lance said nothing more. With a firm click of the latch, he left her alone.

Alone with a passel of dirty dishes and leftovers from the culinary success that had been an absolute failure.

She reached for the wine bottle and filled her glass to the rim.

Chapter Six

Heavy water buckets bulged the muscles in Lance's arms as he carried them, one in each hand, from the pump toward the horse trough behind the cabin. He didn't mind staying at the ranch's scattered line camps for weeks on end. Riding fence and checking cattle wasn't as monotonous as the other cowboys claimed. He rather enjoyed the solitude and never tired of the rolling Wyoming landscape.

A soft moaning sound reached him, a sound at odds with the creak and groan of the towering windmill close by or the muted calls of cows in the distance. Another, deeper and lustier, followed, a puzzling intrusion to the otherwise stillness of the land.

Lance's steps slowed. He approached the cabin warily, tiptoeing to the back with the stealth of a wolf on the prowl. He peered around the structure's corner.

And froze.

A man and woman, both as naked as the day they

were born, lay entwined on a bed of pine needles, their only covering the shadows cast by the breadth of the evergreen branches above them. Lance recognized the wrangler, a drifter recently hired by Vince for the summer; his mate was a willing young girl whisked away from a nearby farmhouse for the tryst.

Blood thundered in Lance's temples. He eased away from the sight, then leaned against the cabin. His fingers lost their grip on the bucket handles; each bucket toppled to the ground with a thud that sloshed water over the toes of his boots.

He was almost twenty. He knew what happened when a man had relations with a woman. Many times he'd heard the men in the bunkhouse boast of their conquests, their fun.

Their power.

His eyes squeezed tight; his belly churned. He trembled with a raw fear that surfaced from somewhere in the deepest core of his being.

A man could bring a woman pain, too. Hurt her with his strength, his demands.

His lust.

Mother.

And Hawthorne.

Why had he thought of them now? Hadn't the memories vanished with time? Would the pain ever dim?

Never. Never would he forget how Mother had suffered and died because of a man who couldn't control his body's greedy lust, a man stronger than she who had overpowered and conquered.

Conquered.

He would never be so weak as to succumb to desire. Passion. To yearnings so strong he would yield to a woman on a bed of pine needles in broad daylight or triumph over her for the sake of some lousy rent.

Never.

*   *   *

Silver Meadow, magnificent even at night, sprawled before Lance. He didn't need the brilliance of the sun to know the gentle lay of the land, a miles-long length of range lush with grass and fed with water from a glistening spur of Chugwater Creek. Moonlight splayed over the valley, painting everything it touched with hues of silver and shadowy grays. Dots of black formed the moving shapes of grazing cattle, and toward the east lay the only blemish to the land, the charred remains of the cabin Clay Ditson had once called home.

A sharp wind tugged at Lance's hat brim, and, absently, he pulled it lower over his forehead. Beside him, Vince sat straight in the saddle, oblivious to the cold, and like a king surveying his kingdom, swept a slow glance over the view below.

Lance waited in silence. He sensed the rage building in Vince, a possessive kind of rage kindled by one man who stole from another. He understood it. He felt the same. But Vince's illness demanded a calmness, a control, that Lance must maintain for the both of them.

The staccato of hooves drew his eye toward Charlie and Cookie riding up from within the darkness of the valley. As they drew closer, obliging beams of moonlight rendered their forms more distinct.

"Campfire's cold, Mr. Mancuso," Charlie said, reining his mount to a stop. "Ditson and Snake are gone. At least for now."

Vince gave no sign he heard him. In the prolonged quiet, Cookie's horse blew and pawed the ground. The two cowboys looked expectantly at Lance.

"Want to go down and have a closer look?" Lance knew full well Vince would settle for little else.

"What right do they have to waltz out here and squat on my land?" Vince exploded as if Lance had never spoken. "Rustle my herd, then use *my* grass and *my* water to graze 'em! I won't stand for it!"

"Easy, Vince," he cautioned. "Your heart."

The older man's breath hissed inward as he visibly strove for composure. "I wish to hell they were here," he muttered in declaration. "They need convincing, and I'm of a mind to do it."

"I'll talk to Ditson again," Lance said.

"Pah! Talk! We tried talk, and he won't listen! We tried threats, and they don't faze him!" With a jerk, he yanked the reins into his hand. "He's forcing us to take stronger measures. Maybe then he'll understand we mean business." Abruptly his heels jabbed his mount's ribs, and he broke away, riding at a brisk canter into the valley.

Lance exchanged a somber glance with Charlie and Cookie. In unison, they took up their own reins and followed him deeper into the darkness.

The blackened carcass of the cabin's foundation sat as a reminder of their last warning to Ditson. A pot-bellied stove sat in what had been the structure's largest room and loomed above the ashes and seared furnishings. A pile of bedrolls and supplies lay heaped in one corner, swept clean for use.

The very sight of Ditson's belongings worried Lance. They told of his obstinacy, of his deliberate rebuff of their attempts to keep peace on Mancuso range.

They told of trouble.

"Look at this, boys." A short distance away from the cabin's rubble, Vince inspected a springboard wagon, its back loaded with fresh-cut lumber, a wide roll of tar paper, tools, and several open-topped cans.

Lance rode closer, adding his inspection to Vince's. Next to the cans stood a lone bottle.

He leaned from the saddle to read the label in the meager light.

It was yellow phosphorous.

Rat poison.

Sonnie had been right. So had he. Clay Ditson had poisoned Mancuso cattle with rat poison.

The son of a bitch.

Vince reached inside his coat and retrieved a cheroot. A match burst into a flare of light, and in the glow of the flame, a slow grin spread beneath his mustache.

Cookie slouched more comfortably in his saddle. "Reckon Ditson's plannin' on nestin' fer a spell," he commented. "Got enough wood here to build himself a right cozy little home."

"Must've cost him a bundle," Charlie grunted.

"Yeah. A bundle," Vince said. One hand cupping the flickering match, he drew in deeply of the expensive tobacco before exhaling a puff of smoke. "He's a fool. A damn fool."

He removed his foot from the stirrup and kicked at one of the cans. Kerosene spilled out, pooling on top of the lumber and tar paper. His arm lowered, and the match arced in the air. Within moments, flames stretched and lunged, engulfing the wagon bed in a hungry fire.

Heat bathed Lance's face. He stared impassively at the waste, the destruction.

It had to be done. Ditson deserved it—poisoned and stolen cattle in exchange for the home he planned to build.

Ditson would know Vince Mancuso had come to call. And there would be repercussions, and revenge and anger—a hit at Vince where he'd hurt the most. The certainty of it tugged a silent curse through Lance's teeth.

"Cold night, eh, boys?" Vince asked with a little smile. The tension had eased from him. He appeared relaxed, pleased with his actions. "Let the fire keep you warm. When it burns out, ride back to the ranch."

"Sure thing, Mr. Mancuso," Cookie and Charlie said.

Vince spurred his horse into a turn, and Lance did the same. Instead of riding out of Silver Meadow, they swung wide and rode slowly into Ditson's small—but growing—herd.

Grimly they studied the stock. Showing the conviction of a man who knew what was his, Vince's expression hardened as he scanned the fatted Hereford cows and calves.

Ditson had chosen well. The animals were ordinary, with no unusual traits to set them apart, animals any other rancher in the area would have. All he had to do was mark each as his own, and no one could prove they once belonged to the Rocking M.

Lance strained to discern the brand marked on the nearest calf. In his mind's eye, he compared it to the original, the Rocking M's, and within seconds he comprehended what Ditson had done with a simple running iron. Circle Double Diamond. A few strokes and the half circle and M had changed into a design belonging only to Ditson.

But guessing the artwork was still not proof enough he had rustled Mancuso stock. Short of killing the animal on the spot and pulling back its hide to see the initial brand burned underneath, it was only one man's word against another's. Clay Ditson was too smart to get caught in the act of rustling. He knew what he was doing, he knew what he wanted and he would continue to steal from the huge herds on the Rocking M to build up his own.

And Vince would not stand for it. Nor would Lance. And therein lay the problem.

"He'll go after Sonnie, you know," Lance said.

"He does, and he hangs. Right along with that damned Indian of his," Vince snorted.

"I want to send her back."

"Send her back?" Vince seemed surprised. He shrugged and tossed aside the stub of his cheroot. "She wants to stay."

"Boston is the safest place for her. At least until we get Ditson thrown into jail."

"Pah! No jail will hold him. He's too shifty. And the juries are against the cattlemen. They won't convict him." Vince fastened the top button of his coat in a gesture that hinted that the matter was settled, that he was ready to leave. "This is Wyoming range. Mancuso range. We'll get rid of Ditson our own way."

"Vince." Lance tried to keep his frustration at bay. "We have do this right. Go by the law, get solid proof that will hold up in court." He leaned forward. "So we can keep Ditson away from Sonnie for good."

"You think I don't know that?" Vince demanded. "We can handle him."

Lance swore inwardly at the defiant confidence. Vince seemed incognizant of all that Ditson was capable of.

But Lance had heard the wily man's determination only yesterday at Gracie's, the vow he'd made, the warning that he would disregard any orders to stay away from Silver Meadow.

Clay Ditson wanted to be a cattleman. He'd stop at nothing to be one.

Abruptly Lance swung from the saddle and dropped to the ground. He walked deeper into the herd, and in the meager light perused each animal closely, trying to find some oddity, some inconsequential characteristic that would set them apart from the rest.

He found several—a slightly swollen left foreleg, a thinning in the curly-haired hide, an oval-shaped white patch over one eye—and memorized them.

Then, with his knife, he carefully made a shallow slit in the hide at their necks. From his hip pocket, he withdrew an equal number of half-dollar coins and inserted them into the openings.

He returned to his horse, mounted, and met Vince's questioning look.

"Proof," he said.

Vince nodded agreeably. "Proof. If we need it."

"*When* we need it," Lance said with a growl. They were on Mancuso land. The day Ditson's pilfered herd showed up at the loading chutes in Cheyenne, they'd be ready for him.

Vince grinned, amused at Lance's stubbornness. He glanced toward Cookie and Charlie and the dwindling fire they guarded before turning back to Lance.

"Let's go home, eh?"

As they drew nearer to the main barn, Stick ran up and took their horses to bed them down for the night. Lance and Vince climbed the porch stairs and entered the Big House. A light shone in the parlor, another in the kitchen, but no sound met them.

It was quiet, Lance thought. Too quiet. Sonnie would have heard them enter. She would have been waiting for them.

Vince sighed and removed his gloves and hat. "The ride wore me out, Lance. You said it would, eh?" He glanced around him, appearing more curious than concerned. "Where do you suppose Sonnie is?"

Lance's heart pumped a little faster. He hid his growing apprehension. "She might be upstairs. It's time for your medicine. I'll get it for you."

"Yes," Vince murmured tiredly, and hung his coat on the wooden rack near the door. "I'll be in my room. Bring it to me there."

Lance let Vince find his own way down the hall. Though the medicine sat in a cupboard in the kitchen,

Lance pivoted in the opposite direction, then took the stairs in long leaps to the top.

"Sonnie?" he called. The rooms were dark, silent. He reined in his budding imagination, refusing to believe Clay Ditson would venture this close. "Sonnie?"

He entered her bedroom, which was illuminated only by the shining moon peeking in through the gossamer curtains at the window.

His gaze scanned the shadows. Everything appeared to be in its place, neat and tidy as usual.

He set his hands on his hips and tried to think of where she might have gone. A late-night ride? The cowboys would never allow it. A visit to the barns? Hardly. Socializing? There were no women nearby.

But there were men.

Lots of men. On a wave of burgeoning disbelief, he strode toward the window and yanked back the curtains.

The bunkhouse sat in plain sight below. Beacons of light shone through the windows. Every cowboy who worked in the Mancuso outfit rose early each morning. The hour was late. They should have ended their day long before now.

But they hadn't.

Because one beautiful, black-eyed woman was keeping them awake.

The wine had given Sonnie courage, of course.

The Rocking M bunkhouse had been denied to her all her life. Her sisters always warned her never to go near it, because Papa would be livid if he ever found out.

But she was grown-up now. A woman of the world. She knew her way with men, and she knew how to take care of herself. Besides, she was perfectly safe here on her father's ranch.

Not that he'd even notice she had gone. He was

too busy shutting her out of his life to care. Clay Ditson and his rustled cattle meant more to Vince Mancuso than she did. So with the evening long and looming before her, she'd buried the hurt, walked over, knocked on the door, and invited herself in.

Now that she was here, Sonnie couldn't understand why everyone insisted she stay away.

The bunkhouse was certainly nothing fancy with its wooden floor, narrow bunks, and scant furnishings. In fact, the place had a rough, homey appeal. Except for the postcards and calendars depicting ladies of questionable reputation tacked about the walls, the atmosphere beckoned with welcome. A stone fireplace radiated warmth to the far corners of the long rectangular room, and the smell of strong coffee flirted with the scent of tobacco. Moose, his head resting on his paws, slept peacefully near the door.

"Reckon it's your play, Miss Sonnie. You know what you're gonna do?"

From his seat across the table from her, Jake McKenna eyed her with insolent amusement. Having just met him, Sonnie couldn't decide whether she liked him or not, but it had been he who'd ushered her inside and convinced the others there was no harm in letting her stay.

"Take your time, ma'am," Red Holmes, one of the young cowboys she'd met earlier that afternoon, advised. He lifted a tall bottle of beer to his mouth and swallowed. "Don't let him rush you."

"Takes a while to learn the game, too. Got a lot ridin' on this hand," Frank Burton, her tutor in this strange game of seven-up, murmured beside her.

Expectant silence fell among the group of men, most of whose names escaped her. They made an avid audience, and Sonnie delighted in having their attention. It seemed they were pleased she'd come, especially since they'd all stopped what they were doing to watch.

Her fingers found her own beer bottle, one of several scattered about the tabletop. Jake hadn't offered her the courtesy of a separate drinking glass; thus she drank the cold brew full-strength and directly from the bottle. She found the menagerie of cards and pennies sprinkled in front of her exciting, but, befuddled by the effects of wine and beer, her concentration lagged. She tried to remember all Frank had told her, and in consternation, heaved an indecisive sigh.

"Now, if I didn't know better," Jake purred at her lack of response, "I'd say you were bluffin' me."

A sprig of boldness pushed a smile onto Sonnie's lips. "Why do you say that, Mr. McKenna?"

"That purty little face of yours is a picture of pure innocence. Makes a man think you don't have a clue as to what you're doin'." He sat with his chair tilted on its back legs, one dusty boot propped on the corner of hers, trapping a swatch of her dinner dress beneath the sole. "But then again," he said, flashing her a big grin resplendent with lazy charm, "could be you know exactly what you're doin' and are just usin' your feminine wiles to make me believe you don't."

Feminine wiles. Sonnie's smile deepened. That was a definite tool in this manly environment.

She took his bait.

"Well, I do declare," she said, affecting an outrageously seductive drawl livened further from the spirits. "That sounds like a challenge to me."

"Call it what you want, honey. But I still think you're bluffin' me."

"Do you now?"

"I do." A cigar rolled across his wind-chapped lips and settled in a corner of his mouth. Several more peeked from his shirt pocket.

"We'll just have to see about that, won't we?" She

fanned her lashes and drew an appreciative murmur from the men, each gazing at her with nothing short of absolute adoration.

Sonnie gloried in it. The heady feeling of being enjoyed in the coveted circle of her new friends, Vince Mancuso's men, gave her a sense of power her besotted mind recognized.

Only Jake McKenna seemed oblivious to her allure. He considered her with an arrogance that was both irritating and perplexing, and he seemed confident of his win.

A challenge, most definitely.

With a final glance at the cards in her hand, she laid them facedown and tugged her dress free of his boot. She rose, pausing a discreet moment until her woozy head cleared.

"What's the matter, Jake?" she taunted softly, glad her words sounded distinct. "Are you so sure you'll defeat Vince Mancuso's daughter in a silly ol' game of seven-up?" She ventured a few steps about the table and let her fingertips trail brazenly along his shoulder blades. "Or"—she came to a stop directly behind him—"do you think that because I'm a woman I'm incapable of defeating *you?*"

At her touch, the cigar quivered against his lower lip. He sat immobile with his chair still tilted back, and Sonnie knew he wasn't as immune to her presence as she'd thought.

Bolstered by the spirits flowing in her veins, she opened her fingers over the curve of his shoulder and slid her hand along the cotton fabric of his shirt. Her shameless flirting kept him distracted, and without a shred of guilt, she looked at the cards he hastily tried to conceal.

"Well, now, Miss Sonnie, bein's this is your first time at gamblin', and bein's a woman of your gentle persuasion don't have the, er, cleverness to outplay someone of my experience—"

"Ah, cleverness, Mr. McKenna." Her husky laughter tossed his explanation aside. Having seen his hand, she knew which of her own cards would give her the point she needed to win the game. "Perhaps my gender is against me. Would you prefer that I be a man instead?" She snatched one of the cigars from his pocket. Holding it between her teeth, she spoke around the rolled tobacco. "A Mancuso son. Would that be better?"

The hem of her dress flared as she twirled, plucking the hat from Frank's head and settling it atop her own. Chuckles flowed about the room, stoking her playfulness. She tilted the hat to a jauntier angle over the coiffure she'd taken such care with before dinner.

"I reckon it don't make any difference whether you're male or female, Miss Sonnie," Jake declared with condescending humor. "Cards are cards. Pennies are pennies. And winnin's all that matters."

"You are right, of course." She removed the cigar from her mouth and tucked it between her fingers. Retaining her new manly role, she swished her skirts aside and propped one foot onto the seat of her chair. The stance gave everyone an unbridled view of her silk-stockinged leg and drew a round of exuberant hoots.

She gave no thought to her actions. It had become imperative to put Jake McKenna in his place, to prove to him and the other cowboys that she could win as easily as any of them.

"My high card," she said. With a flourish, she laid down a queen of spades. "One point to my six make seven. I win."

With the taste of victory sweet on her tongue, she lifted her glance to Jake's.

He was unaware of her accomplishment, but stared,

instead, at a point somewhere behind her.

A jubilant smile froze on her lips. Through her beer-fuzzed state came the realization that the men's raucous laughter had quieted to haunting silence, and no one, absolutely no one, had even looked at her winning card. A pitiful, mewling whine from Moose slathered a wave of apprehension down her spine.

Instinctively, her gaze swept past the coats, boots, and hats cluttering the room, past the flagrant pinups on the wall, past the somber group of men standing about, and rested on Lance.

Lance.

With a burst of panic, she searched for her father beside him, but only Lance's tall, muscular frame filled the doorway. Her gasp of surprise sounded disturbingly, suspiciously, like a hiccup.

His glance raked her from the top of Frank's hat to the toes of her propped foot. All traces of her inebriation evaporated like a raindrop on a hot skillet. The air fairly sizzled with tension.

"Hey, boss," Jake greeted with a tight grin as he carefully righted his chair. "You're back."

"Yeah. I am."

The low, even timbre of his voice betrayed none of the suppressed emotion she sensed in him. Sonnie eased her foot from the chair seat.

He approached the table in a calculated, predatory stroll—a vengeful wolf stalking wary quarry. Her chin lifted, and his glance slammed into hers.

"Don't mind me, Sonnie," he taunted with deceptive smoothness. "Go on with your game."

She refused to let him intimidate her as he'd done the others.

"They were teaching me how to play seven-up," she said. In defiance, she reached for the beer bottle and carried it to her lips. "And I won."

"Really?" His hand snaked out and yanked the bottle from her unresisting grasp. "I'm so impressed." Tilting his head back, he finished off the contents. The strong, bronzed column of his throat bobbed with every swallow.

Sonnie's composure faltered from this new side of him. She hadn't expected his sarcasm, the cold condemnation she was seeing now.

His shadowed gaze ripped over the men. "Who brought in the beer?"

A long, painful minute passed before anyone spoke. Sonnie held her breath. She was unsure of the guilty person, but she understood his reluctance to reveal himself.

Lance moved closer to Jake and dropped the bottle onto the tabletop. The container wobbled and fell on its side. Neither man made an attempt to right it.

"Any ideas, McKenna?"

Jake stood with an abruptness that nearly toppled his chair.

"I did," he said with a snarl.

Lance's jaw hardened. "You know the rules. No drinking. No gambling. No fighting." His imperious glance jerked to Sonnie. "And no women."

Sonnie's hackles rose. "I came of my own free will, Lance Harmon. I have every right as my father's daughter—"

"Shut up, Sonnie," he snapped.

She stiffened at his high-handed treatment of her, and an array of stinging retorts sprang to her tongue. But a warning shake of Red Holmes's crimson-haired head held them in check.

"You'll be accountable for this in the morning, McKenna," Lance promised with a low growl. His sharp-eyed gaze pierced every man. "I want the lights out in five minutes. Anyone still up after that hits the road."

With the exception of Jake, the men nodded in obedience. Lance turned to Sonnie.

"Go on back to the house," he said.

"I will not." She glowered at him from beneath the borrowed hat. "I have five minutes. Just like everyone else."

"You'll go now." His patience seemed at the breaking point.

Sonnie dared to push him to the edge.

"I won't," she said.

"Miss Sonnie." Frank's pleading tone penetrated the dare. "It's best to do as he says, what with him bein' the boss and all."

"Boss to you, maybe, but not me." Yet the cowboy's advice rang in her brain, and her bravado wavered.

She gave up the fight with an ungrateful sigh and a roll of her eyes. She speared Lance with a scathing glare and spun on her heel to leave, but the spirits in her blood bested her.

She swayed and stumbled. From behind her, an iron-thewed arm wrapped about her legs, a rock-hard shoulder hit her belly, and she endured the sensation of being heaved up and over.

Instant nausea rose up from her belly. Frank's hat dropped from her head onto the floor. Her hair loosened, fell, and dangled from the tousled coiffure. Moose, his nose bare inches from hers, sniffed enthusiastically at the beer on her breath.

With a squeal of repugnance, Sonnie reached out her hand to swat at him. Again she nearly lost the contents of her stomach.

"Put me down, Lance," she demanded between clenched teeth. "Now, damn you!"

He ignored her and headed for the door. She kicked and squirmed, but the grip about her legs never loosened.

From her upside-down position, she caught a topsy-turvy view of the men they were leaving behind, their sympathetic expressions and wide-eyed stares.

Humiliated beyond words, beyond insults and pleas, beyond anything she had ever experienced from another man before, Sonnie gave up the fight, flung her arms about Lance's waist, and hung on for dear life.

Chapter Seven

He came upon her by accident.

If not for the softly shaded plum fabric of her dress peeking out from the tangled growth of wildflowers, Lance might have missed her. He drew his horse closer. Sonnie lay on a blanket, cocooned within the beaming warmth of the sun, and slept peacefully, with so much innocence that a part of his heart swelled from the purity of it.

He stared down at her. Her hair, long ago unfurled from the binds of a ribbon, trailed across her shoulder and past her arm. She reclined partially on her side, one cheek turned into the blanket, her hand relaxed across her waist. Lashes, crescent-shaped and richly sable, rested against smooth, ivory skin.

He'd been gone a long time. Trailing cattle kept him away from the main spread of the Rocking M for periods that stretched from weeks into months. Glimpses of Vince's daughters were rare, and those of Sonnie alone were even rarer.

She was growing up.

Breasts not yet flowered into full womanhood rose and fell during her slumber. He dragged his gaze lower to the gentle flare of her hips and downward still farther to slender thighs outlined through the drape of her dress.

Plagued by a strange sense of restlessness, Lance cocked his jaw and looked away. Across the meadow, he caught sight of Vince and his remaining five daughters, all carrying buckets and intent on their pickings from a cluster of crabapple trees and mulberry bushes.

It seemed they'd forgotten their youngest. Lance's glance drifted over Sonnie yet again, and a fragile bond, an understanding, budded inside him. He, too, knew what it was like to be alone. Loved, accepted, but still alone.

A pesky bumblebee hovered and dipped about Sonnie's nose. Her mouth puckered; she shifted and sighed. Lance's lips softened.

He urged his horse back into the shadow of an aging cottonwood tree and settled more comfortably in the saddle. He would stay, he decided, for a little while. He would watch over her when the others were gone so she would not be alone.

He would stay. For just a little while.

The fury burned inside him.

Lance ached to throttle Jake McKenna for breaking Mancuso bunkhouse rules. Red Holmes, Frank Burton, and the other men deserved to be horsewhipped for going along with him. Every damn one of them knew better.

Including Sonnie.

She waltzed in and twisted his men around her perfectly manicured little finger. Good sense left them and typical male weakness with regard to a woman—

especially one as beautiful as Sonnie—took over.

The fury raged.

He loped up the porch stairs with little thought to the bounce he gave her. Her muffled complaint slowed his step, but only slightly. She grasped him tighter as he stomped across the porch and flung open the front door.

"You're a miserable, low-down wretch, Lance Harmon," she choked from behind him.

"Yeah, well," he drawled with cold sarcasm. "You had it coming."

"You don't care, do you?"

"No."

"You don't care about anything but yourself and my father and his—"

He locked the door for the night. "Keep whining and you'll wake him. What do you think he'd say if he saw you drunk and fresh off an illicit card game? In the bunkhouse, no less."

She moaned into the small of his back. A quick glance revealed Vince's bedroom closed and silent. Lance headed for the stairwell.

"What are you going to do?" she asked.

"Put you to bed." He grunted and shifted her to a better position for the climb up.

"Let me down," she commanded in a loud whisper. Her wriggling renewed its fervor. "How dare you treat me like this! I can walk up to my room myself."

"You're in no shape to walk anywhere by yourself, Sonnie," he snorted without sympathy. "And hold still, damn it."

A strangled cry escaped from her throat. She held her body rigid over his; he took his own sweet time in ascending the stairs.

He entered her room and closed the door firmly. She was primed for battle. He didn't want her waking Vince in the fray of it.

A gentle shading of moonlight guided him to the bed. With his free hand he jerked back the covers. Bending, he eased her from his shoulder and let her slide backside-first onto the mattress. Her legs dangled over the edge, and she fell amid the pillows like a rag doll. Her hand fumbled with the unruly hank of hair that had fallen across her face.

His fury flared again. Sonnie—always so graceful and dignified—had toppled to the ranks of a common dance-hall girl. Why had she gone to the bunkhouse?

The crazy fool.

Unceremoniously, he swung her legs up onto the mattress, then grasped a handful of the covers to throw over her. Her protests halted him.

"My dress, Lance," she said in exasperation. "And my shoes!"

He glared at her in the darkness.

"What about 'em?" he said in a growl.

"I can't sleep in them. I need my nightgown." She attempted to sit up. "My hairbrush, too. I must clean my teeth and wash my—"

He reached out and plunked her down into the pillows again.

"You wouldn't make it to the dresser, Sonnie. You're going to have to make do with what you've got on. Here." He bent once more, cupped his hand around the heel of her shiny, bow-topped shoe, and slipped it off. Her toes wriggled; her silk-stockinged foot flexed in sublime provocation.

His foul temper wavered. Even drunk, she had the power to arouse him.

Grimly he removed the other shoe.

"There. Better?" he said.

"Thank you."

Her meekness gave him pause. He guessed the full effects of the liquor were settling in, and she'd feel worse before she'd feel better.

Clutching the covers a second time, he pulled them over her. She lay perfectly still, as if she were afraid to move.

Her pathetic frown tweaked his heart. She watched him, her expression doleful. He realized she was no longer vexed with him, that she wouldn't give him the war of words he'd expected.

He wished she would. He could deal with a heated argument better than he could her inebriation and the discomforts that would come with it.

"Close your eyes, Sonnie. Sleep," he said, his voice rough, raspy in the silence.

Immediately her lashes fluttered downward. The sable crescents joined tight; within seconds, they flew open again.

"Oh, Lance, the room is spinning," she said with a whimper.

Like droplets of water through a sieve, his anger seeped from him.

"Stare at the ceiling," he said. "Don't move your head. The spinning will stop, and then you'll sleep."

"All right," she murmured. She didn't stir a hairbreadth and did exactly as he bade. Lance waited several long moments.

"Better?" he asked finally.

"A little." A stubborn hiccup escaped, and her hands balled the blankets about her stomach. A flicker of alarm went through him.

"You going to be sick?" His glance left her to spear the darkness for a suitable container if he needed it.

"Oh, I couldn't bear it. Not in front of you." Mortification laced the admission. She curled onto her side away from him. "I feel awful."

He knew she did. He'd been in her place a time or two himself. Compassion smothered the rest of his fury.

"I'll stay with you," he said. "Just until you fall asleep."

Finding no chair nearby, he stepped toward the bed. His weight dipped the mattress, and the springs creaked.

Sonnie lay motionless. Silver-tipped shadows outlined the regal shape of her nose, dusted over the gentle curve of her cheek. Her breathing, soft and shallow, whispered in the quiet.

She turned slightly and caught him looking at her. The fullness of her mouth curved downward into a rueful pout.

"Are you going to scold me, Lance?" His brow raised questioningly, but she continued. "Tell me how stupid I am? That I deserve everything I got tonight?"

He shook his head. "Stupid, maybe, but I don't want you hurting because of it."

Her pout deepened. "Jake McKenna said it was okay if I drank a beer or two. He said you wouldn't mind."

"Did he?" Irritation sizzled within him. "What if McKenna said I wouldn't mind if you robbed a bank? Would you do it? You're a smart lady, Sonnie. Don't let McKenna do your thinking for you."

The air hung heavy with the words. From against the pillows, Sonnie released a disheartened sigh and rolled to her back.

"Why do you hate me so?" she asked, the words quavery, uncertain.

The question rocked him. "I don't hate you, Sonnie."

God, no. Never. Never that.

"You're always gruff with me." He detected a tremble in her lower lip. "You hardly look at me. You won't touch me."

"That's not true."

Or was it? Was that how he treated her, as if he

126

hated her, when he'd loved her with every fiber of his being for as long as he could remember?

"It is." She lifted an unsteady hand from her stomach, touched her hair, rubbed her forehead. "You act as if you can hardly stand to be in the same room with me."

"Oh, Sonnie," he said in a frustrated hiss.

How could he tell her that she scared the hell out of him? How would he explain the god-awful fear of getting too close, of hurting, of being hurt?

"Are you sorry I came back?" she asked, her gaze steady.

He struggled with the truth in her demand, searched furtively for a way to answer without wounding her already wounded feelings.

"You are, aren't you?" she said at his lack of reply. "You want me to go back to Boston."

Her intuition dismayed him. His throat worked; tentacles of guilt repressed the words on his tongue. He remembered the conversation he'd had with Vince as they rode out of Silver Meadow earlier tonight. The images of Clay Ditson and Snake lingered vividly in his mind.

He leaned forward. "Sonnie, you have to understand how it is out here. It's too dangerous for you to stay. We're on the brink of a range war."

"Don't send me away, Lance." To his horror, the glimmer of unshed tears shone in her eyes. "Please. I'll stay away from the bunkhouse. I won't drink beer again. I won't fix anchovies again. And I'll have meals ready on time every day."

Her pleas tortured him. "It's more complicated than that, Sonnie. A hell of a lot more complicated."

She studied him, her features troubled. "Why don't you tell me then? I want to learn everything there is to learn about this ranch. And you're fighting me on it."

He swore and drew back. "I'm not one of your damned professors. And the Rocking M isn't a class-room."

"You won't tell me, will you?" she murmured. "You keep everything locked away from me. Just like my father." She drew in a steadying breath. "I can defend myself against Clay Ditson and Snake, if that's what you're worried about."

He couldn't begin to tell her all he worried about, or that all his worries included her.

"They'll use you against Vince. Against me," he said roughly. "Poisoning cattle is just the beginning."

"I can save the ones we saw this morning. I've studied diseases for years and—"

"We put them down this afternoon, Sonnie. Charlie and I. They were too far gone to save."

"Oh." Her lower lip trembled again. "I'm sorry."

"Don't be. It's done. We can't change it."

"Such a waste," she murmured, saddened.

He nodded once in silent agreement.

Her body shifted, rustling the bedclothes. She appeared to hesitate, then reached a hand toward him.

"I'm sorry, too, that I made you angry. I shouldn't have let Mr. McKenna talk me into playing cards. It's just that . . ." She rested her fingers against his chest.

The warmth in her touch drizzled through the fabric of his shirt and onto his skin. She'd touched him before. Now should be no different.

But it was.

His blood stirred.

"What, Sonnie?" His whisper sounded raspy, jagged. "It's just what?"

A fingertip toyed with a button.

"After you left with my father and the others, I didn't want to be alone. I hate being alone. I've always hated it."

128

He held himself taut. His heart stepped up its beat, pounded a steady thrum in his veins.

"Do you know what it's like to have everything you've ever loved or wanted stripped away from you?"

Yes. God, yes. Mother. Father.

You.

"You've probably never been shut out of someone's life, have you? You've never been passed by or denied the only thing you've ever wanted."

He said nothing, kept the old pain of his years at the Children's Aid Society inside him. He refused to share his heartbreak when hers was overflowing.

"I wanted some company tonight. I didn't care who or what kind."

He braced an arm beside her. Her hair tumbled in an obsidian halo about the pillow, glinted in blue-black perfection in the moonlight.

"Right or wrong," she went on in a low, hushed tone, "the bunkhouse gave me that."

Her hand came up, curled around the back of his neck. She tugged him closer. Her breath stroked his chin, teased his nose with the lingering scent of beer.

The familiar rush of waterfalls threatened to overcome him, to drown him with its roar. He fought to stay afloat.

"Don't be angry with me, Lance. Right now I couldn't bear it."

She lifted her head a scant inch. Her mouth, the mouth he'd dreamed about throughout countless nights, found his. He was helpless to draw back, to prevent the kiss she promised to deepen, and he followed her down against the pillow.

Her lips flirted with his, trembled, then grew bolder. The tip of her tongue touched the tip of his.

Sweet Jesus. Her power.

She held a power over him so consuming it devoured his fears, squelched the roar inside him, soothed the pounding of his heart. A power that ignited desire so quickly he could hardly breathe from the force of it.

He groaned her name and thrived on that power. She gave back a portion of the control she'd taken from him; he used it, molded it, and kissed her back with all the pent-up yearning of years of loving without being loved back.

His lips rolled over hers and tasted the response of a woman who was not afraid to kiss a man. She could give him more, and he pleaded for it. Needed it.

Needed her.

His arms moved to pull her closer, to crush her against his chest, to satisfy the cravings she'd stoked inside him, but she pushed against him and ended their kiss when he would have kissed her forever.

Through thick ebony lashes, her gaze found him. He saw the vulnerability in her eyes, the incredulity of what had just happened between them.

His ardor cooled. The liquor had freed her inhibitions, but he'd been sober as hell. The reality of what he might have done appalled him.

"Lance?"

Her voice, soft and uncertain, reached out to him. He drew back, freed himself from her touch, and pulled the bedcovers high to her neck.

"Go to sleep, Sonnie."

Her mouth opened to protest, then closed again.

"Yes," she murmured finally, and rolled to her side. Her lids drifted downward. Within moments her breathing became deep and regular.

He rose slowly from the bed and backed toward the door. All his life he'd struggled for detachment from women—strength, control, common decency. Yet Sonnie was his one weakness. She always had been.

And he wanted her more than ever.

* * *

Sonnie didn't want to wake up.

She clung to oblivion, burrowed deeper into the warmth of the covers, but already daylight filtered through her closed lids, and she relinquished the fight.

She opened one eye. Glaring sun shone through the parted drapes, and she quickly closed her lashes again. The brilliance hurt.

She groaned aloud and turned over. Her temples throbbed. Her mouth was dry as cotton. Her nightgown itched.

Sonnie opened her eyes and stared at the pale blue wool fabric of her dinner dress's sleeve.

She wasn't wearing her embroidered flannel gown.

One by one, her groggy mind sorted through the events of the previous night. The meal she'd prepared for her father and his men. The card game in the bunkhouse. Jake McKenna.

Lance.

Her gaze darted to the edge of the bed, to the precise spot where he'd sat.

And their kiss.

Her belly fluttered. The memory of how she'd pulled him to her rushed forward. She could still feel his mouth moving over hers. Hard. Masculine.

Hungry.

Heat spread through her cheeks.

Lance had shown her vibrant, barely sheathed desire. She'd been almost swept away by it, but had somehow stopped herself.

How had she managed it?

Her head swiveled toward the empty pillow beside her, to blankets rumpled by no one else but her.

If she hadn't . . .

A niggle of disappointment swept through her, in spite of everything.

Another man might have taken advantage of her

131

inebriation and bedded her. But not Lance Harmon. The honorable Boss-man. Her father's favorite.

She should be grateful to him, she supposed.

Even so, the kiss would never have happened if she'd used common sense and resisted Jake McKenna's zealous hospitality. How many bottles of beer had she downed at his urging?

Sonnie didn't want to know.

Now, this morning, she paid the price. She must pull herself together and assume a facade of normalcy for Papa's benefit. Instinctively she knew Lance would not reveal her ill-fated visit to the bunkhouse.

She should be grateful to him for that, too.

With a mammoth effort, she flung aside the covers and sat up, then pushed her toes into the thick carpet. Her head swam, and her stomach lurched.

She waited for the unsavory sensations to pass. Carefully, not yet trusting her balance, she stood. She ventured to the window in her stockinged feet and pulled the drapes closed.

The darkened shadows helped. A splashing of cold water and a refreshing drink for her dry mouth would be even better. She concentrated on getting herself over to the dresser.

She glimpsed herself in the mirror and moaned. Her eyes were puffy and ringed with fatigue; her hair was a virtual rat's nest of tangles and drooping curls. Wrinkles covered her dress from neck to hem, and she detected a definite scent of stale beer and cigarette smoke about herself.

Longing for a leisurely hot bath, she lathered a washcloth instead and cleansed her face and neck, dismantled what was left of her coiffure, and gradually worked the snarls free from her hair.

Her mouth begged for a drink. Having no cup or fresh water at her disposal, she padded gingerly to the door.

The sound of male voices mingled with the aromas of fried steak and potatoes wafting up the stairwell. Her stomach flipped again.

She was in no condition to see her father or anyone else. Her lip curled downward in a frustrated pout, and she retreated back into her room.

And nearly stepped on Jake McKenna's cigar.

The awful thing reminded her once more of the fool she'd made of herself in front of the men in the bunkhouse.

In front of Lance.

How would she ever face them again?

What choice did she have?

More determined than ever to regain her dignity and respect as Vince Mancuso's daughter, she plucked the cigar from the carpet and tossed it into her wastebasket. She shed her mussed dinner gown and retrieved the last fresh one she had from the armoire. From the dresser's drawers she gathered an armful of clean underclothing, from her mirrored tray, an array of cosmetics. She laid them all out on the bed and grimly set to work.

Less than an hour later, she was ready.

Studying her reflection in the mirror, Sonnie ruefully offered thanks for Aunt Josephine's tutelage in the practiced art of ladies' toiletry. Creams and lotions were a godsend; powdered rouge restored color to her pale cheeks. Soap and water had washed away the bunkhouse smells, and her bottle of La Dore perfume replaced them with a delicate carnation scent.

She smoothed the tapered sleeves of her lavender wool gown. Trimmed in darker lavender and black, the gown accented her hair and skin tone favorably, and knowing she looked presentable on the outside helped alleviate some of the discomfort plaguing her on the inside.

Better prepared to meet her father this time, Sonnie left her room and descended the stairwell. She took care not to jar her head unduly and managed each step slowly, methodically. She passed his office and was grateful to find the door closed.

As she passed the formal dining room, however, she noticed that the rectangular oak table held several plates containing remnants of breakfast. The buffet sideboard held silverware and coffee cups, platters and bowls. Drops of moisture beaded on the outside of a crystal water pitcher, hand-engraved with the Rocking M brand.

The icy cold water drew Sonnie like a lifeline. She took a matching tumbler, filled it full, and drank in long gulps.

"Don't drink so much. You'll feel drunk all over again."

She stopped in midswallow at the low, masculine voice behind her. In the sideboard's beveled mirror, she watched Lance approach from the kitchen's direction, a silver-plated coffeepot in his hand.

Her heart did a fast beat. His hair gleamed like honey in the room's sunlight. Clean-shaven, muscular, and rugged in rolled-up shirtsleeves, he looked out of place pouring himself a cup of coffee and setting the expensive, elegant pot aside.

She couldn't hold his cool gaze, not after her brazen behavior the night before. She lowered the glass. An odd wooziness took her, and she leaned against the curved edge of the sideboard.

"Sit down and drink this instead," he said, his tone quiet. "It's better for you."

He handed the steaming cup to her.

"Thank you," she murmured, and sipped.

He made no reply. With prudent movement, she eased into the nearest chair. Lance slid a plate of hot food in front of her.

Daintily she covered her mouth with her fingertips. Any other time, the seasoned beef, hash browns, and eggs would have tasted as delicious as they appeared. But not today.

"I'm sorry," she whispered. "I . . . I can't eat this."

"You have to."

Her eyes closed, and she shook her head slightly.

"You need something in your stomach, Sonnie," he said.

Giving in, knowing he was right, she set her cup down. The first tentative bite of steak was tender and surprisingly tasty. She managed another.

From the corner of her eye, she watched him cover the remaining fare to keep it warm, then pour himself another cup of coffee. He left the sideboard to stand at the window. Long moments passed where only the ticking of the clock broke the silence.

He seemed reluctant to leave. The knowledge brought a measure of relief. She had amends to make.

"Who cooked breakfast?" she asked softly, enduring a new wave of guilt that she had once again failed in that regard.

"Ramon." As he left the window to face her, his glance lighted on her for a brief moment, then skittered away. "Your father has a visitor this morning. He wanted to offer him a good meal."

"Oh." Her spirits plummeted further. She refrained from asking who the visitor was. "I'm sorry I didn't get up in time."

"Forget it."

"If you would've come for me, or . . . or had someone wake me or something—" She halted at the subtle reference to last night, to his presence in her room. . . .

To their kiss.

Lance's whiskey-hot glance burned into her. He

was thinking of it, too. His eyes lowered, settled, dwelled on her mouth.

"I behaved outrageously last night," she said, the words hushed. She couldn't bear the heat of his thoughts when hers traveled the same road. "You must forgive me."

He set his cup on the table, splayed both hands on the starched tablecloth, and leaned toward her.

"Not on your life," he said, his voice low, husky.

His seductive implication flustered her; for the life of her, she could not hold his gaze.

"Where did you learn to drink beer?" he asked.

She grew wary at his sudden shift of conversation. "I prefer flavored brandies and water. I'd never had a beer before Mr. McKenna offered me one."

"You took to it well, then. There were a hell of a lot of empty bottles lying around."

"You finished one for me," she objected in feeble self-defense.

"To keep you from getting any drunker than you already were."

She stiffened. "Why are you scolding me again, Lance? I told you I was sorry for my indiscriminate behavior."

"You were in danger at the bunkhouse."

His words startled her. "Whatever do you mean?"

"All it would take for a roomful of drunken cowboys to slake their lust is one beautiful woman," he said. "Need I say more?"

"Papa would never allow such a thing."

"How would he know, until it was too late?"

Refusing to accept his concern, she shook her head, believing instead that her father, with all his wisdom, influence, and power, would somehow prevent anything of the sort from happening. "No, Lance."

"It happens, Sonnie. You were damned vulnerable going out there by yourself. You broke the rules."

"Why would those men harm me? They're my friends. This is my home."

"Most of those men had never seen you before yesterday. When their bellies are full of liquor, do you think they'd give a damn who you are?"

"I don't believe you," she whispered.

"Believe it. Vince Mancuso is not as invincible as you think he is. He does not control every living soul who walks the land. No one does."

He pushed away from the table in barely controlled frustration.

"You're being far too protective of me, I think," Sonnie said, her wariness increasing tenfold.

"You need protecting, that's why."

"That's silly. What would make you think that?"

He raked a hand through his hair. "Charlie found five more head of cattle poisoned this morning."

His grim-voiced revelation stunned her.

"My God. Where?"

"Just beyond the corrals."

"So close to the Big House," Sonnie said under her breath.

"Ditson is getting reckless, and that scares the hell out of me."

A flicker of pain crossed his features. Then, like a storm cloud passing over a dusky moon, the pain disappeared and somber determination took its place.

"I don't want him getting to you next, Sonnie, so pack your bags. I'm putting you on the first train back to Boston."

Chapter Eight

"You ever had a woman before, Lance?"

From his perch on an aging tree stump, Shorty asked the thoughtful question. At his feet lay a heap of wood shavings fallen from the deft strokes of his whittling knife.

For a moment, the tin of tobacco hovered over a scrap of thin paper between Lance's fingers. He darted a wary glance toward the old cowboy.

"Not sure if that's any of your business, Shorty," he replied.

"Reckon it ain't. But I'm askin' anyway. You ever had a woman?"

Irritation prickled Lance. Tiny bits of tobacco floated onto the paper. Shorty could be as meddlesome as an old hen; Lance doubted he'd give up his persistence.

"Nope," he said finally, his tone terse with the admission.

"Why not?"

"Never needed one." The paper dipped and spilled tobacco between his knees at the blatant lie.

"Never needed a woman?" The knife halted. Shorty's bewhiskered face showed disbelief.

"Nope." He wouldn't think of the thoughts that plagued him at night or the yearnings that were destined to go unfulfilled. He wouldn't think of Mother and all she'd endured because of a man's wretched need for a woman.

"Gawd."

Lance concentrated on adding more tobacco to his cigarette. Even at the age of twenty-one, his desire for feminine warmth and softness haunted him when he least expected it. But he always managed to overcome the weakness through hard work and long hours and buckets of sweat.

"Never needed a woman," the older man said softly, as if he still couldn't believe it. Holding up the misshapen chunk of wood, he considered his handiwork for long seconds. A gap-toothed smile creased his cheeks, and he tossed the creation into Lance's lap, knocking the half-rolled cigarette into the weeds.

Lance swore in exasperation and glanced downward. Shorty had molded a discarded piece of kindling into a crude female shape, complete with curves in all the proper places. He met the cowboy's amused gaze.

"Never needed a woman," Shorty said again, his smile deepening into mischievous determination. *"We're gonna have to do somethin' about that, ain't we?"*

Lance steeled himself against Sonnie's protesting gasp. Dots of color shone on her pale cheeks; her jaw jutted with defiance.

"I'll not leave without a fight," Sonnie said.

Her proclamation, hushed with emphasis, spurred

his resolve. Spine straight, hands clenched in front of her plate, she stared across the table at him.

"I won't let you stay without one, either," he retaliated quietly, hating the argument—any argument—with her.

"I belong here."

"You belong in a safe place. The ranch is not safe."

"I can think of none safer than the Rocking M."

"Damn it, Sonnie." He blew out a frustrated breath and realized she would never listen, would never understand his reasons. She would never agree that he was right and she was wrong.

He refused to let her see how it pained him to have made the decision, but in the absence of sleep the night before, the realization had come, sure and insistent. Charlie's discovery of the poisoned cows just after dawn only intensified it.

She couldn't stay on the Rocking M.

There had been no time to tell Vince of his convictions. Tom Horn had ridden in early this morning without fanfare or announcement. Vince, in his relief and rage, had spent every moment since engrossed in conversation with him about the cattlemen's woes on Wyoming ranges, including his own.

Vince would accept his decision, Lance knew. Sonnie had been gone for a long time. Her presence wouldn't necessarily be missed by her father—or anyone else, most likely. With the Stockmen's Association's meeting to commence in Cheyenne in a few days' time, and with Horn available to help Vince prepare for his appointment with Senator Norbert F. Hickman, Lance expected little resistance.

No, the only one whose heart would be torn in two by her departure would be his own.

Vince's office door opened, and Tom Horn and Vince entered the dining room. Thick-chested and broad-shouldered, Horn stood at an even height with

Lance at two inches past six feet. He moved with the arrogant swagger of a man comfortable with a gun in his hand. A man who held the reins in a fast, hard life.

Just seeing him again annoyed the hell out of Lance.

Possibly because Vince regarded him so highly, as if the sun rose and set on anything Tom Horn said or did. Or maybe it was his reputation for killing and swift enforcement of rangeland law when Lance preferred to use the established judicial system. More probably, though, it was Horn's cool attitude and elevated opinion of himself that made Lance want to stuff his fist down the man's cocky throat.

Horn's keen eyes lighted appreciatively on Sonnie and did little to ease Lance's irritation. Moving away from Vince and toward the table, Horn pulled out a chair and angled it next to Sonnie's.

"Well, Mancuso, you didn't tell me about the lady in the house," he said, a slow, practiced grin spreading across his features. "Pretty little thing, too."

Vince appeared frail next to Horn's bulk. He smiled with pride and sat at the table.

"She's my daughter, Tom. Her name's Sonnie. This is Mr. Tom Horn, Sonnie," he said with a nod. "You remember me talking about him, don't you?"

"The gunfighter?" Her lashes fluttered uncertainly. Her stance was still rigid from the quarrel she'd shared with Lance, and her gaze darted to her father. "Yes, of course."

Horn took Sonnie's hand, her olive-hued hand almost lost in the depth of his bigger one. He dropped a gallant kiss over her knuckles.

Lance wanted to spit in disgust.

"Sonnie," Horn purred. "A strange name for such a beautiful woman. What's it short for?"

"Sonnie Mancuso is my full name," she replied, her

expression demure, yet strained. "Papa christened me at birth."

For the first time, Lance sensed her dislike of the designation. He frowned at its masculine overtone.

"Your ma had all girls, didn't she?" Horn asked, amused, sparing Vince a quick glance before facing Sonnie again. "No sons to use the name on?"

She gave a quick shake of her head. Obviously she found nothing funny about the subject.

"No," she said. "No sons to use it on."

"I've always thought of her name in a different way," Lance said. "Reminds me of the sun that warms and heals." His gaze left the other man, and found Sonnie's already upon him. "And gives life to everything it touches."

Her lips parted in vague surprise.

Horn guffawed. "Damned poetic, Harmon." His mirth faded as a new thought apparently struck him. "You his wife, Sonnie?"

"I'm not married, Mr. Horn."

He appeared pleased. His grin returned, and, oblivious to Vince sitting a short distance away, he curled his fingers over her forearm and squeezed. "Real glad to hear that, Sonnie."

Lance chafed at his flirting, at his continued lack of formal address, a requirement demanded of every cowboy on the ranch.

He snatched his empty cup from the table and headed for the sideboard.

"Back off, Horn," he said in a growl. "She's not feeling well this morning."

"Not feeling well?" Vince asked, running a searching eye over her.

"Late night." Lance watched Horn in the mirror and reached for the coffeepot. "She's still getting used to ranch hours."

"You don't live here at the Rocking M, then, Sonnie?" Horn asked.

"I've lived in Boston for most of the last ten years," she explained with a lift of her chin. "But I've returned. And I've come home to stay."

Lance glared at her in the glass. She pointedly ignored him, as if daring him to deny it in front of her father and Tom Horn.

"The big city, eh?" the gunfighter asked, and absently extended his cup toward Lance. A tiny portion of coffee swirled in the bottom. Irritation surged anew, but Lance filled the cup with fresh black brew. "Never cared for crowds myself. Give me wide-open country and a horse any day."

"We mustn't forget your gunbelt, Mr. Horn," Sonnie said coolly, eying the pair of Smith & Wessons packed about his hips.

"Or a man needin' chasin' down," he replied with a loud slurp of coffee. "That's when I'm happiest."

"I'm sure," she demurred, and unobtrusively leaned back into her chair.

"Tom will be invaluable in helping us deal with some of our problems," Vince said. "The stockmen of Wyoming are in dire need of his services."

"I'd like to check out the neighboring ranges, Mancuso. I need to know if any of the other ranchers have had a problem with their stock being poisoned like yours were." Horn's decisiveness suggested he had no doubt his wish would be honored. "Are you ready to ride with me?"

"Vince, stay here and rest." Lance approached the table. "I'll go with you instead, Horn. Vince has been ill."

"I'm fine, Lance. Don't tell me what I'll do and not do."

Lance stiffened at the sharpness in Vince's tone.

143

"I'm ready anytime you are, Tom," the older man said, and reached for his cane.

"Stick will see that you have a fresh horse," Lance said tersely, forcing himself to be civil, to ignore the sting of Vince's rare indifference toward him. "Take your pick from the corrals."

"I'll do that." The gunfighter rose, gulped one last swallow of coffee, and passed a shrewd glance over Sonnie. "Until later, little lady."

Her lashes lowered in feminine courtesy. "Mr. Horn."

At a slower pace, Vince proceeded to follow him from the dining room. Knowing that an opportunity to discuss her return to Boston wouldn't present itself until later that evening, Lance called him back.

Vince waited expectantly.

"I've told Sonnie I'm putting her on the first train to Boston—"

"No, Lance," Vince interrupted, shaking his head. "Not yet."

The remainder of Lance's sentence stuck in his throat.

"I need her," her father said, passing a noncommital glance her way. "The meeting is Saturday. There will be a banquet and dance, and Tom will need a lovely woman on his arm."

"You want Sonnie and Horn together? He's a hired gun, for God's sake."

Unfazed, Vince nodded. "She's a Mancuso. She can use her . . . influence in a way I can't."

A picture of the tough, hardened killer and Sonnie, eating, dancing, *touching,* turned Lance's blood cold.

"There are women better suited than your own daughter to persuade Horn to your way of thinking," he scowled.

"Like who?"

Lance's chin squared, his roster of qualifying females limited.

"Like Gracie," he said.

"Gracie?" Vince appeared aghast at the thought.

"She could handle him. He's her type."

Vince waved an arm, dismissing the idea. "Sonnie is perfect. My sister Josephine has prepared her for an occasion such as this. That's why I sent her to the East, eh?" As if remembering Sonnie was still in the room, he turned and gave her a tender smile. "You'll help your papa when he needs you, won't you?"

"Yes," she said in a soft voice. "Yes, of course. If you need me, I'll do anything you ask."

"There. You see, Lance? Sonnie is happy to help."

A growl of protest rumbled from his chest. Every fiber of his being fought Vince's intention—a father using his daughter for his own gain.

"Vince, I'll handle this," he grated. "I'll find a way without Sonnie."

"Not this time." Vince's tone stung with finality. "Come, Sonnie. We'll talk on our way out to the corral."

In a rustle of petticoats, lavender wool, and a hint of carnations, she went to him and slipped her arm through his. Together they disappeared beneath the archway and out the front door.

Lance stood frozen with disgust and impatience. Rarely did he and Vince disagree, and to do so now, on an issue as important as Sonnie and a ruthless gunfighter, over a couple of lowlifes like Clay Ditson and Snake, left him quaking with frustration.

Thumps and thuds from the porch drew another scowl, and he strode to the hallway. A courier from the train station struggled with a profusion of leather and brass trunks.

An hour ago Lance would have sent him back to reload Sonnie's luggage and transport it all back to

Boston. Now, he thought with a healthy curse, the damned things were here to stay.

But not for long.

Sonnie had never socialized with a hired gun before.

Indeed, she'd never been in the same room with one, spoken to one, or even seen one before this morning. But now, knowing of Papa's wishes, she knew all that would change.

It was an important task he'd entrusted to her, that of wooing Tom Horn to Vince Mancuso's way of thinking. A man of Horn's rank would surely be the solution to the cattlemen's plight—and Papa's as well. If the reputed gunfighter agreed to accept the job as range detective, stockmen throughout Wyoming and neighboring states would be spared future losses of land and livestock from untold numbers of rustlers' plundering.

And poisoning.

Her responsibilities unnerved her, however, and she leaned back in Papa's leather chair with a sigh. Sequestered in his office for most of the day, the air laced with a lingering scent of his cheroots, she was struck by how sheltered her life had been. Back East her most troublesome worries had been limited to her rigorous academics or which evening gown to wear to which gala affair with whom. The problems of the West had pretty much been lost to her.

Until today.

Upon her lap, the thick, cloth-covered volume of the *Minutes of the Executive Committee* described them in detail. As secretary of the Wyoming Stockmen's Association, Papa's notes, and those of his predecessors, outlined the organization's rise to power, its political advocates and enemies, victories and defeats. Sonnie read the papers in their entirety and came away with an awed understanding of the cattlemen's concerns, their wealth, their love of the land with its bountiful grass and water, and their belief that the range must be policed by ruthless men to protect what was theirs.

A ruthless man like Tom Horn would not be averse to using his gun to uphold their beliefs.

Sonnie couldn't help thinking of the methods he would employ to rid the Mancuso range of Clay Ditson and Snake. Blood would spill, and she abhorred the thought. But Papa knew best how to handle such a troublesome matter. It was what he wanted and what the Association wanted.

But not what Lance wanted.

Unbidden, the certainty came through. His antagonism toward Horn had been a tangible thing this morning, and Sonnie puzzled over it. Despite their close relationship, Papa seemed oblivious to Lance's feelings, yet Lance held his tongue and hadn't made an issue of their differences in front of the gunfighter.

Bemused, Sonnie closed the book and rested it on the desktop. The cluttered office, homey and endearing, encouraged reflection, and she was struck once again by the memories the room held and the years of hard work it represented. All the countless hours Papa spent toiling over financial ledgers, reading the latest in veterinary journals and newspapers, keeping abreast of the cattle market and his involvement in the Stockmen's Association throughout Wyoming's rise from territory to newly established statehood, had been spared her.

But the Rocking M prospered. Her gaze found the huge map on the wall behind the desk, and she pondered the ranch's boundaries. Straddling three counties, the thousands of acres of Mancuso land were almost impossible to comprehend. Yet there it was in the mapmaker's ink, a maze of lines representing forests, hills and canyons, grass-rich pastures, and winding creeks. Her heart swelled with renewed pride in the vastness, in the beauty.

Her heritage.

The Rocking M was hers, given by her father to be shared with her sisters, but it was a heritage no one could take away—not Clay Ditson and Snake, and certainly not a train bound for Boston.

So engrossing were her thoughts that she didn't hear her father's approach until his movement drew her attention, and with a smile, she rose to greet him.

"Is this where you've been all day, *mia bambina?*" he asked, removing his heavy coat and hat and hooking them on the rack near the door.

"Yes, Papa." Inwardly wincing at his endearment, she tapped her finger upon the volume before her. "Reading your minutes from the Association meetings."

"Ah. And what have you learned?"

He appeared preoccupied. With his shoulders hunched, he shuffled toward the liquor cabinet. It seemed to Sonnie he leaned more heavily on his cane than usual. Her smile faded.

"I've learned much," she said quietly, watching him with a concerned eye. "I had no idea the blizzards of '86 and '87 were so devastating. You never mentioned it in your letters."

His hand lifted in a bland gesture. "Why worry you? It was hard on all of us." He shook his head wearily. "Drought in the summer, early snows in the winter. The cattle couldn't find grass to eat or water to drink. Our losses were devastating."

"Oh, Papa." She clucked her tongue in compassion. "I would have come home to help you if I'd known."

"Pah." Again his hand lifted. "The trains would never have made it through. Better you stayed in Boston." He reached for a glass and a bottle of whiskey. "All the stockmen suffered. Some were wiped out completely." Pausing, he appeared to relive the past. "We were one of the lucky ones. Lance and I . . . we built the herds back up again. The Rocking M is still strong."

"Thank goodness," she said, picking up the book to return it to its place beside the family Bible. On the shelf, a yellowed envelope lay askew in the empty spot where the *Minutes of the Executive Committee* belonged.

"The problems never end, Sonnie," he said, his tone sounding unusually defeated. "If not the weather, then a fickle market or rustlers and squatters. Now I'm losing cattle to poisonings. Sometimes I get so tired of the fight."

His fatigue worried her. "Papa, you must rest. Come sit for a spell," she urged, indicating the brocade settee near the desk. "You've been out riding too long. You've worn yourself out."

The whiskey bottle rattled against the edge of the glass as he poured the amber liquid.

"I might have at that, *bambina*," he conceded, his expression wan. "I should've listened to Lance, eh?"

While he spoke, Sonnie stole a curious glance at the envelope. Printed in the upper left-hand corner with the words *Children's Aid Society, New York,* it was addressed to her father and postmarked in 1877, thirteen years earlier. She held it up to the window's light to sneak a peek at the contents.

"Papa, what is this Children's Aid Society?" she asked in growing puzzlement. "May I read the letter?"

Only silence greeted her query. From behind her she heard a muffled thud, as if something heavy had dropped to the floor.

She whirled. Her father lay in a crumpled heap, one hand extended outward, still gripping the bottle. Whiskey seeped into the crimson floral carpet and pooled into a staining puddle. His other hand clutched his chest.

"Oh, dear God!" she gasped in terror, and the envelope slipped unheeded from her fingertips. Sonnie ran to him and fell to her knees at his side. "Papa! Oh, Papa!"

His skin held a deathly pallor. He seemed suddenly old and drained of life.

His lashes fluttered; a rasping cough escaped from his throat. He gulped in air.

"Get Lance, Sonnie," he said in a wheeze.

But she shook her head in refusal and pulled the liquor bottle from his grasp.

"I won't leave you, Papa." A sob welled up, pushed into her throat. "I'm staying right here with you."

Cold, weak fingers curled around her wrist.

"I need . . . my medicine."

She strove hard to keep her panic under wraps and tried to recall where she'd seen the collection of little brown bottles.

Her father struggled for consciousness. Time was precious. He needed help immediately or she'd lose him forever.

"I'll find the medicine. Hang on, Papa. I won't be long."

Yanking at her skirts, she stumbled to her feet and flew down the hall. Her mind whirred to remember which cabinet bore the lifesaving pills.

She jerked open doors and drawers in her search. Somebody had moved it—or had they? Where had she seen the damned medicine?

On a fevered prayer, she finally found the bottles. But which one did he need?

Aconite? Digitalis? Amyl nitrite?

Which one?

She scooped them all up into her skirt. Hugging

the unwieldy bundle to her, she left the kitchen in a run and returned to the office.

Her father hadn't moved. He lay deathly still. She dropped to her knees, let everything tumble onto the carpet.

"Papa, tell me what you need." She held up a miniature bottle, the label printed in tiny letters she could scarcely read or understand. "This one?" His eyes remained closed; he didn't appear to hear her. A hopeless feeling of uselessness and inadequacy washed over her. Her voice rose to a panicked pitch. "Papa, tell me which one!"

She feared giving him the wrong antidote. Or too much or too little. How would she know? His life depended on the right decision, a decision she couldn't make.

But Lance would know.

She had to find him. She hadn't seen him since breakfast, but she had to find him to save her father.

Sonnie rushed from the room and flung open the front door. A flurry of cold air whipped her face and tugged her hair as she raced down the porch steps.

She hadn't a notion where he would be. Her feet flew across the lawn toward the nearest barn.

Please, God. Let him be close.

The massive wooden doors stood partially open, and Sonnie squeezed in sideways without widening them further. A stinging sensation blazed across her arm, but she hurried inside without sparing it a thought.

"Cookie!" she cried. The old cowboy was bent over a dismantled plow. "Where's Lance?"

He blinked up at her, obviously surprised at her frantic state, and frowned. "Well, now, I reckon I saw him last in the corral."

"Which corral?" she demanded, breathless, urgent to keep moving.

"The north 'un." He lifted a greasy finger in the general direction of another door. "What's got you all fired up, young lady?"

Her skirt hem lapped at her heels. She bolted from the building, past Red Holmes and Frank Burton, their arms laden with heavy sacks of feed. Frowning their concern, the two men dropped their burdens and sprinted after her toward the corrals. Cookie hustled close behind.

Sonnie found Lance hunkered over a foal nestled in a bed of straw and engrossed in conversation with Stick.

"Lance," she called without a halt in her run. "Come quickly!"

He rose, half twisting toward her. She stumbled over her hems and nearly fell into him in her haste. Automatically his hands grasped the curve of her waist and steadied her.

"Sonnie." His tawny brows furrowed beneath the shadowed brim of his black cowboy hat. "What is it?"

"It's Papa." She tried to swallow and gather her wits, but tears threatened to overcome her. Her fingers dug into the muscular flesh of his biceps. "Hurry, Lance! He's had another attack, and I-I think he might be dead!"

"Damn." Lance's gaze shot toward the Big House before swinging back to the gathering group of concerned men. "Red and Frank, ride into town and get Doc Tanner. Cookie and Stick, come with me."

He was already moving toward the corral's split-log fence. As he slung orders, each man instantly obeyed, responding to his authority without question. His hand reached out and took Sonnie's, pulling her with him toward the fence in a shortcut back to the Big House.

He bent and slipped between the rails ahead of her. Battling her skirts, she followed with as much grace as she could manage. Once through the fence, she was hard-pressed to keep up with him.

"Where is he, Sonnie?" Lance asked at the back door.

"In the office," she said in a gasp.

He pushed her ahead of him. She scurried through the kitchen and down the hall and found her father just as she'd left him.

Still. So very still.

Lance dropped to a knee beside him and immediately pressed his fingers to her father's neck. Sonnie's gaze clung to Lance's grave features for a sign of what she feared the most.

"He's alive." Lance's glance lighted on her briefly before he turned his attention to loosening Papa's collar. "His pulse is weak but steady."

"Oh, thank God."

"Find the nitroglycerin, Sonnie," he said, making a terse gesture toward the menagerie of medicine strewn about the carpet.

She found the appropriate bottle and tapped a mound of pills into her palm.

"How many?" Her hand shook.

"One. Just one. Take a deep breath, Sonnie."

She did, felt better for it. She slid the remainder of the pills into their container and capped it.

His control soothed her panic. She thanked God he was there.

"I'll tip his head back and keep his mouth open. You put the pill under his tongue," he said.

She held the medicine between two fingers and did as he told her, then warily sat back on her heels. The others stood in respectful silence.

"The pill is so tiny. Is it strong enough to save his life?" she asked in a doubtful whisper.

"Yes." The low, confident timbre of his voice assured her he knew of its power. "The pills are sugar pellets in which a solution of nitroglycerin and alcohol is absorbed. Pretty soon the medicine will strengthen his heartbeat and reduce the pains in his chest. You'll see."

His knowledge of the unfamiliar drug impressed her. She trusted him that it would work, that they'd followed the correct procedure to keep his heart pumping.

Still, she awaited the medicine's cure with bated breath.

Chapter Nine

Everyone stood in the yard waiting for her.

Everyone but Lance. He wanted to watch from the nearest livestock barn when the others chose the front lawn of the Big House. He couldn't tell her good-bye looking dirty, sprinkled with hay and smelling of manure.

She was leaving today. Leaving for a city called Boston located clear across the country. Leaving forever, maybe, and he had no idea when he would see her again.

If he would see her again.

Worse, she didn't want to go. He'd found her crying in the garden behind the house. Though she sobbed her despair, he'd been helpless to offer her comfort. In his usual cowardly way, he remained in the shadows and fought the unexpected lump in his throat.

He remembered the arguments she had had with her father. Through the open window, he had heard every word of her pleas as she begged, screamed, demanded to stay on the Rocking M.

But Vince had refused.

Lance didn't know why. How could a father send his daughter to a strange city so far away? How could he deprive her of the clean air, the rich land, the beauty of the Territory? Wyoming was vastly different from Boston. How would she manage?

The cowboys stood in a somber group, their hats in their hands, their conversation scant and subdued. At last she emerged onto the front porch, and Lance couldn't help sidling just a little closer.

So young, yet so grown-up. Wearing a coat of deep blue wool trimmed in frothy fox fur, she descended the stairs flanked by her sisters. Vince brought up the rear.

Even from where he stood, Lance could see her red eyes swollen from tears shed not long ago. Yet she walked tall, proud, mature for her youthful age.

Her dignity slipped, however, in the group of men. Hugging each one in turn, she cried openly as she bade them farewell. The work-hardened cowboys swallowed hard, rendered emotional by the beautiful wisp of a girl they'd all come to love.

Too soon, she climbed into the waiting buggy. Vince was the last to board the rig. From over the hatted heads of his men, his gaze found Lance's, and he halted.

It seemed to Lance he waited for something, an unspoken message of agreement, perhaps. Or assurance that the all-powerful Vince Mancuso had done the right thing in sending his sixth daughter away.

But Lance could give him nothing. For years, he had been convinced that Vince could do no wrong, that every decision he made was the right one. Today, though, Vince had fallen off his pedestal. With regard to Sonnie, he had failed in the worst way.

Filled with disgust, Lance spun on his heel and walked away.

Papa's lids quivered and opened; a faint degree of color infused his ashen palor. His eyes were glazed and confused.

He stared up at her. A sheepish smile formed beneath his thin mustache. "Guess I passed out, eh, *mia bambina?*"

"You did, Papa. And gave me the scare of my life, too," she admonished softly.

"Shouldn't have . . . gone out with Tom." A wheezing groan escaped with the admission.

"One of these days you'll learn to listen to me, Vince," Lance said.

Her father's head swiveled against the floral carpet. His smile faded. "Too used to giving orders . . . not taking 'em."

"That's going to change." Lance gestured to the sober-faced men standing aside. "Help me get him to his room. It'll be a while before the doc gets here."

With the care normally reserved for the handling of a newborn infant, they lifted Vince from the floor and carried him to his bedroom. Sonnie ran ahead and pulled down the quilts on the bed, fluffed the pillows, and lighted a lamp.

"Okay, lay him down easy."

Under Lance's direction, her father was settled upon the mattress with great care. Charlie removed the expensive boots; Lance draped the covers over him.

"Reckon you ain't gonna be out ridin' fer a spell, Mr. Mancuso," Cookie predicted.

"Best that you stay right here till you're feelin' like new again," Stick said, his young features serious.

Papa managed a weak smile. "I don't think . . .

Lance and Sonnie will let me leave this room till I am. Thanks for your help, boys."

His raspy voice betrayed his fatigue, and, in unison, the men glanced at Lance.

He gave them a silent nod. Touching fingers to their hats, they acknowledged Sonnie and took their leave. Collective boot soles thumped the floor in the hallway; the front door closed with a firm click.

"They're very worried about you, Papa," Sonnie said, moving toward him and sitting on the edge of the mattress. She smoothed the quilt over his chest. "It's important that you rest and get well again. You have a ranch to run."

His gaze flickered past her to where Lance stood at the foot of the bed.

"I'm puttin' the Rocking M in your hands, Lance," he said. "Run it . . . as you see fit."

Sonnie went still.

Had her father considered *her* for the management of the ranch? She was a Mancuso through and through.

And Lance wasn't. He would never claim that birthright.

She forced a stiff smile. "Papa, I'm home now. I can assist Lance whenever he needs it. I'll show you. Both of you."

Lance's eyes rested on her. She could feel the heat, the intensity. She knew it as surely as if she'd turned and faced him.

But she wouldn't look at him. She wouldn't allow him to see the hurt her father's decision inflicted or the misfortune of her inadequacy as the youngest Mancuso daughter.

She couldn't meet his eyes as he watched her beg.

"Pah." Vince lifted a hand in a weak gesture of dismissal. "What can you do, Sonnie? It's a man's world out here. You know nothing of ranch matters."

"I know more than you credit me for. Give me a chance, Papa."

"What's this foolishness I'm hearing from you?" His tone sounded weary, faintly exasperated. "Lance will run the Rocking M. It's all he's ever done."

"Of course." Despite the prickles of keen disappointment, she accepted the command. She had to, in light of his illness.

She stroked his pale cheek.

"Rest, Papa. The doctor will be here soon." The words sounded stilted in the room's silence. "I'll be near if you need me."

He mumbled a feeble compliance, and his lids closed.

She was acutely aware of Lance's presence. Her lashes lowered to keep from meeting his gaze, and she swept aside her skirts to pass him by.

A manly blend of tobacco and leather assailed her. His scent. She closed her mind to it, and quickened her steps down the hall, then busied herself in the kitchen lighting lamps to ward off the evening's shadows gathering in every corner.

Without looking, she knew when he stood in the doorway.

"Don't fight me on this, Sonnie," he said.

Her actions faltered. "Fight you?" She feigned ignorance as she retrieved the coffeepot from the top of the stove. "Whatever do you mean?"

She sensed the tautness in him as he strode closer, his boots striking the wooden floor with a slow, even tread.

"I'm the logical one to run the ranch. Your father knows that. So does everyone else."

"Everyone but me. Is that what you're saying?" From the pump at the sink, she sloshed water into the blue enamel pot.

"Yes." He stood a few feet away from her. Oddly,

it seemed only a few inches. "You've been gone for years. You don't know the first thing about running an outfit this size."

"I've studied hard. But because my learning came from a classroom, I'm incapable." She sliced him with a sharp glance that mirrored the sting of his insinuation.

"I never said that."

"You don't have to."

"Sonnie, damn it." Frustration emanated from him. "You've led one hell of a pampered life up to now. You're not ready—"

"Pampered! As if I had any choice!" To her dismay, tears welled up and rendered the last word shaky. She spun on her heel to flee him, but his lean fingers caught her upper arm.

She cried out at a sudden burst of pain. He swore and immediately let her go; his thumb came away with a smear of blood.

A rip in the lavender wool of her sleeve gaped open and revealed a seeping gash across her skin.

"What happened?" He took the coffeepot from her and set it back on the stove.

Sonnie inspected the wound, feeling its bite now that she knew of it. "The barn door, I think. I was so worried about Papa, I didn't pay attention when it happened."

"Sit down." He opened a drawer and retrieved a clean length of white cotton.

"It's only a scratch," she protested, still eying the unsightly abrasion.

"Scratches get infected. Sit."

The command in his tone allowed no argument. Crossing the kitchen, she sat in the nearest chair and watched him mix alum and water in a bowl before dropping the cloth into the contents.

He strode toward her, positioned another chair in

front of her, and plucked the cotton cloth from the bowl. He wrung it free of excess water.

"Pull up your sleeve," he said.

Fashion dictated a snug fit from her shoulder to her wrist, and she could not easily bare her arm to his tending.

She frowned.

"I can't. It's too tight," she said.

He considered the dilemma only a moment. His eyes met hers. The honey-gold depths darkened to a burnished hue.

"If the sleeve can't go up," he reasoned softly, "then it has to come down."

"Oh." Warmth found her cheeks at what his logic implied, but she could see no other way to allow him access to the wound. "All right, then." She scooted about on the chair seat and presented him with her back. "Please unbutton me."

After a moment's silence, he cleared his throat.

"Why?" he asked with a tad more roughness than she suspected he intended.

She peered at him sideways. "The tiny buttons deal me fits. I can barely manage them on my own." A rueful pout dipped her mouth. "And my arm is beginning to throb now. It hurts to lift it."

The cloth dropped back into the water. Taking the act to be acquiescence, Sonnie scooped the weight of her hair off her nape and waited.

Just when she thought he'd refuse her his assistance after all, his fingers found the first button at her neck. They hovered for a fraction of a second before working it free; then, with hesitant dexterity, he undid several more.

The gown sagged against her shoulder blades. Cool air danced over her bare skin. He continued his trek downward, the touch of his fingertips brushing her spine like teasing flourishes from downy-soft feathers, until he came to the lacy satin barrier of her corset.

A soft curse drifted to her ear.

"You'll have to make do with that, Sonnie," he said, snatching the cotton from the alum solution and wringing it a second time. "I'm not in the habit of undressing women."

His sudden gruff temperament unsettled her, and she refrained from arguing that he was hardly undressing her or that it was *his* idea to pull the gown down in the first place.

Instead she murmured her thanks and managed to tug the sleeve from her arm, all the while clutching the front of the gown to her bosom in a determined attempt at modesty.

Not that he was even looking at her.

"I'm ready," she said finally, eying the cloth clenched in his fist. She took pity on the thing; he seemed intent on wringing it to shreds.

He faced her again, and though his tawny brows remained furrowed, the gruffness seemed to have left him. He laid the cloth against the abrasion and applied gentle pressure to stem the seeping blood. The combination of alum and cold water stung the raw tissues, and she sucked in a gasping breath.

"I know this hurts, Sonnie." His free hand curled around her elbow, holding her arm still. "But we have to make sure the wound is clean to prevent infection."

The task took his full attention, his every touch gentle with compassion. Lean and tanned and dusted with hairs of burnished gold, his hands worked nimbly, efficiently. His sure actions inspired trust, not only in treating her simple wound, but, she guessed, in most anything else as well.

Had she fallen into the same trap her father had, that of trusting Lance Harmon above anyone else? Hadn't she run to him when she needed him most? And, in return, hadn't he responded by taking charge, by being in control, by living up to all she had needed and expected?

Yes, that and more.

"Is there nothing you can't do around here, Lance?" Sonnie asked, her tone pensive.

Tossing aside the cloth, he applied laudanum to the open wound. The opiatic immediately brought relief from the persistent ache.

"What I 'do around here' took years to learn," he said. His gaze caught hers. "Years of hard, backbreaking work. Living with risks. And danger."

She understood his implied meaning.

"Because I've been denied all that, you still want to send me back east."

The container of laudanum rolled across the tabletop.

"Yes."

"I won't go. Not with Papa so sick. You can't possibly think I would."

The strong line of his jaw tightened.

"No," he said finally. "We'll wait until he's better. Then you're going."

She would see about that. The smug thought acknowledged a small victory and gave Sonnie hope. He'd granted her a measure of time to learn, to take care of her father, and to convince Lance she truly belonged on the Rocking M.

But, most important, to prove to him she had no intention of returning to Boston.

Her lips softened in a smile. Reaching out, she trailed a knuckle along his cheek, which was faintly stubbled with the shadow of a beard.

"In the meantime, shall we call a truce, Boss-man?" she challenged quietly.

He seemed unable to resist touching her in return and took her hand. He drew his palm over her wrist to her elbow.

Sonnie held her breath, transfixed by the sheer tenderness of his caress. He did not stop but continued toward her shoulder and onto her back, his work-roughened skin a pleasurable contrast to hers.

His hand splayed, then slid along her shoulder blade, one side and then the other, before ending his journey at the barrier of her corset. He seemed hungry to explore, to learn the feel of her.

Her gaze melded with his. She couldn't pull herself away, though the intimacy of the moment suggested she should.

He fingered the pink satin ribbons, as if he contemplated undoing them as slowly as he'd undone the back of her dress. Unbidden, the feel of his hard mouth rolling over hers the night before flared in her memory, and she longed to feel him again. His whiskey-shaded eyes, smoldering with the desire he held in check, settled on her lips, and his breathing took on a definite ragged edge.

"Truce, Sonnie," he whispered. "But nothing more."

He swore softly and pulled away. He rose to his feet and jammed his thumbs into the snug denim pockets at his hips.

She scrambled for composure.

She'd been far too bold. She should never have let him touch her bare skin so freely or to see and feel something as private as her corset.

But somehow, with him, it was different. The amorous moment invoked no shyness, only the stirrings of a deep need she wanted him to assuage. The memory of last night, and the kiss they'd shared in her bedroom, remained all too vivid.

She refused to be ashamed of her actions. Though he promised her little, she knew that at times a woman had these feelings about a man, and she knew, too, with absolute certainty, that Lance had the same feelings for her.

He was just better at hiding them. The man had the control of steel.

"I fear the torn sleeve has quite ruined my gown." Grateful for her outward calm, she stood, clutching the lavender wool tightly to her bosom. "I'll change before Doc Tanner arrives."

His eyes still smoldering, his desire still strong, he nodded. Perhaps he didn't trust himself to speak. Perhaps he felt as shaken as she.

But for now, it didn't matter.

He'd given her more time, after all. Time to restoke the fires he'd banked. Time for the kiss he denied her. Time enough to make him want her so much that maybe, just maybe, he wouldn't want to send her away.

And if she accomplished nothing else during her reprieve, she would accomplish that.

Doc Tanner pulled up in front of the Big House amid a squeal of buggy brakes and swirling dust. He dismounted from the black rig and hastened to Vince's bedside.

His rank as the Mancuso family's physician from Sonnie's eldest sister's birth on down had fostered a close friendship between the two men. His features, lined from years of devotion to patients, reflected his anxiety.

He examined Vince thoroughly. Lance kept his distance and quietly watched from the bedroom's doorway, while Sonnie hovered nearer, speaking in subdued tones, lending her assistance whenever the good doctor needed it.

At the end of the examination, Vince's fatigue was evident. Doc Tanner returned his stethoscope to the worn medical bag, reached over, and patted Vince's hand in companionable reassurance.

"I'll leave Sonnie instructions, old friend. Mind you, do what she says. Your heart will need a measure of tender loving care for a spell."

A ghost of a smile appeared on Vince's lips. "Don't look so worried, Ed. Got no intention . . . of restin' easy in heaven yet."

The doctor snorted in good-natured disagreement. "You're too stubborn for heaven, Vince. A slow burn in hell would do you some good. Even then, the Almighty would have to do some serious thinkin' to let you into His part of the country."

Lance grinned; Sonnie's mouth crinkled in amusement. The exchange relieved the room of its somber mood, and Doc rose to take his leave.

"I'll check back in a couple of days, Vince," he said. "I want to see your ol' ornery self by then, hear me? Until then, take care."

Vince's hand lifted in a limp wave of farewell, and Sonnie preceded Doc from the room. She gifted Lance with a sable-lashed glance and a soft scent of carnations as she passed him.

He drew in an aching breath and savored it.

After a moment, he joined her in the hall.

"I'm worried," the doctor said, a frown replacing the teasing countenance he had worn for Vince's benefit. "I'm certain Vince's daylong ride in the cold outdoors triggered his attack. He didn't have the stamina for it."

A stab of resentment for Tom Horn's arrival and Vince's adulation of him shot through Lance.

"What are you worried about, Doc?" he asked. "Another attack?"

The doctor shook his head. "Pneumonia."

"Pneumonia!" Sonnie's hand flew to her breast.

"I may be fearing the worst, but his lungs don't

166

sound as clear as they should. Watch him close, Sonnie. If he takes a bad turn, we'll have to put him in the hospital."

Her dismayed gaze touched Lance's before she nodded to the physician.

"In the meantime," he went on, "motherwort tea is a good remedy if he has heart palpitations. Have him drink it freely."

"I will."

He donned his hat and buttoned his coat; Lance reached around him and pulled the front door open.

"It's good to see you again, Sonnie." Doc smiled. "Even if it must be under these circumstances. You've grown into quite a beautiful woman. Spitting image of your mother."

"Thank you." Her head dipped in courteous acceptance of his compliment. "I've been told often of our resemblance."

"Well, I must get back to town." Repeating his promise to make another trip out in two days, he settled himself into his rig and waved good-bye. Lance stood next to Sonnie at the top of the porch stairs, and they watched the buggy drive out of sight.

"I didn't realize he was so sick," Sonnie murmured.

"None of us did." He regretted the worry in her voice. "He's tough. He'll make it through."

The night cloaked them in its chilly embrace, and Sonnie shivered, folding her arms across her chest for warmth. Lance doubted his trite words eased her fretting, and he wished for the right ones that would bring her comfort. They failed him, and a need to hold her close against him grew in their stead.

His courage failed him there, as well. He despised his inability to slash away at his fears of getting too close. What man would deny himself her kiss, as he'd done earlier in the kitchen? What man could keep from touching her now, from giving compassion and comfort when she needed it?

Only a hell of a fool.

He would hurt her in the end. He couldn't lose sight of that. Her departure from the ranch, her return to Boston and the distant, sheltered life Vince intended for her was inevitable.

He took solace in her presence beside him, her nearness a rare pleasure. He couldn't help reliving the feel of her creamy, smooth skin beneath his fingertips and the inviting warmth of her body. Desire flared anew in his loins.

She looked up at him, turned his provocative thoughts into a jumble, and gently touched his arm.

"I'll go in and read to Papa for a while, Lance. Maybe he'll sleep easier."

"Sure, Son," he said, his husky voice implying agreement while his heart yearned for her to stay.

She hesitated, a slight frown on her brow. He expected her to protest his inadvertent shortening of her name.

She said nothing, however, merely withdrew her hand and stepped away.

The brief contact numbed his arm. He watched her go, staring at the enticing sway of her hips as she did, and wondered if she still wore the pink-ribboned corset.

She disappeared inside. Uncomfortable from the growing tautness in his groin, he shifted his stance and reached inside his shirt pocket for a rolled cigarette. In the match's flare, he noticed Charlie Flynn's approach.

"Mind if I bum one off you, boss?" Charlie climbed the porch stairs and relaxed against a whitewashed post.

Lance handed him the one he'd just lit and repeated the process with a second. Both men inhaled leisurely, and Lance forced his thoughts away from Sonnie with great reluctance.

"Where's Horn?" he asked, propping his foot on the bottom railing. He rested an elbow against his knee.

"Decided to stay at the Iron Mountain Ranch." Charlie studied the fiery tip of his cigarette. "Mr. Mancuso came back without him. Said Horn had some friends up there, and he was gonna do some scoutin' on his own before comin' back here."

Not for the first time, Lance inwardly cursed the gunfighter for his lack of concern toward Vince's health.

"Reckon it's a good thing Mr. Mancuso had his attack here and not out on the range alone," Charlie commented.

"Yeah."

"How's he doin'?"

"Lousy. Doc's afraid pneumonia'll set in."

"Damn."

"We'll take it one day at a time. Meanwhile it's business as usual."

Charlie nodded. "Miss Sonnie fussin' about her pa?"

The mere mention of her name tripped the steady beat of Lance's heart. "She is."

The cowboy sighed in understanding, and the conversation fell to ranch affairs until long after the tobacco had been smoked and the stubs flicked into nearby shrubbery. Charlie eventually yawned and departed, shuffling toward the bunkhouse with the tired tread of a man who'd more than earned his wages for the day.

Lance rubbed the back of his neck and went inside the Big House. Though he detected a faint aroma of brewed coffee, no lights shone in the house except from Vince's bedroom. Sauntering down the quiet hall, he halted in the doorway at the sight of Sonnie inside.

She'd fallen asleep in an oversize chair next to the bed. Her stockinged feet were curled beneath her, and her head drooped to one side. An open book, its story abandoned, lay cradled in her lap. Only Vince's deep, steady breathing broke the hush of the room.

Emotion spread through Lance. Moving closer, he squatted on his haunches next to her and took full advantage of the opportunity to simply watch her sleep.

He drank in the sight of her tresses, glinting like black diamonds in the lamp's glow and tumbling in thick confusion about her shoulders. Flawless in its creation, her olive-hued skin accentuated the dark shade, and her bow-shaped lips, softly parted in slumber, beckoned his.

He almost gave in to the temptation. To steal a kiss now, when she slept and was unaware, was all too indicative of his cowardice toward her.

Or any other woman, for that matter.

No, when and if he ever kissed Sonnie Mancuso again, she would be a full participant, willing and wide-awake as hell.

He reached over and carefully pulled the book from her unresisting grasp. Despite his efforts, however, her eyes opened slowly. She focused on him and raked slender fingers through her hair.

"Guess I fell asleep, Boss-man."

The sheer sultriness of her voice tugged at his restraints. A corner of his mouth lifted.

"Guess you did," he said, and set the book aside.

"What time is it?"

He didn't bother to look at the clock on Vince's bedside table. "Late."

She made no effort to rise; instead she burrowed deeper into the chair's brocade.

170

"Have you been outside all this time?" She laid the palm of her hand against his cheek. "You're cold."

He almost turned his face into the warmth of her skin, almost pressed a kiss to the inside of her wrist.

Almost.

"I was talking to Charlie."

"Oh." She withdrew her hand.

"How's your arm?"

"Better. It doesn't throb anymore."

He nodded, reluctant to end the intimacy of their mundane conversation. He wanted her to touch him again.

Her dark head swiveled, and she studied her father. "He's sleeping soundly. I hope he has a good night."

"He will. He's a stronger cuss than you realize." He plucked her shoes from the floor and straightened from his hunkered position. "Time for you to go upstairs."

She pondered him for a moment through her sable lashes, then extended her hand toward him. Her mouth softened.

"Help me up, Lance."

Without hesitation, his fingers closed around hers. She unfurled from the chair's cushion and stood before him, so close the hem of her skirt brushed his pant legs.

He inhaled her sweet scent and stared into the obsidian pools of her eyes, wishing that if he ever were to drown, it would be right here, in them.

He lifted her hand and dropped a kiss over the silken knuckles.

A barely discernible sigh escaped her. Her glance drifted over the skin his lips just touched. The corners of her mouth dipped.

"My shoes, please," she said, as if she wanted something else instead.

Lance had forgotten he still held them. She took

the pair and moved toward the hall, halting within the doorway.

"Sleep well, Boss-man." A little smile softened her mouth.

He watched her leave and doubted he'd sleep worth a damn. He extinguished Vince's lamp and found his way through the blanket of darkness to the office.

After lighting the room, he noticed Sonnie's edition of *Special Report on Diseases of Cattle* on the desk. He picked up the book, skimmed through the chapter titles, and found several that teased his interest.

He began to understand why she put such value in it. The manual brimmed with information on a wide variety of topics. He conceded that he could learn a thing or two himself.

Besides, the report's findings would help keep him from dwelling on *her*.

He stepped to the liquor cabinet and poured himself a shot of bourbon, his attention hooked by a section entitled "Noncontagious Diseases of the Organs of Respiration."

Something on the floor distracted him. Medicine bottles were scattered about the floral carpet. It was little wonder Sonnie, in her panic and fear, hadn't remembered they were there.

An envelope lay near the strewn bottles, its age evident in the room's shadowy light. Lance set aside his drink and book, then knelt to retrieve it.

He read the words printed on the outside. In growing puzzlement, he removed the paper folded inside and scanned its contents.

A ball of dread formed in the pit of his stomach. He read the document again, slower this time. The subject hit him hard with the full potential of its consequence, and he breathed a savage expletive.

What the hell could Vince have been thinking of?

Chapter Ten

"Tell me her name again."

Lance had forgotten. In all the tomfoolery it had taken to get him here, the woman's name escaped him completely.

"Gracie." Shorty said with infinite patience. "Gray-cee."

Lance nodded and shuffled his feet in the dirt. He would remember. He couldn't forget again and look any more stupid than he did right now.

They stood in front of her little house, a whole group of them, Mancuso cowboys fresh off the spring roundup. Full of spirit and wired for fun, they intended to kick off the night with a visit to Gracie's.

But only Lance would be going inside. How he came this far, he had no idea. Why he had agreed, he didn't know.

And his courage left him in a whoosh. He couldn't go through with it, this visit to a woman far more *experienced than he. He couldn't perform the act with her as everyone wanted and expected.*

Lance turned aside to break loose, but they wouldn't let him go. A myriad of hands and hoots of laughter kept him firmly in place, and he cast a helpless look at Shorty.

The cowboy thrust a wad of crumpled bills into Lance's fist. "Here. Just lay these on the table when you git inside. She'll know what you're there fer."

"I can't," he said quietly in a futile attempt to save face in front of the other men. "I don't even know her. I don't love her. She doesn't love me."

"Love!" Shorty seemed amazed at the idea. "Love don't have nothin' to do with it. She's a businesswoman. Everythin' boils down to the almighty dollar and any way she can git it."

"I can't do this." Lance groaned, trying to wrench himself free from the persistent grips holding him.

"She'll teach you all you need to know. Don't you worry about a thing."

"Shorty, you son of a bitch."

"Yeah, well, that might be, but one of these days you're gonna thank me." His gap-toothed grin widened. "Can't have you bein' a virgin all your life, now, can we?"

Lance fairly seethed from frustration. Remaining a virgin would have to be better than the humiliation he endured in front of these men he called friends. What could be worse than being the laughingstock of the entire Mancuso outfit?

Shorty planted a hand on Lance's shoulder and pushed. Lance stumbled forward and found himself a few steps closer to the little house's front door.

"Just remember," Shorty called from behind him, "you ain't a man till you had a woman."

The challenge hit a raw nerve. His pride stung; his

spine stiffened. He closed the distance between himself and the house.

You ain't a man till you had a woman.

He rapped his knuckles on the door and waited.

True to his word, Doc Tanner returned to the Rocking M two days later. Fretfully worried about the cough beginning to plague her father, Sonnie hung back throughout the examination with bated breath, sure her worst fears would be realized.

They were. Doc confirmed her worries of early pneumonia and declared that a stay at County Hospital in Cheyenne was paramount. Sonnie tried to soothe Papa's emphatic protests that he would recuperate just fine from treatment and care right there on the Rocking M, and though the doctor conceded that his admission into the hospital could wait until the morning, neither he nor Sonnie budged from the decision, and Papa fell back into the pillows with wheezy grumbles of complaint.

Even his plea to Lance failed. After the doc's departure, Lance had taken Sonnie's side of the argument, reasoning that, since the Wyoming Stockmen's Association's meeting and dinner would be held the following night, the trip into Cheyenne couldn't be avoided. Whereas Lance and Sonnie would stay in a hotel, Papa's placement in the hospital assured him of prompt updates of the proceedings, and he was finally placated.

Thus Sonnie spent the rest of the day preparing for the important event. As a spokeswoman for her father, it was imperative that she be well dressed and appear poised, confident, and informed of Association matters. Between keeping a watchful eye on Papa and packing trunks she'd only recently unpacked, the time flew with amazing speed.

The next morning dawned bright and clear, with

enough nip in the air to warrant wearing the fashion-
able new cloak and matching velvet hat she'd brought
back from Rome. Lance had ordered the black-and-
gold stagecoach pulled around to the front of the Big
House, and when he noticed the orderly mountain of
baggage waiting on the porch, his tawny brow quirked.

But he said nothing and hefted the largest piece
onto his shoulder. He'd been preoccupied of late, and
Sonnie couldn't fathom why. Though Papa's wors-
ening condition kept him on the ranch, Lance took
his meals at the bunkhouse, rose early, and worked
grueling hours until late, pausing only now and then
to check in on her father.

Sonnie found herself missing him.

Was his mood due to something she'd said or
done? Did he worry unduly over Papa's health? The
uncertainty spawned a frown and an unladylike nibble
on the inside of her lip.

Her glance shifted toward the stagecoach, gleaming
in the bright sunlight. Once again she marveled at its
majestic style and quality. After depositing a basket
of food and a small satchel inside, she ran a discern-
ing hand over the door's shiny paint.

"The coach is magnificent." She took advantage of
the opportunity to converse with Lance. "Whatever
possessed Papa to buy it?"

He shifted her trunk from his shoulder to a storage
compartment at the back of the rig.

"His work with both the Association and the ranch
required frequent trips into Cheyenne and surrounding
states. The coach made traveling easier." He faced her
and hooked a thumb into the hip pocket of his Levi's.
"But it's mine, Sonnie. Bought and paid for with my
own money."

She gaped at him. "Yours?"

He nodded. A touch of wry amusement graced his

lips and softened his somber expression. "Had it built and shipped from Denver to my specifications. Are you surprised I might have some wealth of my own?"

She detected a hint of defensiveness, of challenge, in the quietly voiced question. Her assumption that only Papa could afford such a fine rig flustered her. Her cheeks pinkened, betraying the assumption.

"Your father pays me well, and I've accumulated a tidy sum in my accounts over the years," he said. "I've earned every dime, Sonnie. Never think that Vince Mancuso coddled me or showed me favoritism. Everything I have, I earned with my own sweat."

His tone, earnest and emphatic, quashed the tiny stirring of suspicion that Papa might have, indeed, favored Lance. Lance Harmon, she'd begun to learn, was a man of pride. Decent and principled.

She wanted to tell him so, but his attention left her to focus on someone behind her. She turned to find Jake McKenna approaching with a purposeful, bow-legged stride.

"Am I riding into Cheyenne with you?" he demanded of Lance, not sparing Sonnie a glance. He halted and set his hands on his hips, his glare a tangible show of animosity.

"Hadn't planned on it," Lance replied.

Tension shimmered between the two men.

"Why not?"

"We're shorthanded. I need you to work the ranch while we're gone."

"Work? Damn it, that's all I've done lately is work my butt off around here."

Lance narrowed an eye at the vehement protest. "You broke the rules, McKenna. You had to pay the price."

"I'm entitled to some time off just like everyone else. Half the outfit is going with you. I want to go, too."

In spite of herself, Sonnie took pity on him.

Lance had enacted swift punishment after the card game in the bunkhouse, heaping chore after chore upon him until, in Sonnie's mind, McKenna had paid his dues. Guiltily aware of her own part in the affair, she was moved to step in on his behalf.

"Lance, couldn't you give in and let him go with us?" she asked gently. She rested her hand on his muscular forearm in a subtle plea for compassion. "It wouldn't seem fair to make him stay."

He dragged his gaze from the cowboy and considered her for long moments. She sensed the war he waged within himself; a tiny muscle in his chiseled jawline leaped in evidence of the battle.

Finally he gave her a curt nod and swung his attention back to the cowhand.

"You have Miss Mancuso to thank for my leniency," he said, as if he'd relented against his better judgment. "Grab your things. We're pulling out in ten minutes."

Jake's glance lighted on Sonnie for a brief second, but showed no gratitude or relief. Wordlessly he spun on his heel and stepped toward the bunkhouse.

"McKenna."

The cowboy halted.

"You gonna behave yourself on the trip?" Lance asked with deceptive softness.

"Don't talk down to me, Harmon," Jake said in a snarl.

"Mess up once, and you're out of a job."

Sonnie swallowed at the hard tone of Lance's warning. Jake stormed off in a cursing huff, and, worried she'd been mistaken in intervening, she ventured a tentative peek at Lance.

The flare of his nostrils revealed a lingering distrust for the man. He turned and caught her studying him.

His eyes meshed with hers for several pulsating heart-beats.

Gradually the tawny depths lost their coldness and instead mellowed to the hue of sun-warmed honey. His hand reached out, as if to caress her cheek, but his fingers curled into a fist, and he pulled away.

"I'll load the rest of the baggage," he said.

Sonnie bemoaned the loss. Keen disappointment from the denial of his touch, the hope of it, held her frozen, and she found herself in need of several moments to regain the aplomb that, surprisingly, his heated look had shaken.

Drawing in a breath, she stood a little straighter, pivoted, and returned to the house to tend to her father.

Lance contemplated the Mancuso entourage as it pulled away from the Big House and headed toward Cheyenne. Six outriders rode ahead, each carrying a loaded rifle in a scabbard positioned for easy reach. They flanked the shiny stagecoach, and in spite of the protection they offered, Lance wondered if it was enough.

He couldn't risk another attack on Sonnie like the one during her homecoming—or one on Vince, for that matter—and he'd strictly ordered his men to keep a sharp eye on the Wyoming rangeland for any sign of reprisal.

Especially from Clay Ditson and Snake. Burning their supplies stockpiled in Silver Meadow had produced no response from them, and Lance grew increasingly edgy from their silence. He preferred a confrontation to not knowing their whereabouts; he was certain Ditson wouldn't let the matter go without retaliation.

Nor had Lance heard from Tom Horn. Irritation roiled through him at the gunfighter's arrogance in neglecting to give them a decision. Would he hire on as range detective and help the cattlemen in their war against rustlers, or wouldn't he? Too much time had passed already. They had to get their herds back to recoup their losses and put a stop to the thievery.

The cheerful morning sun kissed the countryside with brilliance. Through eyes shadowed by his hat's brim, he scanned the familiar lay of the land and realized the stagecoach traveled parallel to Silver Meadow.

He decided to make a quick investigative side trip. Setting his spurs to his horse's ribs, Lance rode up beside Charlie, one of the outriders guarding the rear of the stagecoach.

"Want to ride with me to Silver Meadow?" he asked over the rumble of the wheels. "Won't take but a few minutes."

"Sure." Charlie shot a glance in that direction. "Best you don't go by yourself, anyway."

"I want to have a look around. Doubt we'll find much," Lance said. "Ditson's been too quiet, and he's too smart to be lazy. I'll tell Vince and Sonnie we're leaving." He whistled sharply to the man in the driver's seat. "Cookie, pull up."

Cookie lifted a hand in acknowledgment of the command. With a jingle of harnesses, the horses lumbered to a stop, and Lance reined in closer to the stagecoach. Leaning from the saddle, he opened the door.

Inside, Vince sat on the leather seat with a brightly colored afghan over his lap. A week-old copy of the *Cheyenne Daily Sun* engrossed him. From her seat on the opposite side, Sonnie's curious glance met Lance's.

"What is it, Lance?" she asked.

"Charlie and I are riding up to Silver Meadow," he said. "Go on without us. We'll catch up."

Her dark eyes widened. "Silver Meadow! I'd like to come with you."

His heart leaped at the unexpected opportunity to be with her, even if it meant sharing her with Charlie. Still, he hesitated, concerned for her protection.

"Take her, Lance," Vince said. "I'm not good company for her."

The comment triggered a spell of hacking, and the older man coughed repeatedly into a handkerchief pressed against his mouth.

"Lance, please," Sonnie said after her father calmed. She appealed to him, her features eager, confident. "If I'm to speak at tonight's meeting with any sort of authority, I must be familiar with the stolen rangeland. This is a perfect opportunity for me to learn of the troubles the Rocking M is facing with Ditson and Snake. Surely you understand that."

She blatantly challenged him, a black-eyed beauty who knew what she wanted and could give the argument to justify it.

She was good. Damned good.

"Besides, you and Charlie will be right beside me. To protect me, of course," she added, a demure pout on her mouth.

She taunted him with her wiles, mocked him with his worries for her safety, and he was powerless to deny her.

"She can have my horse," Stick offered, unabashedly looking in from a window on the other side. "I'll ride on the box with Cookie."

Vince nodded, approving. "The trip will do her good."

"Guess I have no choice, do I?" He refused to show the others how easily she'd maneuvered him. "Mount up. We're wasting time."

Her delight unabashed, Sonnie dropped her needlework into the satchel at her feet and scrambled from the stagecoach. Brushing aside Stick's offer to help her into the saddle, she slipped one slender foot into the stirrup and swung up onto the mare with sleek agility. She hastily adjusted her skirts about her.

"Well, now, Miss Sonnie," Charie drawled, eying her efforts. He rested a forearm on his saddle horn. "I know that you're a real lady, through and through, and women 'round these parts don't ride them god-awful sidesaddles like they do back east." He made a show of studying a lone cloud in the sky. "Can't say for the others, but I reckon if I can get a peek at a lady's purty little ankle while she's ridin' in a normal saddle, it just might make my day a little brighter."

Sonnie laughed. "Charlie, shame on you!"

But she stopped her fussing, and he heaved an elaborate sigh.

"Can't blame a man for tryin', can you, ma'am?"

Lance released an exasperated breath. The other cowboys chuckled, gazing with unmistakable adoration toward Sonnie during the exchange.

Only Jake, bored and restless, seemed oblivious.

Lance ordered Cookie to pull out. The outriders took their places around the stagecoach, and, lifting a hand in farewell to Vince, Lance promised to return Sonnie shortly and closed the door.

The three left the road and crossed through grass knee-high to their horses. They reached the bluff overlooking the meadow, and Sonnie gasped in pleasure at the sight below.

"It's even more beautiful than I remembered," she said softly. "See the morning dew on the grass and how it sparkles in the sun? Fairies' tears, my sisters would tell me. I always believed them." She sighed at the memory, a wistful smile on her ruby lips. "Is that why they call it Silver Meadow? Because of the morning dew?"

Lance shook his head. "This was your mother's

favorite part of the Mancuso rangeland. Vince told me she named it because of the way the moonlight turned everything it touched silver."

Charlie squinted an eye against the sun.

"Yep. Right beautiful country," he concurred. "Too bad it's causin' us so much trouble."

His comment deflated Sonnie's smile. Lance followed her gaze as it swept the horizon and paused at the blackened debris Vince's flaming match had left behind.

"He has no right to take this from us," she murmured. She turned and faced Lance. "Ditson, I mean. He has no right."

"No, Sonnie," he said. "He doesn't."

Their conversation ceased for a pensive moment, and as he rooted around his shirt pocket for a rolled cigarette, Lance was struck by the stillness—the absolute absence of life.

He didn't have any naive illusions of finding Ditson and Snake within easy view. Still, he saw no evidence of their attempt to rebuild the cabin, not even a heap of new supplies puchased in defiance of Vince's harsh warning to them to stay away.

Where were they now? What was their scheme?

Not knowing only increased his unease.

Sonnie emitted a soft sound of pleasure at the field of wildflowers growing rebelliously amid the gently swaying grass. A riotous display of flora beckoned her.

"I'd like to gather a bouquet for Papa." She touched Lance's arm and indicated the colorful patch of nature. "Some flowers might cheer him."

"Go ahead," he said absently, and tucked the unlit cigarette into the corner of his mouth.

"I'll hurry." She guided her horse toward the flowers. Knowing his protective gaze lingered over her, she dismounted into the thick foliage, bent, and plucked a stem of violet larkspur. She inhaled the delicate scent from the miniature petals.

"How about that there pretty flower?" Charlie called out, pointing toward a cluster of orange-petaled flowers growing close to the soil.

Recognizing the species, rare for this part of the range, she smiled.

"*Lithospermum caroliniense*. Beautiful, isn't it?" she called back, and picked the delicate blooms.

"*Lithosper*—Shit." The cowboy frowned. "I'll just call it a pretty flower."

Sonnie's smile widened. "It's a puccoon, Charlie. And this one is named *Yucca glauca*. Soapweed. And this one, is *Rosa arkansana*."

"You know all them funny names for 'em?" he asked, awed.

"Goodness, no, not all." She added a stem of yellow sand lily to the bunch. "Just some. This is prickly poppy. And over here"—she strode a few feet farther—"is spiderwort."

As he watched her, Lance's mouth quirked. "Smart aleck."

She laughed outright. "I'm not."

He removed his cigarette from the corner of his mouth and studied the unlit end.

"There are more than two hundred species of flora 'round these parts," he drawled. "I heard tell there might be upward of seven hundred identified when it's all said and done. Bet you didn't know that, did you, Charlie?"

Wide-eyed, the cowboy gaped at him. "My Gawd. No, I didn't."

"Well, you do now." Lance tucked the cigarette back into the corner of his mouth.

"Smart aleck." Sonnie wrinkled her nose at him.

Lance grinned back, charming her.

She couldn't hold her amusement. Flaunting her

studies to Lance warranted the teasing. She was willing to take what she handed out.

She made a shooing motion with her free hand.

"Leave me to my picking, you two," she said. "Take a ride around Silver Meadow. I'll be ready to leave when you are."

Lance nodded. "We'll come back in a few minutes, then. Don't stray too far. I want to be able to see you."

"Go. I'll be right here."

His shadowed glance lingered on her a moment more; then he shifted in the saddle and spurred his horse deeper into the meadow, Charlie at his side.

Sonnie adjusted the growing pile of flowers lying in the crook of her arm. She delighted in being gifted with Lance's show of humor, and with a smile tarrying on her lips, she bent to pick some Canada wild rye grass to add to her bouquet.

Troubled by an evasive element he couldn't quite put his finger on, Lance scanned Silver Meadow. Again the stillness struck him. Something was different.

Then he knew.

"The herd," he said softly, drawing Charlie's glance.

"What?"

"The herd is gone. Every damn head of cattle that Ditson stole from us is gone. They were here that night we burned his supplies."

Charlie sat ramrod straight in the saddle. His scrutiny darted across the range in a search Lance had already finished. "Hell."

Lance figured the loss in dollars and cents and winced.

"Suppose he just took 'em somewhere else?" Charlie asked. "A different grazing range, maybe."

"A range better than Silver Meadow?"

Lance grunted in disagreement. He nudged his

horse past the burned cabin shell toward a faint trail farther east. He halted and studied the tracks imprinted in the dirt.

Two horses, one of them unshod, had herded the cattle over the little-used path. He followed their direction and guessed Ditson and Snake were headed for Cheyenne.

"All that beef'll fetch a mighty purty penny for 'em," Charlie said.

Lance scowled. "Ditson's getting back at us for burning him out. By the looks of the tracks, they passed through the day after Vince set the fire."

"Reckon he'll use the money to start up an outfit of his own? A legitimate outfit?"

Lance's lips tightened over the unlit cigarette still tucked in his mouth. He remembered the night at Gracie's.

"Reckon he might at that."

His mind played with several theories, plausible guesses as to Ditson's next move. Most likely he'd head to the Cheyenne stockyards, where he could ship the rustled cattle in railcars to an eastern market and remove the evidence of his theft. Or he could drive the herd to Cheyenne to sell the beef to the meat-dressing plant and flaunt his victory beneath the Rocking M's nose.

One thing was sure: finding a buyer willing to pay top price for the prime Mancuso stock would not be hard.

Clay Ditson would be a rich son of a bitch.

A whisper of a rustle, as if the petals and leaves on the wild-growing flora had brushed against someone's legs, stilled Sonnie's humming. Stems snapped and crunched beneath boot soles.

Even before she turned, her heart began to pound. Even without looking, she knew it wasn't Lance.

She straightened slowly, her gaze riveted to the monstrous shadow looming over her. She turned then, wary.

A huge form blocked the sunlight. Copper skin stretched over harsh, angular features. Black eyes, flat and cold, stared down at her.

She swallowed hard.

"What do you want?" The demand left her throat in a shaky rasp.

He took a step closer. Sonnie's heart pounded faster.

"Get off this land, Snake. Do you hear me?" She took a cautious step back.

His lips thinned into a leer and revealed yellowed teeth. He made a sound, low, grunting, deep in his throat. The primitiveness of it sent shivers up Sonnie's spine.

His knife blade gleamed, then arced in the sun. Powerful fingers tightened over the handle.

He'd been stalking her, she realized in horror. Waiting until Lance and Charlie had ridden away before moving with silent stealth toward her.

"You'll never get away with this. Lance—my father"—she sucked in a breath—"they'll come after you. I swear."

He slid his bulking frame into a crouch. His long, muscle-rippled arm swung once, twice, the knife so close the wind sang across the blade.

She flinched and jumped back with a gasp.

The hard mouth parted. Laughter jerked from his throat, eerie and menacing.

He was toying with her, taunting her until he attacked.

She'd not make it easy for him. She'd not fall victim to his brute strength without a fight.

The laughter died. Yellowed teeth bared in a guttural snarl. He lunged for her.

She screamed and whirled and ran for her life.

*   *   *

Lance's heart lurched within his chest. Her scream clawed at him across Silver Meadow.

Sonnie.

His instincts leaped at the sound. Charlie's anxious features mirrored the fear pounding in Lance's veins. He ripped the unlit cigarette from his mouth and yanked his rifle from its scabbard. In the same motion, he kicked his spurs into the sorrel's ribs and reined him into a sharp turn from the trail.

Their horses broke into a hard gallop. An eternity passed, and he finally saw her.

She was running, searching for him, the hem of her deep blue cloak trailing behind her. Panic paled her face.

She spotted him and cried out his name. One arm clutched the wildflowers to her breast while the other reached out to him. Even before the horse ground to a complete halt, he slid from the saddle and caught her to him, holding her tightly against his chest with his free hand.

"Sonnie, what's wrong?" he demanded into the soft skin at her temple, his embrace so protective his jaw pushed her little velvet hat askew.

She swallowed a sob and tilted her ebony head up to him.

"Snake. He's here. In the flowers." She pulled away from him slightly and peered behind her, as if certain the Indian would suddenly loom into view.

Lance jerked his gaze all around the tops of the tall grass and colorful blossoms, but saw no one. He gestured to Charlie. The cowboy, his rifle ready, nodded and reined his horse into a wide search.

She shuddered. "He came from nowhere. He wouldn't say anything. Just stared at me with those mean black eyes."

Her body trembled, and he held her tighter.

188

"I should never have left you, Sonnie." Regret haunted him. "God, if he hurt you . . ."

Her forehead wobbled back and forth on his chest. "No. He didn't touch me. He had this awful-looking knife, but . . . but he never touched me."

Sweet Jesus. He could have.

"I'll take you back to the stagecoach," Lance said.

Gently he released her and noticed the bedraggled armful of flowers she held in a death grip to her breast.

"Do you want to pick another bunch before we leave?" he asked.

She shook her dark head. "I think not. I'm afraid I've lost the fun of it."

She stepped away from him, but boldly took his hand and curled her fingers around his. His grasp tightened in reassurance.

He kept a sharp eye out for any sign of movement as they traipsed through the wildflowers to retrieve Stick's horse. A swath of broken and leaning stems clearly showed that Snake had stalked Sonnie.

The close call galled him.

After she mounted, he grasped the bridle and led the horse to his own. He swung into the saddle and noticed Charlie's approach.

"Snake's been here all right," the cowboy said, drawing closer. "Must've shimmied on his belly through the grass and flowers from a camp over yonder. Damned Injuns can be as quiet as the dead when they got a mind to be."

"No sign of him, though?"

The question was moot. If Snake wanted to be seen, only then would he be. Still, Lance needed to hear it.

"None." Charlie returned his rifle to its scabbard. "He's probably watchin' us this very minute, laughin' his guts out because we can't see him." His compassionate glance drifted over Sonnie. "If he wanted to hurt you, he'd 'a done it the minute our backs were turned. I reckon he only meant to scare you, Miss Sonnie."

She lifted her chin with a dignified sniff. "Then he did a fine job of it, Charlie."

Lance shoved the Winchester into its scabbard.

"Come on," he said in a growl. "Let's get the hell out of here."

Both men formed a protective shield about Sonnie as they left Silver Meadow and cut through the range-land ahead of the Mancuso entourage. The rig, flanked with its outriders, rumbled in the near distance. They waited three abreast in the road for it to draw nearer.

Lance's gaze strayed often to Sonnie. He studied her delicate profile, the thrust of her chin, the uplifted tilt of her nose, as she watched the approaching stage-coach. A surge of heated possessiveness, of prolonged worry, coursed through him.

Reaching out an arm toward her, he let his fingers gently catch her chin and turned her to him.

"You okay?" he asked softly.

Ebony eyes met his.

"Yes," she murmured. A hint of color had returned to her cheeks, and she seemed to have regained the aplomb she'd lost. "Really, I am," she added, as if she sensed his anxiety.

Lance pulled his hand away, but her index finger hooked with his and kept his full attention.

"Don't say anything to my father about this," she said quietly. "Not with his health so precarious."

His thumb stroked her knuckle in a slow caress. "I won't. But from now on I'm not leaving you alone. If I can't be with you, one of the other men will."

Her lips softened into a provocative smile that

nearly turned his heart on end. "Whatever you say, Boss-man."

He wanted to say many things, all that he was feeling, had always felt, but he held it in. Lifting her knuckle to his lips, he dropped a kiss upon her satin skin, then reluctantly released her.

The black-and-gold stagecoach rumbled to a stop. Stick jumped from the box and loped toward them, an eager grin on his boyish face.

"How was she for you, Miss Sonnie?" he asked, indicating his horse. He stroked her sleek neck. "Gentle enough?"

"Oh, yes, very gentle," she said. "A baby could have ridden her without falling off. Did you train her yourself?"

He glowed from her compliment and gallantly offered her assistance to the ground, no mean feat, considering his initial shyness toward her.

"Started when she was a colt," he declared.

"Thank you for letting me ride her. You're very proud of her, I can tell."

"Yes, ma'am. You're sure welcome to ride her anytime you get the hankerin'."

"I'm touched, Stick." She slipped her hand in his elbow as he escorted her to the stagecoach. "You've always been very kind to me."

"How could any man not be kind to you, Miss Sonnie?" he asked.

"It's easier for some than for others." With a wan smile, she relinquished her hold on his arm and stepped inside the rig to rejoin Vince.

Stick rubbed his jaw in puzzlement, her comment lost on him.

But not on Lance. He knew she spoke of Snake and Ditson, of her tumultous homecoming and the incident in Silver Meadow. Yet again, he regretted putting her in danger.

"Don't be so hard on yourself. She's stronger than you think," Charlie said quietly, his gaze keen on Lance, on what he was thinking. "We're all gonna help you take care of her till this thing is over. Ditson and Snake won't get to her."

"Just let 'em try," Lance said in a growl.

Charlie eyed him. "And if they do?"

He watched the stagecoach pull away toward Cheyenne. His lips spread in a cold, mirthless smile.

"Then I'll kill 'em both."

Chapter Eleven

It had been pleasant enough, he supposed, now that he thought back on it. Lying with Gracie proved to be enjoyable and enlightening, an experience not without its finer moments. She'd been kind, compassionate, even fun. With her gentle guidance, he had shed his virginity with dignity, and they parted in amicable friendship.

Lance sprawled on his bedroll and stared into the star-studded sky. He was a man now, in every sense of the word. In a few carnal minutes, he passed over that coveted masculine threshold into a new world, a world brightened from a glimpse into feminine desires and pleasures. With Gracie as his teacher, he learned another lesson in life; in a fleeting flare of passion, a fresh understanding had dawned.

Their coupling had not been perfect. Even though they performed the physical joining as nature intended, with both achieving mutual satisfaction, something was missing. And Lance, with all the wis-

Pam Crooks

dom of his twenty-two years, knew exactly what.

Feeling. Emotion. That depth of yearning only a man fiercely in love with a woman had.

He didn't yearn for Gracie, nor she him. Gracie shared her body as easily as she would a good drink or a hot meal. She expected little in return, only a small token of payment for her time. Denied the warmth of love, she accepted the coldness of lust.

Lance regretted the travesty. She didn't deserve the loss of a man's care and affection in her life. But had Mother? Being abandoned by his father, her husband, had left her broken, and Hawthorne's vile demands had defeated her even more.

The memories sickened him, as they never failed to do when they slipped back into his mind. Was he any better? Did he use Gracie as Mother had been used, to sate his baser appetite?

Maybe. But Gracie knew the score. She was agreeable. She hadn't suffered from his power. He hadn't hurt her as Hawthorne and his father had hurt Mother.

No, he was different. He didn't want a woman in his life, much as Gracie didn't want a man in hers. He would stay away, refuse himself the love that, at times, he felt he needed. He wouldn't be vulnerable to a woman's softness and touch.

As if to seal the vow, he drew in a long, slow breath and held it inside him. Unbidden, the visage of a young, sable-lashed beauty thousands of miles away appeared. He hadn't seen her for a couple of years, but her memory hovered ever near, haunting him when he least expected it.

Sonnie. His breath left him in a low groan, shattered the vow he just made, and sent the fragments hurtling toward the black Wyoming sky.

* * *

The Mancuso entourage, resonant with its jangle of harnesses and thundering horses, made an impressive entrance into the city of Cheyenne.

From wood-planked boardwalks, townspeople gaped openly at the outriders clustered closely about the polished stagecoach, their rifles in plain sight as they sat straight and somber in their saddles. Awe-stricken youngsters left their mothers' sides to run behind, soiling their clothes with the dust raised from the rolling wheels and clomping hooves.

Cheyenne bustled with activity. Through the coach's window, Sonnie took it all in, enthralled with the changes that had taken place in her absence. False-front buildings had given way to sturdier structures within the business district, and the residential areas she glimpsed bore elegant homes graced with landscaped lawns, wrought-iron fences, and stone walks. The massive cattle industry, despite hard times, distributed its wealth into the city, and Cheyenne benefited from the impact.

As did County Hospital. Newly built at the corner of Twenty-third and Evans, the rambling wood-and-brick facility was a far cry from its beginnings as the tent Sonnie remembered, set up to care for workers building the transcontinental railroad. The hospital would easily rival any in Boston, and she found herself duly impressed by its size and modern appearance.

The stagecoach halted at the front door. Doc Tanner, watching for their arrival, descended the stairs with a nurse at his side. Papa gave them a halfhearted wave and grumbled under his breath his displeasure at having to stay.

"Papa," cajoled Sonnie, taking the afghan from his lap and setting it aside, "Doc knows what's best for you. He'll give you special care here. In a few days' time, you'll feel much stronger."

195

"I could get stronger at the ranch," he rasped, fighting back a cough. "Don't have to come . . . all the way to the city for what I could get at home."

"Promise me you won't be difficult." Her patience was strained from his stubborn repetition of the argument. "You'll frighten the nurses."

"Pah! Don't need 'em, anyway."

"Papa!"

Lance opened the coach door, and Sonnie's exasperated gaze met his. He glanced at Vince, then back at her, and his amber eyes glinted in silent understanding.

"I'll help you down, Vince." He extended a long, muscular arm toward him. "Doc's waiting."

"Indeed, I am," the doctor said in a cheerful voice as he drew closer. He politely acknowledged Sonnie and nodded toward her father. "Have a good trip, my friend?"

"Fine, fine," Papa mumbled. Leaning heavily on Lance's strength, he managed the step down with slow care. Once on the ground, he frowned and rapped his cane against the wheelchair Doc brought. "I'm not using that damn thing, Ed. I can walk in on my own feet."

Nonplussed, Doc gestured to the smiling nurse, and she hastened to remove the offensive chair.

"Sure, you can." He nodded, placating him as if he were an obstinate child. He took Papa's elbow and, with the adroitness of years of experience with difficult patients, led him toward the entrance. "Have you had a tour of the hospital yet, Vince? Grand facility. When you're feeling up to it, we'll show you around."

Both men headed toward the stairs. Sonnie accepted Lance's assistance from the coach, and she contemplated Papa's retreating back.

"He'll have the staff in a tizzy before day's end," she said.

"They'll know how to handle him," Lance said, his low voice bearing traces of amusement.

"But he can be so overbearing. He's not used to someone telling him what he can and can't do." She sighed and watched both doctor and patient disappear inside the hospital doors.

Lance made no further comment. Puzzled that he didn't, she twisted and found his gaze pinned at some point in the distance.

Her own followed. From over her head, he studied two men on horseback, one of whom Sonnie recognized as Tom Horn. They drew closer, and the cluster of Mancuso riders parted, allowing them closer access.

Lance's hand rested easily on the small of her back.

"Been expecting to hear from you, Horn," he said, his tone crisp. "Where you been?"

"Glad to see you, too, Harmon." He ignored Lance's demand and flashed an arrogant grin at Sonnie instead. He leaned forward. "My, you're lookin' especially pretty today."

Her father expected her to treat Tom Horn in a demure—but decidedly feminine—manner. Still, Sonnie knew Lance's dislike of him. Indeed, she harbored no love for the man herself and refused to be swayed by his charm.

"Thank you, Mr. Horn," she said, and managed a smile.

He sat straighter in his saddle and indicated his friend. "John Coble, from the Iron Mountain Ranch. John, meet Sonnie Mancuso and Lance Harmon, from the Rocking M."

Lance inclined his head in greeting. "We've met. Our spreads are next to one another. John, Sonnie is Vince's youngest."

"That a fact?" Coble asked, and touched a finger to his hat. "Glad to meet you, ma'am."

"Likewise, Mr. Coble."

"Been stayin' up there with his outfit," Horn went on in delayed response to Lance's initial question. "Today's the first I've left his place, else I'd'a gotten word to you sooner."

"Good of you to find the time for us now," Lance said, the taunt smooth and cool.

His eyes narrowed a fraction, but the gunfighter let it pass. "We got us a meeting to go to tonight, don't we, Sonnie?"

Despite all the preparation she'd put in for this evening, she remained uneasy at the thought of being in his company. She quashed the feeling, for Papa's sake.

"Yes, we do."

"I'll pick you up at seven. What hotel you stayin' at?"

Lance's hand slid up her spine and settled over her shoulder in definite masculine possession.

"The Railroad Hotel," he said.

She didn't mind him answering for her. His touch was most distracting, whether for its rarity or its pleasure, she wasn't sure.

"Gonna be joinin' us, Harmon?"

"Yes," he said. "I am."

Sonnie glanced at him in surprise. He hadn't mentioned going to the meeting before.

"Good enough," Horn drawled. "We'll make it a foursome." His eyes found Sonnie and raked over her in brazen appraisal. Lance's fingers tightened over her shoulder. "Until later, little lady."

She inclined her head. "Mr. Horn."

With that, he and Coble reined their mounts around the stagecoach and leisurely departed down the street.

"I didn't know you were attending," Sonnie murmured, watching the pair halt in front of the closest saloon, dismount, and saunter inside.

"You think I'd let you go alone? Horn'll have you in bed first chance he gets."

Taken aback, Sonnie stared at him, then tossed her head.

"Not if I have any say-so in the matter." She sniffed.

"He wouldn't give you a chance."

"Papa knows I can handle him."

"Papa knows to expect too much from you," he retorted, and nudged her toward the hospital's doors.

She pursed her mouth at his words. His presence would be valuable, she conceded inwardly. An asset. He would help if she needed it.

Her apprehensions eased.

She considered him a moment. "Who are you taking?"

He shrugged. "I'll ask Gracie."

Gracie. He'd mentioned her once before, to Papa, as a woman better suited to accompany Tom Horn than she. Sonnie frowned.

"She's a friend of mine," he added, glancing at the sky, seeming to gauge the time of day by the sun.

"You're hardly giving her enough notice."

Lance's mouth quirked. "She'll be ready."

"Do you have that effect on women, that they drop what they're doing to go out with you?"

"Hardly," he scoffed.

"It'd serve you right if she turned you down, Lance Harmon," she declared airily, halting at the bottom step. "Any woman in her right mind would demand the courtesy of a proper invitation, with time enough to prepare herself."

"Gracie's not like other women."

His quiet statement stopped her short. She peered up at him, wanting to question him further, finding herself inordinately curious about this unknown lady and the position she held in his life.

"Lance." Charlie's softly spoken call prevented it. "Look yonder." He indicated a mealymouthed bay strutting down Evans Street.

Sonnie gasped. Clay Ditson.

Smoking a cigar as if he didn't have a care in the world, he sat in the saddle like a pompous member of royalty. His clothes appeared new; fold creases were evident in his cotton shirt and dark, stiff-looking Levi's. Seeing him again spawned a fresh wave of revulsion and brought back the memory of her recent encounter with Snake.

Lance's eyes grew cold with contempt. Sonnie sensed his impatience, his need to take care of unfinished business.

"I'll get Papa admitted and settled in his room," she said.

He hesitated, clearly remembering what had happened in Silver Meadow.

"I'll be fine," she said, understanding. "I'll see you at the hotel later this afternoon."

"All right." He nodded curtly and swept his glance over his men. "Cookie. Jake. Stay with her until she's ready to leave her father, then get her checked in at the Railroad Hotel. Wait there. The rest of you, come with me."

In sudden trepidation of what might lay ahead for him, Sonnie reached out her hand and caught his. A run-in with Ditson would only bode ill. "Be careful, Lance."

He gave her a slow grin, one that was a little wild, a little reckless, but very sexy.

"I will, Son."

He squeezed her fingers in farewell, then mounted his sorrel. Taking the lead, he guided the men down Evans Street in Clay Ditson's wake.

From the stagecoach's box, Cookie jumped to the ground, then stretched his legs and arched his back.

"They're gonna be gone a spell. Reckon someone in that there fancy hospital has a cup of black coffee fer an ol' cowboy like me?"

"I imagine they would," she said, her gaze clinging to Lance's retreating back. She tugged it away and forced a smile for Cookie's benefit. "I'd like one myself."

"Hey, Jake," he called to the younger man still on his horse. "Wanna join us?"

"Nope." Jake tucked a wad of tobacco inside his lower lip. "Gonna stay out here with the rig."

"Suit yerself." Cookie shuffled closer to Sonnie. "Dadburned kid has an attitude problem," he muttered in a disgusted whisper. "A right poor outlook on life."

"He's still sulking from Lance's punishment, I think," she said, but her thoughts followed a different course. "Cookie, who is Gracie?"

He appeared taken aback. "Gracie Purcell?"

"Is she . . . associated with Lance?"

He nodded. "Has been fer a long time now. She's got her own place in town. An eatery."

"Oh." Sonnie's spirits fell. She'd always held great admiration for independent women who ran business establishments. She straightened, tilting her nose a little higher. "Is she beautiful?"

He rested a scuffed boot on the bottom step. "She works at it."

"I see."

"Lance takin' her to the Club with y'all?" Though he asked the question, he seemed to already know the answer.

"Yes."

"Well, I wouldn't feel left out 'bout it, Miss Sonnie," he soothed, patting her shoulder. "Lance isn't a womanizer. He pretty much stays away from 'em all. You and Gracie are nigh the only ones he cares fer, and I'd reckon ye're at the top of his list."

Despite his comforting words, Sonnie didn't believe a single one. She couldn't compete with someone who'd known Lance much longer, who held his affection, who was mature and respectable and knew life in the West far better than she.

Sonnie regretted the long years in Boston more than ever. True, there'd been her studies. Luxuries and travel. She'd met important people, attended extravagant parties, owned expensive clothes, things Gracie Purcell most likely would never do or have.

But regardless of all that, Gracie held the advantage.

While Sonnie was gone, Gracie had had Lance.

Cheyenne's stockyards abounded with the cacophony of bellowing steers, squealing pigs, and bleating sheep, creating an atmosphere appropriate only for a parcel of land situated outside city limits. The noise blended with the stench of manure. Endless pens, loading chutes, and low-roofed sheds crisscrossed the sprawling yards.

Cattlemen milled everywhere. Some intended to increase the size of their herds or improve their breeding stock; others planned to sell by cashing in on years of hard work and walking away with the profits.

As Clay Ditson intended to do. Only he hadn't worked worth a damn. And the profits weren't his to spend.

Lance flung aside his third cigarette in disgust and shifted his position on the pen rail. He was tired of waiting, and it was getting late.

After leaving County Hospital, he and his men followed Ditson at a discreet distance, then were forced to sit while he went into Sadler's Dry Goods to buy the most god-awful hat any of them had ever seen. It was already eye-blinding in a brilliant shade of green; then he added an oversize peacock feather to the hatband, and the effect sent them all tumbling into fits of suppressed laughter.

Ditson continued to meander through the city toward the stockyards, the outrageous hat making him an easy target to follow. Not realizing he was being trailed, he appeared to keep an appointment with another cattleman. Lance guessed him to be a foreigner, of English descent judging by his prim suit and jaunty bowler, and totally unaware Ditson attempted to sell him rustled stock.

Mancuso stock.

Lance immediately recognized the fatted Hereford steers and cows in the pen, and though he longed to strangle Ditson for the crime, he held back. He'd make his move when Ditson was ready to cinch the sale; a stay in jail would proclaim the message that Lance had had enough. Though Vince had little faith in the judicial system, Lance believed laws were made for a reason—to be enforced—and he vowed to see Clay Ditson and Snake prosecuted to the fullest extent possible.

"We've been waitin' a long time now, Lance. I got things I gotta be doin'."

Lance glanced over at Wayne Hitchler, Cheyenne's police chief for the past six years. Experienced and dedicated, he was the key to stopping Ditson, and he'd passed the time as patiently as the rest of them. Until now.

"Hang on, Wayne. Just a little longer."

"Lance." The policeman cleared his throat and peered over the length of pens catawampus from where Ditson and the Englishman conducted their business. "I know how rustlin' raises your hackles, just like it does every cowman in the country. But the truth of the matter is—"

"There they go." Lance's eye narrowed as the two men left the penned cattle behind. "Fan out, boys.

Surround 'em. Don't let Ditson make a run for it when he sees we're after him."

Charlie and Stick paired off in one direction; Red Holmes and Frank Burton sprinted in the other. Lance, with Wayne in tow, took a more direct course and reached the cashier's office first.

Ditson looked inordinately pleased with himself. He draped an arm about the Englishman's stiff shoulders, chattering and cackling as if they were the best of friends. He seemed eager to square the deal with his unsuspecting buyer, and he walked a little faster as they drew closer to the office.

"Get the price you wanted, Clay?"

A smile froze on his weasel-like face. Ditson yanked his arm back at the sight of Lance leaning casually against the door. Beads of sweat popped out on his forehead beneath the green cowboy hat's brim. He caught sight of the other Mancuso men moving closer, their feet spread, fists ready.

He snarled a curse. "What the hell do you want, Harmon?"

"I want my cattle back."

"Your cattle? I ain't got none of your damn cattle."

"Don't you?"

"Hell, no."

"You lying son of a bitch." Lance shook his head as Ditson persisted with the sham, even with Police Chief Hitchler listening in.

"The cattle I'm sellin' to the baron here are my own. Anyone can check the brand and see they are."

"That's right, by Jove," the Englishman piped up, his bespectacled eyes wide with outrage. "Registered Circle Double Diamond. I saw it myself." He puffed his chest and assumed a dignified air. "I'm afraid you've made a mistake, sir."

"No," Lance said softly. "No mistake."

"You got proof I stole your stinkin' cattle, Harmon?" demanded Ditson.

"Yeah, I do."

The beads on his forehead grew bigger. "What're you gonna do? Kill them fine animals just to look 'neath the hide?"

"Don't have to."

"What, then?" The question rolled off his tongue; he appeared unnerved from Lance's confidence and the lawman's stern-jawed presence. "I don't have to listen to his false accusations, Wayne," he whined, trying a new tactic. "Charge him with slander against my good name."

"He's got a right to speak his piece, Mr. Ditson, just like you got a right to speak yours."

"I'll give him his proof," Lance said.

He stepped forward and gripped a handful of Ditson's new shirt. A swift shove sent him stumbling back in the direction of the stock pens.

Grim-faced, everyone followed, including the sputtering Englishman who was all but ignored. Lance climbed over the top railing and jumped into the pen housing the Mancuso Herefords. Walking among the animals, he searched for those he'd marked in Silver Meadow.

They were there, each of them. Choosing the cow with an oval-shaped white marking around her eye, Lance led her toward the edge of the pen. While everyone watched, he laid his hand along the back of her broad neck and groped along the hide. Within moments, he'd worked free the hidden half-dollar coin.

Ditson paled.

The Englishman appeared perplexed.

Triumphant, Lance held the coin up for everyone to see.

"Here's proof," he said. "I planted these coins when the herd was on our range."

"Ain't good enough." Ditson scowled. "You coulda planted 'em anytime, anyplace."

Police Chief Hitchler shuffled his feet in the dirt and looked away.

Lance sensed the arrest sliding through his fingers.

In growing desperation, he climbed out of the pen and grabbed a stick from the ground. With brisk strokes, he etched the Rocking M brand into the dirt.

"See, Wayne? One little running iron, and"—his stick scratched the dirt again—"the Rocking M becomes the Circle Double Diamond."

"I believe you, Lance. Honestly, I do." The police chief sighed heavily. "The coins are damned good proof. And I'd reckon if we'd pull back the hides on every one of them cattle, we're gonna find your brand on the inside. But the fact is—" He halted and stared sadly into the sky.

"Is what?" Lance said in a growl, already knowing the answer.

"Fact is you ain't gonna get a jury to convict him."

Rumbles of disbelief went through his men. A relieved grin inched its way across Ditson's homely features, and Lance's fist tightened over the makeshift pencil.

"Why the hell not?"

"Them juries are packed with nesters and rustlers, that's why. They'd all build their spreads and their herds same way as this lowlife is tryin' to do. They're gonna be on his side. They're all against you big cattlemen. They see you as the enemy against the little man."

Lance hurled the stick into the distance and swore.

"It ain't fair, I know." Hitchler's sympathy seemed genuine. "But that's the way it is. Press charges if you want, but I seen it happen too many times not to know what I'm talking about."

Lance's mouth opened to protest, to voice another plan of action, but the lawman held up a hand.

"An expensive lawyer ain't gonna do no good, either," he declared, taking the very words from Lance's mouth. "The best-run prosecution ain't worth a damn if you ain't got a good jury, and them are nigh impossible to find around here."

"Don't expect me to lie down and play dead on this, Wayne," Lance said. "I'm not going to let the bastard go about his business and sell Mancuso beef to some prissy-pants foreigner!"

The Englishman gasped at the insult, but said nothing, the abrupt turn of events evidently too confusing to comprehend.

"I don't expect nothin' of the sort, Lance." The lawman lifted his hat and scratched his head. "Not much I can do for you, but if you want me to throw him in jail, I will, at least till he posts bond. That'll give you and your men some time to trail your herd back to their own range. Leastways, you won't be losing any more money or beef."

Lance thought of Snake and his successful attempt to stalk Sonnie, to frighten her. But the Indian wouldn't stop there. Lance dreaded the lengths he and Ditson would go to in order to hurt her, to get back at him and Vince, to tear down the Mancuso kingdom. How far would they go?

Not far, he vowed. *Not very damn far.*

"All right, Wayne." Years of friendship and a history of fairness convinced Lance the lawman wasn't trying to lead him astray. "Throw this stinkin' piece of shit in a cell and keep him out of my sight."

The police chief planted a firm hand around Ditson's arm and began to pull him away.

Disdain contorted the rustler's features. He glared

at Lance over his shoulder. "Jail ain't gonna keep me from gettin' what I want, Harmon. I'll be out in no time."

His words rang in Lance's ears as Wayne led him away. He set his hands on his hips and glared at their retreating backs while wrestling with his lingering fury.

"Ahem. I do believe my apology is in order." The Englishman's nasal voice drew Lance's cool gaze. "I hadn't the foggiest Mr. Ditson wasn't a legitimate cattleman. If I had, I wouldn't have tried to buy his bloody cattle. Er, *your* bloody cattle."

"Wasn't your fault," he said curtly, giving Ditson one final look before he disappeared from sight.

"Fine stock, though. You wouldn't be interested in selling—"

"No."

"Very well, then." Straight-backed and formal, and obviously reluctant to test Lance's patience further, the Englishman dropped the issue without further ado. "Again, sir. My apologies."

"Accepted."

"Good day."

It'd been a damned *lousy* day, and Lance stubbornly refused to say it was any better than that. He had neither the time nor the desire to engage in conversation with the man, and taking his silence as a wise hint to leave posthaste, the foreigner spun on his expensive-looking boot heel and left.

Frustration registered on his men's faces, and Lance drew comfort from their loyalty. He removed his hat and raked his hand through his hair.

"Who wants to drive the herd back to Mancuso range?" he asked grimly.

Red Holmes and Frank Burton volunteered, and Lance gave them his thanks along with a few last-minute orders. They departed, and with Stick and

Charlie at his side, he made his way through the yards back to his sorrel.

"Can I buy you a beer, boss?" Charlie asked, squeezing Lance's shoulder in mute compassion.

"Or two?" Stick offered tentatively.

"Sounds good, but no." He thought of the envelope he carried in his pocket and the visit he had had no time to make to the ranch's attorney. And even more pressing, he had to stop at Gracie's. "Too much to do before tonight's meeting. I'll take a rain check, though."

"Okay."

The two cowboys left Lance to himself. Though he knew he had to put Clay Ditson from his mind, Wayne Hitchler's words troubled him.

Vince was right. The courts were useless to the Rocking M, and they were on their own in fighting their land and stock losses. With Vince detained at the hospital, Lance had to man the fight alone. He had to change tactics, and, he reluctantly admitted, those tactics would have to include Tom Horn.

And Sonnie.

Thinking of her warmed his loins and softened his keen disappointment from Ditson's failed arrest. He would be with her soon. Anticipation swirled through him, and his steps quickened.

He spared a glance toward the sun and figured the hour.

He'd damn well better hurry, or he'd be late.

Chapter Twelve

She was even more beautiful than he remembered.

Like a delicate Wyoming wildflower kissed by the sun, Sonnie had blossomed into full womanhood, a breathtaking creation of femininity and allure who conquered his heart and sent his blood humming through his veins.

Her first trip back from the East brought her home for Christmas, but she would stay only a short time. A holiday party filled the Big House, and adoring Mancuso cowboys competed for her smile, her touch. From across the crowded room, Lance riveted his gaze to the fluid, swaying motions of her body as she danced with every man in her father's outfit.

Everyone but him.

It mattered little that she hadn't noticed him. He took refuge in the sea of cowboy hats and masculine faces, content to watch her from afar. He hadn't even spoken to her. Until now he'd stayed away.

Yet she drew him. Something beckoned him to her,

a persistent, silent call to stand near her, to study and savor her. The strength of his need baffled him. He doubted she'd ever looked him full in the face.

Her laughter sweetened the air after the music stopped. She turned and, with the grace of an angel, glided toward him. His pulse pounded harder, then harder still, drowning out the voices around him. A rushing sensation erupted inside his head, and he cursed his vulnerability, his weakness, his cowardice.

Hawthorne did this to him, scourged him with this fear so long ago in that decaying slum tenement. Gradually, so gradually he'd hardly noticed, he'd built an unbreachable wall around his heart. He allowed no woman access. As a man, his power to hurt terrified him. Only by staying away could he prevent the pain.

She halted at Vince's elbow instead. Her features radiant, she stroked his cheek and gently led him to the dance floor. She hadn't once glanced at Lance.

The roar inside him faded, calmed, disappeared. Shaken by his reaction to her nearness, he stood frozen for long moments.

Even as she waltzed with her father, she lured Lance in a mute invitation no one else would comprehend. He succumbed to the insatiable thirst and drank in the sight of her, storing the delectable memories inside him to last through the endless months until he would see her again.

All too soon she would leave the Rocking M, board another train, and make the long, tedious trip back to Boston.

And he would wait for as long as he must. The knowledge rocked him almost as much as did the dawning of a strange, new truth.

Maybe it had taken years. Maybe only seconds. But somehow he'd fallen in love with Sonnie Mancuso.

* * *

A late-afternoon breeze swept inward from the second-story window and cooled the air inside the small hotel room. For the hundredth time, Sonnie strode to the door, peered into the hall, and listened for the tread of Lance's bootstep.

Hearing nothing, seeing nothing, she sighed in disappointment and closed it again. A shiver took her, one fraught with worry.

Where could he be? She feared Ditson brewed up new trouble for him, and her imagination ran rampant with visions of fistfights and gunfire and puddles of spilled blood.

God forbid. She closed the window, paced the confines of her room, retraced her steps back and forth around the sturdy, serviceable furniture, and squelched the horrid thoughts. She refused to think of Lance being hurt. He was far too strong and much too smart to fall victim to a weasel of a man like Clay Ditson.

Then where was he?

She chewed on her bottom lip and confronted the notion that had persisted in the back of her mind all afternoon.

He could only be with Gracie.

The certainty left a leaden lump in the pit of her stomach. Obviously he enjoyed the woman's company so much that the lateness of the hour escaped him. He took his responsibilities to the Rocking M seriously, that Sonnie knew, but as the minutes ticked away, she couldn't help but believe Gracie Purcell must be quite a lady to keep him from them.

She fancied the two together, perhaps sharing a meal in her eatery, conversing quietly, or lingering over a drink. Or did they slip away to someplace private, where Lance would take her in his long, sinewy arms and nuzzle his jaw into her hair, ply her with gentle kisses until passion carried them away?

A groan of dismay escaped Sonnie's lips; her gaze darted to the bed positioned against a far wall. She would not think of them in that vein.

She would not.

Not when Lance kept his distance and refrained from touching *her* except in the rarest of circumstances. And she certainly would not think of him kissing Gracie the way he'd kissed her the night he'd slung her over his shoulder and stormed from the bunkhouse.

No, she couldn't bear it.

Suddenly restless, Sonnie paced again. How would she endure the evening with this unfamiliar woman, knowing she held a special place in Lance's heart? How could she compete with Gracie's maturity and her years of friendship with him?

Her pacing halted in front of the dresser mirror. After getting Papa comfortable in his hospital room, Cookie had stayed behind to engage him in a quiet game of checkers. Jake took Sonnie and the mounds of baggage to the Railroad Hotel, and they reserved rooms for her and the other Mancuso men. Thus she had the majority of the afternoon to bathe and dress for the important meeting. Her mouth pursed in a pensive moue, and she studied herself in the glass.

Had she dressed well enough to compare to Gracie? Her gown, of rose-shaded brocade and mousseline de sole, draped her body to the Parisienne seamstress's pleasure and Sonnie's own satisfaction, and a pleated underskirt, featuring embroidered floral bouquets along the right side from waist to hem, brushed her ankles. The square-cut bodice hugged her breasts and plumped them upward to reveal a teasing glimpse of décolletage. Dainty puckered sleeves covered the unsightly scratch on her arm, and as she fluffed them up over the curve of her shoulders, she assured herself that, outwardly at least, she could match Gracie inch for inch.

A knock sounded on the door, and Sonnie glanced at the dresser's clock. The hands read exactly seven, the time she was to leave for the Cheyenne Club. Hoping to see Lance on the other side, she hurried to the door and flung it open wide.

The hotel proprietor's wife stood patiently in the hall, and Sonnie's spirits plummeted.

"Miss Mancuso," the older woman said. "A Mr. Horn is waiting downstairs. He says he has an appointment with you."

"Oh, dear." Sonnie regretted the gunfighter's promptness. Evidently being tardy wasn't included on his list of vices. Regardless, she couldn't leave not knowing Lance's whereabouts.

"I'm afraid I'm not quite ready for Mr. Horn's company," she said. "Serve him a drink, won't you, and make my excuses to him? I'll try not to be long."

"Yes, ma'am."

She stepped away, but Sonnie caught her arm. "By the way, could you tell me"—she hesitated—"has Lance Harmon sent word? I've been expecting him."

"Lance?" She smiled. "He stays with us often. I'm sorry. We've heard nothing."

After the woman returned downstairs, Sonnie leaned against the closed door and released a frustrated sigh. One by one the minutes dragged. What if Lance was in his room after all? She plucked a key from the dresser top and strode from her room to his. With no answer to her knock, she endured a pang of disappointment and went in.

Earlier she'd taken the liberty of unpacking his bag and removing his suit. After steaming the wrinkles from his black worsted jacket and pants, she had laid them neatly upon the bed, then touched up the starch in his shirt. Afterward, she had ordered a tub of hot water brought up for his private bath.

The water had long since cooled. Her gown's brocade train rustled softly against the carpet near the bed. Filled with thoughts of him, she trailed her fingers along the rich woven fabric of his suit jacket.

She was accustomed to seeing him only in Levi's and cotton work shirts. Her mind formed a vision of him in the elegant evening wear and sent her heart thumping against her breast.

He would be . . . devastating.

The door hinge creaked, and Sonnie turned in expectant surprise. Seeing her in his room, Lance halted, one hand still on the doorknob.

He looked in good health, no worse for the wear for his late return, Sonnie thought in relief. Only a concentrated effort kept her from running across the room and flinging her arms about his neck.

"Lance! I've been worried. Where have you been?" she demanded in a breathless rush.

"It's a long story." He sagged against the jamb and hooked a thumb into his waistband. His gaze roamed the room, dwelled briefly on the large metal tub and the clothing spread on the bed, then drifted leisurely over her from head to toe.

A crooked grin crept across his lips. "Ah, Sonnie. You are a sight for sore eyes."

She was uncertain whether he meant to compliment her appearance or if his afternoon had been so harrowing, he was truly glad to see her.

She extended her arm and beckoned him inside. "You must hurry. Mr. Horn is here and has already called for me."

He straightened and pulled the door shut behind him.

"Let him wait." He tossed his hat into a nearby chair.

Her gaze riveted to Lance unbuttoning his shirt. Corded, bronzed flesh appeared beneath the parted fabric. He pulled the shirt free from his waistband.

Her pulse tip-tapped.

"I've readied a bath for you," she said, needing to explain her presence in his room.

"I noticed." He shucked the cotton garment and hurled it onto the chair with his hat. "Thanks."

Muscles rolled and tumbled over his back and shoulders. Sonnie stared, finding it increasingly difficult to breathe around the odd tightening in her throat.

He reached for the top button of the Levi's, and, knowing he intended to remove those as well, she sucked in a sudden breath.

"You won't enjoy a bath in cold water," she said, moving toward the door. "I'll get a maid—"

"Don't bother." His hand curled around her upper arm when she would have passed him. Her gaze flew upward to his.

The air sizzled with incandescent awareness. His touch ignited a spiral of budding warmth deep inside her.

"I could get used to this, you know," he murmured, the whiskey-shaded depths of his eyes darkening to a smoldering hue. "Having a beautiful woman waiting at the end of the day, ready to take care of me." A corner of his mouth lifted, as if he were reluctant to make the admission. "I like having you here with me, Sonnie."

She liked it, too, more and more with every ticking second. The pleasurable feel of his work-roughened palm upon her bare skin stole a proper reply. His scent surrounded her, a masculine scent of horse and leather and tobacco.

And a woman's perfume.

Her lashes lowered, her chin lifted, and she pulled

away. He'd been with Gracie, after all. The certainty stung.

"I only hoped to save you the time of doing it yourself," she said, keeping her back to him as he stepped away. "I had no inkling when you'd return."

"Ditson held me up. The bastard."

The mattress springs squeaked. The bootjack thudded upon the floor. Preferring his explanation of the afternoon's events to thoughts of Gracie, she turned around again.

"What happened?"

He tugged off each boot, peeled away his woolen socks, and launched into a clipped explanation of the failed arrest despite the proof he offered to Police Chief Hitchler. Frustration laced his words and drew her instant sympathy.

"You did all you could, Lance. This same case would have brought a swift conviction in Boston." She lifted a shoulder helplessly. "It's just different out here in the West."

"A law is a law, Sonnie." He rose from the bed. "No matter which part of the country it's made for."

He undid the rest of the buttons of his Levi's, and her eyes widened at his disregard of his own modesty.

She abandoned the conversation, spun, and faced the wall to preserve it for him.

"You are far too bold, Lance Harmon!" she exclaimed in exasperation, and recognized the sound of denim dropping to the floor. "Stripping down buck naked in front of a lady is *not* the behavior of a gentleman!"

His mirth encircled her.

"I reckon if a lady is in a man's hotel room when he's dirty and hard-pressed for time, she wouldn't mind if he used the bath she's readied for him."

"Oh!" Words failed her. Her cheeks flamed. His playful retort hit its mark.

From behind her, the water lapped and splashed against the sides of the tub.

"Damn!" He hissed a swift breath inward.

"I warned you it would be cold." Her lofty declaration softened her embarrassment and carried a vein of amusement to match his.

She dared a peek in his direction. He sat in the water, his knees propped against the sides of the tub.

He glanced at her wryly. "Since you find this bath of mine so funny, maybe you'd like to get in and help me warm the water?"

Her heart thundered at his implication. She couldn't recall his speaking to her with such intimacy before. This provocative side of him quite unsettled her.

"There isn't room for both of us, and you are out of line in making the suggestion, Boss-man," she said with a toss of her coiffed head. "I'd best leave while my honor is intact."

He chuckled heartily, filling the air with the pleasant sound.

"Come on, Sonnie. Don't go gettin' uppity on me. Stay and tell me about Vince."

She should leave. She truly considered it. Her staying in his hotel room would have thrown Aunt Josephine into a dead faint. Papa would've blasted her with a scolding and a fierce frown of displeasure.

But she could think of no man she'd be safer with than Lance. Or whose company she'd enjoy more.

She stayed. While he made short work of his bath and hair washing, she kept her gaze primly averted and busied herself at his dresser mixing shaving soap and water, laying out his razor, tooth powder, and brush.

She told him of getting her father checked into County Hospital and the care Doc Tanner intended to give him, the tests he'd make and the medications needed to treat the pneumonia. Lance listened, asking questions now and again.

Afterward he left the tub, dried himself, and padded barefoot to pause at her side. Their conversation ceased. Of its own accord, her gaze found the droplets of water lingering about his shoulders and chest and the areas he'd missed with the towel. His hair was tousled and wet. He smelled of freshness and soap.

Her pulse pattered a fast beat. She dropped her gaze even lower.

The scrap of linen he'd wrapped about his lean waist failed to hide the bulge marking his blatant masculinity. He wore nothing beneath, and the knowledge rocked her restraint. She knew a sudden, bold desire to pluck the towel from his body and give in to her virginal curiosity.

She took a step back and nearly stumbled on the brocade train. She couldn't trust herself to keep from touching him in places she must not.

"Mr. Horn probably thinks I've deserted him. I've not yet finished my toilette, you see, so I really should return to my room now and . . . finish."

His tawny brow quirked at her sudden move to leave.

"I'll join you there in a few minutes," he said. "We'll go downstairs together."

Managing to nod in agreement, she left. Once she was inside her own quarters, a ragged sigh escaped her, and she strove to mend her tattered wits.

A full half hour later, Lance knocked upon her door. She bade him enter, and at the sight of him, her new-found poise evaporated in a poof.

The worsted suit fit him with a tailor's perfection, its black fabric and weave accenting his height and lean build. Beneath the vest, the white shirt looked crisp and stark against his tanned throat, and Sonnie feared that the evening would be far longer than she ever anticipated.

"Ready?" he asked, approaching with the agile grace so much a part of him. Indeed, the man was a pleasure to see in motion.

In his haste, he'd formed an uneven bow in the suit's narrow black tie.

"Here," she said, moving closer to pull it loose. "Let me fix this for you." He stood perfectly still, keeping his chin tilted high to allow her access. Her fingers worked nimbly to reshape the bow, and she eyed the end result with satisfaction. "There. Much better."

He gazed down at her with a burning intensity that held her frozen. The bay rum cologne upon his just-shaved skin swirled about her senses and restoked the desire she thought she'd banked. She longed to touch him, to run her fingers through his damp hair. She wanted to kiss him and feel him hold her tight against the rock-hard warmth of his chest.

But that was foolish. And there was no time.

"We have to go," she said, her voice whisper-soft between them. "Mr. Horn is waiting."

"Yeah." Slowly, reluctantly, he nodded.

He wanted to stay, too. He longed for the same things she did. She knew it as surely as if he'd spoken the words aloud.

He stepped away from her. "Gracie's waiting, too."

An ironic arrangement for the evening, Sonnie thought. Tonight she would be with Mr. Horn. Tonight Lance would be with Gracie.

It was a disappointingly ironic arrangement.

The gunfighter was not pleased with their tardiness.

In the hotel dining room, which was gaudy with mounted buffalo and mountain sheep heads, Sonnie used her brightest smile to coax away his irritation.

Lance offered a cool apology, took full blame, and

ordered the proprietor to charge all Horn's drinks to the Rocking M's bill. The gesture soothed his ire, and they left the Railroad Hotel to pick up Gracie with the air cleared between them.

Cookie drove the stagecoach, and Horn staked his place on the tufted leather seat beside Sonnie, leaving Lance to occupy the opposite seat by himself. Under different circumstances, the man's stubborn possessiveness would have forced Sonnie to keep a haughty distance, but this time she made an exception.

She had to, for Papa's sake.

She allowed him to put his arm about her shoulders and hold her hand, did not object when he leaned close and murmured suggestively in her ear. She did not pull away when his liquor-tainted breath stroked her cheek and neck.

Because Papa had asked her to. Because Papa needed her help. Because he needed Tom Horn, as much as the Rocking M needed him.

But, during the ride to Gracie's house, she knew Lance's displeasure, sensed his shadowed disapproval. He didn't like the part she played any better than she did herself.

Therefore she kept her eyes averted from him. It was easier that way.

O'Neil Street ran along Union Pacific's railroad tracks and delved into one of the poorer neighborhoods in Cheyenne. The elegant stagecoach seemed out of place among the shabby homes and scruffy lawns. Mongrel dogs raced beside the gold-trimmed wheels and barked their curiosity.

Cookie pulled up in front of a tiny house on the corner. Flower boxes along the two front windows provided color against the whitewashed siding. A fat tomcat sprawled on the top step of the miniature porch. The home's tidiness suggested to Sonnie that

Gracie, despite meager finances, worked hard to maintain a respectable appearance.

At their arrival, a curtain lifted at the window, then dropped back into place. Lance dismounted from the coach and strode toward the house. The tomcat scurried from his perch, and, without knocking, Lance went inside.

Sonnie glanced away on a surge of dismay. He needed no invitation. He entered Gracie's home as easily as he entered the Big House.

Their relationship stirred a boiling pot of questions she longed to have answered. He was certainly entitled to Gracie's company, she assured herself. They were friends, had been for a long time. It was perfectly understandable that he'd be comfortable enough to go into her house without a proper knock.

But how deep did their friendship go?

How intimate was it?

Lance emerged with Gracie on his arm. He assisted her into the rig, then eased his long frame into the empty leather seat beside her.

At once, the coach filled with her flowery perfume, the same scent Sonnie had noticed on Lance at the hotel. He made introductions, and Gracie, her red-lipped smile wide and appealing, reached over and shook the gunfighter's hand first.

"Glad to meet you, Tom," she said, slipping into the familiarity of using his first name immediately. "I hear you can pack a mean gun when you set your mind to it."

Sonnie's eyes widened at her forward way of speaking.

Mr. Horn laughed outright and held her hand longer than was necessary.

"My reputation precedes me, I see." He tossed an ambivalent glance toward Lance. "Or has Harmon been talking me up to you?"

She pulled away and gave Lance a playful nudge. "Lance never tells me nothin' he thinks I don't need to know. I have an eatery in town, and I hear all about the rustlin' problem from my customers. There's some that's hopin' you'll help the cattlemen."

He shrugged, his expression vague. "Not sure yet. I'll decide tonight."

Gracie turned toward Sonnie. For the first time, Sonnie realized the woman was older than she'd assumed. Face powder and rouge accented the beauty lingering from her younger days. Gracie Purcell could hold her own with any man, and Sonnie could easily see her being a friend of Lance's.

"Miss Mancuso." The greeting unexpectedly formal, Gracie thrust a chapped, stubby-nailed hand toward her, and beneath Sonnie's gloved one, it had a slight tremble.

Gracie was nervous, and Sonnie knew she was the cause.

"Please call me Sonnie," she said softly, hoping to put her at ease.

"Been wantin' to meet you for some time now," Gracie said, pulling her hand away and clutching her fringed, crocheted shawl snugly about her generous bosom. "The boys from your pa's outfit talk about you with real reverence. So does Lance."

Sonnie's glance slipped toward him. She wanted to ask Gracie everything he'd ever said about her.

He leaned back in the corner of the coach, his long arm resting on the seat behind Gracie's dark brown head. His brow rose at her questioning look.

"You're too kind," she murmured, returning her attention to the other woman. "I've been gone and—"

"I know. But that don't stop 'em from talkin' about you."

"I see."

A tight silence followed. Sonnie doubted Gracie

223

had ever lacked for conversation until now, and she felt responsible. They had nothing in common—with the exception of Lance—and Sonnie's mind groped for a topic to talk about, but failed.

Mr. Horn dipped his head close to hers and indicated something outside the stagecoach's window. His query forced her to concentrate on a suitable, flirtatious reply, allowed her to ignore how Gracie sidled next to Lance in what could only be described as a snuggle, and immerse herself in quiet conversation with him, but it could not help her forget that she would much rather trade places and snuggle next to him herself.

And, most startling, with every turn of the stagecoach's wheels as they made their way to the exclusive Cheyenne Club, Tom Horn and Gracie Purcell made Sonnie realize she had fallen in love with Lance Harmon.

Chapter Thirteen

Lance had often thought the prestigious Cheyenne Club should be located somewhere more affluent than the dusty, curbless corner of Seventeenth and Dodge. Unmindful of the ungraded streets and less pompous buildings surrounding it, the two-story clubhouse presided in regal splendor and offered an oasis of opulence, companionable pleasure, and dining in a Western frontier desert. Men of prominence paid lofty entrance fees and annual dues to have their expensive tastes satisfied, and they lingered long and often within its walls to be entertained and pampered in high style.

Though he found equal comfort with a bedroll in front of a campfire, Lance enjoyed going as much as anyone. The luxurious atmosphere provided a change of pace from the rigors of cattle season, and when not staying at the humbler Railroad Hotel, he took one of the sleeping rooms provided especially for members. Many times Vince and he had conducted lucrative ranch business with a glass of Rum St. Cruz in one hand and a Reina Victoria cigar in the other.

The stagecoach drew up alongside sleek landaus and broughams, and parked. Through the window, Sonnie stared at the handsome redbrick structure with its numerous chimneys, mansard roof, and tower.

"So this is the Cheyenne Club," she said softly.

Lance had to smile at her awe. She must have frequented resorts of the same caliber during her worldly travels, and having been a part of the Club since its beginning, he felt ridiculously pleased that she found this one just as impressive.

"There's nothing like it for miles," he said.

"I've never been inside," said Gracie, adding her gaze to Sonnie's. "I've always wanted to rub shoulders with rich society people. Now here's my chance."

"So what are we waiting for?"

With a flourish, Horn opened the door and stepped down, lending assistance to both women.

"What time do you want me to come fer y'all?" asked Cookie, peering down at them from his perch on the box.

"Make it eleven," Lance replied, the last to leave the coach. He tugged on the cuff of his shirtsleeve. "The meeting and dinner should be finished by then."

"Okay, boss. See you later."

The old cowboy caught Sonnie's eye and gave her an encouraging wink. Her glance skittered toward Gracie before touching upon Lance; then she looked away.

Lance wondered at their exchange. Horn took her elbow and led her toward the wide stairwell leading to the clubhouse entrance. Lance bristled at the gunfighter's claim upon her as well as Sonnie's calm acceptance of it.

226

From within the confines of the stagecoach, he'd been forced to watch them together. He knew her intent, her need to please her father, but how far would she let the man go?

And who the hell did Horn think he was that he treated her with the same familiarity as a lover?

One overly bold move on Horn's part would give Lance swift cause for a well-deserved punch. He'd deliver it with pleasure, and he didn't give a damn what Vince wanted.

Gracie tugged on his arm and pulled him out of his resentment. He realized Sonnie and Horn waited on the veranda; he fell into step with Gracie to join them.

"She's more beautiful than I thought she'd be," Gracie declared quietly as they climbed. "She makes me feel like an old spinster."

Lance saw Horn bend close and adjust the diamond-and-pearl ornament in Sonnie's hair. She laughed softly at something he said, and Lance's jaw tightened.

"You mean Sonnie?" He tried to remember what Gracie was talking about.

"Yes, I mean Sonnie." Exasperation flitted across her powdered face. "If you'd quit gawking at her long enough, you'd understand."

"Sorry." His hand covered hers in apology.

"Ever since you called for me, you've hardly taken your eyes off her."

"I worry about her with Horn."

"He's been a perfect gentleman," she defended.

"He's not in her league. He'll try anything."

They reached the veranda, and Gracie snorted a disagreement but made no further comment.

"Shall we go inside?" Sonnie asked.

A cool smile tarried on her full lips. Her glance dropped to where his hand rested over Gracie's. He heard the vague challenge in her too-polite query and pulled his hand away.

But before he could reply, Gracie stopped dead in her tracks.

"I can't go in there."

The three of them turned toward her in surprise.

"Look at the ladies," she said with a hint of alarm, indicating the well-heeled couples milling about. "They're dressed like queens. I'll never fit in." She appealed to Lance. "I can't go inside. I can't."

"Oh, Gracie," Sonnie murmured, moving closer. "You look lovely. Nobody will think—"

"Yes, they will." She wouldn't budge. "I won't know what to do or say. My dress is old, and I'm not near as fancy as you. I'm not wearin' diamonds or furs or even a stupid pair of gloves."

"Take mine then." Setting her satchel on the veranda floor and tucking her tiny beaded purse under one arm, Sonnie began tugging off the ivory leather gloves finger by finger. "They'll make you feel elegant. And look, all the ladies are wearing them."

"Oh, but I couldn't." Gracie's eyes were wide as saucers.

"I want you to keep them, truly. I have a dozen more pairs at home."

"Miss Sonnie . . ." Her voice trailed off in indecision.

Sonnie resolutely pried Gracie's hands from their tight grip on her shawl.

"I'll help you put them on. See? They fit you nicely."

"I've never had a pair that go clear past my elbows before."

"And they match the lace on your dress. Your shawl, too. They're perfect."

"Miss Sonnie." Gracie was at a rare loss for words. "Oh, Miss Sonnie. Thank you."

"You're quite welcome." Sonnie seemed pleased with herself. "Don't worry about how to act. Just watch me, and you'll be fine."

"I will." She drew a big breath. "I guess I'm ready now." Flashing a confident smile, she proceeded ahead of them. Horn hastened to open the doors, and the pair disappeared into the main hall.

"You've made a friend for life." A soft scent of carnations drifted up to Lance's nose. He longed to nuzzle her close and breathe her perfume forever.

She shrugged and picked up her satchel. "I think she was a little afraid of me at first. Maybe now she won't be." Her dark eyes considered him a moment. "Will you be nice to Mr. Horn tonight, Lance?"

His brow quirked. "Nice?"

"Civil," she amended. "Engage in a normal conversation with him. The two of you hardly spoke the entire time we were in the stagecoach."

He'd make no promises. "I wish you didn't have to be with him tonight."

Her glance flitted away. "And I wish you didn't have to be with Gracie."

His heart skipped a beat. The admission caught him off guard. She sounded jealous.

His grin must have looked downright smug, but there was no help for it. Gently he took her warm fingers and settled them in the crook of his arm. Feeling damned satisfied, he escorted her into the club-house.

A skylight breathed dusky illumination into the main hall, which was already brightened by glowing chandeliers. Thick carpets lined the foyer and two additional stairways that connected to a grand piazza graced with stunning Victorian French windows. Women in ball gowns and men in dress suits, many of whom carried drinks dispensed from silver trays

229

by efficient waiters, filled the dining room or strolled about the piazza.

Sonnie murmured her pleasure at the scene. Lance paused and let her take it all in, pointing out now and then certain acquaintances of her father's. Though Gracie noticed their arrival, she made no attempt to join them, seeming happy enough to converse with Tom Horn in Lance's absence.

And that suited him fine. Sonnie's beauty and dignity set her apart from the other women present. She was a picture of demure femininity, and Lance reveled in the opportunity to be with her.

From across the hall, the Club's steward hailed them and rushed over.

"Ah, Monsieur Harmon. We have been expecting you," he said, the greeting heavily accented with French. "I am so relieved you have arrived. Your journey went well?"

"Fine, Francois. We came in this morning," Lance replied. "Is everyone here?"

"Yes. They are waiting for you to start the meeting. Please, mademoiselle. Let me take your wrap." He helped Sonnie remove her gray-blue hooded cape, then stepped back and beamed in approval. "This is Vince's daughter, no?"

Lance nodded. "Sonnie, Francois De Prato. He takes good care of all us here at the club."

"*Enchanté,* Monsieur De Prato," she said in French, and inclined her head with the salutation.

The steward exclaimed in delight and replied in turn. Lance, not understanding a single word, listened with fascination and marveled at Sonnie's ease with the language.

"You two must hurry," Francois said finally. "You will come to dine after the meeting, no? We have many delicacies on the menu."

"We'll be there," Lance replied. "Is everyone in the reading room?"

"Yes. If you need anything, I will help you."

"Thanks, Francois."

After the steward left, Lance took Sonnie's elbow.

"He's smitten," he said under his breath, guiding her toward Gracie and Horn. "Just like the rest."

She blinked up at him in surprise. "You're addled to say such a thing, Lance Harmon."

"Just wait." He chuckled wryly. "This place is full of men. You'll conquer nearly all of them before the night is through."

"Think so?" She lifted her chin pertly. "Too bad. There's only one I'm interested in."

Her retort blocked out any further thought. He was afraid to read his own wants and hopes in her words.

Most likely he would only be disappointed in the end.

Sonnie was the only woman seated around the reading room's long walnut table. Straight-backed and proper, she retrieved Vince's notebook from her satchel and acted as secretary of the Stockmen's Association in his place, recording the Executive Committee's minutes in a precise, competent manner.

Gracie had pursed her painted lips and declined to attend with them. She told Lance she'd rather not waste her precious time at the Cheyenne Club sitting through a boring meeting that had nothing to do with her, that she would much rather mingle and make small talk with the rich. It made her feel respectable.

Thus assured, Lance and Horn had escorted Sonnie in, and in the generous hour since passed, Lance conceded that the meeting had definitely taken a boring turn. Senator Hickman held the floor, centering his discussion around passage of a legislative bill he'd introduced and that Lance had long since lost interest in. They hadn't yet touched on the subject of range detectives, and he could only hope the item was next on the agenda.

Tom Horn appeared equally indifferent. Since he was not a member of the Association, he couldn't participate in the meeting, but as Lance's guest he could sit in on the proceedings. He spent the duration fiddling with a toothpick; the other cattlemen fidgeted in their seats, dozed complacently, or simply stared out the heavy-draped windows. Only Sonnie and the Stockmen's Association's president, John Carlisle, gave the senator their undivided attention.

Lance's stomach growled its hunger, and he craved a drink. Past the point of unwillingness to disrupt the meeting, he leaned toward Sonnie.

"Want something from the bar?" he whispered.

She dragged her gaze from Hickman and smiled, seeming to understand his restlessness.

"Yes, water, please," she whispered back.

On the other side of her, the gunfighter's brow raised in curiosity. She discreetly repeated the offer to him; he gave Lance a comradely grin of gratitude, and Sonnie passed his reply back.

Glad for the opportunity to stretch his legs, Lance left his chair and headed toward the ornate bar set up in the back of the room. Generally, Club rules prohibited beverages in the reading room, but Francois made an exception for tonight's meeting. As quietly as possible, he poured two shot glasses of whiskey, then reached for the bottle of water.

The door burst open, and Clay Ditson boldly walked in. Francois, looking aghast and frazzled, followed on his heels. All heads turned at the intrusion. Tom Horn sat straighter in his chair, and the senator's lengthy oration sputtered to a stop.

Lance stood stock-still. *What the hell?* Ditson should be in jail. How had he posted bond so fast?

Because of Lance's partially hidden stance behind the bar, Ditson hadn't seen him. Prudently Lance set the bottle down.

"I beg your pardon, sir!" the Association's president said in a huff, rising from his chair. "We are conducting a meeting here!"

"I know it. I been waitin' nigh an hour to get in so's I can talk to you," Ditson declared.

"Forgive me, Monsieur Carlisle," Francois begged. "He would not listen to me. I could not stop him from . . . from barging in here like a stung bull!"

The group's president thinned his lips in barely concealed outrage.

"Thank you, Francois. I think we have enough manpower to handle this . . . gentleman from now on. Go on with your duties."

The steward was noticably relieved to have Ditson taken off his hands. Seeing Lance at the bar, Francois rolled his eyes and shook his head, then made a swift departure from the room.

Even from where he stood, Lance could tell Ditson needed a good wash. He still wore the same new clothes and the ridiculous green hat from earlier in the day, the very outfit he'd worn to the stockyards and later in jail, and now it was inappropriate as hell in a place like the Cheyenne Club. Lance doubted the fool even realized it.

"Now, fellas, don't go gettin' your dander up," Ditson said, his mouth curling in a semblance of a placating, gap-toothed smile. "I ain't gonna stay long, unless you want me to. I just got a bit of business with you, is all."

"I can't imagine what kind of business you'd have with us," said the senator with a sniff.

"I wanna join the 'ssociation. Long's I'm at it, I might as well join this here Club, too."

A gasp of disbelief went around the table.

"Do you honestly think you can storm in here and demand such a thing?" Carlisle's disdain got the best of him. "Who are you?"

"The man's name is Clay Ditson, John," Lance said, stepping from around the bar. "And I can tell you all you need to know about him."

Ditson's head jerked, and the feathered hat wobbled. His yellow teeth bared in a snarl. "Harmon, you son of a bitch."

"Tsk. Tsk. Your first mistake, Clay," Lance taunted. "Profanity isn't permitted here."

The weasel-like eyes narrowed. "I'm gettin' real tired of you showin' up every time I turn around. I'm a stockman, same as you and everyone else in here. I got just as much right to belong to the 'ssociation. The Club, too."

"You call yourself a stockman?" Lance snapped. "You're a disgrace to the rest of us."

"Is his brand registered?" Carlisle asked, more of Lance than Ditson.

"It is," Ditson defended.

"An artful version of the Rocking M!" Lance retorted.

Collective brows shot up; suspicion set in among the other cattlemen. Everyone present understood what Lance insinuated.

Sonnie's attention darted from man to man during the exchange. She gripped her pen tightly, her cheeks a tad too pale.

Lance moved toward her, whether in reassurance to her or himself, he wasn't sure.

Tom Horn watched Ditson in amused fascination.

"Where's your spread?" demanded Carlisle.

Ditson shifted. Beads of perspiration trickled from beneath the hat brim.

"I got me a right good piece of land for my herd

234

out northwest way." His glare sent daggers of antagonism at Lance.

"So tell them where you squatted, Clay," he urged almost casually, propping a booted foot onto the padded chair seat next to Sonnie's. "Tell them how you claimed Silver Meadow and a few hundred head of prize stock grazing there."

"Perhaps they'd be interested in the poisoned cattle we've discovered, as well, Mr. Ditson," Sonnie said coolly.

"Poisoned cattle!" one of the cattleman exclaimed.

"Silver Meadow?" repeated another. "Mancuso's?"

"Mancuso ain't entitled to all them acres of prime land, I'm tellin' you!" Ditson said in a hiss. "And you!" He rammed Sonnie with his beady-eyed gaze and speared a dirty-nailed finger close to her nose. "Stay out of this!"

Lance's hand lashed out and clamped around Ditson's scrawny forearm.

"Don't get near her," he said in a snarl, and thrust the man's arm from her. "Just stay the hell away."

Several of the cattlemen bolted to their feet.

"What's this about poisoned cattle, Harmon?" Carlisie demanded. "On the Rocking M?"

"Yes. We've lost a dozen head to yellow phosphorus poisoning."

"There may be more we have yet to discover." Sonnie speared Ditson with a haughty glare. "The Rocking M is a very large ranch."

"You can't pin no poisonings on me!" Ditson spat. "I ain't done nothin' of the sort."

"But you know about them, don't you?" Lance said softly.

Red fused the sallow, fleshy cheeks. "Don't accuse me, Harmon, until you got proof, hear me?"

"Get out," Lance said in a low growl. "You've rustled our stock and poisoned our beef. Those are

235

crimes. Maybe the courts won't put you away, but the association has the power to destroy you as a cattleman in the state of Wyoming. You'll never be one of us. Now get out."

Clay Ditson swept a harsh glance over each person in the room. Slowly he nodded his head at Lance.

"All right, I'll leave. But I ain't through." His voice rose steadily with every word until he nearly shouted his vow. "Y'hear me? I ain't through till I've made you and Mancuso pay for all you've taken from the rest of us." His lip curled in contempt, and he glared at Sonnie. "And that includes Mancuso's little piece of fluff."

She froze at his threat. Lance took a warning step forward, but Ditson spun and stormed from the room. Seconds later the clubhouse door slammed.

"What a lowlife!" muttered Carlisle, easing back down into his chair with a grim shake of his head.

The cattlemen concurred grim agreement.

"Can you see, gentlemen, how we must have stronger laws to stop the rustling problem?" Lance demanded. "It's industry-wide, not limited to the Rocking M. Juries are against us. Time is against us." His glance settled on Senator Hickman. "And even the Livestock Commission, with all its power, isn't enough. We have to take action now to guard our herds against theft. We need range detectives who are not afraid to enforce our laws and whose actions will teach the rustlers and squatters to stay off of our land."

"Do you have someone in mind for the job, Lance?" the senator asked.

"I do." From over Sonnie's head, he looked pointedly at the man sitting next to her. "Mr. Tom Horn."

The gunfighter steepled his fingers and leaned back in his chair.

"Well, now," he drawled. "After seeing Mr. Ditson,

I'm wondering how this man can possibly be a threat to someone as powerful as Vince Mancuso."

His words stunned Lance. "He is, Horn. Damn you."

"No swearing in the Club, remember?" A lazy smile crossed the gunfighter's mouth. "C'mon, Harmon. The man is a"—he pursed his lips as if he searched for the proper word without using profanity—"a buffoon."

Lance leaned forward. "It isn't just Ditson. He has an accomplice who is even more dangerous than he. They don't stop at rustling cattle or poisoning them. They attack stagecoaches, too." He thought of Sonnie. Of Snake in the wildflowers. "Among other things."

"One more point to consider, Mr. Horn." Sonnie's hand swept outward in a gesture to indicate their elite surroundings. "He managed to get in here, didn't he? And the Cheyenne Club is very strict about their clientele."

The room fell silent.

A slow, arrogant grin curved Horn's mouth. He stood, took Sonnie's hand, and dropped a gallant kiss across her knuckles.

"Touché, little lady," he purred. "You have a right clever way of swaying a man to your kind of thinking."

"Is that so, Mr. Horn?" she cooed, playing his game.

"It is." He straightened, extended his hand toward Lance. "Well, Harmon, I'd say you and your fellow cattlemen have a real problem."

Lance held his breath.

"And I'd be right happy to solve it for you."

Sonnie sipped a glass of zinfandel and reveled in the glory of the meeting's success. Papa would be most pleased when she told him of Mr. Horn's agreement.

She scanned the crowded dining room for Lance. He'd left her and Mr. Horn to search for Gracie, and in the time he'd been gone, the gunfighter had regaled her with stories of his past adventures with Apache Indians. Sonnie found the tales rather daunting, if not gruesome in parts; worse, they reminded her of Snake, the only real Indian she'd ever seen in her life, and he was quite enough. She had little desire to hear of others.

She listened with only half an ear and continued to watch for Lance. She missed him. She liked being with him. She preferred to sit or stand or talk to him more than any other man in the Club.

The knowledge didn't surprise her. A woman wanted to be with the man she loved. It was only natural and to be expected.

Except that tonight she had to share him with Gracie.

From the general direction of the piazza, he finally appeared with Gracie holding his arm. Sonnie's heart did a funny flip-flop, and her gaze clung to him as he dodged chairs and people en route to their table.

He made a handsome sight. He would fit in anywhere, she mused: on the back of a horse riding the Wyoming range or among crystal chandeliers and plush carpets in the prestigious Cheyenne Club. He stood a head taller than most, and his grace and agility seemed in contrast to his strength and power. His tawny hair, swept back over his bronzed forehead, glinted beneath the incandescent lighting, and Sonnie's palms tingled to run through the satiny thickness.

Her hand tightened into a fist. She had no right to want such things. He wasn't hers to claim.

The oval-shaped table seated four, and he pulled a chair out for Gracie directly across from Sonnie, then settled his lean frame into the one remaining. Gracie, her eyes alight with excitement, sighed loudly.

"What a night! What a wonderful, wonderful night!" she exclaimed.

Sonnie smiled at her enthusiasm. "You sound as if you're having fun, Gracie."

"Fun don't cover it, Miss Sonnie. I've never talked to so many hoity-toity people in all my days, and I loved every minute of it. People are actually nice to me! Leastways, polite. I love the ones with accents, those foreigners, you know? I never get *them* in my eatery. And even if no one wanted to talk, I'd be happy enough just to go around and look at the pretty furniture and rugs and—oh! I could stay forever."

"Cookie is coming for us at eleven," Lance reminded her.

"I know, I know." She grimaced. "Is anyone as warm as I am?" She peered over her shoulder at the radiators along the wall and pulled the crocheted shawl from her shoulders. "They need to shut down the furnace in here."

Perhaps the plunge of the magenta, lace-edged neckline made it seem as if Gracie possessed the most amply rounded, creamy expanse of bosom Sonnie had ever seen. She couldn't help taking a discreet peek down at her own and making a mental comparison.

Gracie won, no doubt about it.

Sonnie's breasts were average, enough to need a corset, plenty to fill out a gown's bodice, but not much more than that. The discovery tweaked her feminine pride. She squared her shoulders just a little to thrust them up a bit.

Men placed great importance on such things as a woman's breasts, Sonnie mused, unable to stop the flow of her thinking. They found them enjoyable and exciting and pleasurable to touch.

Not that she knew firsthand. No man had ever had the privilege with hers.

But the longing was there more and more often of late. And the more she thought of Lance, the stronger the longing became.

She couldn't help sliding a covert glance toward him. His gaze touched Gracie in the casual way anyone would make an appreciative perusal of a woman's gown. Sonnie derived great satisfaction from his indifference.

Far bolder in his appraisal, however, Mr. Horn ran his gaze over Gracie with a lusty glint in his eye. Gracie seemed to know the course of his thoughts—indeed, even encouraged them; she leaned unnecessarily close to speak with him.

The waiter arrived and took their orders. After he left, an amiable mood descended upon them, one far more relaxed than the strained atmosphere in the stagecoach. Spirited conversation circulated about the table with ease.

Lance's antagonism toward Tom Horn seemed to have faded. Sonnie sensed that his joining forces with the gunfighter against Clay Ditson was responsible, and she welcomed the bonding of their friendship. They would need it before the ordeal was over.

A portly gentleman entered the dining room. His bespectacled gaze scanned the crowd in an apparent search for a seat. After a moment his glance lighted on Lance, and his thick brows lifted.

"I think he knows you, Lance," Sonnie murmured, trying not to stare at the man. "He's coming over here."

"I'll be damned." Lance grunted, less discreet in his scrutiny. "It's that Englishman I told you about."

"The one Clay Ditson tried to sell our cattle to?"

"The very same."

"Oh; dear." She feared another confrontation like the one at the Stockmen's Association meeting.

"Mr. Harmon. Fancy seeing you here." Unsmiling,

the foreigner halted at their table. He seemed stiff and wary of Lance's reaction.

Lance rose and extended his hand. "Name's Lance. Didn't expect to see you either. Are you staying at the Club?"

He took Lance's hand in a firm clasp. "I am. As a guest of my friend, Hubert Teschemacher."

"Ol' Tesche, eh?" Lance grinned, and Sonnie recognized the name of the Cheyenne Club's head officer. Papa spoke fondly of him. "Care to join us? We'll find space at the table."

The Englishman relaxed visibly.

"Thank you, sir," he said. "George Leighton, Lord Whitby, Baron of Kettleston, by the way."

"Ooh, a lord!" Gracie said, awestruck.

"Quite." The Englishman smiled.

Introductory small talk ensued, tableware shuffled, and everyone squeezed together to make room for a fifth chair. The arrangement placed Lance closer to Sonnie, Gracie closer to Mr. Horn, and Lord Whitby in between. With Lance's shoulder always brushing hers in their tight quarters, Sonnie found the seating definitely satisfactory.

"About this afternoon," Lord Whitby began, his tone colored with apology, but Lance shook his head.

"Forget it," he said. "You didn't know the cattle were stolen. Ditson thought you were an easy mark because you're not from around here." He paused. "I was a little rough on you. I apologize."

"No, no, no. You acted as any man would. You were only defending what was yours." The baron sighed. "Strange country out here, different from my native England. I'm touring some of the outfits I've invested in. I knew rustling was a problem, but I didn't understand it was on such a bloody grand scale. Seeing it firsthand, I can tell you I'll take greater care to investigate my purchases from now on."

Gracie held up a hand, which was still sheathed in Sonnie's leather glove. Her red lips curled in a pout. "Are cows all anyone ever talks about around here?"

Lord Whitby gave her a tolerant smile. "Forgive us, Miss Purcell. You have an eatery, not a ranch. Choose a topic, then."

She batted her lashes in unabashed flirtation. "I love your accent, George."

Sonnie cringed at the casual address, but the baron didn't seem to mind. Through the lenses of his spectacles, his gaze dropped to Gracie's ample cleavage displayed above the magenta neckline, and his smile widened.

"Tell us about England," she said. "I've never been there and probably never will. I want to hear all about the place."

Lord Whitby appeared happy to oblige. Sonnie recognized many of the areas he described, having traveled them herself. She offered items of interest to him, and in seemingly no time at all, the waiter returned with their meals.

Gracie and Tom Horn delighted over their choice of boiled leg of mutton with caper sauce; the baron complimented his roasted turkey and oysters. Lance had bypassed the more elegant fare and ordered a succulent steak with mashed potatoes, and Sonnie took note of his simple tastes. When they returned to the Big House, she intended to provide him with more of the same.

Lance glanced down at her plate, steaming with creamy macaroni au gratin. A corner of his mouth lifted.

"What?" he teased softly, his voice low so as not to interrupt Lord Whitby's humorous anecdote of some bumbling ancestor in his noble lineage. "Nothing fancier than macaroni?"

She shook her head. "I've had my share of banquets and haute cuisine. Barbara used to fix this for me when I was a child. It's still my favorite." Her fork swirled in the cheese sauce. "We're really not so different, Lance, you and I. We both want the same things from life, I think."

His brow furrowed. "Our backgrounds are different. Very different."

"Yes, but our needs are not."

"Needs? Ah, sweet Sonnie." He emitted a soft, humorless laugh. Oblivious to the three sharing the table, to the clatter of dishes and the hum of conversation in the crowded dining room, he reached out and cupped her cheek with his palm, a touch so rare, so tender, Sonnie held her breath for fear he'd pull away.

"I have only one need," he said. His honey-gold eyes smoldered with want, with unspoken desire.

Sonnie's heart pounded. She was afraid to hope, to read into his fervent words the same need burning inside her.

"One need, Sonnie. And that's you."

Chapter Fourteen

"I don't want to go home yet, Lance."

Gracie's heavy-lashed eyes pleaded with him to let her stay awhile longer. Lance hesitated, reluctant to pull her away from an evening that meant so much to her, but Cookie already waited with the stagecoach outside the Club's entrance. Lord Whitby had long since bidden them good night. And Lance knew Sonnie was tired. He'd seen the yawns she had tried to hide throughout the late meal, and he himself had been up since long before dawn. He wanted to call it a day.

"I'll see her home safely, Harmon," Horn offered. "You won't have to worry about her."

"Please, Lance. There's dancing on the piazza!" Gracie exclaimed.

As if that were reason enough to stay. Being the one to escort her to the Club, Lance felt duty-bound to bring her home again, but he admitted that the gunfighter could be trusted. A fragile code of honor had formed between them, an honor bound by mutual respect. Lance decided, in spite of his initial suspicions, that Tom Horn had his good qualities.

He finally gave in, and Gracie squealed in delight and flung her arms about his neck.

"Oh, thank you, Lance!" She planted a wet kiss on his cheek, turned, and grasped the gunfighter's arm. "Come on, Tom. The music has already begun!"

Both men chuckled, and Horn raised a hand in farewell. Within moments they had disappeared into the throng on the dance floor.

Lance took Sonnie's elbow and ushered her into the main hall.

"Does it bother you to leave her behind?" Sonnie asked, her tone curious.

"No. I wouldn't have agreed if it did." He glanced down at her and wondered why she asked. "Does it bother you to leave Horn behind?"

"Heavens, no! I'd much rather be with you," she declared, her eyes wide.

Lance grinned. She couldn't have given him a better answer.

Several men mingled in the hall, among them C. W. Riner, legal counsel for the association, and the Rocking M's attorney as well. Lance thought of the yellowed envelope in his suit jacket pocket.

"Stay here, Sonnie." He left her in the capable hands of Francois, who was waiting near the club's doors to assist her into the folds of her hooded cape.

"C. W., I have to talk to you." Dispensing with preliminaries, Lance clasped the smaller man's shoulder and firmly guided him away from the others. He halted beside a cluster of tall, potted ferns.

"What is it, Lance?" C. W. asked, his dignified features concerned.

"I need your advice." Lance withdrew the envelope and handed it to him. "Read this. Tell me what you think."

The attorney studied the piece of paper inside.

"I think this is most surprising," he said with a perplexed frown. He scanned it again, then returned the document to the envelope.

"Surprising? Damned inconvenient is more like it," Lance said dryly, placing the envelope back into his pocket. "Check into it for me, will you? Find out if everything is legitimate. Get back to me as soon as you can."

"I will," C. W. promised.

"How soon?"

"It'll take a couple of days for the research. I'll send out a few wires first thing in the morning."

"Couple of days. Hell." Lance hated to wait. He wanted answers now. "Let me know the minute you learn anything."

"Of course." C. W. hesitated. "What does Vince say about this?"

"Nothing. Not a word in all the years I've known him."

"And you haven't asked?"

"No. He's too sick. Had a relapse; then pneumonia set in. He's in County now. I found the envelope by accident."

"Sorry to hear it, Lance." His sympathy was genuine. "I'll see what I can do for you."

"Good. Thanks. And C. W.?"

"Yes?"

"Don't talk to anyone else. Deal only with me."

"You got it."

The attorney stepped away from the privacy of the ferns and returned to his friends. Lance raked a hand through his hair and fought a sense of impending doom.

The devil take him if Sonnie ever found out.

* * *

The Railroad Hotel had long since quieted for the night. Subdued lighting guided Lance and Sonnie up the stairwell to their rooms. A single lamp in the hall shed a muted glow about the walls and created shadows upon the worn carpet runner lining the floor.

Sonnie glanced toward the block of rooms reserved for the Mancuso cowboys, the men who had escorted the stagecoach in from the ranch. Their rooms were silent, and she guessed they'd already turned in, with the exception of Cookie, who'd taken the rig to the livery.

Lance unlocked her door, opened it partway, and gave her the key. He seemed in no hurry to go to his own room; he leaned a shoulder against the wall and crossed his arms over his broad chest.

The softly lit hall, their seclusion, the quiet, all gave birth to a yearning that accentuated Sonnie's reluctance to leave him, to end the evening in which she'd had to share him with so many others when she wanted him only for herself.

It all seemed unfair, somehow: to desire someone as badly as she desired Lance, yet be denied his love, his touch. He rarely touched her except in a polite or comforting manner. A fluttering of hopelessness welled up.

"Good night, Lance," she said, and turned toward the emptiness of her room.

"Hey." His low voice reached out to her. "Not so fast."

She halted in midstep.

Fingers, gentle but firm, tugged her around until she faced him. His hand circled the back of her neck; his thumb stroked the delicate line of her jaw. The light caresses sent waves of tingles clear to her toes.

"Have I told you how beautiful you are?" he asked huskily.

Pam Crooks

"Once or twice," she managed, the reply little more than a breathy whisper.

He trailed a leisurely eye over her features.

"I'm not sure which way I like your hair better," he murmured. "Piled on top all elegant with diamonds and pearls"—his gaze smoldered, as if he considered removing each of the pins holding her curls in place— "or down about your back and shoulders, thick and long and rich. Like black satin."

The provocative tone of his voice held her captive. Her heart pounded wildly one moment, then stopped altogether the next.

It seemed her knees were filled with jelly; she swayed subtly toward him. His arm slipped about her waist and snuffed the distance separating them. He rasped her name, and she trembled with longing.

His mouth, moist and warm, found hers, played and seduced with an expertise that nearly shattered Sonnie's composure. She parted her lips and invited his tongue. He accepted and explored the innermost cavern of her mouth, traced the curve of her teeth, stroked the soft underside of her cheek.

A shuddering moan escaped her. She'd expected a tentative response from him, controlled, restrained, as he always seemed to be. But this—this unbridled passion would be her undoing. If he followed her down to the floor and took her right there in the hall, she would not protest. Indeed, she wanted him to do just that.

He dragged his mouth aside and rubbed his jaw against hers, dropped little nibbles to the sensitive skin beneath her ear and groaned her name again. Sonnie clutched the lapel of his jacket; she needed his strength to stay afloat in the swirling pool of sensations into which he'd thrown her.

"Go, Sonnie," he said even as he rained kisses onto her temple and forehead. "While I can still let you."

Reluctantly she pulled away and peered up at him with unfulfilled desire. With a fingertip, she touched the lingering dampness of his lower lip and debated asking him to her room.

Or following him to his.

"Go," he repeated, as if knowing the way of her thoughts. The gentle command was followed by a rueful smile. "Or I won't be responsible for my actions."

Sonnie's lashes drifted downward to hide her regret. "You needn't be so gallant, you know."

"Yes, I do." His sigh sounded heavy with frustration. "Believe me, I do."

He pushed the door open wider and nudged her into the dark room. Using the meager light borrowed from the hall, Sonnie located the nearest chair and dropped her satchel onto the seat while Lance found the switch to turn on the electric light.

He slid his fingers into the suit pants pockets, and she wondered if he used the gesture to keep from pulling her into his arms again.

"I'll take you to County Hospital in the morning to see your father. About eight, okay?" he asked.

"Yes, thank you." She clasped her hands tightly behind her. "Sleep well, Lance."

His grunted curse adequately indicated his opinion of that. "Lock the door behind me."

Too soon, he left, and in the solitude Sonnie's mouth dipped in disappointment.

How could he leave when he knew she wanted him to stay?

A melancholy emptiness filled her heart. She secured the door, then regarded the bed and its cold, empty sheets.

I have only one need.

She remembered his words from the Club's dining room, fervent in their low-spoken intensity, and how they'd tripped the breath from her lungs.

I have only one need. And that's you.

Did he truly need her? She refused to hope. He would only deny her, just like he denied himself. Hadn't he done so all along?

Pensive, she undid the closures of the gray-blue cape and draped the wrap over the back of the chair. Cool air drifted over her bare arms, raising goose bumps, and she glanced toward the window. The midnight breeze blew inward, billowing the hems of the woven curtains, and she chastised herself for forgetting to close it sooner.

The lamp's subtle glow barely reached the farthermost edges of the room. She moved into the shadows and tugged the window shut, then peered through the glass panes into the railroad yard below. Moonlight bounced off the twin ribbons of tracks lining the rear of the hotel. Union Pacific's Round Hotel, bereft of workers long since gone home, loomed in the distance. An engine's whistle wailed a lonely cry as it chugged toward the next station.

Only then did Sonnie remember.

She *had* closed the window—earlier, when she was waiting for Lance.

A prickle of apprehension raised the fine hairs on her neck. Bending closer to the glass, she strained to see the back porch roof skirting the entire second story of the hotel, checking it right and left just in case someone huddled in hiding. But she saw no one and breathed a little easier.

She yanked the curtains closed so not a wink of the outside peeked in. A shiver took her, a shiver that had nothing to do with the chill in the room, and she knew a sudden need to undress and retreat beneath the safety of the bedcovers.

A grimy hand clamped over her mouth.

The force of the grip hurled her backward into her

captor's chest and smothered the scream bolting to her throat. The stench of dank sweat filled her nostrils. Full-blown terror exploded inside her.

He had come.

He had come to wreak his revenge, just as he'd promised at the Cheyenne Club, revenge against Vince Mancuso or anything that was his.

Including his daughter. Especially his daughter.

Oh, God.

Panic clouded Sonnie's brain and rendered her temporarily motionless. The heat of Clay Ditson's body penetrated her gown; his liquored breath blew hot across her cheek.

"Yell and you're dead, y'hear me?" he said in a hiss.

His grasp over her face prevented a nod. She attempted to speak, but the words came out muffled and useless.

"We're gonna have a little fun, you and me." He cackled in her ear, and Sonnie's eyes closed in her dread. "Yep. A little fun. You'll enjoy it, too. Just wait and see."

His arm tightened about her waist, and he pushed her toward the bed. Her lashes flew open; she whimpered and dug her heels into the carpet. He swore and pushed harder.

"Don't fight me," he said in a snarl. "Git on the bed. You ever had a man before? A real man? Git on the bed, I said!"

He threw her onto the mattress and followed her down. In desperation, Sonnie twisted and writhed beneath his wiry frame, and in the struggle Ditson's fingers moved away from her mouth.

She gulped in a lungful of air and let it all out in a scream, but he clapped a hand over her mouth again.

"You little bitch! Try that again and I'll smack you so hard you'll see stars!"

251

His rank breath billowed over her, and she gagged in revulsion. She flailed her fists, pummeled his arms, chest, and shoulders. He gripped all the harder. She sank her teeth into his palm, tasted the salt and dirty sweat on his skin.

He jerked away with a yelp, and she lurched toward the edge of the bed. He hauled her back, then struck her violently across the side of her face. She cried out, and tears sprang to her eyes.

"She-cat! Damn, you're a fighter!" he said, panting.

"I'd rather die than let you touch me, you filthy bastard!" Her bosom heaved. All her senses laid in readiness to renew the fight.

"Bet you don't say that to Harmon, that connivin', lyin' son of a bitch, do you, pretty lady?" He leered down at her, a glint of lust in his bloodshot eyes, and grabbed her breast roughly, kneading the flesh through the brocade bodice. "Even when he does *this* to you."

A low, feral sound of fury erupted from her throat. Twisting, she raked her nails across his wrist and tried to gouge his face.

He laughed, stoking her wrath more.

"You're too much woman for him, y'know that? He don't deserve you." He grasped one arm, held it above her head, and dodged her swinging fist.

"He's more man than you'll ever be," she said in a gasp. "God, you sicken me!"

Her hissed insult struck a chord with him. His thin lips curled back menacingly.

"Shut up!"

She tried to roll away from him, but he hung on to a section of her hair, loosening the diamond-and-pearl ornament from her coiffure. With a burst of adrenaline, she landed a punch to his belly.

The air left him in a grunt; his hold weakened. She plucked the frill from her hair and reached out wildly to scrape the comb across his cheek. She felt the tines break from the force of her strength. Her legs kicked within her skirts. Her knee connected with his groin.

He swore loudly and curled away from her with a howl of pain. She bounced from the mattress to the floor, landing with a thump. Scrambling to her feet, she sucked in huge breaths.

Some part of her awareness identified the sound of pounding, of someone calling her name, of the door-knob rattling fiercely.

She cursed her puny strength. How could she fend him off much longer? The hotel room offered little chance of escape.

Ditson left the bed, his cheek bloodied, his wrath spewing full-steam, and approached her.

"Stay away from me!" she warned, backing toward the chair. She stumbled over her train and hastily righted herself. "You'll never get away with this. My father will—"

"To hell with your father!" he roared. "The high and mighty Vince Mancuso ain't gonna listen to me unless I got you. You're gonna be my weapon, pretty lady. My ace in the hole to get Silver Meadow."

"No!" The chair halted her step, and she groped blindly behind her. Her fingers found the satchel on the seat and closed around the handle. She hurled it toward him; he lifted a forearm and blocked its flight. The case fell open and dumped her meticulous notes from the Stockmen's Association meeting all over the carpet.

"Sonnie! God, Sonnie!"

Lance.

Sonnie wanted to call out to him, but Ditson had to be her focus. If she took her eyes off of him . . .

"He ain't gonna get in, not before I grab you," Ditson warned, obviously knowing her thoughts. "I saw you lock the door."

The pounding increased a hundredfold. The door quivered within its frame; the wall shook. It seemed Lance threw his whole body into trying to break inside.

"You're a horrid man, Clay Ditson." She licked her lips and fought down panic. Too soon he would have her cornered. Too soon he would win.

Throwing the satchel had deterred him little. He kept coming; she kept backing away. She bumped into the dresser and knew then that there was nowhere else to go.

"Maybe I am," Ditson said tersely. "But I'm plumb broke. Harmon took the last of my herd. I ain't got nothin' else." His mouth snaked into a grin. "Nothin' but you, pretty lady."

Shouted commands rumbled in the hall, but only Lance's voice penetrated her terror. Wood splintered and cracked, yet the door stood solid.

He would never reach her in time.

Ditson lunged toward her. She snatched a crystal perfume decanter from the dresser top and tossed the carnation-scented liquid into his eyes, into the raw gashes in his cheek.

He screamed and cursed and rubbed his sleeve against his face. Sonnie whirled and threw herself at the door. Her fingers fumbled, groped with the lock. And then Ditson had hold of her gown.

Suddenly the door crashed open. Its edge clipped Sonnie's shoulder, spun her about with such force she tumbled to the floor in a tangle of petticoats and brocade.

Momentarily stunned, she lay in a heap, vaguely aware of the blur of men rushing into the room.

"Sweet Jesus. Sonnie, are you okay?"

Lance's strong arms pulled her into a sitting position. Winded, she swiped at the weighty hank of hair that had fallen over her face and peered up at him, his features darkened with anguish and worry. She wanted to cry and hug and kiss him all at once.

A flash of peacock feather drew her eye. Ditson had already opened the window and had one leg on the sill.

"There he goes." She gasped.

Lance twisted. A growl thundered low in his chest. He leaped to his feet and shoved Stick and Charlie, wearing only their union suits, out into the hall.

"Go after him! Try to catch him in the back. I'll follow from up here."

Slipping on the scattered papers in their haste, the barefoot cowboys bolted from the room. Lance ran to the window and maneuvered his tall frame through to the outside.

He paused on the slanted roof and darted a glance into the dark night. He nearly missed seeing Ditson's feathered hat disappear below the roofline. Lance sprinted after him, dropped to his knees and grasped the shingled edge, and swung his body over. He wrapped his legs around a sturdy wooden column bracing the porch roof and slid to the ground.

He searched the blackness in front of him, behind him, and all around.

Nothing.

Only silence.

He hissed a frustrated breath. Like a clever weasel, Ditson had escaped. Disappeared into thin air. Gone. *Damn*.

Charlie and Stick rounded the hotel at a full run, Cookie right behind them.

"Find him, boss?"

"No, damn it."

"He can't be far. We'll get a posse or somethin'."

"No."

It was too late for that. Ditson would make sure

not to be found. Lance scanned the railroad yards and knew there were a thousand places the bastard could hide. Besides, he didn't want to leave Sonnie for the hunt.

He raked a hand through his hair. "Thanks for trying, boys. Might as well go on back to your rooms and try to get some sleep."

"Come for us if you need us. We'll do what we can to keep Miss Sonnie safe," Stick vowed.

The three men left, shaking their heads and murmuring their concern over Sonnie's ordeal. Grimly Lance set his hands on his hips and studied the porch roof.

Ditson had found her so easily.

He stepped onto a ceramic planter placed at the base of the wooden column. Giving a little jump, he grabbed the roof's edge and heaved himself up and over. The ease with which he managed it explained Ditson's break-in from the rear, but as he scanned the long line of windows, Lance wondered how the wily man knew which one was hers.

He reentered Sonnie's room in the same manner he left. He found her on her knees with the proprietor's wife, picking up Vince's notes and her own and placing the sheets in neat stacks. She glanced up. Their eyes met, and her lower lip trembled.

Lance scooped her into his arms, pressing her tightly to his chest. His fingers splayed in the sable thickness of her hair. She buried her face in his shirt.

"You okay?" he demanded against her temple.

"I am now," she said, the words muffled. She drew back slightly. "He got away, didn't he?"

His mouth tightened. He hated telling her. "Yes."

"He'll be back."

"Yes," he said again, without fanfare.

She sighed heavily, accepting it. Her troubled gaze swept the room, the rumpled bed, the overturned chair, toilet articles scattered over the dresser top.

"This place is a mess," she said, and frowned at the ruined door.

"It doesn't matter. We're not staying."

"Where are we going?"

"We'll get a room at the Club." He kept his voice low. Secrecy was paramount. "Throw a few things together. I want to leave now."

She nodded, and he released her.

Within moments the satchel bulged, and she was ready. Lance picked her cape up from the floor and draped it about her. He noticed a rip in the shoulder of her gown; the brocade kept slipping, dipping the neckline low over her breasts.

Sweet Jesus. What she's been through.

"Let's go," he said roughly. He took her elbow and led her briskly from the room. Trying to keep up, she considered his haste with a dark brow raised. She couldn't know the demons of regret, of pain, that haunted him, and he couldn't help hauling her against him and pressing a swift, hard kiss to her lips.

He released her and headed toward the stairwell. Several hotel guests in their nightclothes lingered in the hall, talking quietly about the incident that had awakened them. The proprietor and his wife assured everyone the scare had passed, and asked them to return to their rooms.

Lance ignored them.

"Mr. Harmon," the proprietor called. "The damages—"

His step never slowed. "Put 'em on my bill."

"Yes, sir," the other man said.

Lance hustled Sonnie down the stairs. The protection of the Cheyenne Club called to him; he couldn't wait to get her away from the hotel. It was as if Ditson had tainted the entire establishment.

Hurrying through the lobby and out the door, they

encountered Charlie, Cookie, and Stick lingering over a last cigarette before retiring. The cowboys looked up in surprise.

"We'll be at the club," Lance said, knowing he could trust each of them with their whereabouts. He lifted the hood of Sonnie's cape over her head, the effect offering her a measure of obscurity. "I'll see you in the morning."

"Sure, boss," Charlie said, understanding. "Want to borrow my horse?"

"No. It's only three blocks. We'll walk." He urged Sonnie forward again. As an afterthought, he halted and took a mental head count. "Cookie, who're you bunking with tonight?"

"Stick," the old cowboy said without hesitation.

"Charlie, how about you?"

"Jake."

McKenna. Jake McKenna. Suspicion coiled in Lance's belly. "You seen him lately?"

Charlie seemed taken aback by the question. "Come to think of it, no. Left him at Kapp's Saloon. Haven't seen him since supper."

Lance's eyes narrowed. "Sonnie, when you reserved the block of rooms this afternoon, were any assigned? Or did everyone choose their own?"

She frowned. "We chose our own. No specific names were listed in the hotel registry, just the Rocking M's. I simply charged all the rooms to the ranch's bill and left it at that." Her eyes widened. "Lance, you don't think—"

"Who brought you back from the hospital?" he demanded.

"God Almighty, Jake did," Cookie said tightly, Lance's head jerked toward him. "I stayed behind fer a round of checkers with Mr. Mancuso."

"So McKenna would've known Sonnie's room number."

Lance released a slow breath. He forced himself to stay cool, to sort methodically through the evidence, to keep from jumping to conclusions.

"Cookie, stay with Vince tonight. I want someone at the hospital at all times in case there's trouble. I'll spell you in the morning. Charlie, if Jake shows up, don't say anything. I might be wrong."

But he knew he wasn't. He was right as hell, and by the looks on the others' faces, everyone agreed.

The Rocking M, long known for its loyal men, now had a traitor in its ranks.

Chapter Fifteen

Virtually all of the guests had departed the Cheyenne Club, leaving the place unusually subdued. Even the orchestra on the piazza had quieted, with the remaining dancers enjoying a final drink in one of the public rooms before going home. A few men lingered over games of chess and billiards, but for the most part, no one noticed Lance and Sonnie's arrival.

They stepped into the main hall and spied Francois talking to Lord Whitby. The steward's graying brows shot up, and he exchanged a surprised glance with the Englishman.

"Monsieur Harmon! Mademoiselle Mancuso!" he exclaimed. "I did not expect to see you again this evening. Are you here for your friends—er, the gunfighter and Mademoiselle Purcell?" His tongue clucked in dismay. "I am afraid they have already left."

Lance lifted a hand and waved aside the older

man's mistaken notion. "No. I need a favor, Francois."

"A favor? Just ask."

"We need a room. Now. Tonight."

"A room." Francois swallowed and paled. "But forgive me, monsieur. We have no sleeping rooms available. They are all taken." Panic and chagrin circled his face. "We can fashion something in one of the others, the reading room, perhaps—"

Lance shook his head. "No. Not good enough." He wanted protection for Sonnie. Privacy from the mainly male clientele. "I'll pay whatever it takes."

"I say, that won't be necessary, Lance," Lord Whitby piped up. "Take mine."

Their attention swung to him.

"After our wonderfully pleasant dinner, I went upstairs and wrote a number of letters, but I'm afraid indigestion has set in since then. Ghastly affliction." He rubbed his portly stomach with a grimace. "I'd best not lie down. A chair and a pillow will be my bed tonight. Please take the room."

From beneath the gray-blue hood, Sonnie peered up at Lance. He hesitated, sensing her unwillingness to boot the baron out of his own quarters, yet he knew that if he were in the Englishman's place, he would make the same offer. After a moment he nodded.

"I owe you, sir. Maybe someday I can return the favor."

The baron's gaze twinkled beneath his spectacles. "Give me another chance to buy some of your bloody fine livestock. Then we'll be square."

A side of Lance's mouth lifted in a grin. "Deal."

Moving closer, Sonnie raised up on tiptoe and kissed the baron's cheek.

"Thank you, my lord," she said quietly. She pivoted, then glanced at him over her shoulder. "Perhaps

Francois will prepare an infusion of sage for you. It will help the indigestion, I think." A ghost of a smile appeared on her lips as she turned and patted the steward's arm. "Just a few leaves in a cup of hot water, Francois. Make sure he drinks it all."

Francois bowed, an adoring expression on his dignified features. Lord Whitby beamed in spite of his malady. And Lance had never loved her more.

The Club spared no cost in furnishing its six sleeping rooms. Heavy, well-crafted furniture in polished walnut sat upon plush carpets. Marble topped the commode and dresser, and though the rooms contained fireplaces graced with lovely mantels and grates, radiators provided the inviting warmth.

Wrapping her arms tightly about herself, Sonnie moved deeper into the baron's room. She ran her gaze over the lavish appointments, halting at the tall windows positioned on either side of the fireplace. A visible shiver took her.

"He won't find us here, will he, Lance?" Her voice, hardly more than a whisper, cried out her apprehensions.

Lance's heart constricted.

He locked the door behind him and strode closer. Placing his hands on her shoulders, he turned her about to face him.

"No, Sonnie. He won't. We're safe."

Doubt clouded the obsidian depths of her eyes, and her glance skittered back toward the heavy-draped windows.

"How do you know he didn't follow us from the hotel? How can you be sure he's . . . he's not watching us this very minute?"

"Sonnie." His jaw tightened. Over the fabric of her cape, he ran his palms along her upper arms and tried to find the right words to soothe her fears. "Sweetheart, I won't let him get to you again. He'll have to go through me first. You're safe. Trust me. He won't hurt you anymore."

Her chin quivered, and Lance knew the gallant effort she took to quash the flow of tears. Her lashes lowered. She fiddled with the lapel on his jacket.

"You'll stay with me, then? Tonight?"

"Yes." Only then did he understand the implication of that tiny word: that they were very much alone, that the room contained just one bed, and dawn was a long, long time away.

And he would make love to her.

He waited for the rush, the roar, the sensations inside him that always came whenever he yearned for Sonnie.

They didn't come. Not now. Not ever again.

Maybe it was the scare of nearly losing her. Maybe desperation made him realize how vulnerable they were, that life was full of uncertainties, and he wanted her forever.

Gently he pushed the gray-blue hood down from her dark head. The light from several lamps placed about the room swathed her features and illuminated the swelling over her cheekbone. He sucked in a breath and swore softly.

"Ditson hit you." He brushed a fingertip over the abrasion and winced, feeling her pain as though it were his own. "I'll get some ice from Francois."

"No." Her fingers, cool and smooth, closed around his. "It doesn't hurt anymore. Really."

He debated going anyway, but her hand tightened, keeping him in place. With the other she unfastened the cape and let the folds fall into a heap at their feet.

The brocade gown had a large tear above the sleeve, causing if to sag from her shoulders. Golden light shimmered over the olive tones of her skin and revealed the tantalizing curve of a single breast.

Lance swallowed hard. Desire flickered, flared, raged through him. Lust. A wanting so powerful he could hardly control it.

Ruffled lace and scarlet ribbon peeked above the gaping square-cut bodice. The corset hid the rest of her breast from him, hid the nipple he longed to suckle and the rounded globes he ached to cup in his palms.

"Touch me, Lance," she whispered, seeming to know the way of his thoughts.

His breath quickened. His imagination ran rampant in anticipation of the liberties she allowed him, yet he hesitated.

"Sonnie," he said huskily.

He wanted to give her time, to make sure she understood what was happening between them. He didn't want to take advantage of her emotional state, of the defenses Clay Ditson had weakened with his attack.

"Touch me," she said again. "I want it."

She took his hand and slowly, steadily brought it to rest against her breast. Of their own accord, his fingers moved, flexed over the brocade and lace and supple skin. His palm massaged, stroked, caressed the fullness.

Her lids drifted closed, as if she were savoring the sensations he evoked. Lance covered the other breast, too, working both beneath his palms, until he heard her ragged sigh.

"Turn around," he said.

She obeyed and then lifted the profusion of dark tresses off the slender column of her neck. With fingers unaccustomed to such tiny buttons, he undid them all, only to encounter the tight laces of the corset.

He made a slight sound of frustration.

"Why do women do this?" He eyed the bindings with masculine distaste.

"Do what?"

"Truss themselves up like Christmas turkeys." He grunted and set himself to the task of loosening the strings.

She laughed softly. "To make us look good. Or to tease our men, maybe, by prolonging—"

She halted and peeped at him from over her shoulder. A blush colored her cheeks.

His head lifted. He fought a smile. "By prolonging . . . ?"

Her lashes fluttered. "By prolonging the moment when he will make mad, passionate love to her."

"Ah." The corset fell open. "And how long would a woman want a man to make love to her after he went through all the trouble of unlacing her damned corset?"

She faced him and hugged the layers of garments to her bosom. Her chin lifted in a challenging pose. "All night, of course."

He quirked a brow. "Of course?"

"Until the crest of dawn."

He started to speak, but had to clear his throat and begin again. His loins warmed steadily by degrees.

"Provided he was up to it. Of course."

"But the man I have in mind is very strong. He would definitely be up to it." Her lips twitched. "Of course."

The heat in his groin raged full force. Sonnie reached up and trailed a finger along the bridge of his nose.

"I love you, Lance."

Her quiet announcement knocked the air from his lungs.

How long had he waited to hear her say that? How

long had he hoped, despaired of her returning the same depth of feelings he felt for her?

Forever. A lifetime.

She loved him.

He snared her wrist in a gentle grip and pressed his mouth to the opaque, delicately veined skin there, feeling the wild beat of her pulse, then moved his way slowly upward. He ran his tongue along the sensitive crease in the crook of her arm.

"I've loved you since you were a kid," he said. "I was always just one of your father's men, another cowboy he needed to work the ranch. But I loved you even though you never knew me."

The dark crescents of her brows furrowed. He'd surprised her with the admission.

"And then I went away," she said, her voice hushed with compassion. He nuzzled her neck; she tilted her head to the side and sighed.

"Yeah. For a hell of a long time. But I knew you'd come back eventually. Or at least I hoped you would."

"Oh, Lance." A faint glimmer of emotion shone in her eyes. "I'll never leave again. Not ever."

Unbidden, his vow to send her back to Boston flared in his memory like an evil curse. He quenched the thought, shoved it away to deal with later.

Much later.

He tugged at her bodice until the fabric bunched at her waist. With a wiggle of her hips, the gown left her body in a whisper of brocade, falling to the floor on top of her cape. Petticoats and silk stockings followed. Sonnie lifted her arms, and Lance pulled the corset up over her head, then dropped the feminine contrivance on the heap with everything else.

She stood naked, and ravaged his sanity. A low, animal sound tore from his throat.

"Hey, Boss-man," she purred, a virginal tigress ripe

for the taking. She stepped closer, over the mound of clothing, and splayed her fingers over his shirt and under the lapels of his jacket. "This will never do."

She pushed it down his shoulders and he shook it free, adding to the pile.

"Nor will this." His tie followed.

"Or this." Graceful flicks of her thumb undid each button and parted his shirt. She dragged the garment free of his waistband and took it off him.

The breadth of his shoulders seemed to captivate her. Carefully, as if afraid he'd vanish with her touch, she stroked her palms against his chest in a slow, circular motion, exploring, discovering. They lowered to skim his belly and came around his ribs, clasping his back. Lance guessed she'd never before caressed a man so freely, and the thought pleased him.

She leaned forward and rubbed the tip of her nose against his skin. She inhaled deeply. The sable lashes closed, and her tongue fluttered over his flesh, hot and wet and glorious.

Shudders of sensation rippled through him.

His hands spanned her waist and drew her roughly to him. She melted, flattening her warm, luscious breasts against his chest, and suckled the curve of his neck. Shivers buzzed along his spine. He struggled for control. Her breath came in short pants, her nipples pebbled, and Lance thought he'd die from wanting her.

Bending, he scooped her up into his arms and strode to the bed. He managed to jerk back the covers and lay her down, then step away and make short work of the suit pants and boots. He came to her, one knee on the mattress, one foot on the floor, and halted.

Flowing tresses as dark as midnight spilled about the crisply ironed pillowcase. Her gaze burned with his. Lips—moist, full, inviting—parted and waited for his kiss. She turned partially toward him with slender arms outstretched, and still he hesitated.

He thought of Vince, of the envelope tucked away in his pocket.

Just as swiftly, he thought of the long, lonely years he'd dreamed of this, of beautiful, grown-up Sonnie waiting for him, loving him, and of how he'd hungered for this moment.

This wonderfully sweet moment.

He caught her to him in the breadth of a heartbeat, rolled with her deeper into the mattress. Their mouths locked in a blending of souls and desire, of heat and fire, their tongues seeking and mating in a sensual dance of passion.

Lance clutched her tighter. She mewled a primitive groan. From beneath him, her thighs opened, and he could wait no longer.

But he feared hurting her, though he knew he must. He rose above her, holding himself taut, his heart pounding in anticipation. Her back arched; she rasped his name. Her hands slid along his back and grasped his buttocks.

His arousal throbbed against the petals of her womanhood. He found his rightful place within her and moved gently, slowly. Her hips tilted in a silent plea for him to deepen the thrusts.

"I want you, Lance," she whispered. "I want this."

He sensed she sought to reassure him, that she knew what to expect, and that it would hurt. He pushed a little harder and broke through the virginal veil. She squeezed her lids shut with a soft gasp, but her hips moved again soon, very soon after, and his mouth caught hers in a lingering, comforting kiss.

He drove into her, carefully at first. She was tight. Incredibly tight. She opened her legs wider, lifted and wrapped them about his waist. He was so deep inside her he thought he'd drown from the sensation. Their breath sounded harsh within the silence of the room as he moved faster, unable to help himself, forgetting this was her first time, that he should be more tender, slower, gentler.

Her heat sheathed him, blanketed his skin with a fine mist of perspiration. His blood raced; his pulse pounded. Faster, he moved within her. Closer. God, but he couldn't get close enough.

She stayed with him, meeting his every thrust, matching the tempo he created. The massive bed absorbed the rocking of their bodies as he took her with him to the heights of release. He arched, shuddered against her, filled her with his life and love, and their cries meshed as one.

Like a pair of autumn leaves, they drifted back down to reality, to the lateness of the hour and Lord Whitby's well-lit room. Sonnie held Lance within the circle of her arms and ran her fingers through the silken thickness of his hair, which glinted gold in the lamplight.

She welcomed his weight upon her. His long, hair-dusted legs entwined with hers; his lean belly pressed warmly over her abdomen. She thought she could lie with him like this, intimately joined, yet spent and satisfied, to her last living day.

He seemed to know what she was thinking. Lifting his head, he gazed down at her and looked as content as she felt inside.

"You're mine, Sonnie. Y'know that?" His low voice curled around her, seductive and intense.

"Yes," she said simply. She belonged with him. No other man would command the love she had for Lance.

"Mine. Not Stick's or Charlie's—"

She frowned. "Stick or Charlie?"

"—or Tom Horn's or Francois's or Lord Whitby's—"

"Lord Whitby!" Growing more exasperated by the

minute, she pushed on his shoulders. "Lance Harmon, what are you talking about?"

He grinned down at her, but the possessive look in his honey-gold eyes told her he was serious.

"I won't share you with anyone, Sonnie. I've waited too long for you to have someone else take you away. You have this effect on men where they fall simpering at your feet like lovesick schoolboys—"

"I don't!" she denied, her eyes wide.

"—and I'm the worst—hell, I admit it—but just get used to the idea that I will be the absolute one and only man in your life from now on and forever!"

And with that, he planted a wet smack of a kiss to her mouth.

He rose up, gently pulled himself out of her, then left the bed. Robbed of his warmth, she settled the blankets snugly about her and stewed over his masculine arrogance. Magnificent in his nakedness, he double-checked the locked door before turning out the lights and finding his way back to the bed.

She made room for him, but he slipped his long arm about her and brought her back close to his side. She rested her head on his shoulder and pursed her lips.

"Turnabout's fair play, you know, Boss-man." She sniffed, still thinking about his lofty proclamation of moments ago.

He grunted. "Meaning?"

"Meaning there shall be no other women in your life either. From now on and forever," she said, adding his own words for emphasis.

"Other women aren't a problem for me."

"I beg to differ."

His head turned on the pillow. "What're you saying?"

She heard the puzzlement in his tone. Didn't he

270

know who she was talking about? Their gazes met in the darkness. "Gracie!" she exclaimed.

His jaw dropped, and he stared down at her. Within seconds he filled the air with a hearty chuckle.

"Come here, my darling little idiot."

The muscles in his arms bunched as he lifted her from his side and brought her to lie on top of him. Their sensuous, skin-to-skin position nearly swayed Sonnie from the conversation at hand.

"Let's get one thing straight right now: Gracie is my friend and nothing more. I don't love her. I never have, and I never will."

"But she cares for you," Sonnie protested. "I saw her, all snuggly and cozy and clinging, like she couldn't get enough of you."

"She was the same way with Horn once she got to know him." He shrugged a bare shoulder. "She likes men. It's as simple as that." Not entirely convinced, Sonnie wriggled against him. He clamped his hands low on her hips and held her still. "Careful, woman, or you'll get me hot and wanting all over again."

Sonnie's brow furrowed into a wary frown. "Did you sleep with her, Lance?"

She held her breath, fearing his answer, yet needing to purge her soul of the uppermost worry within her heart.

"Yes."

A squeak of dismay escaped her, and she tried to slide away from him, but he held her fast on top of him.

"Yes, I slept with her," he repeated slowly, succinctly, as if he, too, needed to destroy this obstacle between them. "More than once. But she was the only one; I swear it."

Sonnie's mouth dipped. "That makes her special, then."

"No." The terse denial clipped the air. "It meant

271

nothing to either of us. For me sleeping with her was just an occasional physical release, however cold that must sound to you. For Gracie it was fun and games. And I always paid her well for her time."

"Oh." Absorbed with that new perspective, Sonnie shifted position again.

"Sonnie, doggone it, hold still."

His thickening manhood pressed against the inside of her thigh. Sonnie realized the power she held over him, a power not totally carnal.

The knowledge pleased her.

"Do you believe me?" he asked.

"Yes." In retrospect, she sounded churlish and jealous when she had no need to. It became imperative to make amends. "I believe you, Lance. If she's your friend, then I want her to be mine, as well. It's just that . . ."

Embarrassed, she stopped.

"What, Sonnie?"

She took the plunge.

"Gracie is an attractive woman whose bosom is much larger than most women's. Certainly mine, I might add, and since men seem to like that in a woman, I wasn't sure . . . I thought they might be what attracted you—"

His laughter stopped her rambling explanation abruptly. She blinked down at him.

"Sonnie," he said. "Her breasts could damn well smother a man if he wasn't careful. Yours are perfect."

"You're only saying that to make me feel better."

His mirth faded. "Never let it be said that Lance Harmon isn't completely taken with Sonnie Mancuso's breasts," he said silkily, his tone sensual and intent. He released his clasp about her hips. "See how they fill my hands? Not too large, not too small. Perfect. And they're soft and warm to hold. Just the way they should be."

His callused palms offered a stimulating contrast to the sensitive globes, which had never before been fondled so freely.

Her blood pumped faster in her veins.

"The nipples will bring you pleasure, my sweet, if touched the way they're meant to be touched."

His thumbs stroked the hardening nubs until her breath quickened. She clutched his shoulders and arched her back, wanting more of this new sensation.

"But the pleasure will be even better if they're tasted. . . ."

His words died in the midst of his groan as he took one nipple into his mouth, lightly skimming his teeth, his tongue, over the peak.

Sonnie moaned from sheer ecstasy. Her head fell forward, dropping her hair into a sable curtain about them.

He laved the other, and desire surged strong within her. She recognized the excitement swirling deep inside her, a tidal wave that grew higher and higher with every stroke of his tongue.

Of their own accord, her hips rocked, seeking his thick hardness inside her.

"Lance," she said softly, wanting him. Begging him.

"No," he said when she would have slid onto her back, bringing him with her. "Stay here, and I'll teach you a new way to ride."

She spread her knees on either side of him, and he gently guided his manhood into her. He filled her, filled her to the brink in a way she never thought possible, in a way that stole her breath and kept her heart thundering inside her chest.

She began to move, tentatively at first, to keep the excitement. He joined her, and they learned the beat, caught the excitement together. Their hips moved, pumped fast, faster, until their beat cried out in its fever, and they rode the peaks, rode them and rode them, until together they crested in joyous victory.

Spent, fulfilled, and deliciously sated, Sonnie crumpled on top of Lance. He laughed softly in her ear and circled his arms tight about her, shifting his weight so that they both rolled to their sides on the mattress.

He buried his fist into her hair and kissed her long and deep. Hardly an inch separated them anywhere on their bodies, and Sonnie thought she'd never tire of being this close to him.

"I love you, Son," he murmured.

"I know," she purred on a happy sigh, and nuzzled his chin.

"Does it bother you when I call you that?" He rubbed a shank of her hair between two lean fingers.

She paused, remembering the times he'd shortened her name, turning it into a nickname of sorts. In the past she'd suspected her father gave her a distinctly unfeminine name as a result of his disappointment at failing to sire a male. She recalled, with regret, the instances when she'd turned her resentment toward Lance.

"No," she said truthfully. "You make it sound like an endearment. It doesn't trouble me."

"Good." He sounded relieved, and Sonnie glanced up at him. In the darkness she found his lower lip and traced it with her finger. He drew the tip into his mouth. "Tired?"

"Mmmmm." She liked his warm tongue licking her skin. She thought of the nightgown stuffed in the satchel and decided against retrieving it, finding the idea of lying naked with Lance for the entire night much more appealing.

She slid her knee in between his thighs and drew

contentment from the pleasing heaviness of his body. Her lids drifted closed. Sleep hovered only wispy seconds away.

Lance made her feel needed for the first time in her life. His love, honest and true, held her fast within its grip, and she glowed from the glory of it.

She would not think of the morning with its worries of Papa's health, of Silver Meadow, of turmoil that would inevitably come.

Turmoil reeking of revenge from a weasel of a man named Clay Ditson.

Chapter Sixteen

The persistent hiss and ping of the radiators dragged Lance from the depths of blissful sleep. Mentally resisting the noise, he shifted and became aware of the delicious, silken warmth cuddled next to him.

Sonnie. The love of his life.

They'd slept together in a tangle of arms and legs and a plethora of sable tresses. The scent of her perfume lingered in the bedclothes and on his skin, reminded him of how she'd come to him once more in the night. He'd shared his body as she shared hers; he taught her new ways of loving, of tasting, of giving and taking, until dawn lit the horizon.

He opened an eye. Sunshine filtered through the sheer curtains beneath the drapes, and he could only guess at the time, instinctively knowing a good portion of the morning had already passed. His eye shut again anyway, and he burrowed closer against Sonnie's body.

But his promise to Cookie to relieve him from

guarding Vince at the hospital kept him from falling back to sleep. He resisted the lure of his responsibilities. He didn't want to get up, didn't want to abandon the addictive need to keep Sonnie close.

Her love freed him from his fears, shattered the debilitating vulnerability of his past. She strengthened him when he would have been weak; she made him want to love, to touch, when before he would have stayed away. She gave him peace.

Movement in the hall—the clatter and clink of dishware outside their door—persuaded Lance to give up sleep altogether. Carefully, so as not to disturb her, he removed his arm from around Sonnie's waist and slid his leg out from beneath hers. He dropped a tender kiss to her temple before slipping out of bed.

She stirred and stretched provocatively; her dark lashes fluttered open. Her sleepy gaze found him, and a gentle smile curved the fullness of her lips. He knew she remembered their loving, just as he had, and he couldn't resist going back for another kiss, this one longer, deeper, and infinitely more ardent.

"Mornin', beautiful," he murmured, and rubbed his stubbly chin lightly across her cheek.

She laughed softly and pushed him away. "Why are you up so early?"

"It's not early. Someone is trying to wake us up, I think." Regretfully he left her and strode across the room toward the door.

She scrambled to sit up and pulled the blankets up over her breasts.

"Who? Lance, you're not dressed." She hastily combed her fingers through her hair in an attempt to tame the tousled mane.

He plucked a towel from the commode as he passed and barely had the fabric wrapped about him before he unlocked the door and opened it wide.

"I thought so." A wooden cart, laden with fresh

strawberries, golden croissants, and a bottle of Giesler champagne in a silver-plated ice bucket, waited in the hall. The latest issue of the *Boston Sunday Herald* rested against a crystal vase filled with red roses. "A gift from Francois."

Sonnie exclaimed in delight. "How wonderful! What a dear man!"

"He's smitten, didn't I tell you?" Lance declared wryly. He recognized his leather case sitting on the floor and brought both items into the room before relocking the door. He wheeled the cart next to the bed.

It seemed Charlie had sent over the remainder of Lance's clothes from the Railroad Hotel. The cowboy included a scrawled note reporting that he and the others from the Mancuso outfit would be waiting at Kapp's Saloon until Lance came for them. At his—and Miss Sonnie's—convenience, of course, and Lance had to smile.

He shucked the towel and pulled on a pair of clean Levi's. Shirtless and barefoot, he sprawled on his side next to Sonnie on the bed and propped himself up on an elbow. She handed him a buttered croissant and half of the newspaper.

"Eat quickly, my love," she urged, pouring two glasses of the sparkling champagne. "We have to go to the hospital to see Papa." She glanced at the clock on the dresser and clucked her tongue. "It'll be noon by the time we get over there. He'll wonder what's happened to us."

Despite her words, Lance was in no hurry to leave, to end their stay at the Cheyenne Club, with all its sweet memories of the night they'd shared together. He reached over and curled his fingers behind her neck, bringing her closer for another kiss.

"I want to ask Vince for your hand, Sonnie. Okay?" He nuzzled her jaw, then nibbled on her earlobe.

"I'd be most thrilled if you would," she whispered, then turned slightly and pressed her mouth to his in a fervent acceptance of his proposal.

Apprehension misted the sensations she brewed within him and overshadowed his happiness. He grew wary of those things over which he had no control.

"Suppose he'll agree?" he asked.

"Why wouldn't he?" She shrugged, an impish light in her eyes. "If not, I'll marry you anyway." She kissed the tip of his nose, drew back, and picked up one of the stemmed glasses. "You worry too much, Boss-man."

He took the proffered champagne. He had to settle for her answer, but he wished he possessed the same beguiling innocence and trust that she did.

He couldn't wait to talk to C. W. Even more important, he had to talk to Vince. Either man could give him the answers he needed.

Answers that would tell him if the past would destroy his future.

Sonnie finished the front-page article she'd been reading in her half of the *Herald*, took a bite of a plump strawberry, and gave Lance the rest to finish. She'd dallied long enough; she simply had to get dressed.

Engrossed in a lengthy editorial, Lance let his hand trail her arm in an absent caress as she slid from the bed and sank her toes into the thick, wine-colored carpet.

From the satchel, she pulled out a navy blue shirt-waist with a puritan white collar and articles for her toilette. She took care not to interrupt Lance in his reading and garbed herself in relative haste, then washed her face and cleaned her teeth.

Her glance sought him in the mirror while she brushed her hair. He'd abandoned his part of the paper for hers and studied it intently. Sonnie guessed he didn't often read so leisurely, and she hated to rush him now.

"I'll be ready to go in a few minutes, Lance," she said. "You'd better hurry."

He grunted and turned a page. "You're sounding like a wife already, Miss Mancuso."

His teasing remark invited her indulgent smile, and she decided to give him a little longer, knowing a man needed far less time than a woman to dress. After pulling her hair back with an elaborately scrolled tortoiseshell comb, she determined that their room needed a definite tidying-up before they left.

The heap of clothing at the foot of the bed brought a rush of memories; she almost blushed, remembering how quickly the garments had been shed the night before. The brocade gown was in shambles—wrinkled and torn beyond repair. She'd never wear it again. It would only remind her of Clay Ditson and his frightening attack. She balled the gown up and stuffed it into her satchel; her delicate underthings and patent-leather shoes followed with considerably more care, and only Lance's worsted suit remained.

She folded the pants along their crease and set them aside, righted his boots, and reached for the jacket. In her attempts to smooth the wrinkles, a yellowed envelope slipped out from an inside pocket.

In an instant, Sonnie recognized the paper from her father's office and how she'd discovered it only seconds before his heart attack. She had forgotten about it in the chaotic days that followed.

But the old curiosity returned full force. She removed the document and started to read. *Children's Aid Society, New York.* She frowned. An orphanage? *1876.* Her mother had died a few years earlier. Sonnie would have barely started school. *Vince Mancuso . . .* Why would Papa be in contact with an orphanage so far away? ... *hereby presents his petition to adopt Lance Harmon.* ...

Her hands began to shake.

... *orphan train* ... *Missouri.* ... *Old Opera House. Omaha, Nebraska* ... *territory of Wyoming* ...

The tiny printed words blurred together in a legal jumble. She blinked furiously, but forced herself to keep reading. She focused on Papa's familiar, clipped handwriting at the bottom of the page. Next to his signature was another's, smudged and difficult to decipher, a reverend whose name she didn't even want to know.

"Oh, my God."

Her choking cry, torn from her throat, jerked Lance's attention. She dropped the horrid paper as if it had burst into flame and pressed her fingertips to her mouth. His gaze flew to her face, followed the paper's descent, then jerked back upward.

"Sonnie. Hell, baby."

His skin paled beneath the stubble on his cheeks. The *Herald* fell from his grip. He sat up slowly, warily, and eased from the bed.

"You knew about this, didn't you?" she accused, stepping back when he would have stepped closer.

He froze.

"Yes. No. Oh, damn. Sonnie, you have to listen to me."

"You knew, but you made love to me anyway. Again and again."

"Sonnie, I *didn't* know—"

"My father *adopted* you, and you didn't know?" Her voice raised to a shrill pitch. She wavered on the edge of hysteria.

"I swear on my mother's grave, I did not know anything about this!" He hissed the words desperately, frantically, through his teeth. "I only found the damned document a few days ago."

"And you asked me to marry you anyway. God, I'm such a fool."

Her chin trembled. She prayed for the strength not to break down in front of him.

"Sweetheart, I've got C. W. checking on it to see if everything's legal—"

"Legal? It's *notarized*, Lance, for pity's sake!"

He drew in a terse breath. "He'll find out the truth for me. For us." He exhaled and raked a hand violently through his hair. "We'll go to the hospital now. We'll ask Vince. I don't care how sick he is. He'll tell us. We'll *make* him tell us, but by the grace of heaven, he never told me a thing."

"No. I don't want to see my father."

She would not compete for his affections any longer. He had Lance to love, didn't he? She whirled and scooped up her satchel, glad the bag was packed and sat a fair distance away from where Lance stood.

"I will never be good enough for him. He wanted a son nineteen years ago, not another daughter. I don't care if I ever see him again."

"Sonnie, come on. Please." Lance's tone turned pleading. "We'll work this out together."

She steeled herself against his masculinity, against the love she felt for him and the nearly overpowering desire to throw herself into his strong arms and feel him hold her tight.

Because she hurt so badly she thought she'd never heal again.

"He did it for his precious ranch and rangeland and stupid cattle. My sisters and I were never worthy enough for him. But you obviously were." Her lip curled in disdain; her wounded rage drove her onward, stabbing Lance with the resentment that boiled within her. "Fine. Keep it all. I don't want anything

to do with him or you or this horrible country and its
problems—"

She lied, and Lance knew it, and she could not go
on. Breaking into an agonized sob, Sonnie bolted toward the door, but in an instant he held her arm in a
death grip, preventing her from moving another inch.

Without thinking, without feeling, she lashed out
and struck his face. He took the blow, not making a
sound, not even a curse of surprise; then abruptly,
unexpectedly, his grasp loosened, and she fled.

He let her go.

The sting in his cheek spread like a roaring wildfire
over his skin and into his heart, but left him cold and
dead inside.

He let her go.

He never thought she would find out. He'd been so
careful. From the time he first found it, he wouldn't
let the document out of his sight, carrying the damned
thing with him always so she wouldn't discover it
somehow when he wasn't there to prevent it.

He let her go.

And now she was gone.

He stood where she left him, feet spread, fists
clenched, chest heaving with every burning, painful
breath.

How would he live without her?

She'd been hurt more than he ever thought possible, even in his worst nightmare. He understood how
she felt, how unneeded she must think she was; he
never dreamed it would come to this or that he'd be
responsible.

She'd be alone now, without him or her father or
the Rocking M to love. She lost everything, and all
because a lousy place of paper took it all away.

He loved her with his life, and like a coward he let
her go.

A coward in the worst way.

His mind screamed in protest, refusing to allow it to happen. His aching heart infused him with a surge of strength and raw determination to go after her, to hug and kiss the hurt away and keep loving her forever.

He had to find her and bring her back, even if she hated him and never loved him again. He had to try. Hell, he had to do at least that.

He broke into a run toward the door, then remembered he wore no boots, no shirt. Swearing mightily, he ravaged the leather bag, yanked out something to wear, and grabbed his boots. Balancing on one leg and then the other, he pulled them on, and after a second's thought, clamped his holster around his waist.

He'd hold a gun to her head if he had to, he thought grimly.

He plunged down the stairs two at a time while shoving his arms into the shirt and a hat onto his head. Francois, wringing his hands and looking distressed, met him at the bottom.

"Monsieur, is everything not all right? Mademoiselle, she was crying."

"I know, I know." Without a break in his run, he left the steward to fret in the main hall and lunged out the club's doors.

Lord Whitby stood out front stroking the neck of a saddled, fine-blooded stallion hitched along the row of posts. He lifted a chubby leg into the stirrup, but Lance grasped a handful of his tailored riding jacket and pulled him away. The Englishman stumbled backward; Lance hastily righted him, then lifted his own foot into the stirrup.

"Do you mind? I'm in a hurry," he said tersely, and swung himself up.

The baron sputtered, taken aback by Lance's erratic

behavior. Lance took the reins and nudged the horse into a turn.

"I say, I was just going after Miss Sonnie. She was bloody upset about something—I say, Lance, where are you going with my steed?"

"After her. Which way did she go?"

The Englishman didn't appear to know what to make of it all.

"Which way did she go?" Lance repeated through clenched teeth.

"That way." He pointed a finger toward the south.

The train depot. Instinctively Lance knew Sonnie was going back to Boston.

He kicked the horse into a hard gallop. The need for haste consumed him.

The stallion's hooves clawed up clumps of dirt and dust all along the several-block ride to the Union Pacific train station. A massive black engine pulling a dozen cars squealed to a stop, spilling passengers into the crowd waiting on the platform. Skillful maneuvering through a snarl of rigs and horses brought Lance as close to the depot as he could get.

So many people. What if he couldn't find her?

Twin sets of tracks held trains headed in opposite directions. Curling wisps of steam trailed in the sky from an engine already on its way east. A knot of fear formed in his chest. Had Sonnie already left?

He dismounted and entered the throng of men, women, and children packed in among the clutter of trunks and baggage. His height allowed him a view most would envy, and, frantic, he scanned the crowd for the raven-haired beauty who'd stolen his heart.

He found her at the ticket window.

Relief almost buckled his knees, and he elbowed his way over to her. Mel Timms, the railroad clerk, took the bills Sonnie handed him from inside her small beaded purse, then turned away to make change.

"You're not going anywhere, Sonnie," Lance said in a growl close to her ear.

She started at the sound of his voice. Their gazes clashed. The surprise in her tearstained eyes froze into flashing shards of black ice.

"Yes, I am. You'll not stop me, Lance."

The clerk slipped the ticket and a small bill under the iron-barred window. He acknowledged Lance with a polite nod. "Howdy, Mr. Harmon. There you are, miss. Train leaves in twenty-five minutes." He peered over the edge of his rimless spectacles to the matronly woman wearing a hat with a bird nest on the brim who was waiting behind Sonnie. "Next?"

"Keep the ticket, Mel. She won't need it," Lance said, and slid the printed pass back to him before Sonnie had a chance to protest.

Mel glanced from Lance to Sonnie and frowned. He pushed the ticket back under the bars again, this time holding both it and the bill until Sonnie could take them. "Reckon it's hers, Mr. Harmon. She paid, fair and square."

"Thank you." Sonnie smiled sweetly at the clerk before turning and glaring at Lance. She kept a firm grip on the scrap of paper while she returned the money to her purse, picked up the satchel, and spun on her heel into the crowd.

Striving for patience, Lance took off after her.

"I'm not going to let you leave, Sonnie," he said.

"You can't stop me."

He emitted a humorless laugh. "I'll throw you over my shoulder and take you back home. I've done it before."

Her step faltered; her wary glance considered him as if she pondered whether or not he'd carry through

286

with his threat. She bumped into an elderly gentleman and apologized.

"I'll scream and make a scene, then," she warned, continuing over to a row of benches to await the train. "Don't think I won't."

"Go ahead. Damned if I care."

Her jaw jutted. "I have the ticket. See?" She waved the pass under his nose in gloating defiance of his refusal to see her go. "I'm getting on the train—"

He snatched the ticket from her unresisting fingers and tore it into pieces before tossing them all into the air.

"No, you're not."

She watched the tiny scraps drift down to the platform floor like confetti at a parade. Her back straightened, her chin lifted, and she stood up with stilted dignity.

"Very well." She sniffed and began to retrace her steps back to the ticket window.

His patience nearly at an end, Lance shook his head and followed her. Again.

"Sonnie, you are the most exasperating, stubborn woman I've ever met," he said, and stepped around a toddler hanging on to his mother's skirts.

"And you are the most pigheaded, arrogant, deceitful man to walk the face of the earth!" Once more at the window, she leaned around the bird-nest woman doing business with Mel. "May I have another ticket, please? Mine seems to have been destroyed."

"Excuse me, ma'am." Lance carefully but firmly pushed the indignant older woman aside. "I never meant to deceive you, Sonnie. You know that."

"That'll be thirty-two dollars, miss." Mel's lips thinned in annoyance.

"I don't know what to think anymore." She rummaged inside her purse, frowned, then dumped the contents onto the counter. Counting under her breath, she gathered all the bills she had into her fist. "I don't have enough money," she said, and stomped her foot in frustration.

"Too bad. Sorry to bother you, Mel." Lance quickly swept her belongings back into her bag, took Sonnie's elbow, and pulled her away from the window. "Let's go, sweetheart."

"I'm not your sweetheart." She tried to jerk away. "I'm not your anything."

His grip tightened; he debated throwing her over his shoulder after all.

"You're gonna be my wife as soon as I can get you to a church. Now shut up. People are starting to stare."

She stumbled over somebody's trunk, but Lance's hold kept her from falling. He continued pulling her toward Lord Whitby's horse.

"I'm going back to Boston. That's what you've wanted all along, isn't it, Lance? To get me out of your life?"

"Not anymore. I've changed my mind."

They wound their way around a paint-worn springboard wagon. The stallion waited a short distance away.

"I want to marry you, and you want to marry me, and if you weren't so damned stubborn, you'd admit it." He halted in the street and turned her about to face him. "I need you, Sonnie. I love you. I want you to have my babies, to build a life with me. A future."

Her chin trembled, her ebony eyes glistened with a new set of tears, and he sensed the moment her apprehensions broke free. "Oh, Lance."

Those luscious lips quivered, and he lowered his head to taste their sweetness, to give her comfort, to offer silent reassurance that he would do everything in his power to make her world perfect and right.

The satchel dropped to the street, and she wrapped

her arms snugly about his neck. His arms tightened, enfolding her to his chest. His mouth opened and sought her tongue in a familiar quest. She accommodated him, flirting and teasing, fulfilling her own need to be consoled, to bring him pleasure within the strictures of broad daylight and crowds of people and propriety. Fire flowed in Lance's veins with every thrust and curl, and he knew a burning need to take her back to Lord Whitby's room.

Suddenly Sonnie was wrenched from him, jerked from his embrace with an unexpectedness that dulled his reflexes and numbed his brain. She cried out, as surprised as he, and before he could think, before he could react, someone stronger and larger whipped both his arms behind his back, yanking them as high as they would go until Lance was sure they'd be pulled straight from their sockets.

He hurled a curse from the innermost cavern of his chest. Clay Ditson cackled back at him, his scrawny arm clutched around Sonnie's shoulders, a Smith & Wesson revolver pressed to her temple.

Where seconds before love and yearning had swum in Lance's veins, now only hatred curdled. He fought the man who held him, tried with every muscle he possessed to break free of the powerful grip. He ignored the pain, the very real threat that both his arms could be broken, or that Snake was a hell of a lot stronger than he would ever be.

The Indian muttered a harsh word in Shoshone and pressed a blade to Lance's throat. The glinting, sharp edge pricked Lance's skin just enough to draw blood, deep enough to give him warning. Beads of crimson trickled down his neck.

"Let her go, Ditson," Lance said in a hiss.

His lungs heaved. He strove for control.

"Huh-uh. No way." Ditson's yellow teeth bared in a devilish, valiant grin. "I gotcha now, don't I, Harmon? I'm gonna win this time. And you can't do nothin' about it."

Sonnie's face had paled. Her skin looked luminescent above the prim collar. She stood stiff, frozen in Ditson's clutch, as if afraid to move for fear he'd pull the trigger.

Lance's heart twisted. God, he wanted to spare her this.

"Let her go, y'hear?" He sounded frantic, on the edge of control, but he couldn't help it. "Take me instead."

"Don't reckon I want either one of you real bad." Ditson leered. "It's Silver Meadow I want, but I need her to be my ace in the hole against her pa."

"Silver Meadow? It's yours. We'll sign the land over to you."

Even as he made the proposition, Lance knew it would never work, that the offer would be too easy, that Ditson wasn't gullible enough to take the range and live happily ever after. He would make them all bleed first.

"Y'think I'm stupid?" Ditson roared, and Sonnie flinched. "The old man ain't gonna give Silver Meadow up without a fight. And me and Snake'll be ready for him." He turned slightly, revealing the rows of scabbed-over scratches on his cheek, and Lance guessed Sonnie had been responsible. "Besides, I got a score to settle with the pretty lady." He started to drag Sonnie away, backing her up one step at a time toward his rangy-looking bay. "Come on, Snake. Let's get outta here."

Desperation exploded inside Lance; he feared what Ditson would do. He writhed in the Indian's ironlike hold. Pain shot through his shoulders and down his back. He thought of the Colts strapped to his waist and despaired over his inability to reach them.

"Lance, I'll be okay. You hear me? I'll be okay."

Sonnie's plea reached out to him as she moved farther and farther away. He loved her for trying to reassure him in the midst of her own struggle, for her courage to face what lay ahead, and he had never felt so helpless in his entire life.

"Sonnie, no!"

Again he tried to yank himself free; he pitted his strength against the Indian's brawn and found himself hopelessly outmatched. Wildly he scanned the crowd, hoped, prayed someone would come forward to help, to end this nightmare, to save Sonnie when he couldn't save her himself.

But no one did. A few men watched with wary fascination on their weathered faces; worried mothers fled with their children in tow, and others merely went about their business, preoccupied with their lives and unconcerned with anyone else's.

And Lance despised them all.

Clay Ditson shoved Sonnie toward the bay; she stumbled. He jerked her back up again with a leer curling his gap-toothed mouth, and soon, so soon, she would be gone.

"I'm going after her, Snake," Lance grated out, unable to take his eyes off of her, his chest heaving from the exertion of trying to break free. "You know that, don't you?"

Snake grunted and said something in Shoshone, the guttural sounds indicating acceptance, as if he expected little else. Abruptly the knife's blade left Lance's throat, Snake's grasp loosened, and he spun Lance around so fast, Lance almost lost his balance.

The Indian's mammoth fist reared up, then bore down with a force that sent Lance hurtling into the dirt. Fiery pain, white-hot and searing, erupted over his jaw. Bright lights flashed and blinded his vision.

Sonnie. Sonnie, my love.

And then everything went black.

Chapter Seventeen

Lance clawed his way through the throbbing, whirling blackness upward toward the hazy gray cloud of consciousness. From far away, a woman's voice reached him, gentle but persistent. He clung to the sound; the tones gave him focus, something to concentrate on during his fight through oblivion.

Someone tapped his cheek over and over and over. He moaned, wanting them to stop, to go away, to let him rest until the pain in his jaw disappeared.

"Come on, mister. Wake up. You've got to wake up now. There you go. Come on."

His eyes opened. The haze cleared, faded in and out, and he blinked. A pair of hummingbirds in a nest sat on a hat, a woman's hat, amid a garish creation of velvet loops and grosgrain ribbons.

"He's coming to," the woman said, relieved.

Lance remembered the hat—gaudy, downright ugly. He remembered it from the train depot when Sonnie had tried to buy a ticket.

Sonnie.

Christ, he had to find her.

He groaned and tried to sit up, but strong hands pinned him down.

"Whoa, boss. Take it easy. Not so fast."

Lance swallowed. Drawn to the familiar voice, he swiveled his head in the dirt and squinted at Charlie. Their faces somber, Stick, Red Holmes, and Frank Burton peered over Charlie's shoulder.

"Let me up," Lance ordered, his voice thick. "They . . . took Sonnie."

"I know. I heard. So'd half the town. But you gotta give yourself a little time. You ain't gonna be able to go after her when you can't even see straight."

"That Indian hit you pretty hard, mister. Didn't think you was ever gonna wake up," the woman said, her plump, kind features showing worry. "Get yourself together real quick. Your wife needs you."

"She's not my wife . . . yet."

He shrugged free from Charlie and pushed to a sitting position. His world swam; he cursed the dizziness and managed to stand up. In unison, the others rose with him, ready to catch him should he fall. Lance touched his jaw gingerly, working the joints to make sure nothing had been broken.

"They rode into the yards over there." The woman's chubby finger pointed in the general direction of the railroad tracks. "I saw the whole thing. I felt real bad this had to happen, mister, just when you were gettin' things patched up with your lady."

He narrowed an eye toward the area she indicated. Driven by the need to find Sonnie, Lance felt his strength return by quick degrees. Clear, rational thought followed. He pivoted, wobbled, and headed toward Lord Whitby's stallion.

"Sure you're up to a fast ride, boss?" Charlie asked, scrambling with the others to follow him.

Lance tossed him a black glare to show him the folly of his question.

"No tellin' what Miss Sonnie's been through by now," Stick muttered, anguished.

Lance settled unsteadily in the saddle and laced the reins around his fingers. He fought down the nauseous worry churning in his stomach.

"She's a fighter. She'll hold her own till we get to her."

His gaze swept over the cowboys, each mounted and ready for his command. His men—Mancuso men who loved Sonnie almost as much as he did. Their loyalty filled him with pride. Never had he been as thankful to have them with him. They'd die for Sonnie if they had to.

"I sent for the police," the woman said, brushing the dust off of Lance's hat and handing it to him. "They should be here real soon."

"I'm not waiting."

He didn't need them anyway. He and his men would take care of Clay Ditson.

Raking a hand through his hair, ignoring the ache in his jaw, Lance pushed the hat onto his head and nodded his gratitude to the woman. He vowed to learn her name and thank her properly later, but for now, only Sonnie mattered.

"Anyone can see how much you two are in love," she called out. The curious crowd parted. Lance and the others maneuvered their horses through. "Bring her back safe, y'hear?"

Lance ran an irritable glance over the wide expanse of Union Pacific Railroad yards. Years ago Vince had taught him to read sign, to track down cattle or horses that had strayed from their home range, but the skill proved worthless to him now when he needed it most. Coal and rocks strewn about the ground, which was already packed from the railroad's heavy equipment, prevented any prints from being left behind, and they'd wasted too much time in the search.

"Sons of bitches could've gone any which way," Charlie muttered.

"Yeah."

Lance knew Ditson had fully intended to slow their hunt by fleeing through the yards, and the tactic had worked. Restless and anxious, he shifted in the saddle.

He knew of only one man better at tracking than he.

"Let's go to Gracie's," he said with a grunt, reining the stallion into a turn.

"What the hell for?" Charlie demanded.

"I'm guessing we'll find Tom Horn with her."

O'Neil Street rumbled with the pounding of hooves from their swift ride to Gracie's little house. As they drew nearer, Lance removed his Colt from the holster and fired two shots into the air. Their horses halted on the front lawn, and the gunfighter, wearing nothing but his Levi's, stepped onto the porch with a final buttoning of his pants.

"Harmon, what're you tryin' to do? Wake the dead?"

"Ditson and Snake took Sonnie. I'd be obliged if you'd help me get her back again."

Horn's expression hardened. "Hold on till I get dressed."

He retreated into the house, and Lance chafed at the delay. A few moments later Horn returned fully clothed, and strapped his gun belt around his hips. Gracie emerged with him, fastening a purple satin robe about her.

"You said Snake was part of it?" he asked, all business. At Lance's affirmative reply, he nodded in satisfaction. "His horse'll be unshod, then. Makes him

295

easier to track. Where would they hide out?"

"Who knows? Could be anywhere in the damned state." Impatience swirled through Lance. "But I'd reckon they'd head to Silver Meadow first."

Horn climbed on top of his horse. "Might be a place to start. If Ditson had any sense, he'd know that's where we'd check first."

"Who says the bastard has any sense?" Lance said in a growl.

The miles to Silver Meadow, normally easy to manage, suddenly loomed long and frustrating, and he could hardly wait to get riding again. The stallion pranced from the lawn and onto the street; the other horses followed his lead.

"Lance, I'm sorry about Sonnie," Gracie called. Concerned compassion filled her features. "Is there anything I can do?"

"Yeah. Get word to Vince. He'll want to know."

She nodded and waved and ran back inside, all in one motion. With Horn on one side and Charlie on his other, Lance kicked the stallion's ribs, and the grimly determined posse broke into a hard run toward Silver Meadow.

"Gonna be dark soon. She don't have a coat."

Jake McKenna tied the ends of the neckerchief covering Sonnie's mouth into a tight knot, then pushed her down onto a charred log. Her hands and ankles bound with rope, she landed with a painful thump to her tailbone and speared him with a haughty glare.

"So?" Clay Ditson challenged. "That's her problem."

He moved about what little remained of the burned-out cabin and rooted through scattered dried leaves and debris in search of kindling. A brisk breeze blew over the rubble once claiming to be the structure's walls; grass grew freely up to the foundation. Using blackened chunks of wood, he lit a fire in the sooty potbellied stove standing forlorn among the ashes.

"Why do we have to gag her, anyway? Nobody's gonna know if she hollers all the way out here."

Ditson slammed the stove's door shut in a fit of temper.

"Will you quit your whinin', McKenna? Shit! That's all you bin doin' since we left Cheyenne."

"We're miles from anybody, Clay. And she ain't had nothin' to drink or eat. What's it gonna hurt?"

"I don't want her screamin' or tryin' nothin' stupid. Silver Meadow ain't that far from the main spread. What if somebody thinks they hear somethin' and comes to check us out? 'Sides, I don't trust her. She's a Mancuso, or did you forgit that?"

"I didn't forget."

The trace of sympathy McKenna had for Sonnie disappeared. She could hardly believe he was the same man who had playfully goaded her into a game of seven-up the night she'd slipped into the bunkhouse. His betrayal stung.

Jake sneered down at her. "Your old man ran us off our land when I was just a kid. But I remember like it was yesterday. We had our own herd, bought and paid for clean, and we was stayin' in a cabin this side of the Iron Mountain. Mancuso claimed the land and everthin' on it was his. Shot my pa down in cold blood when he tried to defend the place."

Sonnie's eyes widened in disbelief. Papa would never act so ruthlessly. Through the neckerchief, she attempted a denial. McKenna ignored her.

"I promised Ma the day we buried my pa I'd get even. The old man didn't recognize me when I came back. Bastard don't have a forgivin' bone in his body. And I don't either, not anymore. Not when it comes to Vince Mancuso or his uppity kin." He loomed above her, his bowlegged stance rigid, his mood vengeful. "Poisoning a few of his precious cattle don't cut it, though. But now I got you." Sonnie shivered from the loathing in his eyes.

Abruptly he pursed his lips and hurled a stream of spittle into her face. Startled, Sonnie stiffened; the warm droplets slid from her cheek onto the navy blue shirtwaist. Pride kept her dignity intact, her chin up. She would not give him the satisfaction of seeing her humiliation; she met his venomous gaze evenly.

"You don't know what the old man is really like, do you, Miss Sonnie? You been off livin' a life of luxury wearin' your fancy clothes and expensive jewelry while me and my brothers and sisters been near starvin'. Ma died way before her time workin' harder'n she should." His chapped mouth curled with disgust. "Clay's right, you know? We'll let you spend the night cold and hungry. See how it feels."

Ditson snorted and rammed the tip of a knife into a can of beans.

"You still complainin' over there, McKenna?" he demanded, wrenching the blade until the tin parted. He set the container onto the hot stovetop and reached for a second. "I've heard your sob story before."

"It don't hurt for her to know the way it is," Jake said with a snarl. "Besides, you do your share of complainin', same as me."

Ditson dropped the can and bolted toward Jake. A flash of fear leaped into Jake's eyes a split second before Ditson backhanded him with a savage stroke. The cowboy spun to the floor, and Ditson grabbed for him again.

A sharp, harsh call stopped a subsequent blow. Ditson twisted around toward Snake. The Indian snapped a few words in Shoshone. Ditson swore and let Jake fall.

"I near 'bout had it with you, McKenna," he said. "Now that we got Mancuso's brat, I don't have much

298

use for you anymore, so keep your mouth shut from now on. You rile me another time, you're dead."

His brief bout of rebellion effectively quashed, Jake wiped the blood oozing from his lip with the cuff of his coat. Ditson returned to the stove and the can of beans, showing no more remorse than if he'd scolded a recalcitrant mule.

Sonnie's pulse pounded from the exchange. Violence had never been a part of her life. Her puny strength would provide little protection against three armed men, and she dreaded the darkening of the night.

Lance would come for her. She knew it with the certainty of her love. But when? Snake had struck him so hard. She'd seen him fall, and her heart had cried out in anguish.

Throughout their hectic flight from Cheyenne, Sonnie thought of little else but him. She kept him close in her mind; he gave her courage, the will to hang on until he found her.

She strained against the ropes holding her wrists and hated her helplessness. Her eyes lifted. Snake, his long, coarse hair scattered about his shoulders, his angular features cast in shadows, stared at her mockingly.

They would use her tonight, as violently as Ditson had attempted to the night before at the Railroad Hotel. She vowed to fight them with every muscle she possessed. They would use their lust to punish her for her father's actions; they would make her suffer with the degradation of her body.

Snake pulled his black-eyed gaze away and, with hands still bloody from the rabbit he'd skinned, turned the roasting meat impaled by a spit over the campfire. Succulent juices sizzled over the flames; the smells taunted Sonnie's stomach.

Dusk had fallen, and the autumn breeze pulled her

hair, nipped her with a chill. She squirmed on the log, and her aching limbs screamed in protest. She scanned the Wyoming horizon, remembering how beautiful Silver Meadow looked with its swaying grass and colorful wildflowers. Only yesterday the rangeland had brought her pleasure; tonight apprehension and dread dulled its appeal.

In the distance, a dog barked. Sonnie's ears pricked; her senses heightened.

A spoonful of beans stopped midway to Ditson's mouth. Wariness emanated from him, and he set the can down, then reached for the Smith & Wesson revolver. The Indian and Jake studied the darkness not reached by the campfire's light.

"Someone's out there," Ditson said, and strode to the edge of the cabin's foundation. He cocked his weapon.

The bark came again, this time closer. Ditson shot in the direction of the sound. The deafening pop cracked the silence, and Sonnie flinched.

The dog halted, wary of Ditson's aim, then boldly loped toward them, his tongue lagging to one side. In the fiery light she recognized Moose, and his arrival from the ranch brought a measure of wary comfort. Ignoring Ditson, he trotted right up to her, his tail wagging excitedly; she would have petted him in welcome had her bound wrists allowed her. Ditson leveled the revolver at him, and she held her breath in alarm.

"Hold on, Clay," Jake said in a hiss. "No more shootin'. You want to bring Harmon down on us? Stupid mutt's probably just hungry."

After a moment of deliberate consideration, Ditson lowered the gun and shoved it into his waistband. Receiving no affection from Sonnie, Moose meandered toward him, paused, and growled low in his throat.

"Git away from me, you stinkin' mongrel," Ditson said, and kicked at him.

Moose sidestepped the kick; his growling suddenly stopped. His long nose lifted in the air and sniffed voraciously of the roasting rabbit's aroma. He whimpered and scampered closer to Snake. The Indian swung a muscular arm and swatted him away with an epithet.

"Come here, Moose." Jake scooped out the beans in his can and dumped them in the grass. "Eat, you dumb dog," he said, and left.

In a few swipes of his red tongue, the beans were gone. Moose licked the grass clean and moseyed over to Sonnie, sighed, and rested his head on top of her shoe.

The three men squatted on their haunches around the campfire and devoured the meat. They talked quietly among themselves, ignoring Sonnie and Moose.

She longed for her gray-blue cape with its hood and warm folds. The cold had become almost unbearable. Seated too far away from the fire to receive any heat, she felt shivers rack her body, though she tried to hide them. Rumbles of hunger escaped her stomach, and she tried to hide those, too.

She didn't want the men to know of her discomfort or her fear. She didn't want to think of the hours ahead, of the struggles and humiliation she would endure. She didn't want to be Ditson's pawn in his plan to seek revenge against her father.

Her thoughts turned to Lance and fused into new worries. Why didn't he come? Her despair raged fresh and strong, and she pulled at the rope wrapping her wrists; the raw flesh stung and burned with each effort.

Moose's head lifted from her foot. He whined, a slight sound from his throat that no one but Sonnie heard. His tail, once still, wagged fast and furious.

301

He recognized something, someone, in the rangeland's shadows. Sonnie's heart stepped up its beat; she darted a glance toward the men. A bottle of whiskey kept them occupied; she was sure they hadn't noticed anything to rouse their suspicions.

She braced herself for disappointment as her gaze searched the darkness. What if Moose saw only a squirrel or a pesky fox? Then her eyes found Lance.

He crept through the grass, his stealth hushed, determined, yet reckless. He seemed unbearably far away. She wanted to run to him. Their eyes met for long moments. It was as if he touched her, spoke to her, reassured her everything would be okay.

Yet everything could go wrong.

He held a finger to his lips. She nodded slightly, careful not to give him away with her actions. He disappeared into the darkness.

She hated not being able to see him. She waited, fidgeted, worried—and hoped Moose would stay still.

The cold night failed to chill her skin anymore; her blood raced hot with trepidation. The seconds dragged by like hours. Where was he?

A twig snapped, and Sonnie ventured a peek to the side of the cabin's foundation. There, amid the rubble, the skeleton of a springboard wagon stood in the darkness. Lance hunkered beside it and pulled a bowie knife from its sheath; he dropped soundlessly to his belly and shimmied through the weeds toward her.

A round of whiskey-laced laughter erupted from the campfire, and Lance froze. Sonnie's breath hitched, but none of the men glanced over. She swallowed down her anxiety, and he continued toward her.

Sheer willpower kept her from squirming or from calling his name through the wad of neckerchief.

And then he was there, in front of her, slicing the knife's blade through the ropes around her ankles, then behind her to cut through the ones about her wrists. Moose, in his excitement, wiggled and twitched; his tail thumped the cabin's floor. Sonnie feared he would start barking at any moment.

She knew Lance's impatience with the dog and the very real possibility that Moose would give them away. Lance tossed his knife aside. With one hand, he clamped Moose's jaws closed; with the other he fumbled with the neckerchief, tied so tightly that the corners of Sonnie's mouth ached. Her arms, numb from lack of circulation, lifted to lend assistance, but the binding proved unexpectedly stubborn.

Moose pulled away and began to yip and dance and proclaim Lance's arrival with maddening exuberance.

Shouts exploded from around the campfire. Lance hissed a curse, gave a final yank, and the neckerchief fell away. He pressed a pistol into Sonnie's hand and jerked her to her feet.

"Get the hell out of here!" he yelled over the chaos, and pushed her away.

"Harmon! You slime-bellied bastard!"

His teeth bared in a snarl, Jake McKenna stood wide-legged with a raised gun pointed at Lance's back. His finger moved; Lance spun and lifted his own weapon. McKenna's body jerked from the force of the striking bullet, blood spurted over the front of his chest, and he fell dead in a sprawled heap.

Sonnie cried out, but no one seemed to hear. Shrieking like a hyena, Snake leaped forward and hurtled through the air toward Lance. The Indian's brawn toppled him, the force knocking the gun from Lance's grip, and the two men rolled and scuffled in the grass.

"Move, Snake, damn you!" Ditson shouted, waving the Smith & Wesson in his agitation. "Get off him. Let me kill him!" He ran closer, pointing the revolver's barrel scant feet from the wrestling men. "Give me a clear shot, y'hear?"

Moose growled with a ferocity Sonnie had never heard. His sharp teeth protruded from his open mouth, and he vaulted toward Ditson, clamping his jaws firmly around a scrawny forearm. Ditson screamed and tried to push him off. Moose held on all the tighter, and man and beast tumbled over the cabin's floor.

Fear for Lance's life choked the air in Sonnie's lungs. The pistol's cold metal burned her palms; she lifted it higher. She must shoot and save him, but he wouldn't hold still, wouldn't stay in one place to give her a chance.

Dear God, what if she missed Snake and hit Lance instead?

From out of nowhere, the Indian pulled out a knife, its ominous blade already stained with blood. His powerful body straddled Lance's; his muscle-thewed arm shot upward, fingers curled around the handle, the deadly tip turned downward. His chest heaving, Lance gripped Snake's wrist to prevent its descent. His muscles quivered from the effort; perspiration beaded his forehead. He was at a disadvantage; he would not outlast the Indian's formidable strength much longer.

She had to shoot or Lance would be lost to her forever.

Nothing in her tender upbringing had prepared her for this moment. She leveled the pistol at Snake, held it with both hands, and pulled the trigger. The Indian grunted, and he fell forward in a heap on top of Lance.

Tom Horn burst through the shadows. Stick and Charlie. Red Holmes. Frank Burton. Lance sucked in mammoth breaths before shoving Snake's lifeless body away. He staggered to his feet, dirty and disheveled, but blessedly alive. A sob rent Sonnie. The pistol fell from her hands, and she flew into his arms.

Ditson sliced the night with a mighty curse, and another shot exploded. Moose yelped and whined, bounded off of him, and limped into a corner to nurse the graze on his flank. His features demonic, Ditson cackled in gap-toothed glee, and ran toward Lance and Sonnie, who were locked in an embrace.

Firelight jumped off the revolver's barrel. As if in slow motion, Ditson kept coming closer, closer. His wild, triumphant screams echoed in Sonnie's ears, but they sounded far, so far away.

A bullet whined. Ditson's back arched, but still he kept coming. Looking stunned, Tom Horn, Charlie, and all the Mancuso men whirled to search the darkness behind them.

Ditson bettered his aim. He was frighteningly close, but Sonnie couldn't move, couldn't scream in warning. Lance yelled and twisted, putting himself between her and Ditson's gun, shielding her from what was to come. His arms tightened about her; she buried her face into his neck and waited to die.

Bullets pelted—three, four, five, six in succession. Blood spattered over their clothes, and Ditson dropped dead with a final gasp.

The haze of spent gunpowder hung over Silver Meadow like an acrid cloud. The well-stoked campfire brightened the darkness and illuminated the sheet-draped bodies lying in the coroner's wagon. Dancing, flickering flames chased away the autumn night's chill, warming Sonnie and the group of men huddled around the cabin's abandoned shell. Their voices, subdued but relaxed, softened the range's stark silence. Moose, his hind leg duly bandaged, basked in the limelight of attention and care.

Sonnie watched Lance fill a tin cup with black coffee and hand the steaming brew to her father, seated near the fire. Looking gaunt yet animated, Papa wore a hospital robe beneath his suede coat; a woolen blanket covered his lap.

"Another two seconds, Vince, and Sonnie and I would have been goners," Lance said wryly, moving next to her and slipping his arm around her waist. She snuggled closer and shuddered from the memory. "What the hell took you so long to shoot?"

"I wanted to savor the pleasure." Papa slurped loudly, winced, and swallowed. His eyes gleamed, as if he were reliving the moments just before Clay Ditson died. "After Gracie came and told us about Sonnie's kidnapping, I couldn't get out here fast enough. I'd waited a long time to get Ditson off of Mancuso land my way. I had to make it last, eh?"

He clearly derived great satisfaction from the act. Had he worried about her at all? Sonnie wondered.

"If I'd known you carried a weapon into my hospital, Vince—" The words trailed off of Doc Tanner's tongue threateningly.

Papa shrugged. "A cattleman must protect what is his, Ed. He can't do it without a gun."

A cattleman must protect what is his. Did he, as her father, mean to protect her, as well?

Sonnie couldn't be sure, and that saddened her.

She recalled Jake McKenna's story of how his father had died under Papa's gun. Throughout the long years she'd been gone, Papa had evolved into a different man—harder, ruthless, driven. Had he lost his capacity to love his own flesh and blood?

And she could not forget the yellowed envelope with its shattering document inside.

A spasm of coughing took Papa, and Doc Tanner rose, waiting patiently until the spell passed.

"We have to get you back to Cheyenne, Vince. This cold and excitement will be the end of you yet."

"I'll sleep good tonight, eh?" Papa smiled and allowed the doctor to take his elbow. He turned. "Are you coming back with us, Sonnie?"

"No. I'll stay at the Big House tonight."

A flicker of surprise passed over his features, but he nodded. "Suit yourself, *mia bambina.*"

"I am not your baby, Papa." Her simple statement, softly spoken, yet firm, emphatic, and more than a little rebellious, raised his brow. "I am a woman now. But, more important, I am your daughter. Or have you forgotten?"

"Of course I haven't forgotten," he said, frowning sternly. "Why would you say that?"

She pulled away from Lance, even though he tried to hold her near him. "Did you adopt Lance, Papa?"

Her point-blank question startled him. He glanced at Lance, then back at her. "You found the paper, then."

"I did."

His nostrils flared slightly, as if he disliked explaining his actions. "I gave him my love, but not my name, Sonnie. I intended to go through with the adoption, but I never made it to probate court."

"Why not? Then you would have had the son you always wanted." She couldn't keep the bitterness out of her tone.

"Yes." He showed no regret, no apology, no sensitivity to her wounded feelings. "He was very young when I brought him out here. He was hungry. He needed a home. I would have filed the legal papers to keep him on the ranch with me, but he loved the country so much. He thrived on the land, the work. He couldn't get enough of the fresh air. Soon I could see he would never leave." Papa spoke of Lance as if he were in the next county instead of only a few feet away, listening intently. "Besides, after you came home that first time, I could tell he had fallen in love

307

with you. I knew he would marry you, and then he would always stay, because you loved the ranch, too. I was right, eh?"

"You knew how much I loved you and the Rocking M, and still you sent me away." Sonnie fought to keep her lower lip from quivering. "Why, Papa?"

He shrugged. "After your mother died, I had nothing left in my heart to live for."

"You had me. You had six daughters who adored you."

His smile looked wan in the firelight. "Maybe it wasn't enough, eh?"

"I think not, Papa." She steadied her breathing, forcing herself to ask a final question. "Why did you name me Sonnie? Were you so disappointed that I turned out to be another girl?"

A long moment went by. He seemed buried in the past, then roused himself to the present with a little shake. He reached over and patted her shoulder. "So many questions, *mia bambina*. It's not such a terrible name, is it?"

He evaded the truth, and she knew the answer, as she always had. With Doc Tanner's gentle prodding, her father turned and walked slowly across his precious rangeland to the ambulance waiting to return him to the hospital.

The campfire's giant flames had dwindled to almost nothing, but Sonnie felt no loss of their heat. Snug and secure against the warmth of Lance's body, he held her close against him after nearly everyone had left Silver Meadow to return to Cheyenne. Only Tom Horn and the most trusted of the Mancuso men lingered.

The gunfighter stretched and yawned. "Guess I'll head back, too. Gracie'll be wonderin' what happened to me."

"Fill her in on all the details," Lance said. "She'll give you no rest until you do. And thanks, Tom. For everything."

The two men shook hands, their clasp firm and strong. "Don't mention it." Horn's gaze scanned the dark horizon. "The rustling problem is far from over. You cattlemen'll be needing me for a while yet." He grinned. "I'll be back."

He touched the brim of his hat to Sonnie and left.

"Reckon I'm close enough to the main spread, I'll just head on home," Charlie said. "I've had enough excitement in town to last me for a spell."

"Me, too," Cookie concurred, as he scratched his head and replaced his hat.

"Phew!" Stick gasped, jumping to his feet and moving away in search of fresher air. "What's that smell?"

Everyone grimaced, wrinkled their noses, and followed his lead. Only Moose, heaving a contented sigh, remained near the fire.

Sonnie's cheeks pinkened. Laughter bubbled in her throat. "Jake McKenna . . . he, uh, fed Moose some beans."

"Gawd." Cookie's features registered full-blown disgust. "Come on, you good-fer-nuthin' dog. Let's take you where you can pass your stinkin' wind someplace more private." With a gentleness that belied his gruff words, the old cowboy picked him up, mounted his horse, and settled Moose on his lap for the ride back to the bunkhouse, ever careful of the furry, injured leg. "Mind you, be a gentleman till we git you there. Stupid mutt."

The cowboys left amid waves and sleepy goodbyes. Sonnie and Lance lingered in the solitude of the Wyoming night.

"Cold?" he asked, coming behind her and wrapping his arms around her waist. She leaned into his warmth, his strength, and relished the feel of his body through the thin shirtwaist.

"No. Not with you."

"Doin' okay?" He nuzzled his chin against her jaw.

"Yes." She'd killed a man tonight, an Indian as ruthless as any depicted in Jeffrey's novels. And she'd survived. "Yes, I'm fine."

"Vince loves you in his own way. You know that, don't you, Sonnie?" The tender reassurance came through little nibbles on her earlobe.

"I suppose he does." Papa would never need her as long as he had the ranch. She accepted it. She'd lived many years without him, and he'd lived many more without her.

But Sonnie had Lance now. She understood Papa's love for him. Didn't she love him just as much?

Yes, that and more. A million times more.

She turned and lifted her mouth to his, spilling her love into the kiss in a way the little words never could.

Lance's breath grew ragged. "We'll get married as soon as we can. We'll live at the Big House—"

Sonnie drew back. "No, not there."

A tawny brow rose. She shook her head emphatically.

"The Big House is my father's. I want to start fresh with you, Lance. I want you to build us a home"— she paused and thought of fairies' tears in the morning—"here. Right here in Silver Meadow."

AUTHOR'S NOTE

Many thanks to Ms. Jean Brainerd, senior historian at the Wyoming State Museum in Cheyenne, for her invaluable help in providing me with photographs and research materials for *Wyoming Wildflower*, among them Agnes W. Spring's fascinating and detailed "The Cheyenne Club."

With Ms. Brainerd's assistance, I have been able to depict the woes of the cattlemen, the political power of the Wyoming Stockgrowers Association, and the elite Cheyenne Club with reasonable clarity. Several of the characters brought to life in *Wyoming Wildflower* once graced the Club, including John Carlisle, Hubert Teschemacher, John Coble, and the French steward, François De Prato.

The famous club once stood proudly on the corner of what is today Seventeenth and Warren streets in Cheyenne. In 1936, the building was torn down and a new structure to house the Chamber of Commerce was built. The Cheyenne Frontier Days committee kept its headquarters there for many years until moving to its present location.

The CHANGELING BRIDE

LISA CACH

In order to procure the cash necessary to rebuild his estate, the Earl of Allsbrook decides to barter his title and his future: He will marry the willful daughter of a wealthy merchant. True, she is pleasing in form and face, and she has an eye for fashion. Still, deep in his heart, Henry wishes for a happy marriage. Wilhelmina March is leery of the importance her brother puts upon marriage, and she certainly never dreams of being wed to an earl in Georgian England—or of the fairy debt that gives her just such an opportunity. But suddenly, with one sweet kiss in a long-ago time and a faraway place, Elle wonders if the much ado is about something after all.

___52342-6 $4.99 US/$5.99 CAN

Bewitching the Baron

Lisa Cach

Valerian has always known before that she will never marry. While the townsfolk of her Yorkshire village are grateful for her abilities, the price of her gift is solitude. But it never bothered her until now. Nathaniel Warrington is the new baron of Ravenall, and he has never wanted anything the way he desires his people's enigmatic healer. Her exotic beauty fans flames in him that feel unnaturally fierce. Their first kiss flares hotter still. Opposed by those who seek to destroy her, compelled by a love that will never die, Nathaniel fights to earn the lone beauty's trust. And Valerian will learn the only thing more dangerous—or heavenly—than bewitching a baron, is being bewitched by one.

___52368-X $5.50 US/$6.50 CAN

Dorchester Publishing Co., Inc.
P.O. Box 6640
Wayne, PA 19087-8640

Duchess For A Day

Peggy Waide

To save her life and her inheritance, Mary Jocelyn Garnett does what she must. She marries Reynolds Blackburn—without his knowledge. And all goes well, until the Duke of Wilcott returns to find he is no longer the king of bachelors. As long as the marriage is never consummated, Jocelyn knows, it can be annulled—just as soon as she has avenged her family and reacquired her birthright. Unfortunately, her blasted husband appears to be attracted to her! Worse, Reyn is handsome and clever, and she fears her husband might assume that she is one of many women who are simply after his title. After one breathless kiss, however, Jocelyn swears that she will not be duchess for a day, but Reyn's for a lifetime.

___4554-0 $4.99 US/$5.99 CAN

PEGGY WAIDE
POTENT CHARMS

She is the most frustrating woman Stephen Lambert has ever met—and the most beguiling. But a Gypsy curse has doomed the esteemed duke of Badrick to a life without a happy marriage, and not even a strong-willed colonial heiress with a tendency to find trouble can change that. Stephen decides that since he cannot have her for a wife, he will convince her to be the next best thing: his mistress. But Phoebe Rafferty needs a husband, and fast. She has four weeks to get married and claim her inheritance. Phoebe only has eyes for the most wildly attractive and equally aggravating duke. But he refuses to marry her, mumbling nonsense about a curse. With time running out, Phoebe vows to persuade the stubborn aristocrat that curses are poppycock and the only spell he has fallen under is love.

___4694-6 $4.99 US/$5.99 CAN

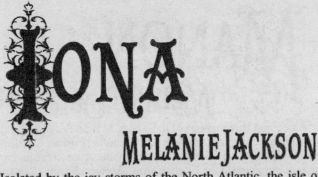

IONA

MELANIE JACKSON

Isolated by the icy storms of the North Atlantic, the isle of Iona is only a temporary haven for its mistress. Lona MacLean, daughter of a rebel and traitor to the crown, knows that it is only a matter of time before the bloody Sasannachs come for her. But she has a stout Scottish heart, and the fiery beauty gave up dreams of happiness years before. One task remains—to protect her people. But the man who lands upon Iona's rain-swept shores is not an Englishman. The handsome intruder is a Scot, and a crafty one at that. His clever words leave her tossing and turning in her bed long into the night. His kiss promises an end to the ghosts that plague both her people and her heart. And in his powerful embrace, Lona finds an ecstasy she'd long ago forsworn.

___4614-8 $4.99 US/$5.99 CAN

Dorchester Publishing Co., Inc.
P.O. Box 6640
Wayne, PA 19087-8640

Please add $1.75 for shipping and handling for the first book and $.50 for each book thereafter. NY, NYC, and PA residents, please add appropriate sales tax. No cash, stamps, or C.O.D.s. All orders shipped within 6 weeks via postal service book rate. Canadian orders require $2.00 extra postage and must be paid in U.S. dollars through a U.S. banking facility.

Name_____
Address_____
City_____State_____Zip_____
I have enclosed $_____ in payment for the checked book(s).
Payment <u>must</u> accompany all orders. ❑ Please send a free catalog.
   CHECK OUT OUR WEBSITE! www.dorchesterpub.com

MANON
MELANIE JACKSON

Alone and barely ahead of the storm, Manon flees Scotland; the insurrection has failed and Bonnie Prince Charlie's rebellion has been thrown down. Innocent of treason, yet sought by agents of the English king, the Scots beauty dons the guise of a man and rides to London—and into the hands of the sexiest Sassanach she's ever seen. But she has no time to dally, especially not with an English baronet. Nor can she indulge fantasies of his strong male arms about her or his heated lips pressed against her own. She fears that despite her precautions, this rake may uncover her as no man but *Manon*, and she may learn of something more dangerous than an Englishman's sword—his heart.

Lair of the Wolf

Also includes the eighth installment of *Lair of the Wolf*, a serialized romance set in medieval Wales. Be sure to look for future chapters of this exciting story featured in Leisure books and written by the industry's top authors.

___4737-3 $4.99 US/$5.99 CAN

Dorchester Publishing Co., Inc.
P.O. Box 6640
Wayne, PA 19087-8640

Please add $1.75 for shipping and handling for the first book and $.50 for each book thereafter. NY, NYC, and PA residents, please add appropriate sales tax. No cash, stamps, or C.O.D.s. All orders shipped within 6 weeks via postal service book rate. Canadian orders require $2.00 extra postage and must be paid in U.S. dollars through a U.S. banking facility.

Name_____

Address_____

City_____ State_____ Zip_____

I have enclosed $_____ in payment for the checked book(s).

Payment <u>must</u> accompany all orders. ❑ Please send a free catalog.

CHECK OUT OUR WEBSITE! www.dorchesterpub.com

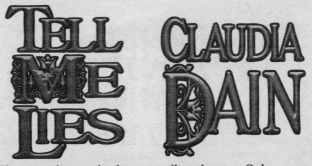

They are pirates—lawless, merciless, hungry. Only one way offers hope of escaping death, and worse, at their hands. Their captain must claim her for his own, risk his command, his ship, his very life, to take her. And so she puts her soul into a seduction like no other—a virgin, playing the whore in a desperate bid for survival. As the blazing sun descends into the wide blue sea, she is alone, gazing into the eyes of the man who must lay his heart at her feet. . . .

Lair of the Wolf

Also includes the fourth installment of *Lair of the Wolf*, a serialized romance set in medieval Wales. Be sure to look for future chapters of this exciting story featured in Leisure books and written by the industry's top authors.

___4692-X $5.50 US/$6.50 CAN

Dorchester Publishing Co., Inc.
P.O. Box 6640
Wayne, PA 19087-8640

Please add $1.75 for shipping and handling for the first book and $.50 for each book thereafter. NY, NYC, and PA residents, please add appropriate sales tax. No cash, stamps, or C.O.D.s. All orders shipped within 6 weeks via postal service book rate. Canadian orders require $2.00 extra postage and must be paid in U.S. dollars through a U.S. banking facility.

Name_____
Address_____
City_____State_____Zip_____
I have enclosed $_____ in payment for the checked book(s).
Payment <u>must</u> accompany all orders. ❏ Please send a free catalog.